A Far
Better Rest

A Far
Better Rest

Susanne Alleyn

Published by
Soho Press, Inc.
853 Broadway
New York, NY 10003

Library of Congress Cataloging-in-Publication Data

Alleyn, Susanne, 1963–
A far better rest / Susanne Alleyn.
p. cm.
Features Sydney Carton and other characters from
Charles Dickens' A tale of two cities.
ISBN 1-56947-197-5 (alk. paper)
I. France—History—Revolution, 1789-1799—Fiction. 2. British—
France—History—18th century—Fiction. I Dickens, Charles, 1812-
1870. Tale of two cities. II. Title.
PS3551.L4484 F37 2000
813'.54—dc21   99-087103

10 9 8 7 6 5 4 3 2 I

For my mother

ACKNOWLEDGMENTS

ABUNDANT THANKS ARE due to the many friends whose encouragement over the years prodded me to keep writing, especially Darline Gay Levy, Greg Robinson, Leonora Perry, Trace Edward Zaber, Don Sakers, Jenny Philips, and Gloria Terwilliger; also to David Plotkin, without the use of whose spare bedroom in London I probably would never have idly begun to ponder Dickens's "two cities."

I owe a particular debt of gratitude and affection to Berenice and Walt McDayter, whose constant support has helped me through some bad times, and who with their generosity and hospitality have also shared some very good times (and many, many enjoyable hours of research, discussion, and speculation). And a very special thank you must go to my editor, Melanie Fleishman, and to my splendid and persevering literary agent, Don Congdon, for taking a chance.

How many things, that we would never do for ourselves,
do we do for the sake of our friends!
—Cicero, *De Amicitia*

Principal Characters

In order of appearance
*denotes character in *A Tale of Two Cities*
**denotes historical character

*Sydney Carton

In France, 1770–1771

*Charles Darnay, pupil at the Collège Louis-le-Grand
**Maximilien Robespierre, pupil at Louis-le-Grand
**Camille Desmoulins, pupil at Louis-le-Grand

In England, 1771–1789

Joseph Carton, Sydney's father, a prosperous manufacturer
Sarah Kenyon, daughter of Sir Mallory Kenyon, Bt.
*Clarence Stryver, a barrister
Molly, a bar-maid
*John Barsad, an informer
*Lucie Manette, a young woman of French birth
*Dr. Alexandre Manette, her father
*Jarvis Lorry, a banker
*Pross, Lucie's housekeeper and companion
*Lucie-Anne, Lucie and Darnay's daughter

In France, 1789–1794

Eléonore de Clairville, née Ambert, Darnay's cousin
Laurent d'Ambert, her brother
Julien Fleutry, a journalist

**Anne Théroigne, a revolutionary agitator

*The Marquis de Saint-Evrémonde, Darnay's late uncle

Baptistine, Eléonore's maid

The Comte d'Aubincourt, a leader of the National Assembly

**Madame de Pontécoulant, Abbess of the Abbaye-aux-Dames in Caen

**Marie d'Armont, a pupil at the Abbey

**Gustave Le Doulcet de Pontécoulant, the Abbess's nephew

**Henri de Belsunce, officer second in command of Caen's garrison

**Lucile Desmoulins, Camille's wife

**Jean-Marie Hérault de Séchelles, an aristocratic revolutionist

**Georges Danton, a bourgeois revolutionist

**Antoine Saint-Just, an ambitious provincial revolutionist

The Vicomte de Clairville, Eléonore's estranged husband

**Jean Paul Marat, radical journalist, deputy to the National Convention

**Fouquier-Tinville, prosecutor at the Revolutionary Tribunal

*Gabelle, former steward to the Marquis de Saint-Evrémonde

Elisabeth Gabelle, his wife

*Ernest Defarge, a tavern-keeper of the Montreuil section of Paris

*Thérèse Defarge, his wife

*Toinette, a seamstress

A Far
Better Rest

Not in Our Stars

1770–1789

1

Paris
16 Germinal, Year II of the Republic
5 April 1794 old style

TO-DAY THEY GUILLOTINED Danton; and with him died the fragile dream of Clemency, and all my hopes and prayers. For if Danton the Colossus has succumbed to the Terror, this ravenous Goddess who has devoured or corrupted the best of France, what chance of enduring has any of us?

Wanting hope, two paths now stretch before me, one towards Love and the other towards Honour, and I know not which I should choose. For I made a solemn vow once to Lucie, and once again to myself this very day, and despite my many faults, I do not break my word. Yet the man who made that long-ago vow to Lucie was not the same man who writes these words to-day.

What a tangled path has led me to this moment, from my father's country estate to the gin-shops and stews and back-alleys of London, from London to the *salons* and parliaments of Paris, and at last to this dreary Parisian lodging-house. Or perhaps my story truly began—as I think it shall end—not in England, not in my father's fine brick mansion, but in Paris. Perhaps my path began to twist and turn, through the ravaged landscape of my life, on the day I met Charles Darnay.

"NEW BOY," SAID one of my fellow senior students, jerking his head at the slender figure who stood irresolute in the door of the rhetoric-hall at the Collège Louis-le-Grand. "A relative of yours?"

"Why do you say that?" said I. All my relatives with whom I was on speaking terms—my father, his brother and nephew, my sister Bella, and my elder brother Oliver—were on the other side of the Channel, in England.

"Why, I merely thought . . . but go and take a look at him, then."

My curiosity piqued, I strolled over to the new student's side. He was two or three years younger than I, sixteen perhaps, handsome and fine-boned with an air of quiet assurance. And indeed I knew his face, tho' I could not, for a moment, think how we might have met. But in another moment I realised (I know not how, for are we not more accustomed to the faces of our closest companions than to our own?) that the visage opposite me might have been that of my brother. No, not my brother, for I and my brother Oliver were little like—not my brother, but myself, my own looking-glass image.

"My name is Carton," I said, offering my hand.

He nodded. "Darnay." He spared us both discomfort by giving me as frankly curious a glance as I imagine I was casting his way. "Have . . . have we met?" he enquired, at length.

"No," said I, "we've not met. But I imagine you've glanced in a glass of late?"

He stared at me a moment ere laughing out loud in astonishment. "*Mon Dieu*," he murmured, adding: "I don't suppose you could be one of my relatives?"

"That depends who your relatives may be," said I, carelessly.

"O—nobody in particular."

"It scarce seems likely, nevertheless, since I am English."

"English! Then what a quirk of Fate it was, that has placed us together here in Paris."

"Who knows the workings of Fate, or of Providence?" said I, with a laugh. "But a fellow ought not be shy with his looking-glass twin; I hope we may be friends, Darnay. Come, I'll show you about."

"I CAN'T HELP but observe that your French is nearly perfect," Darnay told me, a few days later, as we strolled together along the perimeter of the central courtyard, where the younger boys were playing ball under the watchful eye of two of the masters. "The other English and Irish students speak French as if they were talking thro' a mouthful of porridge."

I laughed. "A compliment indeed! I must thank my mother, who taught me. She was a Frenchwoman. My father met her whilst visiting France on a matter of Business and wedded her six weeks later. His first wife had died, you see, and his little daughter, my half-sister Bella, needed a mother."

My poor mother, wedded in her blooming youth to a gruff and exacting man twice her age! I cherish fond memories of her to this day, my gentle, kind, pretty mamma, whom as a child I thought the most beautiful lady in the world (tho' at times I believed Sarah, the golden-haired little daughter of our nearest neighbour Sir Mallory, was near as lovely).

"And she wished you to come here, to Louis-le-Grand?"

"Yes. It was her fondest wish for me, that I should attend the finest school in France, and then go on to the University of Paris. But she is dead, now, too, and never saw me here; indeed never saw France again."

"I am sorry."

"I don't believe she ever felt herself truly at home in England," I mused. "Though she never would return to France. It was as if she had cut herself off from her family."

"Or they from her," Darnay suggested. "Did you never ask her?"

"No. And she never spoke of them, beyond their name and their province. I think she was determined to make the best of her lot, and raise her children, and shut her eyes to whatsoever it was she had quitted in France."

"Perhaps. My mother did the same. I don't remember my father, for I was only four years old when he died, but sometimes . . . one hears things. From the elder servants, you know. Abominable rumours."

"Rumours?" said I, my curiosity whetted.

"They say he was lewd and immoral, that decent women would take care not to be alone with him. He was killed in a duel by the husband of a lady he had dishonoured, I believe, or so they tell me. But everybody knew my mother was unhappy in her marriage. She turned her back on my father's family after he died, and returned with me to her own people. I was educated with my cousins and I dare say I was the better for it."

"Were you not sent away to school?"

"No, we had a tutor. Louis-le-Grand is my first taste of boarding-school."

"And what do you think of dormitory life, and boarding-school food?"

"The food isn't quite as bad as my cousin Eléonore assured me it would be," said he, with a grin.

"Truly! Well, speak for yourself. I am mightily glad to be free of it when I choose, and free of dormitory beds, and schoolmasters prowling the corridors."

"You don't dwell here at the *Collège?*"

"No, I've my own lodgings on rue de la Parcheminerie. It was my father's doing. I told him that I'd been out of school in England for near a year, and that I had no taste for the dormitory life once again, particularly at a school governed by priests. One needs special permission to live outside the *Collège*—my father very nearly had to obtain a papal dispensation!"

Darnay laughed. "Your father must indulge you, then."

"Yes, I suppose he does, or so might a stranger say," I reflected. "He gives me everything I could ask for, so long as I give him no trouble in return."

"But . . ." said my companion, hearing the hesitation in my voice.

"But . . . he does not love me. He gives me all I wish, very nearly, because he will not . . . or cannot . . . give me affection." I looked away, praying that the autumn sunshine would not catch the glint of tears in my eyes. "He loved me once, in his own rough way; there's the rub of it. But since my mother died, and even ere that, we have been strangers to one another." My mother had died of consumption the year Bella wed, when I was yet a lad of twelve, and with her into her grave had gone my boyhood's happiness and any illusion of tenderness my father might have attempted.

The boys' ball came skidding towards us, to an accompanying chorus of "Hi, look out, there!" I scooped up the ball and flung it back at them, perhaps with more force than I had intended. "What did I ever do," I continued, "to deserve such coldness? I have been asking myself that question since I was ten years old. O, I grant you, I was not a model pupil at Shrewsbury School . . . but should a few poor marks, and a few schoolboy scrapes, turn a father against his son? And I tried, Darnay, I truly tried: I applied myself and earned prizes for Latin, for Composition, for History, yet nothing I did could please him. When I showed him the prize book I had won for taking first place in Latin, he only grunted and said 'You'd better turn your attention, then, and improve your Arithmetic'. Perhaps he grew indifferent to me when in my school-work I showed no commercial aspirations or talents whatsoever—for what use, to a manufacturer and merchant of porcelain, is a first prize in Latin? Perhaps," I added bitterly, "since my brother Oliver is to inherit his property and his fortune . . . perhaps he regards me as so much superfluous baggage that must still be fed, clothed, and educated. He is a monstrous practical man, after all."

"I doubt that's the circumstance," said Darnay mildly, "if he is as rich as you have led me to believe."

I winced. Tho' I had suspected, from his courteous and graceful bearing, that Darnay was sprung from the lesser Nobility rather than from the *bourgeoisie* and the professions as were most of the boys at Louis-le-Grand, I had guessed, also, that his family was only of modest fortune. "I am sorry," I said. "I oughtn't to have spoken so."

"You needn't apologise."

"Are you here on a scholarship? It's nothing to be in the least ashamed of, you know, not here. Half the boys have scholarships. It's an honour, rather."

"No," said he, "I am not here on a scholarship. My mother's family can afford the fees." He turned to me. "Are you indeed as good at Latin as all the seniors say you are? Perhaps you could help me; I'm struggling through Virgil at present."

"If you like," said I, with a smile. Tho' his abrupt change of subject baffled me, I thought it better not to pry. "Of course; whatsoever you like."

IN ALL I spent three years, perhaps the gayest of my life, as a student in Paris. Glittering, unforgiving, fascinating Paris, then and ever the centre of European civilisation! My father might have done worse for me; I will readily admit that he never deprived me of the benefits that a man of his wealth might bestow upon his children. In truth, he gave me all I needed but approval, and affection.

What a remarkable place the Collège Louis-le-Grand was, and what a remarkable collection of Alumni it produced. I speak not of myself, nor of Darnay, but rather of the host of native-born students who, long afterward, would overturn a Kingdom. I speak, in fact, of Robespierre himself, at that time a pale, solemn eleven-year-old scholarship-boy from Arras; for the masters, upon his arrival, unceremoniously placed him in my care for his first week or two at the school, until he should learn his way about the buildings and the rules.

During my last year at the *Collège* I befriended a small boy very different from Robespierre. I came upon him in a courtyard where the younger pupils often played, but he was not playing. He was, rather, braving a half-dozen boys of his own age who were taunting him. I had no liking for bullies and with a few sharp words sent them packing. The thought that his saviour was one of the senior students, an elder of the lofty age of nineteen, must have over-awed the lad, for he stept back a pace and attempted to swallow his tears as I approached him.

Taking his hand, I sat on a stone bench and drew him beside me, suffering him to sob into my shoulder. Soon he calmed and raised his head, gazing at me with a pair of splendid black eyes that must, at better times, have sparkled with merriment.

"Why were they teasing you?" I asked him.

"B-Because I stutter," he faltered, his nether lip trembling. "They c-call me *s-stupid stammerer*, and I'm n-not! I'm c-cleverer than any of them!"

"Well, they are envious then, aren't they?" said I. "They would like to be as clever as you are, but they choose to be cruel to you out of spite, because they know they are not. Boys are horrible little creatures, you know. I was one myself once."

"*I'm* a boy," said he, indignant.

I stared at him in mock astonishment. "Why, so you are. What's your name?"

"Desmoulins . . . C-Camille Desmoulins."

"Mine is Carton."

"That's a funny n-name," he declared, brightening, attempting to pronounce it in the French fashion.

"It's an English name."

"Are you English? I'm from G-Guise. It's in P-Picardy."

"Guise, you say?" I echoed him. My erstwhile acquaintance, young Maximilien de Robespierre, was from a northern province also. Though shy and solitary, he seemed the sort of boy who might take a younger lad under his wing. "Well, Desmoulins, I can see you want a friend, and I happen to know a boy from Arras who I think also wants a friend. Would you care to meet him?"

"Will he l-laugh at m-my stutter?"

"I am sure he will not," said I. "He seems a very quiet, gentle boy, and rather lonely."

I escorted the lad inside and found Robespierre. They quickly struck up a friendship, although Robespierre's habitual gravity stood in odd contrast to Camille's sunny, lively disposition. How could I have imagined, then, what those two boys would become, and how our lives would touch again?

THO' INTIMATE ASSOCIATIONS amongst the boys were frowned

upon at Louis-le-Grand, the masters could not prevent Darnay and me from spending many hours in each other's company. Even the elder students were allowed only limited freedom away from the *Collège*, so he came but infrequently to my lodgings. We soon discovered, however, an attic that lay forgotten beneath a high-peaked roof in one of the *Collège's* lesser buildings, and there often retreated of an evening to pore over our books, or perfect each other's Latin (or Darnay's English), or argue some point of rhetoric or philosophy from the day's lectures. Lest it be thought by some that we had overnight become monks, I may add that we spent many more hours, and drank down many bottles of good red wine, in talk of pretty women, and in talk of the newest sensations at the theatre and the opera, and in news of Court and town, and in chattering of nothing of import whatsoever.

How well, and how fondly, I remember those few golden years in Paris, undoubtedly the most dazzling city on the face of the Earth. And how I gloried in it! I confess I ran wild, like any other young scapegrace whose ample allowance burnt a hole in his pocket. Free of the dormitory's restrictions, I enjoyed the liberty to haunt theatres, cafés, gambling-hells; to drink coffee and Cognac at Zoppi's, read the forbidden books of the fashionable new Philosophers, dream of becoming an author like Voltaire or Diderot; to visit the most notorious bawdy-house in the city and there be initiated into its mysteries, after which I promptly kept a saucy shop-girl as a mistress; and somehow thro' it all I attended the lectures, read a heap of dusty books, learnt my share of French Law, and discovered a profound kinship of minds (if not always of opinions) with my looking-glass twin.

"Tell me about your brother and sister," said Darnay to me one day in our attic retreat, after lectures were done.

"What is there to tell?" said I, laughing.

"Whatsoever you wish. I have no brothers or sisters myself, only three cousins . . . and one of them is in his cradle still. My cousin Gilbert is a dreadful little priggish boy, and my cousin Eléonore is but thirteen years old, and far too clever for her years—she is the very devil!"

"O, I have cousins, too—my father's brother's children, Elijah and his three sisters. My uncle is no more than a lazy, good-natured drunkard, if truth be told, but Elijah seems likely to get on. As for my brother, Oliver, he is a splendid fellow, all that my father could ask for. He is tall and ruddy and handsome, just as an English gentleman should be; my mother used to say that he would grow to be *a true John Bull Englishman,* and that one would never guess he was half French. He rides hard, drinks hard, and works hard. But he would spring to my defence in an instant, whether against some school-yard bully or against our father himself when he is ill-tempered."

"And your sister?"

"I scarce know Bella. She is nine years older than I and is wedded to a ship-owner in Bristol, and they don't often spare time for a visit. I remember that she was rather vain, and selfish, but quite shrewd, and had little patience for small brothers who might be underfoot. She assists her husband in managing his concerns and evidently does well at it, for they are enormously rich." I poured out another glass of red wine for him and grinned. "You are more fortunate than you know, Darnay, not to have had some imperious elder sister ordering you about."

"Won't you call me Charles, in private? Are we not good enough friends for that, by now?"

"If you wish," said I. "If you will call me Sydney in return."

"Willingly."

"Darnay . . . Charles," I ventured, "since we are friends, and speaking of our families, may I ask you a question?"

"Anything. You know that."

"Well then . . . Darnay is not your true name, is it?"

"No," said he after a moment's silence. "It's not. How do you know?"

I shrugged. "Darnay is not the name of a Nobleman, and you are manifestly one of the *Noblesse.* You are no more an ordinary Advocate's son, or a provincial Banker's son, than I am the First Prince of the Blood Royal."

To my surprise, he crimsoned. "To me," he whispered at last, "that word

Noblesse is more a term of shame than of honour . . . tho' I ought not brand all the Aristocracy with the same stigma."

"I-I meant only that you carry yourself like a gentleman born: in a courtly manner, like one taught to observe honour and courtesy in all things—"

"And as so many do not!" he exclaimed, fiercely. I stared at him, all amazement.

"Darnay?"

"Forgive me. But if you knew what I know, or merely suspect, about my own family, the people whose name I bear . . ."

It was my own turn to change colour. "I didn't mean to pry."

"No, it will be a relief to speak of it to someone. And who better than you, whom I know I can trust?"

"If you wish, then."

"Well . . . do you remember, we once spoke of our kinfolk, and I told you my father had gained an ill reputation? He was only one of a bad family. They have always been judged callous landlords and harsh masters. And there were others who were far worse than my father. My uncle, his elder brother, was banished from Court for his—his private conduct."

"Banished from Court?" I echoed him. "From *this* Court, from Versailles? From the court of the Lecher-King, who keeps a brothel on the Palace grounds?"

He nodded. "Banished by Louis XV himself. So you can imagine how very vile my uncle's behaviour must have been. If it were only debauchery and lechery . . . but I've heard other rumours, ugly rumours of how he gets his women, and how he treats them." He lowered his voice, though no one could have overheard us. "Whipping, bloodletting, rape . . . and they say he prefers little girls, of no more than thirteen, tho' he'll take any woman who strikes his fancy . . . he enjoys deflowering them, corrupting them, hurting them. I've heard that he is diseased, as well, and that's why he has no living children. It's no more than I would expect. Of course," he added hastily,

"I've scarce met him, nor do I wish to. But if you were I, would you care to know that such a man is your blood-kin?"

"*Mordieu*," I murmured, "it's an ugly story you tell me. We all imagine our own troubles are the worst . . . until we hear another's."

"I wish nothing to do with him, or his tainted name. So, with my mother's blessing, here at Louis-le-Grand, and probably elsewhere, I am and shall be merely Charles Darnay, son of nobody in particular."

"I won't tell a soul. Word of honour."

He smiled and clasped my hand. "Thank you, Carton."

"Sydney," I corrected him.

"Sydney. That's not a very common name, is it? In England?"

"No," I agreed, refilling our glasses once again, relieved to have changed the subject of our conversation. "It's more common as a surname, I expect."

"Sir Philip Sydney," said Darnay, nodding, "he was a poet, was he not?"

"Yes. But I was named for his descendant. Algernon Sydney."

"Algernon Sydney?"

"A comrade of Cromwell's—"

"Ah, your Civil Wars."

"—who fought against the King, even tho' he was himself an Earl's son," I told him. "He was a great man. Long after the Restoration, he spoke out against the King and was at last condemned and put to death, because the King feared him. He died for the cause of Liberty."

"A great man indeed," murmured Darnay.

"My father has always held with the rights of Parliament, and the people, above the rule of Aristocracy. He named my brother after Cromwell, and me after Sydney."

"Did you know," said Darnay suddenly, "that there are tidings from America of a riot in Boston, in the British colonies, some months since? They are calling it a massacre, it's said. It's rumoured that dozens of folk, perhaps hundreds, were killed by British troops."

"What of it?"

"What of it? You, who a moment ago spoke of the cause of Liberty, can ask that? Carton, their taxes lay too heavy a burthen upon them. Once again an oppressed people are speaking out against unjust rule."

"Very well; but nothing that you or I can do will make a whit of difference," said I.

"It's the fruit of the modern Philosophy, Carton! A hundred years ago such a thing couldn't have happened. But to-day . . . to-day change is everywhere—change and reform. Soon folk like my uncle will have to answer for their outrages. Ere you and I have passed our prime, we'll be dwelling in a new world."

"And you are going to take part in this great endeavour, are you?"

"Perhaps. Perhaps I shall. You needn't smile. When one sees the Injustice carried on here in France, the Nobility's detestable privileges—yes, and in England, too—"

"Not so inequitably, and not by me."

"Seeing a wrong done, and doing nothing to correct it, is near as bad as committing a wrong oneself. You will be a Barrister one day; why not defend the victims of Injustice? Think on it. You can't sit idly by forever, Carton."

"I'll think on it," said I, smiling, and drank down my glass.

MY PARISIAN IDYLL came to an abrupt close when I had scarce turned twenty. "We have received a letter from your father in England," said Father Bérard to me, after having called me into his study. "He tells us that you are to return home immediately, and permanently."

"Return home?" I stammered. "For what reason?"

"He does not say. He merely includes a draught on the bank of Tellson et Fils to pay for your passage to England. We shall miss you, Carton."

Mystified, and monstrous disappointed, I ordered my servant to pack my belongings, bade adieu to Célie (my pretty shop-girl) with a handsome present, and at last went in search of Darnay. "I don't know why I'm to go home now," I complained, after divulging my ill tidings in a secluded corner of the library. "I was to stop on in Paris. I was to go on to the University here, as my mother wished. I'd rather be here, where my friends are."

"I'll miss you," said Darnay. "This place will be empty without you. But you know that. Do you think you will ever return?"

"How should I know? I don't know, even, why my father has called me back. But perhaps you could come to England. Some day."

"Perhaps. If circumstances don't keep me in France."

"What circumstances?"

"Property I may inherit, if my uncle has no more children, which seems likely."

"Property?" said I. "You never before mentioned property. Where is it?"

"A country estate east of Paris. Nothing remarkable about it. But it may be mine, some day, and then I shall have obligations, particularly to put right what my uncle and his family have made wrong."

"Always so grave and responsible!" said I, laughing despite my gloomy temper. "You make me almost delighted that I shan't inherit my father's estate. Charles, take care you don't grow old too soon."

"And you, take care that you don't linger in your youth too long," returned Darnay, gently, as we embraced. "We will see each other again, Sydney; I am sure of it."

2

I ACHED FOR Paris, and my student's life, and my friend, from the moment the diligence passed the customs-barriers and set out upon the Calais road. My unwilling steps led me back to Staffordshire by way of packet-boat and public coach, at last to find Bridge House silent, its dozens of windows black-draped as they had been at my mother's death years since. My father met me in the doorway, unsmiling. "You'll be asking why I sent for you, I suppose," said he. "Look about you, then. Your brother's dead, God rest him."

"Oliver?" I whispered. "Dead?" The very idea was impossible. Though we had shared few interests as we grew older, I had ever adored my sturdy, staunch, genial, hard-riding elder brother.

"Aye, Oliver. 'Twas the Typhoid. Swept through the village, it did, and carried him off, the poor lad." He stared at me, stout callused fists on thick-set hips, assessing me. My father, tho' he aspired to the landed Gentry, and across the years had purchased many hundred acres and built a fine new country seat well away from the belching, sooty smoke-stacks at the kilns, was in truth a self-made man of humble origin; he had risen, by virtue of a shrewd and inventive mind and much hard work, from potter's apprentice to master-potter to owner of a famous manufactory of fine porcelain.

"Well, boy, you'll have to do, won't you?" said he at last, in a grudging tone (I really cannot think of a word that would better describe his manner). "No more of your Frenchy nonsense for you. You're my only heir now save Bella, worse luck, so you'd better come inside with your traps, hadn't you? To-morrow you go to the Pottery, boy, and you set about learning the business of China-ware."

☙ ☙ ☙

16

I was returned to Staffordshire to a rôle for which I had no inclination. I imagine the world, or at least the County, thought me a spoilt and ungrateful young puppy. Yet I would have exchanged the greater part of the wealth around me for my father's good opinion. In trade as in school-work, nothing I did pleased him, and I cannot in any event claim that overseeing the kilns and selling biscuit-ware to the Gentry was to my taste, though to be sure the prospect of inheriting the estate was a pleasant one.

Had I inherited all, sold the manufactory, and put the money from the sale into improving and increasing the land, I dare say I might have made a creditable landlord, content to be a scholarly country squireen. For at twenty I spent my idle hours reading Horace, Shakespeare, and Voltaire, or scribbling love-poems never sent. My head was crammed full of rebellious notions and literary pretensions and my father's clear opinion, that I had no taste or talent for Commerce, was soon confirmed.

Let it suffice to say that we did not get on, my father and I. "Begod," he would exclaim, when exercised with my want of commercial aptitude, "with all I've spent educating you, why can't you have half as much sense as my brother's boy?" (My uncle Daniel's son Elijah, by then an industrious young man of thirty, was already chief clerk at the manufactory and was expected to go far.)

And, of course, there was Sarah.

I see her still sometimes, the phantom of a golden-haired girl that bubbles up unbidden from the depths of my cess-pit memory. Sometimes, despite all my efforts to forget, I remember her, Sarah with her blue eyes and her dazzling smile, her slender figure, her laughter, her facility for making the shabbiest of twice-turned, twenty-year-old gowns seem the most elegant of London or Paris fashions. I do not think of her often, not after so many years have passed. But like it or not, she is a part of my history, and I find I cannot pretend that she never was there.

Shortly after my reluctant return to Staffordshire, I must confess that despite my plaints to Darnay I forgot Paris entirely, for I had discovered

Sarah Kenyon. Perhaps I was merely in love with love, a callow boy adoring a childhood sweetheart now the prettiest creature in the County, yet not daring to speak to her of his passion. Despite all the wealth about me I was but a *parvenu* tradesman's son, and she the daughter of a Baronet whose family had dwelt at Fairfax Hall since the days of Queen Elizabeth. But the knowledge that a quarter-hour's canter would bring me to her doorstep compensated me for all I had left behind me in Paris, and all I was obliged to tolerate at home.

It was not so many months after my return to England that Sarah began to cast her gaze my way. It was a fine bright morning in early Summer, I remember, a day fragrant with wild-flowers. Sarah awaited me on a bench along the drive as was our custom, idly dangling her straw hat by its ribbons as her mare cropped the grass behind her.

"*Cui flavam religas comam, simplex munditiis?*" I enquired, approaching her.

She turned, laughing. "You and your Latin! What dreadful things are you saying to me?"

"I merely asked you: *For whom are you dressing your golden tresses, simply but with such style?*"

"Why, for you, of course. Sydney, what do you think? Papa is going to send me to London to stop a month or more with my Aunt Graham and my cousins."

"To catch yourself a husband, you mean." The Kenyons were not rich, and Sarah was hard-pressed to find a young man of good breeding and respectable fortune when she had no fortune of her own.

"Will you miss me?" she enquired, dimpling.

"You know I shall."

"I'll miss you, in dirty old London."

"Nonsense," said I, "you'll have a splendid time."

"You don't know my Aunt Graham! She is the stiffest old stick-in-the-mud that ever was."

I offered her my hand, laughing. "Come. It's cooler in the garden." Arm in arm, we strolled along the flagged path that led around Bridge House's graceful east wing.

"Sydney," she began, "only last night my father spoke very well of you."

"Did he?" At the time I did not recognise Sarah's tentative overture for what it was, a veiled hint that the son of a wealthy tradesman might, despite his birth, be a suitable husband for a Baronet's daughter.

"He said—he didn't mean it to be slighting, so you mustn't receive it so—he said that you are as much a gentleman as any young man in the County who possesses a considerably longer pedigree."

My father interrupted us, his deep voice booming through the garden, to find some fault with the accounts that he had set me to tending. "Begod, I should have sent you to Cambridge with proper Englishmen, or kept you close by to learn your business," he concluded, withdrawing his head from the window. "Ciphering's your business now, boy, never forget it! I'll not have the money I've spent on your high-nosed Frenchy education frittered away in rhymes and such rubbish."

"Lord above," I sighed, as he slammed shut the window behind us. "When will he realise I'm a man grown, and not a schoolboy?" I looked at Sarah, my spirits rising once more. "What do you say we escape for a while, ere he chains me to a desk and sets me to calculating next year's price per cart-load for Dutch clay."

Laughing like conspirators, we ran to the stables. Ten minutes later we were galloping through the rich red earth of the hay-fields and towards the wood that separated Carton land and Kenyon land. "I wonder who is more the Autocrat," I shouted, above pounding hooves and jingling harness, "your father or mine?"

"O, yours, to be sure!" cried Sarah. "Papa has never succeeded in making me do any thing I didn't wish to do myself!"

I SUPPOSE, AS I gaze back across a score of years, that Sarah cannot be blamed entirely for being what she was. The Kenyons were our nearest neighbours, long-established county Gentry who had failed to move with the times; as enterprising, ambitious folk like my father climbed the ladder of success, they slowly slipped down it. The Kenyon family seat, Fairfax Hall, was a rambling Tudor manor-house in want of repair, and a handful of impoverished crofters and cowherds were the estate's sole tenants. Sarah, old Sir Mallory's only child, was expected to make the best marriage possible in order to prevent her family from sliding ever deeper into genteel poverty. Could the Kenyons shut their eyes to my common origins, I, as the young, handsome, agreeable, and eminently eligible heir of the richest man within twenty miles, was without doubt first prize in the matrimonial stakes.

Sarah returned empty-handed from her month's sojourn in London. I took a guilty pleasure in the fact and welcomed her home with rather more enthusiasm than was suitable. How could she not have seized upon the opportunity offered her?

The Summer days rolled by, lush and golden as the ripening corn. I stole hours, then days to saddle my sleek chestnut gelding and go riding through the meadows and woodlands, to my father's exasperation. What he did not know, for I sensed he had little use for such a fragile, ethereal creature as she (*that thin-blooded porcelain doll*, he styled her), was that I spent those stolen hours and days with Sarah.

I have not yet forgotten those drowsy sweet mornings and afternoons we squandered, walking hand in hand amongst the daisies and the dancing white butterflies, or conversing together beneath a shady tree as I lay with my head pillowed upon my arms, gazing up at her. I found her a sympathetic audience when I chafed beneath my father's merciless fault-finding, for I will not deny I was poor at figures and loathed the negotiations necessary to Commerce more even than I loathed ciphering. My destiny, I imagined, was to be a man of letters: Poet, Playwright, Essayist, Historian, it did not matter. "And if ever I should breathe a word of that to my father," I told Sarah one warm bright day in early September as our horses ambled through the wood, "I should never hear the last of it."

"Why so?"

"Because his precious China-ware, his d__ned manufactory is all in this life that matters to him!"

"Are you not a trifle unjust to him? He *is* your father."

"Sarah, in frankness, he doesn't like me. We are poles apart. He wishes to mould me into a man of Business, and that I shall never be." We rode on in silence for a while longer, skirting the fields at the borders of Fairfax land, and followed the path once more into the forest, towards the neighbouring village of King's Berwyck and its ruined mediæval fortress.

"Ought we ride all the way to the Castle?" enquired Sarah, at length. Its still, sun-washed courtyard was a favourite spot for picnics. "You know we shan't have time to ride thither, and return, ere supper-time."

"Let's stop here, then, in the clearing." I scrambled from my mount and offered my hand to help her down from her side-saddle. In dismounting, she slipped and would have fallen had I not caught her. She remained a moment in my arms, clinging to me as she caught her breath. We were face to face, closer than ever we had been. An electric thrill coursed through me as her slender body pressed against my own.

"Well," she exclaimed (an instant too late), with a strained laugh, "I very nearly fell on my face, didn't I?"

I handed her down onto a fallen log. Fetching the old blanket I carried strapt to my saddle for such occasions, I spread it over the thin long grass that grew in the glade and threw myself down upon it, gazing up at her. After a moment, unpinning her riding-hat and tossing it aside, she slipped from the log to sit opposite me on the blanket. Above us, the sunlight filtered in a green haze through the trees, dappling the sparse grass with patches of brilliant gold.

"What a lovely spot. Listen to the birds. There—wasn't that a thrush?"

I gazed at her, drinking in the sapphire splendour of her eyes, a tight little knot of desire twisting in the pit of my stomach—and elsewhere. "It's not as lovely as you are."

She laughed softly, colouring, and looked away. "You are a flatterer, Sydney."

"You are the most beautiful thing I ever have seen," said I.

"Don't tease me so—"

"Sarah—" The memory of her body pressed against mine was too much for me. I scrambled up and knelt beside her, taking her hand. "I—I love you." At last I had blurted it out, that foolish little phrase that changed everything.

"Do you?" she whispered, her eyes wide and lustrous. "O Sydney, I've loved you for ages, since we were children I think. I've gone about all this year past thinking of nothing but you. When I was in London I thought I'd die of missing you."

I touched her cheek and drew her nearer me. Our lips brushed, met, became one for a long moment. I found myself framing her face with my hands, kissing her over and over again.

"Sarah, I—O God, I love you—you know that, don't you? Never anybody else. Always you." Scarce knowing what I did, I reached a hand towards her bodice, towards the laces that held it snugly closed. She did not resist me and suddenly I was touching her beautiful breasts, stroking them, kissing them, until I thought I might go mad with desire. At last, gathering to me the shreds of my prudence, I tore myself away from her. "No—I shan't do this. God knows I desire you, more than I've desired any woman—but it's not right. You're a lady."

"But I will," said she. "I will lie with you. I—I wish to."

"Sarah—have you—have you ever before—"

"No! What do you take me for?"

"Then it's not right. Your reputation—"

"I don't care. I love you." She cupped her palm about my cheek and suddenly kissed my lips, demurely at first, then with more license and passion, and I responded as any man would. "Sydney," she gasped, between kisses, "I shall never love anybody but you . . ."

"And I you," said I, nuzzling at her neck.

"I have always known that, I think, since we were small, and we all played battledore and shuttlecock together in mother's garden. Do you remember?"

"I've never forgotten a moment of the time I have spent with you." I bent over her hands, brushing my lips across them, tracing the length of each slender finger; then, with kisses, following the curve of her arm upward to her breasts once again. I ached to touch her, to possess her, to feel her small soft body moving beneath my own. At last my hand found its way beneath her skirts and she said not a word in protest, only whimpered as I kissed her breasts, her throat, her quivering mouth.

"I can't bear this a moment longer," I panted, after we had spent some time more in frantic kisses and caresses. "I shall go mad. I shall tear off your clothes in a moment, if we don't stop this."

"Why stop?" she whispered. "Don't you imagine I might go mad, too?"

"It's not right. It's impossible. I should have to make promises to you to make it right, and your father would never suffer me to wed you—"

"No, Sydney," she cried, "he would! He thinks very highly of you. Don't you remember?"

"No matter that your father is a Baronet and mine—well!"

"Plenty of respectable folk are in trade these days! We must move with the times. My father'd not object, I know it."

I stared at her, seeing the world, glittering like a jewel, reflected in her eyes. "And . . . would you?"

"Would I what, Sydney?"

"Would you . . . wed me?"

"O yes," she breathed. "Yes. *Yes.*"

Then we both, I think, went mad at the same instant, flinging off all restraints. She was indeed a maiden, yet a moment later she clung to me like a wanton, writhing beneath me and gasping her ardour. I had some experience in such matters, having learnt *finesse* from Célie, my willing Parisian shop-girl, but Sarah's slim young body was far sweeter than ever any jaded mistress's could be. At last we lay breathless together as the shadows lengthened, smiling at each other, saying not a word as we dreamt of the radiant future stretching before us.

BOTH SARAH AND I, for our various reasons, for the ensuing weeks felt ourselves the happiest folk on Earth. My father, however, was not so delighted. As a self-made man, he held a solid contempt for those of the Gentry, like Sarah's family, who clung to their fading eminence yet had not the enterprise to hold onto their fortunes, or to beget new ones. Having learnt unexpectedly of our engagement from Sarah's feather-headed aunt, without warning he hailed me into his study and commenced upon the severest berating he ever had troubled to give me.

"If you must wed to cool your loins," he stormed, "at least wed a wench who will bring you a good few thousand pound, or a flock of titled kin-folk. Wed some Earl's daughter with a name that goes back to the Conquest, boy, not that fool Kenyon's conniving chit who will bring you no more than a few acres that would cost more to improve than they're worth! Begod, have you no wish to be judged one of the Gentry?"

"The Kenyons have been Gentry here for two hundred years—" I returned, hotly.

"Aye, and in another generation the fine Kenyons will be played out and their fine manor-house will be falling to rack and ruin. You can do better, boy. D__n me, if you've no head for Business, as you've proved to me ere now, I hope you have some ambition for your children, at least. Bring some old blood into the family and give your brats cousins with titles. The Kenyons may have lived at Fairfax for two hundred year, but Sir Mallory is still no more than a tuppenny Baronet."

What a disappointment and a trial I was to him. I shared neither his commercial nor his social ambitions; I would have been quite satisfied as a landed gentleman of modest means and standing, content to ride my acres, write pretty verses of tolerable literary value, and increase my library whilst watching a houseful of handsome children grow up about me. I told him as much and he flew into a rage, as countless other fathers have done who discover that their sons reject that for which they have laboured all their lives.

"You love that sly yellow-haired minx, do you, and you think you'll live happy ever after with her?" he snorted. "Does she love you?"

"Of course," said I. Had she not proven it in the most profound fashion a woman may prove her love?

"What she loves is your money, boy, or rather *my* money. Are you too starry-eyed to see it, then? Begod, for a book-learnt lad, you're such a dunderhead in that as matters most."

"And what is that?" I retorted, incautiously. "Money? Business? There are more important objects to living than the accumulation of wealth, father."

He glared at me as if I had blasphemed during Sunday services. "Aye, perhaps; but don't ever you sneer at wealth honestly earned thro' hard work! Now I'm not saying wedding for money is a bad thing—but let it be an honest arrangement, not the result of some d__n-fool love-affair that will cool in six months. When I wedded your mother, d'ye think we were a pair of mooning lovers, I at fifty and she a lass of twenty-two? We each of us knew what we were getting: I a pretty wife, a lady with fine Frenchy manners, and a mother for Bella—and she a fine house and servants, and a rich husband who would cast a blind eye towards a dowry divided to nothing betwixt three sisters. But we never pretended we were in love; that came later."

He shook his finger at me, like a school-master chastising an errant pupil, and seized hold of my collar as if to prevent me from escaping. "Now I'll warrant you that for all your cooing and your dainty verses," he continued, "your Miss Kenyon cares no more for you than she might for any handsome lad who has expectations of three thousand a year. Wed her, and in five years' time Sarah Kenyon will be flying her true colours and you'll be writing her no more love-poetry."

Sarah had succeeded better than she knew, in securing me with bonds not only of love but also of honour. I made my father a very sharp reply and he, irascible at the best of times, lost control of his temper.

"Wed Sarah Kenyon and I will turn you out without a shilling," he told me, his visage purple. "And if you've no more sense than to spend your days scribbling when you could be increasing a fine fortune—begod, why can't you have half as much sense as my brother's boy?"

Sarah, when I told her of the quarrel, suggested we wait at least a year ere we wed. Perhaps, said she, the delay would give my father an opportunity to re-think the matter. I should have seen then what was foremost in her mind—the question of my inheritance, just as my father had said, for he was seventy-six and in poor health. But during the following months my father and I quarrelled often, and bitterly, and perhaps in a moment of anger he altered his Will; for he suddenly fell ill and died not so long afterward without lifting pen to alter it once again. Let it suffice to say that a week after he was laid to rest in the crypt beneath the village church, I learnt that he had bequeathed the Pottery, his fortune, and all his property to my cousin Elijah.

How could I blame Elijah? He never had sought to ingratiate himself unduly with my father or poison his mind against me. He might have refused the inheritance altogether had not a certain clause in my father's Will stipulated that should he refuse it, it was to descend not to me but to my sister Arabella. A thoroughly honourable fellow, Elijah did the best he could for me. He proposed I should remain at Bridge House for as long as I wished, for the rest of my life if I liked, and go into partnership with him in the Pottery if I so desired.

I was young, and angry, and proud. I refused Elijah's generous offer and told him, with imprudent but forgivable bitterness, that I would not accept charity from an inheritance that ought to have been mine. I would take up the Law, I swore, as my father had once meant me to do, and I would make my own fortune and my own fame without aid from anybody.

The negligible portion my father had left me, in order that no one might say he had cut me off without a farthing, consisted of two hundred pounds outright and an income of fifty pounds a year: a tiny income indeed for a gentleman. I wished no other support save Sarah's love. Like the fool I was, I imagined Sarah at my side, softening, with a thousand little womanly tricks, the hardships we would undoubtedly endure ere I found a situation and succeeded in making a name for myself. I had no illusions that our first years as man and wife would be easy; when my earliest anger had cooled, despite my desperate love I resolved to free her, if she wished, from our engagement. But within a week of the reading of my father's Will, whilst the scandalous tidings still buzzed up and down the County, it was she who came to me.

She had ridden across the meadows to Bridge House and stood awaiting me in the hall, twisting her gloves in her hands, the riding-crop that dangled by its loop from her wrist dancing jerkily as her hands continued their restless motion.

"Sydney," she faltered, upon seeing me, "Mr. Carton . . . I do not know any proper and polite manner of saying—what I must say to you. But I must say it. I am sorry, Mr. Carton. I am very sorry indeed." She tugged at the diamond ring I had given her, fumbled and dropt it as I stood unmoving, already hearing the words she was about to say. The ring remained lying betwixt us on the Turkish carpet, winking up at me in the pale morning sunshine. "I cannot wed you."

"You said—you swore you loved me," said I at last, numb.

She leant a little towards me, her lips trembling. "I do, Sydney, I do! You must believe that."

"The money," said I. "It's the money, isn't it?"

"You must understand. Father has no sons to support him. He has withdrawn his consent. What choice have I?"

"I do understand." My voice was harsh, a stranger's voice. "Miss Kenyon, you cast your pretty eyes my way almost ere my brother was below ground. But now that I am no longer a fine catch, you can do far better than a student of Law living on a pound a week, and thus you drop me like a live coal. I understand perfectly."

She gazed appealingly at me, the cornflower eyes very bright and clear beneath her dark blue riding-hat. Strange that those wide-open eyes had so deceived me!

"Suffer me to offer you some parting advice, Miss Kenyon," I found myself adding. "Why not wed my cousin Elijah? Then you will have my inheritance, just as you planned: my fortune, and the manufactory, and Bridge House, and all. Surely, since I was evidently the least part of the bargain, for a husband my cousin will do as well as I."

She flushed a deep unbecoming red. "Trollop," I spat. "Get out. Get out of my sight. You will be back soon enough, I imagine, once I'm gone to London."

She turned without a word and hurried, running almost, out the door and back across the drive to the groom who held her mare. My last glimpse of her was of her wheaten curls bobbing behind her as she galloped away.

She did wed Elijah. She was brazen strumpet enough to secure him ten months later, or so I overheard from some source or other, for I never saw her since.

I CLOSED MY eyes to the past, caught the stage-coach to London as does every footloose young man, paid my fees to the Middle Temple with my trifling patrimony, and attached myself to the Law.

I might yet have made a modest success of myself had I not one day, in the Temple gardens, encountered an old school-mate, Clarence Stryver, then a newly-minted, impecunious Attorney. (At Shrewsbury he was not yet what he has since become; at ten or fifteen he was still the charity-pupil, the grocer's son, a fleshy, glib, ambitious boy acutely aware of his shabby clothes and humble station. It was not until he began to make a name and fortune for himself as a Barrister that he acquired the appalling complacency with which we are so familiar.)

Though no one could deny his audacity and his measure of cleverness, Stryver was not the success he ought to have been. Whilst his great talent lay in performing before a Court of Law, bullying and cajoling Witnesses and Juries alike (he would have enjoyed endless prosperity as a character-man upon the stage), he had not the facility for concocting a solid case of briefs and statements. I was precisely his opposite, gifted with a shrewd mind but with neither taste nor talent for the performance. In short, we soon agreed that the two of us together would make an admirable Barrister where, apart, there were none but a glib and unscrupulous pettifogger and an undistinguished plodder.

For I *was* a plodder. Despite my quick wit and the promise I had shown both at Shrewsbury School and at Louis-le-Grand, I did not shine in the practice of Law. I had not my father's nature, able to seize any opportunity and make the most of it; I was instead one of the many who are content enough with an unprofitable security, *fallentis semita vitae*, as Horace puts it, *the pathway of a life unnoticed.*

Content? No. I was not content. But neither did I know what would content me, now that my dream of a placid, comfortable country life had been snatched from me. Every man, I think, has his particular talent, the one path he was truly born to walk, and should he not discover it—as so many men do not—he will live out his days in vague dissatisfaction, or worse. The Law did not satisfy me and I knew not where my true path might lie.

Stryver made the most of the opportunity I offered him. As in our schoolboy days, he led, and I followed. I followed him still when everyone of our acquaintance grew to recognise Stryver as the coming man, and me as the dispirited ne'er-do-well who laboured for him, the failed lawyer who served in a mongrel capacity somewhere between clerk and very much inferior partner. He paid me well enough for my thankless labour that my former desire to set up a practice for myself faded and, at last, flickered out. When a road is safe and familiar, who but the enterprising, audacious man will strike out for himself thro' a wilderness in search of the treasure he may never find?

But neither did that safe, dull life of an unambitious drudge content me. My only refuge from that gnawing discontent of mine was in whores and in drink, first in jolly, noisy good-fellowship with Stryver, then more often alone with a bottle in the dim corner of a tavern, perhaps with the night's work spread out before me.

Thus the man I was, six years after my father's death. The man I was, who cared for nothing and no one and who wished for nothing but to drink himself to Oblivion. The man I was, who would spend fifteen wasted years suffering a man like Stryver to take full advantage of the talents he did not possess himself, and offer little enough in return. The hard truth is that Stryver needed me in order to appear the prodigy he pretended to be, and I needed him in return because I had lost all will to aspire to a career more profitable or rewarding. We were seen together nine days out of ten, worked together, drank together, wenched together; were inseparable as Damon and Pythias, and we each of us despised the other.

3

I MUST PAUSE here a moment in my account of my youth, and return to the bleak present. I did not take up my pen yesternight, for yesterday afternoon I saw a sight that so tore at my heart that I could do nothing but return to this dreary room and drink down a bottle of the wretched vinegar that passes for wine in these meagre times. It banished not an instant of the memory—the memory of a fair young woman going smiling to her death, as if she were going to her wedding. What I saw served but to strengthen my wavering resolve in proceeding, should the worst come to pass, with what I must do. For would Lucie, in her grief, choose a path different from the road that extraordinary young woman, who bears her name, so fearlessly chose to follow?

THE DAYS OF my young prime passed by me, one very much like the other, as did the years. In 1780 I was twenty-eight years old, and as bitter and jaded as an old *roué* of fifty.

"Truly I don't know why I bring you to these meetings," Stryver grumbled one March morning as we picked our way through the murky, stinking corridors of Newgate Prison. "Since meetings betwixt Counsel and client proceed in the hours of *daylight*," he added, peevishly, "you are generally more hindrance than help."

I yawned, screwing up my eyes against a head-ache. "You sound like my father."

"I mean to. It's for your own good—"

"Nothing I do is for my own good. Have you not perceived that by now?"

"I don't know why I keep you at all, in fact."

"Because you know full well, in your heart of hearts," said I, "that you couldn't do without me?"

"Pah! If I needed the smell of Port wine in order to live, perhaps."

"Don't speak ill of Port wine, or of punch; were it not for that, you'd not keep me at work."

"Work!" He snorted. "As if in Court you ever did more than fall asleep."

"Ah, but I'm there, am I not? You need only elbow me to avail yourself of my brilliancy. What's the case, then?"

"Treason," said he, patting the despatch-case under his arm. "Some Frog, caught with lists of his Majesty's forces in America . . ." He broke off, frowning. "Surely the charge should be Spying, not Treason, if the fellow is a foreign subject."

"Is he resident in England?" I enquired, without much interest.

"Three years, I believe."

"A foreign subject resident in England owes allegiance and fidelity to the British Crown, which shelters him," said I, "and should he betray the Crown he is as much a Traitor, in the eyes of the Law, as any man who is English-born." I gazed at Stryver, all innocency. "Why, I do believe that's why you keep me on, Stryver: to sort out the Law for you when you find yourself in over your head."

He grunted. "Well then, Treason it is. A quartering case, Carton. One doesn't see many of *them*."

"They gave up quartering sometime about the reign of the first George, if I don't mistake myself," said I, with another tremendous yawn, as I shook the lank hair from my eyes. "They'll hang the fellow at Tyburn, and there will be an end to it."

"*If* he is found Guilty."

"Indeed. Your legal acuity never ceases to amaze me."

"I do not intend that he shall be found Guilty."

"A commendable position for the Counsel for the Defence. *Bravissimo.* I would quite agree with you, could I muster up enough enthusiasm to care."

The turnkey ahead of us unlocked the door to the cell and gestured us inside. I slouched in behind Stryver, with scarce a glance at the young man who rose from his chair at the other side of the rough table, and leant against the wall, hands in my pockets. "Now, then," Stryver began, "Mr., er . . . d__n me, Sir, you do speak English, don't you? *Parley-voo?*"

"Yes, I speak English."

"Splendid. Otherwise I'd have had to prevail upon my colleague here to translate, for my French was never—good God!"

"Sir?" said the prisoner.

"Turn your face towards the light again, won't you? By God, Carton, look at this."

I raised my indifferent gaze towards the prisoner, and beheld the face that confronted me, clouded by tarnish, when at times I gathered the courage to glare into my cracked looking-glass.

My own face? Yes. And no. My own face, had my complexion not faded to the unhealthy pallor of those who, in keeping late and wearying hours, rarely saw the Sun, or had I taken the trouble to be properly shaved; my own face accented by its aquiline nose, ere discontent, self-pity, and hard living had carved the two channels slashing relentlessly downward from my nose to the corners of my mouth; my own dark eyes, had my eyes not been blood-shot and aching from the Port wine and brandy of the previous night, and the night ere that, and a hundred, a thousand nights ere that.

"Darnay," I said.

HE GAZED AT me a moment, uncomprehending. The disreputable fellow before him cannot, I know, have much resembled the companion he remembered from Louis-le-Grand.

"Carton?" he murmured at last, and despite his perilous circumstances broke into a smile of sheer pleasure. "*Carton . . .*"

I nodded. "You did say we would meet again. I wish it were not in such disagreeable surroundings."

"You see me here in a predicament not of my own making. It seems I have an unknown enemy . . ."

I turned to Stryver, who stood observing us, mouth a little open in amazement. "Mr. Darnay and I are old acquaintances."

"More than acquaintances, surely," said Darnay. "Carton, I never dreamt—but I could wish for none other as my defence counsel—"

"You are mistaken," said I. "I am not your counsel, Mr. Stryver is. Pray allow him to proceed."

Puzzled by my reticence, he gestured Stryver to the other chair and seated himself once more. Whilst Stryver fired questions at his client and fussed with his sheaf of documents, growing ever redder with his exertions, I took Darnay's measure. He was pale beneath his Sun-tanned complexion, though that was but to be expected in such an ill-omened spot as Newgate Prison. Despite the signs of wear brought about by his sojourn in Newgate, his clothes were of fine quality, and well though simply cut. And he had grown into a comely fellow, that looking-glass twin of mine, with the intelligence I remembered in his calm eyes: an eminently accomplished, principled, clean-living young man of modest but comfortable circumstances, no doubt innocent as any new-born lamb of the frightful charges against him.

My looking-glass image? thought I. No, no longer, not in the least. He had fulfilled his promise, it seemed, the promise we both had demonstrated in those carefree days in Paris, whilst I—I, thrust into the unforgiving world, had so quickly come to nothing. What, I brooded, could I and that Paragon possibly hold now in common? Darnay, plain as day, was an industrious, abstemious sort of fellow; whilst I was one who more likely than not would awaken at midday with a throbbing head-ache and a blacked eye—or perhaps a dose of clap. (Stryver told me more often than once, when in a school-masterish humour, that my loose and dissolute habits but hardened his persuasion that I was born to be hanged.) This after toiling through my days at drudgery I despised, in a thwarted career I never had desired, in a shoddy grey existence of blighted dreams.

I gazed at my looking-glass image, once my dearest friend, and all at once hated him.

Stryver, concluding his interview, gathered up his papers and beckoned me away. "A moment," I muttered, and held my tongue until my employer had left us alone together. Then I turned to Darnay, who approached me, offering his hand.

"What the Devil do you do in England?" said I, hands in my pockets still. "Did you not have obligations in France?"

"I dwell here," said he, his smile fading. "I teach the French language to private students here in London. I have no property in France, not yet. Carton, you cannot believe that I would have so quickly forgotten you, and our friendship, even tho' I had no word from you. Three years since, when first I arrived in England, I went to Staffordshire, hoping to find you . . . they told me you were gone to London, with no address . . ."

"Were I you, Darnay," I drawled, "at this precarious moment, I should worry less about obsolete acquaintanceships, and more about my own neck."

He paused a moment, disconcerted, but blundered on. "I—I see you have become a Barrister, just as you expected . . . how do you fare, then?"

"How do I fare?" I echoed him. "D__n you, take a look at me. How do you imagine I fare?" Without another word I strode out of the chamber, leaving him staring, ashen, behind me.

"THAT CURSED SECRET business of his," Stryver repeated, over his mutton-chop at the Tudor Rose. "He cannons betwixt Dover and Calais like a Kentish smuggler, and then refuses to divulge his secrets to his own Counsel! Could you get nothing out of him?"

"Why should I?" said I, glowering at my plate.

"Well, d__n me, you know the fellow."

"I once knew him."

"Well? What's his secret?"

"He is of the petty Nobility," I told him, thinking back on all the confidences Darnay and I had shared. "His name is not Darnay, tho' he never did tell me the true one."

"A Nobleman?" said Stryver, thro' a mouthful of mutton and potatoes. "Why the deuce is he teaching French in London, then? —Here, Moll, another bottle." He tossed a farthing at the bar-maid, who deftly caught it and pulled a face at him behind his back ere giving me a grin and a wink. "Hasn't he a château to keep up, and a place at King Louis's Court, like all those mincing Frenchies?"

"Not all the French Nobility dwell at Versailles," said I, with laborious patience, "any more than all the English Gentry dwell in London. Most do not. Most are worrying how they can afford to mend the roofs on their manor-houses. All that keeps the poorest of them apart from their peasants is their ancient privileges, and their pride. When Darnay and I were at school together in Paris, my family was by far the wealthier of the two."

Stryver grunted and filled his glass from the bottle of Bordeaux wine that Molly thumped down before him. "But why," he persisted, "must the fellow forever be dashing back and forth? It's d__n' suspicious-looking, you know. He'll say only that it's a matter of family obligation: his dying mother begged him to right some dreadful wrong committed by his father, and his father's family. What do you know of that?"

"Nothing." I could have told him, perhaps, of all that Darnay had divulged to me about his family's ill reputation, and his father's; but I had given Darnay my word of honour, those several years ago, and my honour, whatsoever its worth, was all that remained to me. "Nothing at all."

"Hasn't our principled dunce reckoned that if found Guilty—and at the Old Bailey it's more likely than not that he will be—he'll have little opportunity to make his confounded amends after he is hauled away by the Tyburn mare?" He drank down the glassful and poured out more.

"Confound them all, I say. Frenchies—pah!"

HOW, I WONDER now, gazing back across the years, could I have guessed on that March day of 1780 that Darnay's trial would transform my existence once again?

Perhaps she scarce noticed me that morning, so intent was she on Darnay's plight. But I noticed her. And I must confess my first glimpse of her inspired in me not admiration but aversion. Not thro' any fault of hers, God knows, but for the mere circumstance that Nature had blest her with a fragile beauty, with hair like ripe wheat and eyes of cerulean blue.

That morning I had scarce bestirred myself to take more than a passing interest even in the Prisoner, the object of my diligent and head-splitting travail of the nine nights past. Why, then, should the entrance of a few Witnesses have disturbed my bored and blurred contemplation of the chamber's ceiling? Yet something, perhaps the malicious Angel or demon that has played its tricks upon me all my life, prompted me to look away from the sooty plaster to the Witnesses' bench.

My God, can it be Sarah? thought I, with a flush of contempt and desire all mingled. But of course it was not, I told myself an instant later. Sarah must have been, by 1780, an elegant brittle young matron nearer thirty than twenty; whilst Lucie, at twenty-two, shone with a delicate sweet innocency that Sarah, even at seventeen, never had truly possessed.

"Lovely . . . lovely," muttered Stryver.

Lovely, lovely, I echoed him silently, *a perfect little golden-haired doll.* I attempted to look away, for I had had too much already in my life of golden hair and limpid blue eyes, but found I could not, found my gaze betraying me.

Stryver elbowed me hard in the ribs and I returned to the present, tearing my gaze from Lucie and once again turning it unwillingly towards Darnay, accused of Treason before the Bar. Sir Robert Hetherington, the Judge, entered, and the solemn ceremonious Tom-foolery of the judicial ritual began. I confess I did not listen to it, for I was remembering once again how Sarah, lovely Sarah, had so coldly spurned and betrayed me. Only when old Sharpe, the Attorney-General, rose and began to vent his spleen, claiming Darnay's frequent travels were of a treasonable nature, did I take any notice of the process.

I found, to my sour surprise, that despite my bitterness I cared profoundly about Darnay's fate. They hang, rather than disembowel, traitors in England these days, but in truth no law prohibits the full severity of the judgment—and perhaps a Judge might not extend a foreigner such leniency. Quartering aside, to hang a fellow by the neck until dead, to leave him to strangle and writhe and piss his breeches for twenty minutes at the end of a rope, is sheer barbarity in itself: not even a traitor deserves so foul a death. Yet my concern went beyond that of merely sparing any fellow human creature such an end. In seeing this man who once had been almost a brother to me, this man who bore my face, I seemed to see myself there in the dock, and to feel on my own flesh all that he might suffer. Should Darnay be condemned, would I not see myself led to the scaffold, sense some part of me dying as well?

I shook off such grisly fancies and returned to the present, tho' I could not so easily banish the memories he held for me. The Attorney-General continued to blare on, as he presented the chief Witnesses for the Prosecution. (To what villainous lengths the Courts would resort in our enlightened age, in order to reap their quota of condemnations! I doubt many folk are aware that a sessions in which none of the Accused are condemned to Death is, amongst the legal fraternity, derisively styled *a maiden sessions.*)

The two Witnesses the Prosecution presented to us were manifestly of the worst species of Affidavit-men, members of that disreputable brotherhood always to be found hovering near Newgate and Westminster Hall, their trade (Witness willing to swear to anything for the right price) advertised by the straws thrust in their shoes. Roger Cly, domestic servant, and John Barsad, gentleman, were in truth no more than a pair of knights of the post, at one's disposal for any unsavoury tasks one might wish performed. The affair smelt very strong indeed of a clumsy plot, the Devil only knew why, concocted against Darnay.

The case at its simplest rested upon the nature of Darnay's travels betwixt England and France. Barsad and Cly had brought false evidence against him, claiming he was passing lists of his Majesty's troops and their deployments in North America to agents of France. And as England was at war still with the odious Colonies, which were, now aided by the equally obnoxious French, tenaciously fighting the King's troops still after five weary years, this charge was a very severe one indeed.

I glanced at Darnay as Sharpe thundered to a conclusion. Composed still, Darnay had, nonetheless, gone a trifle paler.

So, Darnay, I mused, *you are not quite perfect after all?*

The patriotic Barsad, of doggedly respectable appearance (but whose broken nose and long narrow visage lent him an undoubted weaselly shiftiness), rattled off his unimpeachable testimony with far too much precision. My egregious employer bounded to his feet like a top-heavy Jack-in-the-Box as the Witness concluded, commencing his cross-examination with the bullying, cozening, cajoling *politesse* that was his particular Genius, and made mince-meat of him. It was a pleasure to see the villain squirm as he reluctantly recalled his various sojourns in debtors' prisons and the various denunciations levelled against him regarding knavery at gaming-tables.

So, Messrs. Barsad and Cly, I mused, *we have your measure, and we have you.* If the Jurymen could not conclude that a man of such a monstrous irregular memory was patently one of that species whose aforementioned memory was best jogged by coin of the Realm, they were more fat-headed even than their appearance proclaimed them.

Stryver, having disposed of Barsad, set to work upon Roger Cly, irreproachable patriot. I confess I did not much listen to their exchange. This once, at least, my easy acquaintance with London's less reputable taverns had stood me in good stead, for the gossip I had gathered about the two scoundrels would be telling, I knew. That Stryver would turn the ruffian inside-out, and flay him in the bargain, I did not doubt.

I DOZED, AS the examinations and cross-examinations and ceaseless commentary from the gallery settled into a wordless roaring in my ears. Only when the roar swelled unexpectedly did I withdraw my gaze from the ceiling, though without troubling to move in the least, and cast about for its source. I soon found it, as I espied Lucie standing in the Witness-box, a Witness for the Prosecution.

Lucie Manette, spinster, aged twenty-two, born a French subject, resident in England since childhood. I heard her name for the first time then, tho' at first glance I thought little enough of her. *Truly,* I brooded, *this Miss Manette is no more than a pink and gold dress-maker's doll.* Sarah had looked so once, too, had been equally lovely as she coldly shattered all my dreams, and shattered, too, my faith in women's constancy. What heedless, indifferent damage, I wondered, would the mantua-maker's doll do the Prisoner? Stryver, beside me, shook his head in vexation.

I was wrong, of course. Could anybody have felt more anguish at the thought of the terrible consequences that might arise from her innocent testimony? I shall never forget the beseeching, compassionate gaze she turned upon Darnay as Sharpe requested her to describe their first meeting on a crossing from Calais to Dover five years previous.

No, I realised, she was not in the least like Sarah. Sarah would never have gazed at any human creature with such concern and compassion as Lucie lavished on the young man in the dock. Sarah Kenyon, wheaten-haired and cornflower-eyed, exquisite and cold as porcelain, would wash her hands of such a matter and hope most sincerely that her reputation should remain untainted; would not weep publicly in the Witness-box for sympathy for a man likely doomed to the most degrading of deaths.

Perhaps human nature is not entirely contemptible, I reflected.

"Mr. Darnay—the Prisoner—told me," she stated, "that he was travelling on personal business of a delicate nature, which might endanger him, and others, and that therefore he was making his journeys betwixt France and England under an assumed name." How could I not have perceived how her glance wavered from Sharpe's scowling visage to that of the Prisoner?

If only Stryver could have persuaded Darnay to reveal the nature of his mysterious private business! What family secret could be of so scandalous a nature, I yet wonder, that it was worth risking death for?

The Prosecution done, Stryver approached the Witness-box, clad in his most soothing manner. "Could you indeed swear that the incriminating papers in the Attorney-General's keeping, those lists of his Majesty's forces of which so much has been said, were those selfsame papers that you had seen in the Prisoner's possession?"

Lucie had gone paler and paler during the Prosecution's interrogatory, but a faint eager flush of pink appeared on her cheeks as some hope returned to her eyes and she hastened to dissent.

"They might have been anything?" continued Stryver. "Private letters of the Prisoner's, perhaps?"

Her distress was apparent as she shook her head and repeated that she did not know. But Stryver was sufficiently satisfied.

"We have them!" he gloated, plumping into his seat beside me. "By gad, we've got them! Did you see, Carton? The Prosecution's Witness became the best Witness we could have had. *She* knows he's no spy, and those two scurvy rascals hindered Sharpe's case more than they aided it. Darnay is a free man."

I shrugged. Other testimony remained to be heard. But I perceived that in returning to the Witnesses' bench, Lucie cast a backward glance at the Prisoner, who met it, and the compassion and encouragement in her glance brought a tender smile to Darnay's lips. I found myself observing her beneath half-closed eyelids, alert but unsurprised a moment later when, distress at last overcoming her, she abruptly changed colour and clutched at her father's shoulder.

I promptly called for an officer and told him to conduct her outside.

When they had assisted her into the fresh air, I settled once more into my chair, tipping it precariously backward, evincing far more detachment than I felt.

Her father took the stand. Alexandre Manette, Physician, aged fifty— tho' he looked seventy—French-born, resident in England for the five years past. He gave his brief testimony very softly and reluctantly, I recall, "that during the voyage in question he had been ill, owing to a long and unjust imprisonment in his native land—in the infamous Bastille in fact—and had no memory of his encounter with the Prisoner."

Mr. Lorry, the Banker, provided little more meat for the Prosecution's case. "During his return journey from Paris to London on the twenty-third of November 1775 as an agent of Tellson's Bank—in keeping with his errand in France with the aforesaid Witness, Miss Manette, that of claiming her newly-released father—owing to a certain indisposition when on board ship, he had been obliged to retreat promptly to a cabin, and thus did not meet the Prisoner until landfall at Dover."

Such testimony was of little value to either side. But as a parting blow the Prosecution presented a Witness whose disinterest in the matter was undeniable: Obadiah Goodwin, waiter at the King's Arms, Canterbury, who swore "that on the nineteenth of November 1775, in the course of his duties, he had seen the Prisoner loitering about the coffee-room of the Hotel, as if waiting for some unknown person". Upon being pressed, he insisted that he could not have been mistaken, whereupon the Prosecution smugly returned to its bench.

Stryver handled him with great care, as a Witness of some credibility. Despite Stryver's determined battering at him, however, Goodwin continued to insist that the man he had seen (on a single occasion, five years previous, at a distance of some thirty feet, on a busy Friday night) was the Prisoner.

Stryver shot me a hasty glance that said *D__n me, Carton, give me something.* For myself, I could not imagine how he had overlooked the most obvious card to play in his predicament. (But then Stryver has never been the most perceptive of men.) I scrawled *Ask him if he would recognise me as surely as he does Darnay* on a scrap of paper, screwed it up, and tossed it to him. He caught it and stood tapping it into his palm as he awaited the Witness's latest response. Unfolding the note at last, Stryver smirked, and very pleasantly asked the Witness if ever he had seen anybody who resembled the Prisoner.

"No, Sir," replied the fool, confident as ever. "Not so as I couldn't have told the difference."

"You couldn't have mistaken the Prisoner for somebody else? For the Attorney-General, for instance, or for me?" He cleared his throat as the onlookers snickered. "Then why not look at my learned friend there, Mr. Goodwin. Could you have mistaken the Prisoner for him? —If m'Lud would suffer Mr. Carton to remove his wig?"

The fellow gaped at me as I rose to my feet, pulling off my unkempt old peruke. "Look at my learned friend, Mr. Goodwin, don't be hasty," Stryver persisted, "and then look at the Prisoner again. Would you say they resemble each other?"

The Court evidently thought so. The roar swelled, stabbing at my skull. Wincing, I slouched to the dock and leant against it, hands in my pockets, my visage an arm's length from Darnay's.

"Mr. Stryver," enquired Sir Robert, testily, "do you intend that next we shall try Mr. Carton for Treason?"

"Certainly not, m'Lud, begging your pardon," bellowed Stryver, above the ensuing laughter, "but I should like to ask the Witness if what has happened once might not happen again. Mr. Goodwin, might you have taken Mr. Carton for the Prisoner on the occasion we are discussing?"

"Tell the truth, Sir,"—and he appeared uneasy—"I might have done."

"And might you have seen another man, some unknown man, who sufficiently resembled the Prisoner, at a distance of thirty feet, in the course of a busy evening *five years ago?* Think carefully, Mr. Goodwin: a man's life hangs upon your testimony!"

"Yes, Sir," he admitted, "I might have done."

"No more questions, m'Lud," said Stryver, primly, adding with a hiss: "For God's sake, Carton, sit down!"

I obeyed: clapping my peruke askew onto my throbbing head, folding my arms, and leaning backward on my chair once again. Stryver presented our Witnesses (men of far more honest aspect than those of the Prosecution, I may add) and cross-examination proceeded with no very fruitful result. Prosecution and Defence presented their closing statements; the Judge, in a manner not calculated to reassure the Prisoner, instructed the Jury; the Jurymen turned to confer.

It was ever my custom to doze off during the deliberations. Yet sleep, or the blank-eyed lethargy that so often took its place, did not come to me so easily as on other days. To my confusion, I found myself thinking of Lucie, whilst about me the Attorneys fretted and fidgeted. At length I drowsed a while, a golden-haired vision haunting my dreams; I cannot in truth state if that dream-creature were she or if it were Sarah.

The renewed commotion awoke me. The Jury appeared uncertain and Sir Robert waved a dismissive hand towards the Jury-room. Stryver blotted his brow.

"I believe I shall have some dinner," said I, with a glance at my watch.

He glared at me. "Now?"

"Why not?"

"They may be out only a quarter-hour."

"Unlikely, if they are asking to retire."

"You may miss the verdict."

I reflected a moment, shrugged, and slouched away. Tho' I was indeed praying most fervently for Darnay's life, I had now done all I could to deliver him from the Law's clutches; his fate, whether he went free or was hanged at Tyburn, was no longer in my hands.

"How is the young lady?" I enquired, encountering Lorry in passing.

"She is recovering, Mr.—er—Sir," he told me, reaching fretfully up to tug his little flaxen peruke down at the ears. "She will do very well. The air is doing her good."

"I will tell Darnay she is better," said I, perceiving the old gentleman glancing dubiously in the Prisoner's direction. "It wouldn't do, would it, for a respectable man of Business to be seen talking to a fellow in the dock?" I left Lorry puffing in embarrassed indignation behind me. What an impertinent puppy he thought me!

"Mr. Darnay," I drawled, approaching the Bar, "I expect you are concerned for the young lady. She is well, will recover."

"I am glad to hear it."

"What do you expect, then, from the Jury?"

"The worst."

"You are very likely right," said I, envy—of every upright quality he so manifestly possessed that I did not—goading me to spiteful, petty cruelty. "Yet I think this delay probably speaks in your favour." I inclined my head, in a manner more insolent than civil, and turned on my heel.

I DINED AND wined at the Tudor Rose and returned to discover Stryver prowling anxiously still betwixt Lorry's seat and his own. To my secret relief, I perceived Lucie at her father's side once again, as he spoke animatedly to her. I spent another half-hour dozing on the edge of my chair ere the Jury reappeared, solemn and not a little embarrassed at the gravity of their civic duty.

Not Guilty, else I would not be writing this to-day.

Darnay, who I suspect would not have moved a muscle or shed a tear had the solemn sentence of Death been read to him, bent his head and hid his face in his arms, trembling.

So, Darnay, I mused once again, with a species of queer malicious triumph, *you are not quite perfect after all?*

4

I RETURNED FROM the robing-room, and two rapid glasses of Port wine to ease my head-ache, to discover a crowd clustered about Darnay, congratulating him. I espied Lucie there, and saw the gazes she exchanged with him as she expressed her relief at his deliverance. Retreating a pace, I waited in the shadows until the group proceeded to the open air and with an encouraging Good-bye to Darnay she led her father to a carriage.

"Well, Mr. Lorry," said I, without turning, gazing at her chariot as it drove away, "respectable men of Business may now be seen with Mr. Darnay?"

"I have my duty to Tellson's to consider, Mr. . . . ."

"Carton."

"Mr. Carton," he sputtered, patting his peruke into place, "though really I don't see what business it is of yours—"

"Business! Bless you, Sir, I *have* no business."

"It's a pity you've not, Mr. Carton," said he. "If you had, perhaps you—would attend to it." He bit off the remainder of his address and gave me a keen glance. "Forgive me," said he, with a nod. "I bid you Good-night, Sir. And Mr. Darnay, I trust God has preserved you for a long, happy, and prosperous life." As his sedan-chair disappeared into the gloom, Darnay and I, left alone, gazed at each other.

"I have not yet thanked you for your rôle in my acquittal," said Darnay at last.

"You don't look at all well, Darnay," said I, ignoring his words. "When did they feed you last?"

"Midday."

"You ought to dine." Long-denied memories would not suffer me to part once again from my looking-glass image, or what might have been my image had the malicious Angel of my destiny been kinder to me. "*I* dined," I added, "whilst those numskulls were debating your fate. Permit me to show you to a good dinner, at least."

The landlord at the Tudor Rose, who knew me well, gave me no more than a passing glance and a nod as I called for a bottle of Port. Allowing my companion a half-hour to dine undisturbed, at length I poured myself a fourth glass and hooked my elbow about the back of the chair. "Are you recovering your equilibrium, then?"

He nodded. "I am. Thank you."

I already had drunk more than I ought to have, and the wine was making me (as it often did) both loquacious and bitter. "I am gratified to see you take such pleasure in the world to which you are returned. As for me, I would be as well out of it."

Darnay glanced at me, unsure of how to reply, and gazed deliberately at his plate.

"This world," I persisted, "has treated me most unkindly. Now don't deny it—I know you too well—don't deny that you'd care to learn by what black miracle I was translated into the shabby sottish fellow you see before you. Perhaps you are burning to discover why the good Mr. Lorry should blush like a virgin pinched on the arse. Aren't you?" I added, when Darnay made me no reply. "Of course you are. Well, Mr. Darnay, I shall tell you why, whether you care or no. I believe Lorry belatedly recognised me as the former heir of a certain prosperous gentleman of Business, a client of Tellson's in fact, who, some years since, unexpectedly disinherited his only surviving son in favour of his nephew. What do you think of that, Mr. Darnay?"

"Why do you tell me this?" said he.

"Why indeed? To illustrate how Fortune shapes a man: how she may take two men cast in the same mould, and fling one about, to bruise and batter him. You, Mr. Darnay, have not been flung about, I think, until quite recently; and your adventure at the Old Bailey isn't likely to leave a permanent dent."

"Could you not," Darnay ventured, "be reconciled with your father?"

"I could not."

"Surely—"

"Not in this world, Mr. Darnay. He died, some six years since, and left a Will cutting me off with a shilling—namely: a nominal sum to meet the expenses of completing my education and buying my way to the Bar, and a trifling allowance that more or less keeps me in Port wine and brandy, and then I might go to the Inns of Court or to the Devil. So there you have it. Do you expect me to have much fondness for Mankind? Or Life itself, for that matter?"

"I am sorry for your misfortune, Carton."

"No, you are thinking I might have set my teeth and made something of myself through my own efforts, as many others have done without benefit of patrimony. Are you not?" I laughed, disagreeably. "*You* have done so, it seems, and quite successfully. But whilst Chance gave us the same countenance, it was more capricious in doling out our other qualities. God saw fit to mock me, old friend, by bestowing upon me more than the usual modicum of natural gifts . . . yet denying me the ability to make proper use of them." I shook my head. "No, Mr. Darnay, we are not very much alike after all, you and I."

I took a bitter pleasure in provoking him, as if I could assuage the acid envy churning in my belly by reassuring myself that he was capable at least of stooping to a sharp retort. "Come," I suggested, "why don't we have a toast? To your freedom, perhaps. Or—to old friendships. Yes, that's very good. Or, to . . ." I shrugged.

"To—"

"Don't be obtuse, Darnay; to the name on the tip of your tongue. To the name of that golden-haired china-doll who was so distressed by your peril."

"To Miss Manette, then."

"Miss Manette, then!" I echoed him, and emptied the glass to fling it crashing into the hearth. "Waiter, another glass! Well, Darnay, is she worth being tried for one's life?"

With the faintest of frowns, Darnay said: "You and Mr. Stryver saved my life to-day. Again, I must offer you my thanks, inadequate as they are."

"You needn't offer *me* any thanks," I drawled. "D'you think I cared a tinker's d__n what became of you? I exercised my wits towards your acquittal because Stryver paid me to do so. And I don't care to see an innocent man hanged from Tyburn tree . . . but there end my sympathies. Tell me, do you think I like you?"

"You once did."

"Ah, but that's all water under the bridge now, isn't it? Long past. D'you think I like you—to-day?"

"You did act for a moment as though you do . . ."

"Did I? I must be drunk. But you, accomplished fellow that you are, you must have come to *that* conclusion already."

"To answer your question . . . no, I don't think you like me, and I am heartily sorry for it."

"*I* don't think I do, either," I agreed.

"Nevertheless, I hope it will not prevent me from calling the reckoning," said Darnay, ringing for the waiter.

When Darnay had quitted me I sat unmoving, gazing into the candle-flame as if I could extract some wisdom from it. I had failed even to provoke his temper. *The capable and faultless Darnay*, I brooded once again. *Had I been born in his skin, and he in mine, would I have made more of myself, to be gazed at by those pretty blue china-doll eyes, and to be thought worthy of pity and compassion?*

I ran both hands through the hair that hung straggling across my shoulders and reached for my bottle and glass. "To the Devil with Darnay," I muttered, scowling at the distorted reflexion leering back at me from the bottle's side. *And to the Devil, too*, I added, *with Miss Lucie Manette for waking me, when I was content enough to sleep-walk my way through this botched life of mine; and d___n father and Sarah and the whole world entirely, and d___n me.*

I WOKE, STILL in my clothes, the following noon-tide, flinging an arm across my eyes as the sunlight creeping through the shutters assailed them. It was my habit to forget a case as soon as ever the trial ended, yet to my sullen surprise I found that memories of the day previous nagged at me still. I could not banish Lucie's lovely face, and the gentle, compassionate look she had cast Darnay's way, from my thoughts.

Rising, I surveyed my image in the cracked looking-glass. I could claim still to be a well-favoured fellow, tho' hard living had left its mark about my eyes in lines and shadows too soon acquired. I poured myself a glass of Port from the bottle I kept in my wardrobe and drank it off in a few swallows ere stumbling to the wash-stand.

The walk to Frith-street in Soho cleared my head. Biting my lip, I stood irresolute for a moment outside the house before putting hand to the door-knocker.

Pross answered the door and, to my mingled vexation and embarrassment, first mistook me for Darnay. I promptly disabused her of her error and she stared astounded at me, clapping a hand to her heart as I turned a moment towards the light. It was so uncharacteristic a gesture for such a tall, raw-boned, mannish woman as she, whom a fashionable witticism of the day would unkindly have styled *a horse's Godmother,* that I very nearly laughed. Dear ugly, loyal Pross!

Gesturing me inside to the sitting-room, she told me that Miss Lucie and her father were out but were expected back within half an hour. After demanding of me (in a most aggressive tone) if I would care for a glass of Sherry, she quitted me, not without a dubious backward glance at me.

I slowly gazed about the chamber, savouring its charm, for its air soothed me as cool water soothes a parched throat. The subtle signs of a woman's presence were everywhere, from the silk flowers in a vase on the mantel-shelf to the half-completed embroidery peeping from her work-basket. A faint scent of lavender caressed the air. I had not seen such a room, tended with love and care, since my father's death. Or rather, I realised with a pang, since my mother's death, long ere that, when my home had been given over to a stern housekeeper who was intolerant of dust but indifferent to flowers.

Voices in the hallway cut short my reminiscences. Lucie entered a moment later, smiling as she saw me. "Mr. Carton," said she, offering me her hand. "Of course I remember you. You had a rôle in Mr. Darnay's acquittal yesterday, as Mr. Stryver's associate, did you not?"

"I took some small part in it, yes," I muttered. I pressed her hand and, as she moved away, drew both my own hands back and clasped them very tightly behind me to still their trembling. "I came to express my hopes," I added, "that you and your father had recovered from the strain of the trial."

She smiled, nodding. "Indeed we have, with such a happy conclusion to it. You are very kind to enquire, Mr. Carton."

"It's you who are kind to remember me, Miss Manette."

"O, but I could never forget you, Mr. Carton: not after seeing you and Mr. Darnay together."

I winced, imperceptibly. How could she have known what sentiments I harboured towards Darnay at that moment, and towards her?

Her father joined us. To my surprise he paused in the doorway, clutching suddenly at the door-post as if he could no longer support his own frail-seeming frame. He gazed at me intently, a frown that seemed almost a look of fear furrowing his pallid brow. Lucie was quick to notice his distraction and hurried to him to take his hand in hers.

"It's Mr. Carton, father. Don't you remember? He assisted Mr. Stryver in saving Mr. Darnay's life yesterday."

"Yes . . . yes," he murmured, raising a hand to his eyes. "I . . . I seem to see them everywhere . . ."

I could make nothing of his statement and neither, I think, could Lucie.

"Mr. Carton strongly resembles Mr. Darnay," she told him gently. "The resemblance perhaps saved him, father."

"Yes," said he, more confident, "of course. Pray forgive me, Mr. Carton. Will you not stop and take a dish of tea with us?"

I accepted, though tea was not a beverage I was in the habit of drinking. I confess I found myself tongue-tied before the two of them, her father by reason of his long ordeal in the Bastille (for what might one say in all innocency that would remind him of that horror?) and Lucie for reasons I could not yet shape into words.

"Tell me, Mr. Carton," she enquired, after some polite and trivial conversation, "whose was the idea to point out the resemblance between you and Mr. Darnay—yours or Mr. Stryver's?"

"Mine, Miss Manette; one cannot long disregard one's own looking-glass image."

"How fortunate for Mr. Darnay that you are so like!"

"Indeed, Miss Manette."

"And how fortunate, too, for Mr. Stryver, that he may call you his associate."

That old perverse spirit of mine seemed determined she should know the worst about me ere she knew the best. I cocked a sardonic eyebrow and said, "You could scarce call me his associate."

"His colleague, then."

"Say *drudge*, rather," I persisted.

"'Drudge', Mr. Carton?" Her smooth brow furrowed with a trace of that concern I had seen in her visage when she had gazed at Darnay. If only she could have guessed how such compassion, directed towards me, soothed my bruised spirit!

I told her the bald truth, that Stryver and I together made a fine Attorney, whilst apart we were no more than a couple of pettifoggers.

"I think, Sir, you do yourself an injustice," she told me, with a reassuring smile.

"Not at all," said I. "I have no illusions, Miss Manette."

Then her father, all unsuspecting, rescued me and Lucie both from a bitter and self-pitying recital of my life by enquiring what a pettifogger was. "*Un avocassier,* Doctor," I translated. "A wrangling, unscrupulous, unduly conceited lawyer." At Lucie's pleased surprise that I spoke French, I admitted that my mother had been French and that I had studied at Louis-le-Grand.

"I expect you speak better French than do I," she told me, laughing. "I have dwelt so long in England—but of course I have used it often since God returned my father to me," she added, with a tender glance at the Doctor. He reached out a bony hand and patted hers, saying nothing. With a sudden pang I remembered how I had longed for just such a trifling token of affection from my own father, and had never, almost since the days I was riding a hobby-horse about the nursery still, received it.

"Your home is charming," I declared. "No, that's not what I mean to say—tho' it is charming—but that is too trivial a description. I mean rather . . . welcoming, and delightful. I have seen little enough of that, of late, that it warms me as well as a fire might."

"You are not married, Mr. Carton?" she enquired.

"No." I could scarce have looked it, slovenly, careless fellow that I was, though that day I had taken some pains to appear presentable for her.

"If our home can offer you some cheer, Mr. Carton," said she, "we would be most gratified. Will you not call on us again?"

Court her, I thought, yearning suddenly for a settled, tranquil life. *Court her and win her, start afresh, seize the chance for happiness whilst yet you can.* For Lucie, I thought, for a fleeting moment at least, I could be a sober, hard-working, domesticated fellow.

"I thank you, Miss Manette," was all I said.

I knew not what else to say and neither, it seemed, did she. She poured out another dish of tea, talking hastily of the Italian operas that she and her father were fond of attending.

Pross swept into the room, announced "Mr. Darnay" very much as if she were accusing him of some great crime, and disappeared once more. He entered, pausing as he saw me there, and made me a civil nod.

"Mr. Darnay is a frequent visitor here," said Lucie, dimpling from him to me. "But of course, you have met, have you not?"

"We've met," said I, rising.

"Yes, we are acquainted." Darnay bowed to me most cordially. "Good day, Mr. Carton." His civility, following hard upon my insolence of the night previous, vexed me beyond measure.

"You are fully recovered from your ordeal, Msr. Darnay?" enquired Dr. Manette, in French.

"Completely, *Monsieur le Docteur*," he assented, with a polite nod. "I thank you. I shall be none the worse for my trouble, I think," he added, in English.

"You may speak French if you wish, Mr. Darnay," I drawled (for I knew I was his equal in that one small capacity at least), "without exceeding the bounds of *politesse*. I speak it tolerable well myself, as you know."

"Mr. Carton was educated in Paris," Lucie added, "and he has just told us his mother was French." She clapt her hands to her mouth, astonished. "O my . . . do you think, Mr. Darnay, Mr. Carton, since you are both French, or part French: do you think in some fashion you might be related?"

"I think not," said Darnay, too hastily.

"No," I echoed him, "no relation indeed."

He is in love with her, I mused, as I drank the last of my cooling tea. *Any fool could see it. He is besotted, and who would not be, with such care and concern lavished upon him, and from such a beauty as she?*

"I must take my leave of you," I declared, suddenly brusque.

"You will call upon us again, won't you, Mr. Carton?" said Lucie, as she escorted me to the door. "You would be most welcome. And Mr. Stryver, too, of course."

"Stryver?"

"After having done Mr. Darnay such a service, we must of course count both you and he amongst our friends."

"O yes, of course," said I, nodding, and bade her Good-day.

He loves her, but does she love him? The question pounded at me in cadence with my footsteps as I trudged through Soho towards the Strand. In truth, what qualities did Darnay possess, I mused, that I did not? He was a fine-looking, well-made man; but then so was I, when I cared to be. He had an easy, pleasant manner about him, and an undeniable generosity of spirit, I conceded unwillingly; whilst I cared not who might fall victim, now and then, to my sarcastic tongue. I had not such an easy manner as Darnay, to be sure, but I could be affable, when it pleased me to be, and had a certain wit that I thought he had always lacked.

Hard-working? Undoubtedly he was . . . and so was I, tho' I got no credit, or profit, or satisfaction of it. Were I to shake off this lethargy of spirit, I thought, fulfil the promise they said I showed in my youth . . . what then? Old Willoughby, at Shrewsbury, once said he would see me a Judge some day. I had sorely disappointed his expectations, but who was to say I could not yet rise to the top of my profession, if I put my mind and heart to it?

I paused in my route and laughed aloud. An old woman hawking buns from a tray turned to stare at me.

There you go again, Carton, I told myself, *building castles in the air. You day-dream, and fail to act; will you truly, do you think, find the will to shake off your apathy, swear off brandy and Port wine forever, leave Stryver to flounder thro' as best he can, and shamelessly thrust yourself into the public gaze as does he? For what goal, Carton? For the love of a sweet-natured, tender-hearted woman, or for the satisfaction of stealing her from under the nose of the man who desires her? Would you make such an effort, merely to score off a fellow who shows you what you might have been?*

Be dispassionate, Carton, I told myself, *and admit the truth.*

I RESOLVED, AND strengthened my resolve with two glasses of brandy in quick succession, that I would never again visit Lucie's house. Yet the next night, when we (or rather I) had done with the legal work of the day, and Stryver had announced his intention of paying a call, the following Sunday afternoon, *to drink a dish of cat-lap with that charming little Miss Manette,* I agreed, less reluctantly than I might have done, to keep him company. And thus, I meditated, as Pross grimly ushered us into the sitting-room, were my wisest resolutions invariably broken.

I assured myself I wished but to gaze at her, to ease my spirit in feeling myself welcome in her household as I might warm myself in the sunshine. With that thought in mind, I lounged in a chair, hands in my pockets and my back to the window, whilst Stryver proceeded to ingratiate himself with her father.

Stryver was more than usually bumptious that afternoon; more often than once I saw the good Doctor, though perfectly courteous, turn to hide a smile beneath a sudden cough. Lucie, too, appeared uncharacteristically demure, as if she were biting her lips to keep herself from bursting out in gales of merriment as C. J. Stryver extolled the virtues and accomplishments of C. J. Stryver.

"And what was the purpose of your coming, may I ask?" demanded my learned friend afterward, when we were seated out of the March wind in a hackney-coach jolting back to chambers. "Skulking in a corner and keeping mum as a statue! I know you've a pretty wit when you've a mind to, Carton. You needn't mope about with such a hangdog manner."

"I might have said a word or two," I muttered, "if you'd not used all the air in the room."

He snorted. "Well, d__n me! We must all blow our own horns, mustn't we? You will never get anywhere by dawdling about, Carton. Speak up and be noticed, I say."

"And you say it very loud indeed, as you say everything," I returned. I rapped on the roof as our chariot turned onto Fleet-street. "Hold on, driver; I'll get out here."

"The Rose, again?" said Stryver, scowling at the butter-yellow tavern windows. "You ought to save more of your pay—you'll want it for your old age."

I alighted from the hack and glanced quizzically back at him. *"Vitae summa brevis spem nos vetat incohare longam."* I often amused myself by vexing Stryver with snatches of classical verse, for to his great mortification he never had succeeded in mastering more than a barbarous Law-Latin.

"For God's sake, speak English, Carton," he grumbled.

"Life's brief span forbids us to cherish far-reaching hopes. Who is to say I shall have an old age, or wish one?"

"Very well, drink yourself senseless, die of barrel-fever! *I* shan't pay for your funeral," he added, hauling the door to with a bang.

"Dinner, Mr. Carton?" enquired the landlord, catching sight of me as I slouched into the common-room.

"No, not to-night." I hungered for companionship, not nourishment. For two or three years I had visited the Rose not only for its ample dinners and its good Port wine but also for Molly's company.

The man winked and sent the pot-boy scurrying off. A moment later Molly came out the kitchen door, wiping her hands on her apron, and stood sucking her teeth beside the beer-barrels. "God's teeth, love," she exclaimed, "what's brought on such a Friday-face? You look glum as a thief on the way to his hangin'."

I shrugged, unwilling to speak of my confused sensibilities. "Nothing out of the ordinary."

"Then the ordinary ought to cure it," said she, untying her apron. "Come on up-stairs, then."

Wordless, I followed her to her room, a small one under the eaves. She began to unlace her bodice, but I seized her wrists and held them before me. "Wait."

"Well, love," said she, with an uneasy little laugh, "you're mute as Mumchance, who was hanged for saying nothing. Out with it, then." She kissed my lips and pushed me, not ungently, into the lone chair. "'Tisn't shag you want to-night. What's the matter, then? Sick with the mulligrubs again, from wishing you was somebody else?"

"You don't waste much pity on me, do you?" said I.

"Seems like you've enough and to spare for the both of us."

"*A hit, a very palpable hit,*" I murmured. "Molly, chick, you have a devilish unerring sense of the truth."

She shrugged, opening a cupboard. "I say what I see, is all. Come on, love; what you want is a dram o' sky-blue."

"Gin?" I echoed her, with a grimace. "Take it away; that stuff's poison."

"No more poison than Port wine or brandy."

"No," I told her. "I've not yet fallen so low as to seek consolation from sucking on a gin-bottle."

"Lor', you are in a bad way to-night," she sighed. She poured herself out a splash of gin, gulped it down, and sat on my lap, straddling my legs. "You're a queer one, Syd. Never know what to make of you."

"I shall be thirty years old soon," said I, "and have nothing to show for it but a dozen grey hairs. Where did my youth go?"

"Where mine went, and everybody else's."

"Thirty years old," I continued, scarce hearing her. "It makes a fellow think. A man should be settled and prosperous by thirty. Married. One or two brats in the nursery, and another on the way. Stryver will wed in a year or two, I expect . . . wed a fat fortune, if I know him, and push his way upward to the Bench. God! Of all men on Earth to be in thrall to!"

"That puffed-up limb o' the Law," Molly scoffed. "No regard for anybody, he hasn't. *Girl, fetch me this* and *Wench, fetch me that* and no thanks for it, and precious little chink left for your pains, the stingy bastard."

I laughed. "You do well to remind me," said I, feeling in my pocket for a half-crown.

"Never mind that, love. Haven't we better to do?"

"I shan't take advantage of your good nature by slipping away without paying my bill."

She put an end to my protests by seizing my hands and kissing me full on the mouth. "What's chewing at your vitals to-night, then?" she enquired, when she had done. "'Tisn't me you're thinkin' on, off wheresoever it is you are."

"I was thinking of a boy . . . a man I once knew," I admitted, "and a young lady . . ."

"A woman?" she exclaimed. "I never heard you talk of women these three years, but to say you'd never trust any mort who claimed to call herself a lady. Who is she, then?"

"A French Doctor's daughter."

"Why her, of all the wenches in the wide world?"

"She . . . she is kind."

"There's more kindness in the world than you might think, if you'd once trouble yourself to look for it. *I'm* kind, or I try to be. Who else would stand for your ill humours these three years and more?"

"You are the soul of kindness," said I, attempting to pacify her. "Truly. But you take me for what I am, don't you?"

"How else should I take you but how I find you? You're not such a bad cove as you make yourself out to be, Syd."

"Miss Manette sees me not for what I am, but for what I might have been. And I thank her for that, and hate her for it, all at once."

"Hate her?" she echoed me. "Well, that's as may be. But you can't be denyin', I think, that you're closer to fallin' in love with her. And she, did she give you the glad eye?"

My sullen silence was answer enough. "See, love, it all comes round again to you," she added, smoothing back my straggling hair. Slowly she untied the knot in my cravat and pushed my collar wide. "Truth is, Syd, that's what's the matter with you. You don't know what you want. You never did know what you wanted, so you never fought for it."

"Don't I?" I murmured. "Perhaps not. And you, do you know what you want?"

"Me? I want to leave off mopping vomit and pouring blue ruin for a lot of nazy cullies." She tossed her head, sending her black hair flying. "I will, sooner or later, when I've put away a bit more chink for me dowry. I want to wed some good decent cove who won't drink away all his wages at the dram-shops come Saturday night, and come home to beat me; and I want to live in clean lodgings on the second floor somewhere and have a baby every year; and hope a few of 'em live long enough to see me into me grave."

"That's a simple dream . . . a reasonable dream. You are the most reasonable creature I know, Moll." I felt once again in my pocket. "But ere I forget, I must make my customary contribution to your dowry."

"O, let it alone, Syd!" she exclaimed, her tone a trifle sharper than was usual. I stared at her and her colour deepened as she snatched up the gin-bottle and took another swallow from it. "The Devil take you," said she, "have you never thought that I prefer your company to your money?"

I gazed at her, surprised, for indeed the notion had never occurred to me. "You—you've a good heart," she added, "and a generous one. But you don't know how to make yourself happy. You'd not admit it, but you'd do anything for anybody, save your own self. You use yourself so ill, Syd, it hurts me to see you." She paused for an instant, as I silently pondered the truth of her words. "Won't you—couldn't I try to make you happy?"

"You do offer me some cheer, Moll," I assured her, "for an hour at least. Would I have returned to you so often, had you not brightened my spirits a little?"

"I don't mean that," said she. "Not for an hour now and then. I mean all the time. 'Cause I always had a special fondness for you; you're not like the rest."

Astonished, I suddenly comprehended her meaning. "It don't have to be marriage," she hurried on, ere I could speak. "An eddicated gentleman like you oughtn't to go weddin' the likes of me. But housekeeping, we could do that, together, and be friendly-like . . . there's me dowry I've been saving, near eighty pound; and I'd do all a wife would do for you, and ask for nothing . . ."

I knew not what to say. At length I kissed her and smoothed back her hair. "O Molly," I murmured. "Your generosity . . . I cannot accept it; it would be unjust to you. I fear there is more that blights me than you could heal."

Poor Molly—she tried her best. I believe she genuinely loved me, despite all my faults. Yet some pride remained to me still, pride that would not suffer me to abide with a low-born, ill-schooled mistress who was more or less a light woman. (No, confess the truth, Carton: would I have scrupled so, had she made her generous offer a fortnight earlier, ere Lucie had captured my bruised heart?) Visit her I might; but live with her I could not.

She sighed, but no more, for she was a practical wench, not given to fruitless outbursts. "Well, we'll have Sunday nights still, shan't we?" said she. "And Wednesdays too." She grinned and locked her arms about my neck. Rising, I gathered her up and carried her to the bed.

Midnight had long since struck when I quitted her and wandered my solitary way slowly towards my cheerless lodgings in Temple-court. None but a few late-going hackney-coaches were abroad on Fleet-street, and the turd-men with their noisome waggons fresh from the necessary houses, and a handful of whores and villains skulking here and there in the shadows. A pair of Tom-cats screeched in an alley as I passed. I paused for a moment, my thoughts flying back to Lucie's peaceful house in Soho and to all the reasons why she and her tranquil happy life could never be mine, ere slinking onward.

Perhaps my motto ought to be the famed verse spoken by Cassius in *Julius Cæsar*, which I know to be the truest words that ever the Poet wrote. I remembered them that night, and murmured them under my breath, as I stood there alone in the chill darkness.

> *Men at some time are masters of their fates:*
> *The fault, dear Brutus, is not in our stars,*
> *But in ourselves, that we are underlings.*

5

I FOUND MYSELF, as Spring softened the air and blossomed into Summer, drawn inevitably to Lucie's quiet corner of Soho. Remembering the home lost to me long ere my father's Will had shattered my expectations, I craved the contentment she and her father shared in the comfortable little house. Remembering emotions once thrust from me, I craved the sight of her, craved her soft voice, craved the compassion I saw in her eyes when, despite my best intention to be agreeable, a bitter phrase escaped me.

"Your father and your friends must wonder why I come so often a-visiting," I told her one warm afternoon in early July, when we found ourselves alone together in the garden as she mended her father's waistcoat.

"Ought they to?" said she, turning pensive blue eyes from her sewing.

"They never hear me speak a word that a young man might ordinarily exchange with a charming young lady." I leant against the plane-tree, hands in my pockets, thankful for its concealing shade. "Most folk, seeing you, would consider me mad."

"I thank you for the compliment, Sir. But you are reticent by nature, I think. Where is the harm in that?"

"I was not always so. But what I would say to you . . . is not light discourse upon the state of the weather, or the theatre, or your flower-beds." I essayed a glance at her, and found her blushing. "And yet," I continued, staring at the roses whose fragrance hung heavy and sweet all about us, "why should I waste my breath, when Darnay is present to offer the gallant little compliments, the tender smiles, the gentlemanly arm?"

She glanced at me, lips twitching in gentle amusement. "Mr. Darnay is not present to-day, Mr. Carton."

"What does it matter? He eclipses me as the Sun out-shines the dark of the Moon. I am no more than a drunken prodigal. I know full well I don't deserve one such as you; had you never met Darnay, I would have shone no brighter by his absence."

"I have told you, more often than once, that you think far too little of yourself, Mr. Carton. You say you are a drunken prodigal, yet you have never once paid a call upon us when drink has you in its grip."

"I should be ashamed to, Miss Manette."

"A man who is ashamed of his vices is not altogether irredeemable, I suspect," said she, with a smile. "And you must look at the balance-sheet, Sir. You possess attributes of which any man would be proud."

"And other attributes," said I, "by which I mean frailties—habits and omissions for which any self-respecting fellow would crimson for shame. But I thank you for your kindly opinion of me. It is . . . consoling."

"Mr. Carton," said she, looking up from her needle once again, "pray believe that I am not merely kind when I tell you these things. I truly respect you, and admire your intellect and your gifts, and—and pity you—a little—for I think you are capable of much more than you believe yourself; and I do like you, very much."

"You do me too much honour, Miss Manette," I murmured. "But Darnay deserves your admiration far more than I."

"Mr. Darnay is a fine man, with many excellent qualities. But then so are you. We all have many admirable traits hidden away in us, and likewise many faults. Who knows what chance series of events might have touched upon his frailties rather than his better qualities?" Her grave pensive gaze stayed fixed upon me a moment, assessing me. "I believe that even the worst of us, with the guidance and kindness of others, is capable of reform . . . and you are far from being a wicked man, Mr. Carton. I—I think you are terribly unhappy, and have merely lost your way in your melancholy and your solitude; and . . . has no one told you the tale of my poor father's *dementia?*" she asked me suddenly.

"I know only that he was a prisoner in the Bastille for many years, and that his memory was affected by it," said I, wondering at her sudden change of subject.

"He was held close in a solitary cell for eighteen years, Mr. Carton, for no crime, or pretended crime, that we have ever been able to discover. During those eighteen years he scarce exchanged a word with another human creature save his gaolers. And at last, when Mr. Lorry and I found him, newly released for no one knows what reason, he had sunk into some other world, some far darker prison, some black prison of the mind brought about by loneliness and idleness, and had forgotten even his own name. But that, thank God, is past him now, and he is whole once more."

"That is a terrible tale," said I, "but—"

"Don't you see, Mr. Carton? Your greatest sin is not one of mere bad habits, of dissipation . . . of drunkenness and of—of frequenting light women. Your true sin is that of despair. My poor father's ordeal has taught me that misery, and loneliness, and utter despair of deliverance may indeed drive a man to the verge of madness—and not all prisons are built of stone and iron. I think you, too, are held fast in some dark prison of your own creating. But I think also that you need but a friend—a constant and loving friend—to encourage you and guide you for a while on your path, until you can see your way clear once again. You ought not to imagine yourself less worthy of respect, and admiration, and—yes, and of love, than is Mr. Darnay."

I gazed at her, speechless. I might have said *I love you* in return, but I could not, for fear that she would only smile. I might have told her how, for her sake, I had envisioned reforming myself, and might even—dare I say it?—might even have asked her then to do me the honour of becoming my wife; but could not, for fear that she would politely and swiftly refuse me.

"Where *is* Darnay, these days?" I enquired, abruptly. "I've not seen him, now that I think on it."

"I—I believe Mr. Darnay is gone to France again," said she, bending her head once more to her sewing. "He assured us he would return ere the month is out."

Ere the month was out—Carton, Carton, in truth you were but a coward: you might have seized your advantage then, and used Darnay's long absence to further yourself in Lucie's favour. For I believe her encouraging words to me were encouragement indeed, from one not unwilling to consider the petition of even such a sorry suitor as I. But I dreaded still that she would rebuff me, and I said nothing.

DARNAY WAS NEAR a fortnight late when at last he returned, unscathed but uncommonly distracted. He told us, on the Sunday following, when our little company was all gathered once more beneath the plane-tree's shade, naught but that the death of a relative had extended his sojourn in France. I sensed, however, that some greater disquiet was plaguing him. After we made our Farewells that evening I trailed, curious, behind him along Frith-street to Soho-square. Pausing restless in the shadow of an old linden-tree, at last he saw me, and crossed the road once again to meet me.

"Carton," said he, not without some uncertainty, "I know we've not spoken much in the months past . . ."

"That was my doing, not yours," said I, sullenly. Tho' envy still soured my belly and my spirits whenever we were thrown together, in truth Darnay had done me no injury save that of being the perfectly amiable fellow he was. "But I see something is gnawing at you . . ."

He dismissed my reluctant near-apology with a wave of his hand and beckoned me on to the silence of the square. "Do you remember once, when we were boys together, how I found it a relief to share with you some of—some of my family's darker secrets?"

"Of course."

"My uncle, the uncle I once spoke of, was just now murdered in his bed."

"Murdered!" I echoed him. "By whom?"

"No one knows. But for a while they suspected me."

"You!" The notion that Darnay might be a cold-blooded murderer was so absurd that I could do naught but laugh.

"I was there, sleeping in his house. He had injured so many folk, though, that the constables soon turned their attention from me, thank God. But—you remember, I told you—I was his heir."

"So his estates are now yours."

"Yes."

"And a title?"

"Meaningless. But . . . the estates are mine: the lands, and the tenants, and the responsibility. Not a rich property, I fear; the land is mortgaged, and the earth is very poor, played out. It scarce supports the folk who work it." He turned away a moment, biting his lip, whilst I silently waited. "I shall give it up, I think."

"Give it up?"

"Renounce it . . . no, that would merely pass it on to the next heir, would it not, whosoever he may be? And he may not have my scruples. Better to leave it to itself. What good would it do me, or my tenants, were I to assume my ancestors' place in that blood-stained house? I could not, in good conscience, demand the rents and dues that my uncle lived on, and how else am I to live? O, I might work a portion of the land myself, but I know nothing of farming. Here in England I can earn my own living very well, by teaching. In France I would be no more than a leech, a parasite."

"At Louis-le-Grand," said I, "you spoke of duty, and obligations. Do you not have a duty to guide your tenants, and care for them?"

"How?" he asked me, quite simply.

I shook my head at that, and laughed. "I am the last fellow you ought to be quizzing in that regard. Responsibility? Most folk would swear I don't know the meaning of the word. But I think you should not turn your back altogether on France."

He sighed. "I'll think on it," said he at last. "I pray you, Carton, keep this to yourself—"

"I have always respected your confidences."

"So you have. I ought not to have doubted it." He pressed my hand and, with a nod, strode away into the twilight.

OUR REGULAR SUNDAY afternoons became a ritual over the course of that halcyon Summer and Autumn. Darnay and Lorry came invariably, whilst Pross often emerged from her domain in the kitchen and her private chamber to add a pungent remark now and then to the conversation. Stryver, too, appeared drawn to the Manettes' modest household, much to my amusement. Chest thrust forward like an amorous cock-pigeon, he expressed his irrefutable opinions of the week's news. Ever kind-hearted, Lucie neither laughed nor yawned at his spouting, though Stryver had never taken to heart the trenchant advice of Voltaire, that the quickest way to be a bore is to say everything.

My learned friend, I sensed, was treading a line as fine as a rope-dancer's. It had ever been his intention to make a profitable marriage and thus augment the comfortable fortune he had accumulated. (When, as I expect it will happen some day, the Heralds' College invites him to choose a coat-of-arms, I cannot but suggest the most fitting motto that might run beneath his blazon: *Si possis recte, si non, quocumque modo rem*—*if possible honestly, if not, somehow: make money*.) Yet despite these practical intentions his heart, it seemed, had betrayed him.

He informed me at last, one sultry night, that he had resolved to wed. Then he added (somewhat abruptly) that he did not, however, intend to marry for money.

"Don't you?" said I. "Who is the fortunate lady?"

He did not reveal his strategy to me straightaway, but first proceeded to reprove me for not myself considering marriage. This antipathy of mine towards women, he maintained, was no obstacle to a profitable union, tho' I ought to make an effort to seem more agreeable to them. "You want delicacy, Carton," he concluded. "Look at you! One would think you'd been bred in the back-parlour of a bawdy-house. You are not such an ill-favoured fellow, you know, when you make an effort. Put yourself forward, as I do, and flatter the ladies, and you may yet come away with a good catch."

I shut my ears to his braying, muttered "Indeed" into my cup of punch, and suffered him to continue. "You ought to wed, you know," said he, barging on. "It's a wonder you've not died already of drink or the French pox. You will be a pretty sight in another twenty years, I dare say! You take my advice and find a decent woman with a little property, and settle down ere you find yourself dying alone in a garret."

"Just like my father," I muttered, rubbing my aching eyes. "Though my father had greater ambitions for me, it's true. Tell me your matrimonial intentions, then, and be done with it. My bed's calling me."

"I intend to wed a young lady whom we both know, and, I may say, have admired. I intend to wed," and he puffed himself up more even than was usual, "Miss Lucie Manette. So what do you say to that, eh, Carton?"

What I would have said, had I not governed my tongue, would have startled him.

"You surprise me," said I. I suffered him to drivel on, whilst my thoughts seethed as furiously as a boiling kettle. At last I pushed his papers aside and slouched to the door. "Good-night, Stryver," said I, interrupting him, and slammed the door behind me with a resounding bang.

A day or two later Stryver, evidently smarting from a courteous refusal of his hand, made an abrupt *volte-face* and carelessly declared to me that he had thought better of *that marrying matter.* He then quitted London for a month's holiday in Devonshire, and left me in peace.

I PAID ONE of my regular visits to Molly late one hot night in August. At length learning that she was busy serving customers in the common-room still, I climbed the stair to her room and threw off my stifling coat. Fumbling with the knot in my cravat, I glimpsed my reflexion in her tarnished looking-glass and paused to scowl at it. Why, I thought sourly, and not for the first time, could it not be Darnay's face gazing back at me from its murky depths?

Molly interrupted my brooding. "Back again, are you, love?" she enquired cheerfully. "Is it Wednesday already, then?" She wrapt her arms about my neck and kissed me. I scarce responded to the kiss, provocative tho' it was, and she pouted as she stared into my eyes. "You're in one of your ill humours to-night. Is the old puzzle-cause givin' you worry again, love?"

"Stryver is on holiday," said I, disengaging her arms from about my neck and continuing to fumble at my cravat.

"Here, love, let me at it," Molly told me, her deft fingers working at the knot. "You tied it too tight is all. No wonder it's put you in such a crotchet, and on such a plaguey hot day and all."

I twisted away from her, impatient. "Must you keep on with your eternal prattling?"

"O, Syd," she sighed. "What's the matter this time, then? Is it cropsick you are to-night, from too many glasses o' kill-priest?"

I had, indeed, done away with a pint of Port whilst awaiting her downstairs, but my ill temper owed more to the heat and the Vacation; tho' I despised my dreary labour, its periodic absence often left me gloomier and more purposeless than did its presence. "I am quite well," I snapped, "or at least as well—and happy—and prosperous—as I ever shall be."

"Come now, don't go working yourself up into a lather again, love. It does you no good to be sittin' there forever broodin' over your wrongs and your frailties. Enjoy the moment, at least. I'll wager you've never said No to a good tumble with a rompish wench."

"Can you think of nothing else?" I demanded. "To hear you, one would think a shagging were the solution to all of Mankind's woes."

"Well, it's not a bad one, love, for lifting the spirits."

"And what if one is seeking more than a ready c__nt?"

She recoiled, as if I had slapped her. "I hope I'm more to you than that," said she, laying a hand on my shoulder. "I try to be, Syd, I truly do."

"You might try, and try, all your life, and still you would not be what I seek."

"It's *her*, a'n't it?" she exclaimed suddenly. "You're mooning still for that Frenchy wench o' yours, who doesn't care tuppence for you."

"Don't you speak of her like that!" I snapped, thrusting her from me. "Miss Manette is a lady. I'll not have her spoken of in such a manner by a creature like you."

"By a creature like me?" she echoed me, arms all a-kimbaw. "And what manner of creature might that be?"

"What but what you are?"

"I'm not a whore!"

"Indeed!"

"I'm just a girl tryin' to make ends meet. I have me self-respect; I don't walk the streets like the Drury-lane screws, do I? I keep to a few gentlemen I like is all. And for the life of me I don't know why I put up with *you*."

"I have always been given to understand," I sneered, "that any woman who takes payment for what a wife gives willingly may be termed a whore. Perhaps you prefer a different word: *harlot, strumpet, drab?*"

"God's teeth, you can be a cruel bastard when you've a mind to be," she hissed. "Sure an' I've had my fill of you, you and your mopin' and your comin' on with the hum-durgeons whensoever you've had a dram too much, and your ever-lasting sorry-for-yourselfing! There's nothing wrong with you but that your thickest part of your thigh is nearest your arse, that's to say nothing at all!" She snatched up my coat and thrust it at me. "Get out and take your Friday-face some place else; I can't stomach you to-night."

I quitted her without a word, turning only to toss a shilling at her feet. She flung it back at me and slammed the door shut behind me.

I had been unjust to her, I grudgingly admitted, and unkind. (From a dozen years' distance I must own that I had been unforgivably cruel to her, to the one human creature who for so long had offered me a little warmth in my bleak existence.) I slouched my way along Fleet-street, shame and the wine I had drunk lying like a stone in my gut.

At length I turned towards Drury-lane and soon found myself amidst the back-alley taverns and the back-alley drabs who lie in wait for the young bloods quitting the theatres. At that moment any wench would have sufficed for me, any common, slatternly three-penny upright. In a dram-shop I found a likely whore, shared a few glasses of gin with her, and outside in the darkness roughly sampled her wares against the brick wall until I was spent. A moment or two later, as she was pocketing her sixpence and straightening her skirts, the gin I had swilled, mingling ill with the pint of Port wine I had drunk at the Rose, soured in my belly. I lurched aside to puke it into the stinking kennel at my feet. When I could look up once more, the drab had disappeared and I was alone.

I blundered my way out of the alley and stumbled away: past the playhouses, past the velvet-clad young bucks fondling the molls on the street-corners, past the whining beggars in their flapping rags, past the noisy gin-shops reeking of vomit and sweat. Somehow I crossed the innumerable little streets and alleys without being accosted by the footpads who skulked in the doorways; I suppose I cannot have looked as if I were much worth robbing.

And suddenly, as if crossing an invisible line, I was in Soho and the night's gentle silence, interrupted by the murmur of crickets and the clip-clopping of a coach-horse some streets away, struck me like a blow. A yearning seized me and I turned my steps towards Frith-street.

I know not what I intended when at length I reached the Manettes' house. I cannot truly have conceived ringing her bell at two o'clock in the morning, when decent, quiet-living folk are long abed. Be that as it may, upon arriving before her door, I was content merely to rest on the mounting-block at the far side of the street and gaze up in the wan moonlight towards the second-floor windows.

What thoughts must have possessed me that wretched night? My wine-

clouded memory is dim. I remember naught but that I imagined her beside
me. Even then, nevertheless, even then, despite my brutish habits and
desires, I pictured her not naked in my bed but sitting beside me in her garden, that fragrant sheltered retreat, her hand upon mine, her smile and her
gentle voice as soothing as cool water on my brow.

I remained there until the first chattering birds heralded the grey-pink
light of dawn. Then I rose, weary but my thoughts a little more at peace,
caught an early-going hack clattering its way towards the Strand, and
regained my lodging to sleep a heavy, dream-wracked slumber till midday.

I wonder if ever Lucie espied the solitary figure loitering before her
house after the Sun had set, in all seasons and all weathers. For I returned,
the next night, and many nights after that, when drink brought me no
escape from self-loathing and self-pity.

I was repaid for my contemptible behaviour towards poor Molly with a
token by which I might remember that six-penny drab: a severe dose of
clap and gleet, and its attendant indignities. I endured a sweating-cure
from a quack in Salisbury-court, tho' it did me little good. After six
months of pissing pins and needles (as they say in the taverns), when
Nature had cured me in her own time of the obnoxious malady, I returned
to Molly with an abject apology on my lips. She suffered me to return to
her; she was more forgiving than I deserved. But she could not fill the void
in me whose ache seemed eased a little by the sight of Lucie's fleeting
shadow at her window.

SURELY IT WAS the guilty memory of that night (without doubt one
of the most shamefully wretched of my life), and the consolation that I
drew from her presence, which gave me the resolution to reveal my heart to
Lucie one evening shortly after, come what might of it.

"Miss Manette, may I tell you an unhappy tale?" I asked her, after Pross
had quitted us and we had exchanged a few polite empty phrases. "It's not
pretty, I warn you, but it is true."

"I should be glad to hear anything you wish to tell me, Mr. Carton," said she, gravely. "Will you not sit down?"

"No, I should prefer to stand, I think." I slipped my hands into my pockets and stared fixedly out the window into the deepening Summer twilight. "Well then . . . once a young man—a boy, rather—" I faltered and drew a long breath, glad that she could not see how my hands trembled. "Suffer me to tell the tale another way, a simpler way, as if a child were telling it. Once upon a time . . . a callow young prince, and a lovely but penniless princess, dwelt in a beautiful, prosperous kingdom. They had loved each other, or so it seemed, since they were little children. The prince and princess grew older together, and at last the princess gave the prince to understand, by deed as well as word, that she loved only him. And thus the prince thought that the princess was the loveliest and dearest creature in the world, and proposed marriage to her, and was accepted. But the prince's father, the king, wished the prince to wed another."

"Go on," Lucie murmured, as I paused.

"The prince, who was very much in love with his princess, rebelled against the king. Soon the king decided that the prince would be but a poor ruler for his kingdom, and so disinherited the prince and gave the kingdom to a cousin instead. It was then that the prince discovered that his beloved princess loved a crown far more than she loved him, for she abandoned him without a second thought, and wedded the new king. And the dispossessed prince disappeared into the night, cursing her name."

"That is the end of the tale?" said Lucie, breaking the silence that had fallen.

"Yes."

"And you . . . are the prince."

"Yes, Miss Manette; I was that foolish prince."

"I am sorry, Mr. Carton," she whispered. "So very sorry . . ."

At last I turned my gaze and found her eyes full of tears. I went to her and lifted her hand to my lips. "Pray don't weep for me; a long time has passed since that day."

"I suspected that once someone had terribly wronged you. Only such a cruel betrayal could embitter one so deeply. And now—now you trust no one?"

"I had thought never again to reveal my secret heart to anyone."

"But you reveal it to me."

"Yes."

"You honour me, Mr. Carton. I could be offered no greater honour, I think."

I held her hand still in my own, I found, and clutched at it like a drowning man clutching at a straw in the vast merciless sea. "Miss Manette—I've not said *I love you* to a living soul since Sarah played me false. During these past months, though, after seeing you here in your home, and after spending time in your company, and treasuring the privilege of your friendship— I have wished to say it. But I never dared say it, for fear you would spurn me as she did. And what could you find in me to love?"

"O, a very great deal, Mr. Carton, if you would only believe me!"

"I wish to believe you, as I wish to tell you what you are to me; yet I cannot find the words . . ." I clasped her hand between my own two hands and drew another long breath. Then, without the least premeditation, I bent my head and kissed her on the mouth.

She did not shrink from me. Instead she responded to my kiss, hesitantly at first, then with shy but eager pleasure. At last her soft lips withdrew from mine and she retreated, but only a pace, our hands still clasped.

"Mr. Carton," said she, her eyes very wide and her colour high, "Mr. Carton—I know not what to say, what to do—but I feel I must tell you straightaway . . . that yesterday Mr. Darnay asked me to marry him."

I do not believe I flinched; but nevertheless I felt as if ice-water had been poured into all my veins. "Darnay," said I, after an instant's pause. "I ought not be surprised."

"I have not yet made him an answer."

This latter intelligence was far more startling to me than was the former. I gazed down at her hand as it lay still in mine and at last stammered: "And what, then, will your answer to him be?"

"What should it be, Mr. Carton?"

Her quiet question astounded me so that I could scarce speak. Could it be that she would have me? For an instant I saw all the world before me, painted in the brilliant colours of the sunrise; saw my dark night at an end. Then cold Reason raised its head and I knew I must speak the truth.

"I am no fit husband for any woman," said I, shaking my head, "most of all an incomparable woman like you, Miss Manette . . . Lucie. I am a worthless fellow, whatsoever you may say: a prodigal, prostituted, self-pitying creature. I know the flaws in my character too well. I might try to reform myself for your sake—and I did think on it, not so long since—but such flaws are not to be amended, no matter how we try. I am incapable of pursuing even my own interests; how could I give you all that you deserve?"

Tho' I was sober as a Judge that day and not maudlin-drunk, or lewd-drunk, as I have been on more than one occasion, still some other force within me than my own urged me onward. I drew Lucie towards me and she came willingly. "And yet . . ." I bent, framed her face with my two hands and kissed her again, and for a long sweet moment she did not resist me.

"No," said she at length, with a gasp, or a sob. "I pray you, no . . ." I released her and she turned from me, trembling.

"Forgive me," said I, appalled at my temerity. "I have offended you. I'll quit you now, if you give the word, and never return, never speak of this to a soul—"

"No—you mis-understand me. You are wrong. You are wrong when you say you are no fit husband for any woman. You are no fit husband for *me*—because I am no fit wife for you. You—I—you . . . you are not *safe.*"

"Safe?" I echoed her.

"You—I don't know who you are, what it is that you want, in your heart, and yet I—my own heart decrees I must love you, despite all the warnings of my reason. But Charles Darnay—I know who he is, and I know I love him also with all my heart, without question, for all that he is—and with my reason, too, for he is a kind, admirable, honourable gentleman, and he loves me. He is safe, and good, and his heart keeps no secrets from me. I shall never know you, or what you truly wish for yourself—not entirely— and thus you frighten me. Charles and I share one heart, and one desire, to live a simple happy life together; whilst you—in your search for happiness, you would lead me down paths I don't wish to follow." She turned back to me at last, and I saw that she was very white. "I pray that you may comprehend me, Mr. Carton."

"Yes," said I, softly, "I believe I do."

I ought then, I suppose, to have tendered her some polite commonplace and quitted her forever, preserving some measure of my self-respect in a politic retreat—the traditional way of the rejected suitor. But what self-respect had I to preserve, pray?

"Wed Darnay," I told her. "Of course you must. That way lies your happiness, and you could not wed a better man. But for the brief moment of happiness you have given me, I am and shall always be in your debt."

"You owe me nothing, Sir," said she, with a melancholy smile, as some colour returned to her visage.

"I owe you everything—for you have just now led me to recognise that perhaps there is a scrap of me that is not altogether worthless. Miss Manette," I continued, all at once bold in my dread that I might lose her entirely and forever, "Lucie . . . let the words that have passed between us to-day be forgotten by the both of us. But would you suffer me to call upon you still, now and then? For I hope that we may remain friends . . ."

"With all my heart," said she. I could not help but notice that she blinked away a few tears. "You need a friend, Mr. Carton, of that I am sure. A friend to give you encouragement—"

"You have given me more than ever you could know," I told her. "More than ever I could repay."

"There is no need—"

I plunged onward, scarce knowing what I said, my words tumbling out. "I have nothing save my life—and I deem that of little value—to offer you in return. Yet offer it I will. I would do anything—give my life—for you, or for your happiness. I swear it. Upon my honour, I swear it."

Such a pledge, after such an exchange, would acutely embarrass most folk, and I think it did Lucie. She gazed at me a moment, her eyes shining with tears. "I thank you, Mr. Carton," she whispered, and without warning turned and fled the room.

I wonder if, on that Summer's evening so long ago, she believed me?

6

ON THE DAY, the following Spring, that Lucie and Darnay arrived home from their honeymoon, I drew Darnay aside. "I wish to apologise to you," said I.

"Apologise?" he echoed me, perplexed. "For what, pray?"

"For that notorious conversation of ours, following your trial."

"*Mon Dieu*, Carton, that was above a year since. Surely you'd not think I would harbour that against you?"

"Well, it sits hard upon me still, and I wish to banish it and start anew with you. I wish to offer you my apology for my behaviour, and for any other such drunken—or, indeed, sober—insolence; and I hope we might once again be friends."

"We have always been friends."

"Perhaps you may have imagined it so," I told him. "But as for me, I must confess that for a while I hated you . . . for you had every thing I wished, and I had nothing. Sheer envy, it was, and self-pity, and most contemptible of me."

He was silent a moment, perhaps reflecting upon all that he enjoyed, his cherished new wife's love most of all, that I did not. But with an earnest smile he offered me his hand. "You need apologise for nothing," said he. "After saving my life, in truth you ask little enough of me."

"If truth be told, on the day of your trial, I cared very little what might become of you. But I would do it again in an instant, Darnay; pray believe that."

"I'd never believe otherwise."

"And I may call uninvited upon you and Mrs. Darnay, now and then?"

"Why, I would insist upon it."

"That's a polite answer, such as any well-bred fellow might give . . . but truly, might I be tolerated as an occasional visitor to your household, much as I was before?"

For reply he embraced me. "There is no one I'd rather welcome to our house. Come whensoever you wish; Lucie and I will expect you."

IS THERE SO little to tell of those eight years betwixt the day of Lucie's wedding and that astonishing year 1789? I cannot recall any but homely and trifling details. I toiled away at my thankless labour without any thought of moving on to more profitable pursuits. Wine and brandy, however, offered less solace than once they had. I cannot say this betokened any great improvement in me, yet whilst I was the hard-drinking wastrel still, as perverse as a she-cat, I was no longer quite so often the drunkard.

By the time of little Lucie-Anne's birth it at last struck Stryver that I cherished some special regard towards her mother. He and I came visiting to pay our respects, a month or two after her christening. I knelt by Lucie-Anne's cradle as Lucie laid her in it and lifted one tiny, chubby hand in my own. Her little fingers curled about mine and she unexpectedly gave me a broad, toothless smile.

"Evidently the child likes you," said Stryver, as we quitted the house and strolled down Frith-street. He was a trifle put out because he had received naught but a grave stare for all his cooing and gibberish. "I never knew you had a way with children, Carton. Of course," he added, eyeing me, "the child may have taken you for her father."

"What mean you by that?" I demanded, too quickly.

"Nothing," said he, all amazement. "Nothing at all, save that you resemble Darnay, as you know full well, and one can't expect a mewling brat in its mother's arms to tell the difference. D__n me, Carton, you are the most capricious fellow for flying into an ill humour."

I muttered some vague apology and continued down the street. Nevertheless, from that moment I believe he realised, if but slightly, the depth of my feeling for Lucie. The matter being a source of no conceivable advantage to him, he never mentioned it; but he remembered it.

I CONTINUED TO visit Molly until the Spring of '84, when one Sunday evening I tapped on her door. She gazed unsmiling at me a moment as she opened the door to me and then, reluctantly it seemed, stept back that I might enter.

"I can't," she told me, ere I could speak a word. "You'll have to go, love."

"But your sick days were scarce a fortnight ago," I began.

"'Tisn't that," said she. "I can't, not any more. Not ever. I'm to be wed, you see."

"Wed?"

"He's a good man, a peruke-maker in Spitalfields. You'd not know him. He asked me day before yesterday to wed him, and I shall. So it wouldn't be right, you see, you and me, now as I'm promised." I could think of nothing to say to her and she hurriedly continued. "They put up the banns to-day. We've arranged for a month this Tuesday."

After a moment I bent and kissed her brow. "I shall wish you happiness, then," I murmured. "You surely deserve it."

"I'd wish you the same, Syd, for you deserve it as much as I, no matter how you may punish yourself for bein' yourself."

"I'll say Good-bye, then," said I, turning to the door.

"Syd, this might be our last meetin', and I wanted—well, I wanted to give you some advice, if you'll take it."

"Advice?"

"Make up your mind on what it is you want, and then go take hold of it with both hands."

"Mrs. Darnay—"

"Not your everlastin' Mrs. Darnay. But you'll know it when you find it." She gave me a rueful grin. "It's been grand, for all in all, Syd. But it's time I went on."

"A good decent fellow," said I, "and clean lodgings, and a baby every year?"

She nodded. "That's what I want. And you, you find what *you* want."

"Perhaps I shall," said I, as I put hand to the stair-rail. "Some day. Who knows?"

I NEVER SAW Molly again but once, four years later, in the City on the day of the Lord Mayor's procession. By sheer chance we jostled up against one another in the crowd and she turned to give me a sharp word, which died on her lips as she recognised me.

"Why, Syd," cried she, "as I live and breathe. Come back to plague me, have you?"

"How do you do, then, Molly?" said I, amused. "You're looking very well."

"Aye, I've no complaints. Syd—Mr. Carton—my husband, Tim Lynch." She followed the inadvertent glance I gave her swollen belly and nodded. "Aye, another on the way. 'Tis a boy we're hoping for, this time."

I shook hands with her husband, who seemed a decent young tradesman, and would have gone on my way had I not had a clearer look at the little girl he carried pick-a-back upon his shoulders. At first glance I thought she was the image of her mother, for she had Molly's black hair, and Molly's grey eyes. The small mischievous face beneath the tangled mop of hair was not Molly's, though, nor that of the man who carried her, but mine, even to the hint of an aquiline nose.

"Your daughter?" said I, carelessly, after an instant's pause. "She seems a fine child."

"Aye, that she is." She stared at me, as if challenging me to speak further. "Her name's Kitty."

I felt in my pocket. "Buy her some sweetmeats," I told Molly, pressing a few farthings into her hand. "I am very glad to have seen you this once again, Moll." I gazed at my daughter a moment longer, for I knew I should probably never see her more, ere turning away and losing myself in the restless crowd.

THRICE BLEST AND more, Horace tells us, *are those whom an unbroken bond unites and whose love, never strained by quarrels, will not release them until their dying day.* I watched Lucie amidst her family, so content and happy, and often for a few hours could forget my own discontent. Perhaps I held thoughts of Kitty secret in the recesses of my memory, for I came to adore little Lucie-Anne as if she were my own, and she me, as the decade crept to its close.

It was she who, all unknowing, was the cause of my forsaking London in the Spring of 1789. Lucie and Darnay, I suppose, have quite forgotten the incident, for it was trivial enough—though not for me.

Stryver and I were taking tea at Frith-street on a fine Sunday towards the end of May, a fortnight or more after the Estates-General were to meet at Versailles. I remember that our conversation had consisted of speculation upon that Assembly's success or failure in replenishing France's depleted Treasury.

"I say King Louis should tax a few items more, like hair-powder or coffee, and be done with it," snorted Stryver. "Those d__ned Frenchies worry too much about trifles. Who the Devil cares what a lot of peasants complain about?"

"The peasants and *bourgeoisie* have been over-taxed for decades," returned Darnay pleasantly, pouring out another round of wine for the gentlemen. "The Estates-General come none too soon. The Nobility and Clergy *must* agree to be taxed, or the French Government will collapse. It cannot go on borrowing money and subsisting upon a deficit forever."

"It was a question of taxes that lost us the American colonies, Stryver," I drawled. "Would you not agree, Darnay?"

"Absolutely. The British Government thought it could tax the Colonies with impunity, and instead found a rebellion on its hands. Who is to say a Washington or a Jefferson is not awaiting his moment in France?"

Stryver grunted. "Nonsense! A lot of upstarts, who were lucky to win because the Frogs came in on their side to tweak King George's nose."

"Washington was scarce an upstart, Sir. And perhaps the Marquis de la Fayette, after winning such renown in America, will be that French Washington."

"He was merely lucky," declared Stryver. "Lucky, the lot of them, not to be swinging from a gibbet at Tyburn, or worse."

"I believe still, now that he is to be President of the United States, that George Washington will leave behind him at least as great a name as George III."

"Now that, Sir, is a species of remark that very nearly brought you to Tyburn yourself nine years ago!"

"A fate from which I was preserved by your legal brilliancy, Mr. Stryver," conceded Darnay, smiling. He caught my eye and we exchanged wry shrugs as Stryver, mollified, settled more comfortably in his chair.

"What is it, my love?" I enquired, discovering Lucie-Anne waiting at my side, pouting most charmingly.

"Play with me," said she.

I reached out to tousle her curls, ready to oblige her. "What do you wish to play?"

"Will you be my horsey again," she asked me, with a fetching smile, "and give me a ride?"

"Whatsoever you like, my pet," I told her, and swung her onto my back, where she clung to my shoulders and shrieked with delight. After her ride was done, she flung her arms about me, declaring that I was the best horse in all the world. "Miss Pross is a nice horse, too," she concluded, "but you're bigger and fiercer and you neigh. Miss Pross won't neigh. She says it's not proper."

"Well, when have *I* ever been quite proper? You need but command me," I told her, dropping to one knee beside her, "and I shall neigh and whinny and snort to your heart's delight."

She embraced me once again and kissed my cheek. "I do love you, Mr. Carton! Why can't you live here with us *all* the time?"

"Well, my pet," said I, "because I am not one of your family."

"Couldn't you be?" she demanded. "Miss Pross isn't a relative, but she's one of the family."

"Miss Pross has no other relations."

"Do you have relations? A papa and mamma, and brothers and sisters?"

"No," I admitted, "none worth speaking of." I had not seen Arabella since my father's funeral, fifteen years previous; we had never been close. Perhaps I had cousins in France from my mother's family, but I knew nothing of them.

Lucie-Anne frowned. "Is that why you always look so lonely?"

"Do I?" said I, touched by her childish concern.

"Yes. When you come to call, you always look so sad and lonely. I don't want you to be lonely, Mr. Carton."

"But when I am with you, and your mamma and papa, I am no longer lonely."

"Are you married, like papa and mamma?"

"No."

"Would you be lonely if you were married?" she persisted.

"I suppose not," said I, gravely.

"*I'll* marry you, when I'm big," she declared. "Then you shan't be lonely any more."

I could not but smile at her proposal and she glared at me. "I *will.* You'll see. I love you more than anybody else in the whole world, but mamma and papa and grandfather."

"If you wish to, then of course you shall," I told her, laughing, and sent her running in search of Pross and some newly-baked gingerbread.

I, TOO, MIGHT have forgotten such a harmless incident had Stryver and I not returned to chambers late that evening, in order to work at a particularly complex case of forgery and fraud. As I shuffled through the statements, eyes sore and head pounding, Stryver settled back upon his couch and let out a long sigh.

"*Out of the mouths of babes,* they say. Perhaps the child had a point there, Carton."

"What on Earth are you talking about?" said I, disagreeably, glancing up at him from the heap of statements.

"The child. Little Lucie. She expressed a desire to wed you, did she not?"

"Lucie-Anne," I reminded him, "is not quite six years old. What nonsense are you talking?"

He sat up and gazed censoriously at me. "Carton, evidently you are determined not to take my advice and provide for your old age by wedding somebody who will take care of you. You seem to cling, as well as I can tell, to some sentimental attachment towards Mrs. Darnay."

I stared hard at the papers before me and said, very quietly, "What of it?"

"Well, barring some unforeseen accident to Darnay, she's out of your reach. But why not wait a dozen years and wed the daughter instead?"

I could do no more than turn and stare at him. Taking my silence for acquiescence, he continued blithely on. "In ten or a dozen years she'll be marriageable, and I expect you'll last that long, even with your hard manner of living. How old are you, Carton, thirty-eight?"

"Thirty-seven," said I, fascinated by his utter shamelessness.

He patted triumphantly at the paunch he had nurtured across the years. "There you are: in thirteen years you'll be fifty. Men of that age have taken brides of nineteen ere now, and got children on them, too. Little Lucie is very fond of you, and she should remain so, if you cultivate her. And the girl should have a nice little fortune by then, I expect, for the Doctor is sure to have put something by. It really would be most advantageous for you."

God help him, he could not in the least comprehend my revulsion. To take my affection for Lucie and her beautiful child and translate it to crude carnal desire, or to some thing as sordid as pounds, shillings, and pence—the very thought offended me. I told him the matter was out of the question and that, moreover, I should not welcome further talk of it.

Naturally he did not take my objections to heart. He nagged on about his clever notion, insisting that only my sheer perversity kept me from considering such a convenient solution to my woes. At last, goaded beyond endurance, I smacked down my bundle of papers with a crash.

"By God," I shouted, "will you never cease your infernal witless braying?"

He gaped at me. "What are you working yourself into such an ill humour for? I make a perfectly reasonable suggestion, and you bite my head off."

I snatched up my hat and made for the door. "D__n you and your Tom-fool cases," I snapped. "I can't stomach either of you to-night."

"What on Earth—" he began. "Why should you be so set against benefiting from the child's affection?" He abruptly seized the door-handle ere I could reach for it. "Unless—Carton!—*is* she Darnay's daughter?"

"What?" said I, pausing in my tracks as I attempted to dodge his bulk.

"No one would ordinarily have cause to question the child's parentage," said he, primly, "for she looks as much like her father as her mother. But I suppose it's possible she might resemble *you*, instead, and no one would be the wiser . . ."

In my confoundment I wanted a moment to comprehend his vile inference. Then I plunged towards him, a white-hot rage blazing within me, for in honest truth I had never touched Lucie since the day I kissed her, so many years past. "You unspeakable swine," I hissed. "How dare you insult Mrs. Darnay so!"

He never had seen me truly exercised and he shrank back, alarmed. "I meant only . . . you seemed so set against the notion of wedding the girl, a perfectly reasonable notion," he stammered. "I could make no sense of it save to—to suppose that—that you knew the child might—be yours—"

"Mrs. Darnay is never to hear a word of what has passed between us here," I told him, seizing his over-broad lapels and jerking him towards me. "You keep your filthy notions to yourself. If ever she or anybody hears a whisper of this, I swear I will kill you, and gut you like the fat pig you are. Do you understand me?"

"Anybody would think, to hear you," said he, with an uneasy giggle, "that you had a—a cuckolded husband on your conscience, Carton—"

And with that, I lost the tenuous control of my temper. I snatched up one of Stryver's gloves and struck him across the face with it. "Hyde Park," said I. "The day after to-morrow. The choice of weapons is yours."

It is a measure of the blinding rage that possessed me that I considered something so preposterous as challenging Stryver. He goggled at me with his gooseberry eyes and babbled a few breathless words to the effect that assuredly he would do nothing of the sort.

"Then you are a worse coward than ever I suspected," I snapped. "An ill-bred, braying, pettifogging mountebank is all you are, Clarence Stryver, a pitiful excuse for an Attorney! Where do you think you would be to-day if you'd not had me to do your work for you and put the words in your vulgar mouth? Only where a fat-headed pompous boor like you deserves to be, and I—I'll be d__ned if I have any more of it!"

And so saying, I rushed out and down the stair. I paused when I attained the courtyard, where the cool Spring night awaited me. My heart thumping in my breast, I stood there a moment as the breeze fanned my hot face. I could feel, to my astonishment, only the most exhilarating sense of freedom.

STRYVER VISITED ME the following day and all but abased himself at my feet, entreating me to return to his employ. Panic-stricken, he dangled any number of enticements before me to induce me to remain his drudge: more pay, a full partnership, the benefit of his not inconsiderable influence. I listened stonily to his pleas and told him that I wished nothing further to do with him. Having at long last crossed my Rubicon, I knew I could never turn back. I preferred to take my chances in America, I concluded, for I had some vague idea of taking ship for Boston, whither an enterprising colleague of ours had recently emigrated. Stryver quitted me like a beaten cur, all his pomposity deflated.

Whither, indeed, would I go? I had scarce thought of my destination, tho' I knew I must quit London. The sole remaining tie that bound me there was Lucie, a tie I knew I must sever, for if one man could discover dishonour in my chaste devotion to her, then so might others. I could no longer suffer my presence near her to invite the faintest breath of slander, altho' I knew not how I could endure living without the sight of her to sustain me.

"I AM QUITTING England," I told Lucie, after Pross had conducted me into her sitting-room and left us alone together, for Darnay and Lucie-Anne had gone out for a stroll in the square. "I wished to bid you Farewell."

"Whither shall you go?" she asked me, rising and taking my hands in her own. It was true to her character that she never asked me why suddenly I had chosen to abandon all I knew.

"The New World, I think. The United States. New opportunity lies there for the taking, I should imagine."

Her face lit like the Sun emerging from behind the clouds. "My faith in your talents and your integrity has never faltered, Mr. Carton. I hope you will never forget that."

I shook my head. "I shall not."

"Go with all my best wishes for your prosperity and your happiness."

I confess I had no very firm design of starting my mis-spent life over again in the New World, as she seemed to think. But I did not care to disappoint her unswerving faith in me. "You know, I think, what you have meant to me," said I. "I need say nothing else."

"Shall we see you again?"

"I think not. For better or worse, I am leaving England behind me. After all," I added, with a flash of my old wry temper, "I could scarce do worse than I have done already."

"Perhaps the wheel of Fortune is now turning in your favour," she suggested, with a smile.

"Perhaps. But I shall accept whatsoever may befall me." I pressed her hand to my lips. "Thank you . . . Lucie."

"Good-bye . . . Sydney."

As if in accord, we came together, and our lips met, and met again. She clung to me for a moment, her heart beating fast beneath her gown. "I shall never forget you," she told me, as reluctantly I released her.

"Nor I you."

She murmured "Good-bye" again as I quitted her, heavy with the certainty that I never would see her more.

I encountered Darnay and Lucie-Anne, arriving home from their walk, in the passage and Lucie-Anne flung her arms about my waist, asking me if I had come to take tea with her. Kissing her, I told her that I could not play with her that day, for I was going away for a long time.

"Will you be gone more than a month?" said she, pouting.

"I fear it will be much longer than a month," I admitted, bending on one knee to her. "I am travelling to Boston, in America, and the voyage alone will want six weeks at least."

"Won't you ever come back?"

"Perhaps I will," said I, tho' I doubted it. "In a few years, when you are a beautiful young lady. You will have other playmates, my pet; but promise me you'll not forget me."

"I won't ever," she sobbed, and burst into tears. I suffered her to cry on my shoulder for a while, until she quietened, and then kissed her once more and handed her to Darnay.

"You are quitting England, truly?" said he. "For America?"

"Yes. It is . . . a private matter."

"You must write to us, and send us tidings of the new Government there . . ." said he, with a regretful smile. *"Mon Dieu,* Carton—once again you quit your friends at a moment's notice, and once again I shall miss you. We all shall miss you. I shan't say adieu, however, but *au revoir.* I said once before that we would meet again, and I suspect we have not seen the last of each other."

"Perhaps not."

He pressed my hand. *"Bonne chance,* Carton."

"Au revoir, old friend," said I, pressing his hand in my turn, and let myself out.

I scarce knew why I had chosen Boston. It seemed as good a destination as any, I suppose. I bought a copy of the *Times* from a hawker at a street-corner and paused to look at the list of ships offering passage to America.

No ships, I found, were sailing to Boston that week, tho' one was bound for Charleston and another for New-York. Glancing at the next page and the intelligence from abroad, I noticed the Editors had published a letter from Versailles, which described the slow and contentious progress of the Estates-General.

Why, I realised, should I not return instead to Paris?

PART II

The Augean Stables

1789

7

I ARRIVED IN Paris on the 6th of June 1789. I found a cheap Left Bank lodging near the church of St. André-des-Arts, published an advertisement in the *Mercure* (for I thought to find work as a translator and tutor of the English language), and within three days was as established as ever I had been in my dingy room in Temple-court.

My sojourn in Paris must in truth begin, as the Revolution began, at the Palais-Royal. I had never seen the great pleasure-garden of which so much has been spoken and rumoured, for the Duc d'Orléans had opened his beautiful gardens to the public many years after I had quitted Louis-le-Grand. In '89 it was nothing less than the pulsing heart of Paris, and of the Revolution.

It was the most fashionable, and notorious, gathering-place in Paris. As the private property of the first Prince of the Blood Royal, no police were permitted within its walls; left unmolested, the cafés and book-sellers fostered the freest speech and print in France. Everyone who wished to ride the heights of Fashion gathered at the Palais-Royal to hear the latest tidings or observe the newest styles, worn by Duchesses and courtesans alike.

I satisfied my own curiosity at last, choosing a fine afternoon—the last day of June—to stroll for the first time down the long arcades. What a whirl of excitement it was! Shops, hawkers, sights of every variety stretched before me. Acrobats performed for a delighted crowd beside the great central fountain, whilst applause and music rose from the colourful indoor riding-circus occupying one end of the enclosure. All along the galleries, a dozen cafés, from a modest establishment serving beer at long trestle tables to the gilded Café Italien, served countless glasses of wine or cheap *eau-de-vie*, or strong black coffee and steaming chocolate in tiny porcelain cups.

Folk of every description passed before me: working-men and their families abroad for their Sunday holiday, gawking at the luxuries they never could afford; servants running errands; soberly-clad professional gentlemen absorbed in an argument; gossiping ladies clad in silk gowns and enormous, beplumed bonnets proceeding from one stylish *modiste* or *parfumerie* to another; painted women leaning out of mezzanine windows, beckoning to the passing men. It was a shimmering, dizzying, wonderful circus, a delirious quadrille danced to snatches of conversation and scraps of laughter.

A pair of fashionable ladies swept past me, their lackeys, laden with bundles, trotting along behind. "—And, my dear, her *hair*," one said breathlessly to the other as they passed, "just as if the birds had been nesting in it—"

"Sweet oranges," cried a hawker, "only two sous for a sweet fresh Portuguese orange!"

"Eh, Monsieur, come look!" beckoned a well-rouged young woman who leant from a window. (Above the smart shops, theatres, and cafés are *restaurateurs'* establishments, hotels, gambling-hells, and, above all, expensive brothels, where a man may indulge any taste, even the most perverted.) A trollop in a competing house leant farther out and added her own voice to the clamour. "Only ten livres for the sweetest night you'll ever spend awake, Monsieur!"

I ignored the courtesans and continued my stroll down the arcade. "I don't believe La Fayette knows what he is talking about," said one earnest, shabby young man to his equally earnest and shabby companion. "Now Mirabeau, he is another matter, but everybody loathes him—"

"We should be glad at least that Necker is the Finance Minister. If anybody can pull us out of this mess, it's he—"

"And if the National Assembly can truly persuade the Aristos and the priests that everyone must give up his privileges for the good of the Kingdom—"

"Three sous only for a rose for your lady," cried the pedlars and stallkeepers, "two sous to see the puppet-show, a sou for the finest sugared almonds in Paris, buttons, hot fried cakes, toy wind-mills, ices, *boutonnières*, combs, fresh roses, paper violets, coloured portraits of the King, coloured portraits of Msr. Necker, the list of winners in the Lottery!"

I threw myself into a chair at one of the cheaper cafés, a haunt of students and seedy, literary young men, and watched the crowds wash by, measureless as the sea, as glass by glass I drank a pint of Burgundy wine. I could not help but eavesdrop upon all the indignant political talk that surrounded me, for since the mutinous Commons of the Estates-General had declared itself the National Assembly not a fortnight previous, Paris chattered of nothing else.

The latest outrage committed against the new-born Assembly, the unjust imprisonment of fourteen patriotic French Guards, had the Palais-Royal buzzing on that last day of June. Even I knew the tale: The *Gardes françaises* had publicly announced that they would never fire on Frenchmen. On the 28th, two Guards had gone to bear witness before the Assembly, denouncing their commanders for threatening to attack the People. The officers had promptly arrested them for this impertinence, claiming they were plotting sedition, and locked them and a dozen of their fellows in the prison of the Abbaye.

I was pouring out my fourth glass and indifferently pondering the Injustice of the world when abruptly a passing woman stopt, gave me a hard stare, and swept over to me. "Marbois!" she exclaimed. "*Is* it you?"

I rose and doffed my hat to her, for she was clearly a lady of some quality, tho' I felt sure I never had seen her before in my life, nor had I ever heard the name Marbois. "Madame," I began, "I think you must be mistaken."

"Nonsense," said she. "I would know you anywhere, though you look as if Circumstance has treated you rather shabbily. But of course you are no longer just Marbois since your uncle was murdered. Do you not know me? Léo d'Ambert. Don't tell me you don't recognise me!"

I imagine I must have resembled a gaffed pike as I stared at her, wondering who she might be. "Laurent!" she cried, turning from me for an instant to address a young man who came hurrying to join her, "look, whom do you think I have found? Charles, of all folk! Our cousin Charles de Marbois!"

Once again a stranger had mistaken me for my looking-glass image, I realised, for quite foolishly I never had considered I might encounter his kin or his friends in France. I had well-nigh forgotten, too, across the years, that Darnay was not his true name.

I was about to disabuse the lady of her mistaken notion when that old perversity of mine seized me. Why not play the rôle she insisted on assigning me? It would be an amusing jest.

"Forgive me," said I, bowing. "After so many years—"

"Don't tell me you're choosing to be stiff and formal," protested she. "Not after all the games we played together at Boissières!" She threw her arms about me and embraced me, then stept back and with a critical but good-humoured eye took my measure from my loose hair (which I never did care to gather back) to my dusty riding-boots.

I took her measure in return, remembering all of a sudden that, long ago at Louis-le-Grand, Darnay had now and then spoken of his spirited, forthright cousin Eléonore. She was a slender woman of perhaps thirty or more, elegantly though simply clad, with fine dark eyes and a great quantity of glossy chestnut-brown hair, drest and extravagantly curled in the fashionable wide *coiffure* that the French call *un hérisson*, a hedgehog. She was not beautiful—if by *beauty* one means the exquisite, fragile prettiness of a little porcelain princess or shepherdess from the royal manufactory at Sèvres (of which our Staffordshire creations are mere clumsy counterfeits). She had not Lucie's delicate beauty, or Sarah's, it is true; but the liveliness of those dark eyes and the spirit and intelligence in her countenance all mingled to provide her with a striking grace and charm.

I forged ahead with the charade. "I knew not how you might greet me after so much time had passed . . . cousin."

"Won't you greet Laurent, too?" she asked me, with a glance at her companion, who was far younger than she but who seemed sufficiently like her to be her brother. I obediently bowed.

"Laurent. I should not have recognised you," I improvised, "for . . . you were a child still when I quitted France."

"I am glad to meet you once again, cousin," he told me briskly, and turned to my new acquaintance. "Léo—"

"But where have you been all these years, without a word to any of us?" Eléonore demanded of me, ignoring the young man. "Have you dwelt in England this whole long while? You must have; you sound a trifle like an Englishman now. Five years since, when Anglomania was the rage, your accent would have been terribly fashionable. It was most ludicrous to hear all those witless popinjays affecting hideous English accents. You look a bit shabby—what have you been living on? And have you never returned to La Tenèvre? The place is falling to ruin, you know."

"*Léo*—" Laurent insisted.

"O, what *is* it, Laurent?" cried she, impatient.

"I have found Fleutry."

"You've found him?" she gasped, promptly ignoring me to turn and seize her brother (for that is indeed who he was) by the shoulders. "Where? Where is he?"

"In the Abbaye. I might have learnt his whereabouts much sooner, but evidently he was imprisoned by *lettre de cachet* rather than by formal trial, so everything was very discreet. You may imagine who requested the filthy thing," he added sourly. "Our beloved brother, to be sure."

"In the Abbaye?" Eléonore echoed him softly, an angry light kindling in her eyes. "D__n Gilbert. May he stew in the lowest reaches of Hell, the prying, arrogant, sanctimonious little wretch!"

"Léo," continued Laurent, attempting to placate her, "I made a friend in one of the turnkeys. I bought him a few glasses of *eau-de-vie* and he confirmed my suspicions. For the right price, Baudouin will carry in any thing you wish to send to Fleutry: food, clothes, perhaps even letters—"

"I don't wish to *send* things to him," Eléonore interrupted him, with a scornful toss of her head that set the plumes in her broad-brimmed hat to nodding. "I wish him out of that place. He's no criminal; he's done nothing wrong save to offend Gilbert's delicate sensibilities."

"Who," I enquired, despite my better judgment to keep myself out of these strangers' private matters, "is Fleutry?"

Eléonore stared at me as if she had forgotten my existence. "He is . . . a dear friend."

"He is Léo's present lover," Laurent told me. "I don't suppose you know that Léo and her husband have been separated for seven years now. And my dear elder brother does not approve of Fleutry, because he is *bourgeois*, and writes slanderous pamphlets about the Court, and so he ordered him arrested six weeks since."

"And we are going to free him," declared Eléonore.

"You can scarce knock on the gate and politely ask them to release him," objected Laurent, cocking an eyebrow. "Be reasonable. Unless you have made a bosom friend of the Minister of Justice, perhaps?"

She let out an exasperated "Bah!" and flung herself down at the table to sit glowering at my three-quarters-empty bottle. I seated myself once more, acutely aware my petty masquerade had gone too far, but ignorant of how to end it gracefully.

A news-crier came striding by at that instant, a bundle of pamphlets tucked under his arm. "The French Guards' complaint against the tyranny of their officers!" he shouted. During the weeks past, as Censorship's grip upon the newspapers loosened, the Journalists had grown ever bolder in setting the popular discontent to print. "Read about the Injustice served to the fourteen Grenadiers! Only two sous! The Guards demand Justice! Reports that the French Guards will be transferred from the Abbaye tonight and hanged!"

"See, Fleutry is scarce the only one to suffer," muttered Laurent.

"And no more should they," said Eléonore, a restless hand drumming a tattoo on the table-top. "They *cannot* hang those poor men!"

"The Guards demand Justice!" continued the news-crier, pushing onward through the crowds and the din. "The complaint of the fourteen against the tyranny of their officers!"

"*Mon Dieu!* Folk must do something about this."

Laurent shrugged. "What can anybody do? Send a petition to the Assembly?"

Eléonore glanced from her brother to me. "No, we can act, as decent folk ought to have done long ere this."

"What mean you?" said Laurent, suspicious.

"Laurent, the *Gardes françaises* are imprisoned in the Abbaye, too! How much encouragement do you think would raise a crowd to break them out?"

"Raise a crowd?"

"Yes, curse it, stir them up! Look about you. All they want is one push."

"You speak of inciting a riot," Laurent warned her. "Not even a title will protect you entirely, should you be arrested for it."

"Inciting Justice! Those men have been imprisoned for—for the crime of *patriotism*, and Julien for nothing at all. Did your turnkey friend tell you nothing about the French Guards?"

"Only that they were to be transferred to Bicêtre to-night."

"That foul Hell-pit," she spat. "Are the Ministers hoping to make them appear common cut-throats now? Perhaps the rumour is true and they *will* hang the Guards! And that's horrible—it's intolerable!"

Scarce knowing what I did, aware only that I admired this woman's spirit, I rose, fumbling in my pocket. I had one silver écu and a few sous. "Laurent," said I, "how much money have you?"

"Two or three dozen livres, I suppose," said he, puzzled.

"Give me a few," I told him. "I am going to buy all that pamphlet-pedlar's stock."

Laurent cast me a dubious glance, then slowly grinned and thrust a handful of silver and copper at me. "Very well, then. Pray you're not arrested."

"In the Palais-Royal?" I heard Eléonore say, with an incredulous laugh, as I hurried after the news-crier, at last catching his elbow. "You!" I bawled, above the incessant din. "How many have you left?"

He stared at me. "Left, M'sieur?"

"How many pamphlets have you?"

"Might be, say, forty or fifty," he admitted, gauging the thickness of his bundle.

"Four . . . five livres for all of them," said I, thrusting the money in his face.

"All of them, M'sieur?" he echoed me stupidly.

"I wish to buy everything you have," I repeated. "Don't you understand?"

"Yes, M'sieur. Right away, M'sieur." The news-crier thrust the coins into a pocket, pushed the bundle of pamphlets at me, and dodged away through the pressing multitude ere this daft fellow (for so he must have thought me) could regret his purchase.

"Cousin," I asked Laurent, returning to my new companions, "where do folk talk the loudest about Politics?"

"Well, they argue very fluently at the Café de Foy, but I would say they are drunker and louder at the Caveau."

"Then we will go to the Caveau." I strode down the length of the long arcade, Eléonore and Laurent hurrying behind me. Arriving at the café, I shouldered my way amongst the outside tables and the loiterers clustered about. The patrons of the Caveau—*petit bourgeois* almost to a man—were an ideal audience for my purposes, I thought.

A tall man in the plain decent clothes of a petty tradesman was haranguing the patrons already about the Grenadiers' plight. I brandished a few pamphlets overhead, waving, catching the attention of the man's excited audience. "Free for the taking, Mesdames, Messieurs! Take one and read about the French

Guards, the victims of Tyranny!" I pressed the pamphlets by handfuls on curious drinkers as I passed. "Free the French Guards who have been imprisoned for no other crime than patriotism!"

"Free all political prisoners in the Abbaye!" cried Eléonore. "They mean to take the Guards away to-night and hang them! Will you suffer the Tyrants to hang the honest men whose only crime was to refuse to fire on their brothers?"

"No!" came the answer: first a mutter, then a rumble, then a roar. "Free the Guards!"

"Long live the French Guards!" others echoed them. "Long live Justice!"

"Take Justice into your own hands, Citizens!" shouted the tall trades-man, above the clamour. "I say we go to the Abbaye and demand their release! Break down the doors if we must!"

"Then take us thither!" cried somebody.

"To the Abbaye!"

"Aye, break down the doors!" shouted a young woman clad in a smart crimson riding-habit, climbing onto a table. The crowd was on its feet, swelling by the moment as curious passers-by joined us. "March to the Abbaye, Citizens, and free the fourteen!"

"Free all political prisoners, all victims of Tyranny!"

"Down with the Ministry!" howled a woman.

"To the Abbaye! Who's with us?"

"Free the French Guards! Long live Justice!"

"To the Abbaye!" rose the thunderous cry.

8

MY NEW-FOUND companions and I joined the throng that poured away from the café, attracting others as we marched along rue St-Honoré until we were two or three thousand strong. This crowd, I suspected, would not be cowed by a few guards; though cheerful, they were in a combative humour, prepared to take the prison were their demands denied.

The young woman in crimson marched near us, shouting still, and belabouring those who attempted to slip away with a *barrage* of vulgar epithets in French, English, and Italian. (I learnt, long afterward, that she was none other than the courtesan whom later the royalist journals would contemptuously christen *the Amazon of the Revolution*, Anne Théroigne.) Her fierce bright eyes met Eléonore's and she grinned impudently.

"You and your chums stirred 'em up proper, *chérie!* Bravo!"

I laughed, perhaps at the absurdity of it all. Had anybody told me, a month ere that, that I—*I*, Algernon Sydney Carton, who scoffed at earnest Ideals and who cared for little—would be encouraging a Parisian mob to break into a prison, I would have thought him an escaped Bedlamite.

Beside me, Laurent attempted to persuade Eléonore away from the march. "I pray you," he begged her, "come away from this, ere you're hurt! These are rough folk."

She tossed her head, in what I would soon come to recognise as a characteristic gesture. "Certainly not! I intend to see the prisoners freed. With you and Charles beside me, I am in no danger. Come with me or not, but I will not abandon Julien!" She turned to me, taking my arm. "Laurent imagines his sole duty is to protect me from my own folly. You will protect me, won't you, cousin?"

"I should be honoured," said I.

We descended upon the Abbaye within half an hour and streamed into the courtyard past the astonished sentries. A dozen men hammered at the great iron-bound doors. "We've come for our brothers the French Guards!" our leader's deep voice boomed out, silencing the rest to a murmur as the doors opened a crack.

"Bring out the fourteen French Guards," cried a second fellow, "and all the political prisoners, or let us pass!"

A few uneasy soldiers hovered before the great doors, muskets ready. The tall tradesman, half a head taller than their young commander and face to face with him, stood at the fore of the crowd.

"We've come for the Guards and we mean to take them, Lieutenant!" he bellowed. "D'you think your muskets can hold off this lot?"

"We do not release felons at the demand of a drunken mob," snapped the officer. "Be off and about your business ere my men fire on you."

"No, Sir," declared one of the soldiers. "We won't. The Guards said they never would fire on Frenchmen and no more will we." The others nodded their assent, glancing uneasily at the jeering throng before them. Livid with anger, the officer ordered his men inside the prison and the heavy door swung shut behind them.

"Well then, friends?" the tall man roared. Half a dozen brawny smiths rushed forward, armed with axes, crow-bars, and sledge-hammers. The door soon gave way beneath their determined hacking and the delighted crowd poured inside, shouting their triumph.

Eléonore and I were swept inside with the rest. "He will be in a separate cell somewhere, not in the common cells," she told me. "We must find a guide—"

"There," I interrupted her, espying a man dodging towards the nearest stair. I overtook the frightened turnkey and seized him by the collar. "Take us through this place," I ordered him, "and find a certain prisoner for us, and you shan't be harmed."

Unnerved by the echoing shouts, the turnkey was only too happy to direct us anywhere we liked. Eléonore pressed a handkerchief to her nose as we hurried through dark corridors and up narrow spiral stair-ways. Though no worse than that at Newgate, the stink of piss, ordure, and unwashed Humanity was appalling.

The turnkey led us through more corridors and halted before a massive barred door. "This is the one, Monsieur. Fleutry, held in secret."

"Well, you fool," exclaimed Eléonore, "don't stand there gaping, open it."

"O Madame, they'll have my job sure. Like as not arrest me, too—"

"*Diable!* I am the Vicomtesse de Clairville and my brother the Comte de Valette is a member of the National Assembly," Eléonore told him. "And my companion is the Marquis de Saint-Evrémonde. You may do this on our authority. Hurry!"

"Very well, Madame, if you say so . . ." The key ground in the lock as our guide glanced uneasily over his shoulder at us. "You'll not let these folk hurt us, will you, Monseigneur?"

"Of course not," I assured him, endeavouring to conceal my very natural astonishment at hearing Darnay's true title. "Go on, open it."

The door swung open with a hideous creak and groan of rusty hinges. "Julien?" said Eléonore, her whisper echoing from the masonry.

"Who is that?" The prisoner's voice was harsh, uncertain, as he approached us. The sharp bones of his face, smudged with a week's growth of beard, were all of a sudden sketched in the flickering torch-light from the corridor. "Good God—"

Eléonore flung herself into the fellow's arms. "O Julien, it's all right, we have come for you!" she told him breathlessly. "Come with us—we are going to take you out of this horrible place!"

He drew her close and held her for a moment, unmoving, murmuring: "My love, I thought never to see you again . . ." At last he glanced from Eléonore to me. "I don't understand. What is happening? Who are you, Monsieur?"

"Julien, wonderful things are happening!" cried Eléonore. "A Revolution—the National Assembly—"

"A mob is breaking open this cess-pit," I interrupted her, without offering Fleutry my name, "and freeing the political prisoners. Come along, Monsieur, make haste. We should be away ere they take a notion to free cutthroats and thieves, too, and lest more troops arrive."

Fleutry uttered no more than a dazed "I see," as he seized Eléonore's hand to kiss it once more and hurried into the passage. We made our way without hindrance through the dim, stinking corridors. Laurent halloaed to us by the shattered door, as he busily shepherded the gleeful mob once more into the courtyard. There they milled about, cheering, shouting, weeping as, one by one, uniformed men appeared in the archway, clutching bundles to them, blinking like owls in the sunlight. A few others shuffled out after them, filthy, bewildered, not a little fearful. One man, pale and starved, was too weak to walk far; welcoming hands reached for him and hoisted him on the nearest shoulders.

"You have grown so thin," gasped Eléonore, dismayed, as she saw Fleutry in the daylight. He was a well-favoured fellow of thirty, with a restless, bony, intelligent countenance. "*Mon Dieu*, what did they do to you?"

"Nothing but under-feed me," said he, raising her slim hands to his lips and holding them there as if he could draw sustenance from her touch. "I am one of the fortunate ones here. Disease sweeps through these Hell-holes like fire."

"And rotten food and cold and filth guarantee that once they fall sick, precious few will survive," muttered Laurent, joining us. "Thank God you are well, Fleutry."

From a short distance away I watched them. This was now, I thought, my opportunity to cease my play-acting and let these strangers alone.

"Take them back to the Palais-Royal!" shouted somebody above the hubbub. "They'll be safe there!"

"Aye, let them sleep there to-night!" cried another voice. "A free dinner from my eating-house to-night, for our honest brothers the French Guards!"

"And as much wine as they can drink!" bellowed a third. The crowd streamed from the gates, singing, the former prisoners swaying as they rode upon eager shoulders.

"I fear the police have sealed your lodgings tight as a drum, Fleutry," said Laurent. "You must go with Léo, I think. Unless you have kinfolk here who should know you are free and safe?"

"No, no one in Paris."

"You must come home with me, of course," Eléonore told him. "All you want is a decent meal—several of them—and a bath, and clean clothes." She perceived his curious glance at me and smiled. "My cousin, Charles de Saint-Evrémonde."

"Pardon me, Madame," said I, "but it is time I ended this charade. I am not your cousin, tho' I have the honour of his friendship, and I know we resemble each other greatly. Forgive me if my pleasantry has distressed you. I bid you Good-day, Madame, Messieurs." So saying, I bowed to them and strode off, following the straggling marchers.

I had proceeded a few steps only when Eléonore overtook me, seizing my wrist in a remarkably firm grip. "Charles, don't be ridiculous. What manner of silly game is this you are playing?" Abruptly her smile vanished and a spark of anger glittered in her dark eyes. "Don't tell me you are ashamed to be seen with me and my *bourgeois* lover!"

"I assure you, Madame," I repeated, "I am not Charles Darnay, or Charles de Marbois, whatsoever his name may be. My name is Carton, an Englishman, at your service."

"English!" she exclaimed. "Nonsense. Your French is perfect."

"I learnt French as a child, from my mother," I told her, speaking in English. "My father was English but my mother French, and I am equally at home in either language. But I am not your cousin."

My easy command of English persuaded her that I spoke truth and she released me. "The resemblance—it's remarkable. You are one of my cousin's kinsmen, then? Your mother must have been a Saint-Evrémonde."

I shook my head. "I sincerely doubt that, Madame. She was merely the daughter of a Champenois Notary named Leblanc."

"Leblanc," she echoed me, thoughtful. "From Champagne?"

"Yes, from some small village; I don't know the name."

She stared at me a moment, then abruptly shrugged. "I don't know of anybody named Leblanc. It must be coincidence. Nevertheless," she added, the corners of her mouth twitching once again into a charming smile, "I absolutely refuse to suffer you to walk away with no more ado, after you did me such a service, Monsieur. You will oblige us all by coming to dine with us to-morrow, and by bringing me tidings of my cousin Charles. Number twenty-seven rue St-André-des-Arts—opposite the corner of rue Gil-Cœur—the first floor, above the mezzanine. Ask for Mdme. de Clairville. Half past two." And without awaiting my answer, she swept away. I stared after her and once again began to chuckle, at length laughing there in the midst of the busy street until the tears sprang to my eyes.

1 *Floréal* (*20 April 1794*)

I MUST DIGRESS again from my account, for the daily bloodshed grows ever more disheartening. Yesterday and to-day I watched the Executioner's carts depart once again for the place de la Révolution. To support myself I have sought employment with an Advocate; often whilst occupied with his errands I am obliged to visit the criminal tribunal at the Châtelet, or the Palais de Justice. To-day, and yesterday too, I quitted the sessions at the very moment the carts were departing the courtyard for the scaffold. Seventeen yesterday and thirty-one to-day—and folk once, scant months ago, complained and muttered of Tyranny when the daily harvest reaped a dozen a week! When will this end?

I LEARNT MUCH about Darnay's ancestry on the following day at rue St-André-des-Arts. (Eléonore and I proved to be neighbours, for my lodgings were no more than five minutes' walk from her comfortable apartment.) Fleutry joined us for an excellent dinner and then, pleading exhaustion, retired, leaving Eléonore and her brother in sole possession of me. Eléonore proceeded to enlighten me in extensive detail about the Saint-Evrémondes and the Amberts, her own family, who were related by marriage.

It seemed Darnay's mother and her own were sisters by the name of d'Aulnais: the origin of the humbler name he chose to bear, I should think. "Charles and I were children together at Boissières, my father's favourite estate, after his father died," she told me. "He was only the Chevalier de Marbois then, of course."

"Did ever he mention," I enquired, remembering Darnay's mysterious journeys to France, "a duty his mother had begged him to perform, on her death-bed?"

"Yes . . . yes, he did. Something having to do with his father and uncle, to redress some particular wrong they had committed, tho' he would tell me no more than that. I don't doubt it in the least; his uncle was a consummate beast, and I understand his father was scarce better."

"Saint-Evrémonde was a filthy libertine, and a murderer, on moral grounds if not on legal, two or three times over," declared Laurent, his lip curling in distaste. "His own murderer was some miserable journeyman whose child the old brute had killed in a carriage accident. His end was no more than he deserved. His wife bore him five children and none of them lived a year, and because of that—as if it were her fault!—he made her so wretched an existence that at last she poisoned herself. The family kept the tale quiet, of course, so she could be buried in consecrated ground, but everybody knew the truth of it."

"And I imagine his rather individual taste in depravity improved matters not a bit," Eléonore interrupted him. "We have all heard rumours."

"Yes, there was an ugly story about a couple of prostitutes, whom he'd beaten nearly to death. And rumours about peasant girls, often children, whom he had raped in his youth. But who outside his own family would dare accuse a Marquis of any crime short of murder? And the family, of course, said nothing."

"But by then no one of good family would suffer his daughter or sister to wed a man with such a horrible reputation. They might have overlooked the reputation had Saint-Evrémonde been richer, but his fortune had been eaten away across the years and the estate that was left was not much of a prize—"

"And thus Saint-Evrémonde never was given an opportunity to produce another heir—"

"A legitimate one, at least," said Eléonore with a laugh. "I imagine he left a few dozen bastards scattered the length of the Marne valley—" She abruptly paused, grimacing. "One oughtn't laugh, when he inspired such terror and hatred in his tenants."

"Well," continued Laurent, "he had no heir, and thus he was obliged to be content with his brother's son—Charles—which was a fitting punishment, as they detested each other."

"Charles was the living image of his father and uncle—I shan't deny Saint-Evrémonde was a handsome fellow, for all his depravity—but Charles possessed every good quality they lacked." She stared at me a moment and shook her head, as if to clear it. "It's uncanny, the resemblance. I shall show you." She jumped to her feet and disappeared into an adjoining chamber, returning shortly with a flat jewel-case under her arm. "Charles gave me all these when he inherited the property, ere he returned to England for the last time," she told me, opening the case to reveal a set of exquisite, gold-framed miniatures. "He said he wished to take nothing of his old life to England with him. This is Charles when he was a boy of fourteen or fifteen, and here are his parents, their wedding portraits. And these," she continued, turning to another compartment, "are Saint-Evrémonde and his wife."

I scrutinised the tiny portraits and beheld my image reflected three-fold in them: the grave, handsome lad I remembered from our youth at Louis-le-Grand; the powdered, petulant man of twenty who had been his father; the elegant, disdainful young Nobleman who stared insolently back at me, eyes hooded above aquiline nose. I studied the Marquis's visage a trifle longer. It was Darnay's countenance, to be sure—and my own—but for the frigid contempt in the expression and a certain indefinable air of decadence and cruelty about the mouth.

"It *is* uncanny," I agreed. "But—to return to Darnay—you never knew the history of his promise to his mother?"

"No. Tho' it must have been something uncommonly revolting, mustn't it? Above and beyond the old man's usual depravity. Charles must have found it too shameful, or disgustful, to speak of, even to me."

"Or to me," I mused.

"Tho' I think that by now he has fulfilled his errand, or abandoned it. And meanwhile La Tenèvre, the château, sits there empty, and at present must be in quite a bad way. Probably the villagers have stolen all there remained to take."

"Let it crumble, I say," muttered Laurent. "That château was built with the sweat and blood of hundreds of serfs. The Saint-Evrémondes were never any too kindly to their tenants."

Eléonore and her brother were, I suspected, far truer representatives of the French Nobility than were conscienceless libertines like the late Marquis de Saint-Evrémonde. Broad-minded and affable, they thought nothing of promptly welcoming me into their circle of friends.

Eléonore, Laurent, and their brother Gilbert were (as I pieced it together) the children of the late Comte de Valette, upon whose death Gilbert had succeeded to the title. Eléonore had wedded the Vicomte de Clairville at sixteen and had separated from him some years later, the couple finding themselves childless and incompatible. Clairville had offered her a handsome allowance and, being of an independent spirit, she had chosen to dwell in her own household, under the care of a devoted maidservant, cook, and lackey, rather than endure the priggish Gilbert's constant disapproval of her liberal opinions and her frequently unsuitable friendships. It was not her several love-affairs that had nettled her brother the Count into using his influence at Court to imprison Fleutry, but rather the fact that she had chosen to disgrace the family by taking a mere *bourgeois* scribbler (as he termed him) into her bed.

She had enjoyed her share of lovers, Eléonore told me some while later, without a blush, for the Aristocrats of France were, and are still, far less fettered in their private conduct than are the English Gentry. *Marriage is a matter of Business, love a matter of pleasure,* many folk blithely say; the French think nothing of public *liaisons* outside the marriage-bed, for in France, far more so even than in England, marriages amongst the wealthy are merely contracts of dowries and properties. Infidelity, when discreet, in the modish circles here is more a fashion than a sin. In truth, often ladies of the highest birth and most delicate breeding comport themselves in a manner that we English would consider fitting only for courtesans, and no one in Paris thinks anything of it.

I HAD KNOWN Eléonore for little above a week when she swept into my lodgings one hot July day and leant eagerly across my rickety work-table. "Julien and I have resolved to publish a political journal of our own," she told me without preamble, her dark eyes dancing. "What do you think? Julien says, with all the uproar in the Assembly, very soon everybody will be reading and writing about Politics and nothing will be sent past the Censors any longer. He thinks we could earn a tidy profit, if we do a good job of it."

"Is Fleutry not wanted still by the police?" said I, pushing aside the manuscript I had been translating and rising to my feet. "He ought to be thinking more of prudently quitting Paris, not of calling attention to himself by putting his name on a journal that the authorities are sure to find seditious."

"O, look about you, Carton! The police have more to worry them than one author who was imprisoned owing to a private grudge. He is no criminal; they will ignore him. And as to putting his name on the journal, if we think it best, only my name will appear, or none at all."

"Where is Fleutry to find the money to start it?" I enquired.

"Where do you think? I cannot imagine a better use for the generous allowance my husband's bankers send me every quarter. Can you?"

"I suppose the cost of hiring a printer, or buying a press, and bribing book-sellers to offer the thing is not much more than you would ordinarily spend on a few new hats."

"Carton," she told me, laughing, "you are monstrous impertinent! If you're not more polite, I shan't tell you what else I had to tell you."

I fetched a bottle of Chambertin and two glasses. "I am hanging on your every word, Madame."

"Now you are teasing me, and if you don't stop I may change my mind. But we wish you to write for our journal."

"Me?" I said. "You wish *me* to write?"

"You do know the letters of the alphabet, do you not?" she demanded.

"I've not composed anything in French since I quitted Louis-le-Grand, seventeen years since."

"I don't ask you to produce prose worthy of Voltaire, Carton. But I do think, as an Englishman, you have a different perspective towards our French affairs. You write what you think, whatsoever you like, and Julien or

I will make it fit to read." She poured herself a glass of wine and drank half of it in a swallow. "Say yes. Say you will do it."

I was somewhat taken aback by this abrupt summons, for I had not yet become quite accustomed to Eléonore's high spirits and forceful character. They say French ladies of gentle birth are, all told, rather more assertive than are English ladies; it was they, after all, who truly ruled France for the century past, in the bed-chambers of the mighty, and in their all-powerful *salons* that governed the worlds of Literature, Philosophy, Science, and Statecraft. "How can I resist," said I, laughing, "after such an invitation?"

"I knew you would agree!" she exclaimed, clapping her hands. "O Carton, it's going to be splendid. Julien and I shall edit it, of course, and write most of it, although we will invite selected friends, like you, and my friend Mdlle. de Kéralio, the authoress, to contribute. We have plenty of grist for our mill, Heaven knows, with Julien's description of his six weeks in the Abbaye, and naturally with all the nonsense the Ministers spout! Do you know," she began indignantly, "that some of the noble Deputies deliberately do their best to hamper the efforts of the rest? No, of course you know that. Everybody does, or guesses it. It's scarce surprising, is it?"

"Has the Censor approved this venture of yours?" I interrupted her, without much hope.

"No one worries himself about the Censors, these days," she scoffed, and I left it at that.

9

ON THE FOLLOWING Sunday noon, the fateful 12th of July, Eléonore invited me to accompany her and Fleutry to the Palais-Royal, in order to learn the latest intelligence from Versailles. As Eléonore's invitations resembled nothing so much as royal commands, I hastened to comply.

The Summer heat scorched us that day, even beneath the chestnut trees lining the gravelled paths. Around us, folk blotted perspiring foreheads with handkerchiefs and sleeves. Ignoring the heat, one young man atop a chair outside the Café Italien wiped the dust from his face and continued his harangue. Curious, I paused to listen.

"Folk may say: *Heaven preserve us from Revolution, from trouble and uprisings,*" he cried. "But we don't want trouble, do we, Citizens? We simply want Justice! Look how the King's Ministers fear the power of Paris! When we offer our support to our National Assembly, the Court surrounds Paris with foreign troops who'd not think twice about making war on Parisians were they ordered to do so! And now this, Citizens, this is the final affront!"

He paused, glancing over the throng that had gathered. Eléonore and Fleutry had strolled on, leaving me behind, but other folk had heard and clustered about him: fashionable beaux and belles, workmen on a Sunday outing, a few respectable *bourgeois* with their wives and daughters, several pairs of sweethearts of every quality and description—the usual patrons of the Palais-Royal, anxious and thirsty for tidings.

Heartened, he continued. "Citizens, friends, Parisians: all the reports from Versailles to-day claim the King has dismissed Msr. Necker! Your last friend has been sent away in the middle of the night, like a servant caught stealing pocket-handkerchiefs!"

A rumble of outrage echoed his last statement. Most Parisians idolised the Minister of Finance, an immensely wealthy Swiss Banker. The Court, however, loathed Necker because as a foreigner, a *bourgeois*, and a Protestant, he would not hesitate to propose that the Nobility and Clergy pay their share of taxes.

The orator waved vaguely towards the South-west, towards Versailles. "Do you know the Assembly will have no more of the decrees forced on us by our King's precious Ministers? Friends, who do you think speaks for you? Your Deputies at the National Assembly, or the Comte d'Artois?" Laughter and applause rewarded his sally. Artois, the King's youngest brother and perhaps the most stubborn and reactionary member of the Court, was an easy target for the pamphleteers' scorn. The young man tugged a bundle of hand-bills from his pocket and thrust them at the men and women nearest him.

"All we ask," he continued, "is that you lend your support to the men who are risking all to take a stand for Justice. Is that so much to ask of you? Look at La Fayette! Look at Mirabeau! They have nothing to gain by taking the side of the Nation. If they can risk all for the Third Estate, for the People of France, is it not your duty to uphold them? Will you join us and stand behind the National Assembly? Will you prove to the Court that they cannot keep us down forever?"

Farther along the arcade, near the Café de Foy, a resounding cheer erupted. Shouting, whistling, applauding, dozens of folk abruptly scrambled onto tables to reach into the branches above them. Eléonore came hurrying towards me a moment later, flushed with excitement. "Carton! Did you hear him! Did you *hear* him?"

"Hear whom?" said I. "What has happened?"

"Desmoulins!"

"Who?"

"Camille Desmoulins!" she panted. "Don't you know him? You must know him. He dwells very near you. The lawyer who never gets a case, and who writes wonderful essays. He was magnificent! He climbed onto a table, told them he had just come from Versailles and the rumours about Necker were true, and called them to arms! He had them on their feet in an instant—they're going mad!"

"Camille Desmoulins," I murmured, a long-forgotten memory awakening. "I believe I do know him."

"Of course you do, everybody in our district knows Camille—"

"Though when I saw him last," I concluded, smiling, "he was not quite twelve years old. Very well, then, Madame, let us see what trouble he is managing to stir up. Where is Fleutry?"

Eléonore stamped her foot. "Heaven knows! We lost each other in the crush. Never mind that! Don't you understand? Camille has succeeded in doing what none of these other wind-bags have done, Carton! Something is going to *happen* at last."

A dozen hands, clutching bunches of chestnut leaves, reached out to me as we approached the Café de Foy. "Green cockades so we can recognise each other as patriots!" cried a man. "Take a green cockade and join us!"

I fastened a leaf in my hat-band and continued doggedly onward. Packed in a tight restless mass, a vast crowd pressed forward, applauding and shouting. At length I made out the speaker balanced most precariously on a rickety table-top—a thin, shabby young man with lank dark hair tumbled about his shoulders, unquestionably the animated black-eyed child I had once known.

"To arms, Citizens!" he cried. He seemed to have overcome his stutter, or perhaps the excitement of the moment had banished it. "Necker's dismissal is but the first outrage! This is the signal for another St. Bartholomew's Massacre of patriots! Don't you know the Queen's party wishes to slaughter every inhabitant of Paris, to the last man? We must arm ourselves and prepare for the worst! Arm yourselves ere the German soldiers come out of their camps to-night to murder us all! Arm yourselves, and wear green cockades, Citizens, so you will know your fellow patriots: green, the colour of Hope!"

Eléonore turned and clutched my arm. "Can it be true? Will they attack the city?"

"I doubt it. But if Necker is truly gone, then it *might* be true . . ."

"I see the infamous police watching me," continued Camille, scornful. To my utter stupefaction, the young lunatic pulled a pair of pistols from his coat and brandished them overhead. "Let them try to arrest me, for calling my fellow citizens to take up arms! I will die first! In the name of Liberty, friends—to arms, Citizens, to arms!"

"Where can we find arms?" demanded somebody near me.

"The Invalides, the Arsenal—"

"The Hôtel de Ville!"

"I hear there are a thousand barrels of powder at the Arsenal—"

"There are muskets at the Invalides, in the cellars, thousands of them, I've seen them with my own eyes—"

"The Château de Vincennes—"

"Try the Treasury!"

To Eléonore's exasperation, I insisted she go home. At last she capitulated. She spent the afternoon prowling restlessly about her apartment until Laurent hastened in, late that night, with the intelligence he had gleaned of the growing unrest. The near-riot at the Palais-Royal had swelled almost to Insurrection, he told us. German cavalry had dispersed a thousand angry marchers at the place Louis XV, killing a few and sending the rest fleeing into the Tuileries gardens, but the incensed crowd had rallied and forced the Hussars to retreat in the face of a hail of stones. In the course of a day, the people of Paris had gone mad in their frantic determination to arm themselves, to defend the city against certain invasion.

EARLY THE NEXT day I heard sporadic musket-shots and then the incessant *clang-clang-clang* of every church-bell in Paris, now alarum-bells sounding a warning and calling the city to arms. I kept to my lodgings, avoiding the frenzy prevailing in the streets. Had I chosen to take sail for the New World, I reflected wryly, I might still have been aboard a ship ploughing the Atlantic that day, not dwelling in the midst of a city gone mad. What business of mine was their cursed Revolution?

After learning what tidings I could at a café, I called at Eléonore's apartment the next morning, concerned for her safety. Her middle-aged maidservant opened the door to me, her face white and pinched. "What's the matter, Baptistine?" I asked her, immediately concluding that Eléonore had rushed out alone on some impetuous errand. "Is your mistress safe?"

"Yes, M'sieur," she whispered, bobbing a courtesy, "she's safe, but—O M'sieur, you're her friend—go to her!"

Bewildered, I proceeded to the *salon* and found Eléonore staring out the window, clad still in her *peignoir,* her thick dark hair tumbling down her back. She did not turn as I approached.

"Madame?" said I. "What has happened?"

She turned to look at me then. Her countenance might have been sculpted of marble, it was so pale and still. "Julien is dead," she told me.

"Dead? How?"

"He must have joined in the uproar at the Palais-Royal after we were separated yesterday," she continued, in the same lifeless tone. "Sunday, rather. It's Tuesday, isn't it. The Royal-Allemand Regiment attacked them at the place Louis XV. Most folk escaped, or fought back. They found him there afterward. He had a book I had lent him in his pocket, and they sent word to me. Last night. Laurent is gone to the Morgue, to make arrangements. I shall have to bury him, and write to his family. They are in Nîmes. It's much too far; the weather is too hot. They will never see him again, and neither will I." She paused in her numb recitation and stood silent for a moment, clenching and unclenching her fists.

"I would better have left him in the Abbaye," she murmured at last. "O Carton, we brought him out to let him be killed!"

"We did nothing of the kind," I told her. "He joined that mob of his own free will."

"Had I never taken him from prison, he would be alive and safe to-day. A fortnight . . . that's all it was. No more time than that. A fortnight."

"Because we rescued him from the Abbaye, it does not inevitably follow he should be killed in a riot two weeks later," said I. "You are not responsible for his death, Madame."

"I—it was *I* who wished to visit the Palais-Royal on Sunday," said she. "If we'd not gone—"

"Stop it!" I ordered her. "What's done is done. You could not have known what was about to happen. The Hussars killed Fleutry, not you."

She drew a deep, shuddering breath and put her hands to her face for a moment. When she withdrew them, I saw she was dry-eyed and tight-lipped.

"You are right. And whosoever gave the order to attack, and whosoever ordered *him*, whosoever it was, to the King himself—he will pay for it." At last she met my eyes. "What is happening?"

I told her of the prevailing rumour, that the cellar store-rooms of the Hôtel des Invalides were full of muskets, and that many folk already had gone thither in search of arms.

"Then that is where I shall go," said she.

"To the Invalides?" said I. "Amidst a rough crowd? You don't know what you say, Madame. You should take a sleeping-potion and try to rest."

She jerked her chin upward, defiant. "If they have muskets, then I shall go to the Invalides and get me one—"

"A musket!"

"I know how to use one, Mr. Carton. My husband's greatest passion, far greater than his passion for me or even for his mistresses, is hunting. He taught me to shoot in order that we might be able to exchange a few words on one theme at least. And at present I am very much in a humour to shoot down a few Hussars, and if need be I shall go to the Invalides alone, or else I will surely go mad!"

Albeit reluctantly, whilst Laurent was occupied elsewhere I felt myself responsible for her safety. I submitted, for even at the best of times surrender to Eléonore's demands was far easier than resistance.

We were obliged to walk to the Invalides. No carriages were abroad and Eléonore's coachman warned us that it might be dangerous to drive when the population's anxiety and anger were at such a fever-pitch. Eléonore, clad in a plain brown dress borrowed from her cook, walked the long way without a word, her step firm and measured. We found the square before the soldiers' Hospital swarming. An immense crowd shouted encouragement to a band of men spilling from the *hôtel's* gates, which stood ajar, the sentry-boxes empty.

We pressed forward through the milling crowd, towards a handful of men who were passing out muskets and bayonets from crates stamped with the royal arms. A man came staggering towards us, carrying another crate, which he swung with a grunt to the ground. "What do you think?" he demanded of no one in particular. "We pushed our way in and we carried off forty or fifty crates ere the Governor could try even to force us out!" He gingerly prodded a swollen, purpling bruise on one cheek and turned his attention to passing out the pistols from his crate.

Somebody thrust a gun into my hands. I glanced at the story-teller. "What of powder and shot?"

"None, curse it! All we have is the barge-load of powder-casks they took yesterday. But they must have powder somewhere!"

"The Arsenal?" suggested one fellow. "The Provost of Merchants said there was plenty—"

"Not a grain! That scum Flesselles was purposely misleading us."

"Citizens, the soldiers say the powder-supply is stored at the Bastille!" cried a third. "They claim it's all been transferred from the Arsenal."

"Aye, I heard that too!" exclaimed another, overhearing. "My brother-in-law, he's in the Guards—"

"We have to go to the Bastille for our powder, lads!"

"Our gunpowder is at the Bastille, Citizens!" cried the first man, jumping onto a crate. "We'll have to go and politely ask the Prison-Governor to give it us, if we want to be armed proper!"

Those within earshot applauded, whooping. "Who's for the Bastille?" cried somebody. Within a few minutes a determined band of two hundred had formed amidst the enthusiastic crowd. They set off for the long walk across the length of Paris, lustily singing snatches of a crude popular song. I relieved Eléonore of the musket she had seized and thrust it and my own into the nearest empty hands.

"You are *not*," I told her, as she opened her mouth to remonstrate with me, "going to the Bastille. It will be no place for a woman, with hundreds of rough folk up in arms."

Eléonore glared at me. "I am not about to stew for another day in those rooms, with nothing to think on but Julien, and the bells driving me mad! Don't you understand? I must *do* something or lose my senses."

At length I persuaded her to go instead to the Palais-Royal, where we might await the latest intelligence. Arriving towards eleven o'clock at the Café Corazza, I ordered Cognac and made Eléonore take a few swallows. She stared unseeing over my shoulder, absently sipping the brandy, her eyes hard. "We would have called it *Le Flambeau Parisien*," she said at last. "Our journal. Julien's journal. He never had a chance to write a single word."

I nodded. "I am sorry."

"I shall start it by myself. It was his dream. It's all I have left that was his. He wished to tear away all the mummery, hypocrisy, stupidity. He wished to do away with all the greedy corrupt scoundrels at Court who govern the country to their own advantage, and all the incompetent fools who never did anything but be born Noblemen's sons. Is that such a foolish dream?"

I poured myself a glass of Cognac and drank it down ere replying. "His dream of Reform, or your dream of revenge?"

"That too. Why not? And you will help me? I need you more than ever, Carton."

"You scarce know me, Madame," said I. "I am not as dependable, perhaps, as you may imagine. For fifteen years I have been a disappointed, thwarted drunkard, who chose wine above action to escape a world I found unbearable, because acting seemed too much worthless effort to me." I proceeded to tell her of my youth: of my father and my vanished inheritance and my final downward slide to apathy and drunkenness as Stryver's drudge. I said nothing, however, of Sarah, that black memory, for I had no wish to reveal the darker reaches of my heart to this woman whom already I esteemed. Nor could I bring myself to lay my heart so bare as to speak of my love for Lucie, of that secret she and I alone shared.

"What brought you back to France?" Eléonore asked me, when I had done.

"I quarrelled with Stryver," I said. "And because of the nature of our quarrel, I was obliged to quit London."

"Well? You could more easily have gone no more than five leagues from London. Why France? It was not the easiest road you might have chosen."

"I wished to return to a place I'd not seen since my youth, that held my fondest memories."

"You were unwilling ere then to make the effort to escape your life; why would you have wished suddenly to return? Carton, we all of us change—sometimes even for the better. I think you are not quite the same man who was a failed lawyer in London."

I mulled over her words, acknowledging the truth of them. "Yet I am a man without great energy or ambition still," said I. "That I have always been, and I suspect always will be."

She smiled for the first time that day. "I don't need your ambition. I need your gifts—and I know you possess them. Your conversation is not that of a stupid man, or an uneducated one. Carton, if you could suffer that blockhead to impose shamelessly upon your talents for fifteen years, surely you can suffer me to do the same. I am an easier taskmaster, and the reward will be infinitely greater. Fame, perhaps. Satisfaction, certainly. The knowledge that you have taken part in this Revolution, which is going to renew France."

Renew France! They thought so, they truly thought so, in 1789. How rosy were their dreams, and how cruelly were their illusions shattered!

"Why should I care what becomes of France?" said I.

"Because you are half French. Because you are here."

"I might pack my valise and quit France for America in a month, or a week, or to-morrow."

"You might," she agreed, "but until you do, you are going to help me, are you not?"

"I have little else of interest to occupy my days," I admitted.

Eléonore nodded. "I thank you."

She fell silent then, and without a word rose and walked away towards the arcades. Suspecting she wished to be alone with her thoughts, I did not follow her save with my eyes, as she wandered slowly past the shop windows.

The quarter-hours passed. The day was overcast, a thin dull blanket of cloud obscuring the Sun. Noon came and went; the little cannon fixed to a pedestal in one of the flower-gardens, whose charge was ignited by the heat of the midday Sun concentrated thro' a lens, failed to fire. Eléonore returned at last with a handful of pamphlets.

"They are besieging the Bastille," she told me. "Seven or eight hundred men. They are attacking the central keep with muskets. You might as easily try to dig a canal with a coffee-spoon. They haven't a hope." She sat and stared glumly into the trees.

"You think not?" I enquired, for I had not yet seen the Bastille.

"The walls are eight feet thick and seventy feet high, and then there's the dry-moat. Not even cannon could do much."

At length we partook of a belated, silent luncheon at a *restaurateur's.* Awaiting we knew not what, we sat and strolled and sat again for some time more, each absorbed in his own thoughts. At last a hubbub a short distance away distracted me from one of Eléonore's pamphlets. I looked up to discover two or three dozen men and women clustering about Camille Desmoulins.

Curious, I excused myself to Eléonore and ambled towards the gathering. My old acquaintance had evidently become the Idol of the moment, for half a dozen ladies of Fashion were pressing in upon him, reacting to his every word with little shrieks of laughter or admiration. For his part, he was preening, drinking in his new-found celebrity as a cat laps cream.

After a moment I caught his eye. "Good day to you, Desmoulins," I said. "You have changed remarkably since we spoke last."

He smiled, tho' his gaze was blank. "I don't know you, d-do I?"

"You knew me quite a long time ago. I see you are thoroughly aware still that you are cleverer than all the other boys."

"*Mon Dieu!*" he exclaimed, after a moment. His stutter had grown less burthensome, tho' it had not vanished entirely. "C-Carton? Or is it Darnay?"

"Carton."

"But what on Earth . . ." He shrugged aside his audience and clasped my hand. "You—in Paris again, after all this time! Tell me, what brings you here? —O, let me be, c-can't you?" he added, over his shoulder, as several of the women resumed their chatter. Linking arms with me, he drew me away. "They won't leave me in peace. All the time yesterday, this morning, they c-come flocking about me, c-clacking like hens."

"You don't seem to dislike the attention," I observed.

He laughed. "If truth be told, I enjoy it immensely!"

Eléonore rose as we approached her. "Well, Camille," said she, "I saw you make a spectacle of yourself on Sunday. What do you think may come of it?"

"Who knows, Madame?" said he, with a shrug and an easy grin. "But certainly something will c-come of it."

"Change?"

"Yes, I think so."

"You think Paris will save the National Assembly?"

"Of c-course. The Ministers will take one look at the intelligence the c-couriers bring them and—"

He never finished his sentence, for at that moment a horseman came pounding in through the arched passage from rue de Valois, provoking a few startled screams and sending the pigeons flapping in a rush of wings. "The Bastille!" we heard him shout as he galloped nearer, gravel flying from beneath the horse's hooves. "The Bastille has surrendered! Gunpowder for all! The Bastille is ours!" Wheeling his mount about, he galloped back down the length of the arcade and vanished through the Montpensier passage. "The Bastille has surrendered!"

I believe dead silence reigned for the space of a breath. Then Pandæmonium arose as everyone in the gardens began babbling at once.

"Good God!" whispered Eléonore, turning to me. "Carton, take me to the Bastille. I wish to see it. I wish to see the Bastille in the hands of the People."

"It may be dangerous," I objected.

"Why should it be dangerous if the fighting is done? I wish to be able to say I have seen this day, Carton. For Julien, for *Le Flambeau*. I pray you— you *must* take me to the Bastille."

"I'll take you, Mdme. de Clairville," said Camille. I gave him a doubtful glance. After witnessing his histrionic and thoroughly irresponsible performance on the 12th—*pistols*, for the love of Heaven!—I scarce pictured him a model of steadiness.

"I will accompany you, Madame," I told her firmly. "Though you are welcome to come with us if you wish, Desmoulins."

At length we found one of the very few fiacres available for hire that day. Clattering eastward along rue St-Antoine, at the place de Grève we came upon a vast raucous crowd, brandishing pikes and muskets overhead as they milled about the steps of the Town Hall.

Our driver reined his horse into a side-street, avoiding the whooping, shouting mob. Above the tumult I heard gun-shots and a few howls of pure savagery. Through the carriage window I glimpsed, for an instant only, some dripping thing affixed on the point of a pike that a tall man swung from side to side amidst the squeals and jeers of the mob; and I knew then that the day's triumph had been sealed already with a vengeful blood-offering.

10

CAMILLE CHATTERED INCESSANTLY as we jolted along. (For all that he was hampered by his stutter, I never have heard a fellow so enamoured of the sound of his own voice.) He maintained a polite fiction of pursuing Law-work, he said, whilst scribbling essays; he had recently completed his best work yet, a pamphlet titled *Free France*, which Msr. Momoro, his publisher, after printing, had decided was too daring to sell, and for which Momoro refused to pay him. He was in love, but his darling's parents would not hear of Lucile wedding him, for she was rich and he poor and, moreover, a very dubious character.

O yes, and Robespierre was in Versailles, a member of the National Assembly. Imagine becoming sufficiently enthusiastic about *Robespierre*, of all folk, an excellent fellow but so thoroughly prosy, to elect him a Deputy! And many of the Deputies he had met had expressed surprise that he, Camille, had not been elected one of them. But after to-day, after lighting the spark that had enflamed Paris and brought the Bastille into the hands of the People, no one could say he was a feckless ne'er-do-well who, despite his cleverness, would never amount to anything.

We discovered, as we arrived at the place de la Bastille, that many folk had conceived the same fancy as Eléonore. The two courtyards leading to the draw-bridge teemed with curious onlookers. Above them, on the highest tower's battlements, a handful of men had pulled down the royal banner with its golden *fleur-de-lys* and had replaced it with the blue-and-red banner of Paris.

The tide swept us through the open gates towards the wide cobbled courtyard within the fortress walls, where workmen swarmed about the doors to the eight massive towers, shouting for powder and shot. Others ran

back and forth from the towers to the barracks to the stables, pushing furiously towards the doors of the Governor's residence in the outer court.
Three men stood their ground there, grimly aiming their muskets at the
mob and shouting words lost in the furor.

"Keep back, d__n you!" snapped a flustered, decently-clad man as he levelled his musket at us, bayonet gleaming. "We'll have no looting!"

"Do you not know who I am?" demanded Camille. "I am Camille
Desmoulins, who called the city to arms at the Palais-Royal!"

In an instant a crowd gathered about us. Disdaining Eléonore and me,
they hoisted Camille on their shoulders, applauding, and carried him off
towards the keep to show him the glorious result of his patriotism.

"Who is in command, if any one?" Eléonore asked the guard.

"Hulin, of the militia. He's a good head on his shoulders——" He stiffened suddenly and barked a curt order to the others as he stared past the
outer draw-bridge to the public court beyond. We followed his gaze to discover three riders approaching in a haze of dust.

The men posted amidst the rubble in the outer court stirred uneasily as
they watched the horsemen approach. No longer smartly uniformed soldiers, the new sentinels were an oddly assorted group: a wizened, leathery
little man, a boy of no more than sixteen, a handful of journeymen artisans.

"Who are they?" the boy asked me as I joined them. "Do you know?
They'd better plan no tricks," he added, cradling his gleaming new musket
more comfortably.

"Have you any spare arms here?" I enquired, mistrustful of the strange
horsemen, my eyes never quitting them. Their leader was a stern, fine-looking man of fifty, with a remarkable head of thick white hair that wanted no
powdering. I had seen portraits enough of La Fayette to know this was not
he, but I did not recognise him.

A safe distance away still, they reined in their horses. The man at their
head dismounted, tossing his reins to a companion, and proceeded on foot
towards the gate.

"That is Msr. d'Aubincourt," said somebody. "The Deputy!"

I had, of course, heard of the Comte d'Aubincourt, for he was one of the leaders in the National Assembly, though not so famous as Mirabeau or Bailly. A faint amazed murmur rippled through the group as the Count drew closer. He paused a few paces from us, evaluating the sentries, I thought, with a dispassionate but not unfriendly gaze.

"Who has taken charge here?" he enquired. "Does anybody know? I pray you, Messieurs, direct me to whomever is in command here—if, indeed, anybody is."

"I believe they are in the Governor's quarters, Monseigneur," I ventured.

"And is anything done here beside looting?"

"They are trying to prevent it, and attempting to keep some semblance of order until the militia may arrive."

"Good. Least of all this city wants a cellarful of weapons and powder in the hands of a lot of ignorant labourers. They will essay to defend the city against the King's troops and end by shooting each other." He sighed and gazed upward at the towers, where tiny, jubilant figures waved coats and muskets overhead. "I believe the city is gone quite mad. Messieurs, whether the Assembly ought to recognise this rebellion is open to debate still."

"But there were rumours everywhere," interrupted the boy-sentry.

"Yes," I agreed. "The French Guards were talking of plans to surround the National Assembly with Switzers and Germans, who were to arrest all the Commons and everyone who had taken their part—you too, Monseigneur. And Msr. de Mirabeau and Msr. Bailly, and possibly even Msr. de la Fayette."

"And now I suppose this mob expects the Assembly to approve its actions?"

"Would that not depend on whether or not those rumours were true?" I suggested.

Aubincourt unexpectedly smiled. "Well, Monsieur, perhaps you can do me the favour of taking me to these brave men who are holding the Bastille for Paris." With a nod, he strode past the sentries.

One of the guards hurried towards us as Aubincourt approached them. "Inside, Monseigneur," he told him, "in the Governor's lodgings. Word spread that you were here. We'll have the Devil to pay if we don't restore order soon."

Aubincourt nodded. "Come with me, if you will," he told me. "You seem to have a grasp of matters."

I turned to beckon Eléonore inside but, to my alarm, could see her nowhere. Cursing myself for bringing her to the heart of such Chaos, I babbled an excuse to Aubincourt and plunged once more into the crowd.

All about me men streamed from the keep, clutching weapons to them. I shouldered my way in amongst them, guessing that Eléonore had gone in search of the musket I had denied her that morning. Powder-blackened men and wild-eyed women hurried past me, shouting to each other. How was I to find her amidst such turmoil? I climbed onto an empty crate, the better to see about me, and as I did so heard a woman's scream not far from me.

A big man clad still in his smith's apron had hold of Eléonore, laughing as she struggled in his grip. "Whosoever you be," he told her, "you're not one of us, not with those dainty hands! What'll we do with the treacherous slut, then? Strip her and give her a good whipping?"

"How dare you!" she shrieked. I heard cloth tear as a second man snatched at her bodice, hooting. She clawed at her captor, at last sinking her teeth into one brawny arm.

"Hoo," he roared, with a curse, "the bitch bites!" He cuffed her and flung her over his shoulder.

Sick with dread lest they hurt her, I looked frantically about me, but I would have trusted not one of the frenzied throng hastening past. At last I caught sight of a tiny pocket-pistol, half-concealed beneath an officer's bloody corpse. I seized it, praying that both its barrels were loaded, and the sword hanging at the dead man's side, and doggedly pushed my way towards Eléonore.

As I neared them, the big man heaved her into an empty cart. She staggered to her feet but yet another of her tormentors seized her and flung her backward, laughing as her skirt tore in his hands.

My heart was pounding as though it might burst. Forcing away the fear that clutched at my vitals, I thrust myself betwixt them, aiming my pistol at the fellow's heart. "Let her be, you swine," I ordered him. "Be off with you."

"Why, it was just a bit of fun," he ventured, cringing, "just a bit of sport with the trollop—"

"Be off with you!" I repeated, much astonished at my own boldness, for I am not and have never been a man of action. "You are not fit to polish the boots of the men who fought here to-day." When none of them budged, I struck the nearest a stinging blow with the flat of the naked sword I carried. "Go back to the gutters where you belong!"

Paling, he and his companions turned and fled. The brawny smith remained, however, laughing as he eyed me, and with one arm seized Eléonore about the waist as she tried once again to climb from the cart. "Who's to make me—you?" he demanded, taking a swallow from the flask he carried and spitting at my feet.

"If I must." All at once I felt no fear, only an intoxicating, trembling anger. As he lunged for me, I raised the pistol—quite calm despite my fury—and squeezed the trigger. To my immense relief a shot rang out.

"Pray take note this pistol has two barrels," I told him, as with a roar and an oath he staggered and clutched at his shoulder. "If you advance another step, the second bullet will go through your vile face. I hope you will not doubt me."

He spat again and stumbled away, muttering and clutching at the wound. Flinging the pistol and sword from me, I reached for Eléonore with hands that suddenly shook as if palsied. "Are you hurt?"

"Only shaken. O Carton, bless you."

We hurried together from the keep, pausing to draw breath in the outer courtyard. Eléonore was pale and trembling still. "Madame," I enquired, "are you personally acquainted with the Comte d'Aubincourt?"

"We have met," said she, staring at me.

"Come, then." I led her to the door of the Governor's residence and told the guard both our names, demanding entry. "You cannot go on without rest," I told Eléonore, as she glanced at me, "and you will be safe here."

The guard returned a moment later and beckoned us inside, pointing out our way. I found Eléonore a chair in a corner of the dining-room, where a number of armed men had gathered, Aubincourt amongst them. She smiled at me, murmuring that she would be much herself in a moment, and pushed me gently towards the assemblage.

The gilded looking-glasses and chairs in the Governor's residence provided sharp contrast to the muskets and ammunition-boxes of the men who stood stiffly about the long dining-table. "You must understand, Messieurs," Aubincourt told them as I approached, "that this has placed the National Assembly in a d__nably awkward position. Ere to-day, we were in disagreement with the Crown, had resisted tyrannical decrees, yet we had no thought of armed revolt. This, Messieurs, this is patently an act of rebellion against the Crown. The Ministry has every justification, at least in its own eyes, to attack Paris with that army everyone has feared, and kindle a civil war."

"Would you say it's likely they will, Monseigneur?" asked the man opposite him.

"I'd not trust them very far, would you?"

The men about me snickered. "So you see, Messieurs," continued the Count, "should the National Assembly dare to applaud this uprising, Paris may be besieged, which at best would lead to frightful loss of life and terrible misery. On the other hand, should we condemn it, the population will assuredly lose faith in us, which will leave us open to any measures the Court wishes to take in order to muzzle us. You see my dilemma?"

"The true question is how to reconcile an illegal rebellion with a legal one," I murmured, slipping into an empty space at the table. "Msr.

d'Aubincourt, you don't believe the Parisians could fight off any foreign mercenaries the Court might set at us?"

"A handful of shopkeepers and tradesmen? Certainly not."

"No, Monsieur, I don't mean only the few hundreds who were sufficiently exercised to take up arms to-day. I mean all of them. The half-million ordinary folk whose only political ambition is to have fewer and gentler laws, and lower taxes. They believe in the National Assembly. Most of them would fight to their last breath for it."

"Don't you visit the Palais-Royal, Monseigneur?" demanded one man, interrupting me.

I nodded. "Monsieur is right. You know how the spectators in the public galleries cheer the Assembly. At the Palais-Royal, that enthusiasm is a hundred times stronger. On the streets, on the Left Bank, everywhere you go they talk about Liberty, how the King and the Assembly will free France from the clutches of the Nobility. Msr. d'Aubincourt, men who have dared attack the Bastille and capture it will not stop there."

Aubincourt gazed across the table at us, thoughtfully nodding. "Well, Monseigneur," said the man who appeared to be in command of the rest, "will you aid us or not?"

"Now that I see how matters lie, I expect the Assembly won't fail to take every political advantage from this insurrection."

A few whooped and clapt their fellows on the back as a palpable thrill, quick as thought, seemed to crackle amongst us like lightning. "Bravo, Aubincourt!" cried one man. "Long live the Assembly!"

"Long live Paris, and Liberty!"

"Now," added the Count briskly, "what of that gunpowder? I suggest you take as many men as you can and ensure that the powder is well-guarded. Paris will be dangerous enough to-night." Aubincourt paced to the nearest window and stood observing the disorderly scene in the court below as the men noisily trooped out.

"Monsieur," he said abruptly, turning and fixing me with a stern gaze, "who are you?"

"I, Monsieur?" said I.

"You. You have an unmistakable look of old Saint-Evrémonde about you, yet you talk like no Saint-Evrémonde I ever met. Are you the nephew, who abandoned his estates after the old Marquis was murdered, and disappeared?"

"No, Monsieur. I am an Englishman; my name is Carton."

"An Englishman!" he exclaimed. "Why concern yourself with our French affairs? This is not your fight."

"I am half French . . . and as for the rest, I don't mean to concern myself with your Revolution, but it seems Fate, or Providence, has determined otherwise."

"I see." Aubincourt turned to the window once again. "Mdme. de Clairville, this gentleman is a friend of yours?"

"Yes, Monsieur."

"And you hold him in high regard?"

"We've not been acquainted long, but I've found him a faithful and trustworthy friend," said Eléonore, puzzled.

"I thank you. Mr. Carton," he enquired, after a moment of silence, "are you in want of a situation?"

I stared at him. "What mean you, Monsieur?"

"I need a secretary, an aide: a man who is trustworthy, intelligent, and believes as I do. If we have, indeed, furthered our Revolution to-day, our work will be twice as hard as before: a suitable reward for having sown our dragons' teeth," he added, with a dry smile. "Revolutions, as I am sure you have learnt from your own history of a century since, are a dangerous business, Mr. Carton. They bring out the worst in folk but they also bring out the best. Those who can ride out the storm become the leaders we need, and I wish those men on my side. Including you, whether you be French, or English, or Hindoo."

"You flatter me," said I, colouring.

"Am I to understand you accept?"

"Monsieur, truly, I am honoured . . . but you scarce know me," I protested. "I am but an English Attorney, and an indifferent one at that. What use could I be to you?"

"I don't need the experience—that will come. I need the man. Will you consider it?"

Eléonore seized my hand and drew me into a corner. "Carton! Of course you must accept."

"He would not be so eager to employ me if he knew me better."

She folded her arms and scowled at me. "Msr. d'Aubincourt is an excellent judge of character. And so, I think, am I. How often must I tell you that you are not the man you were in England?"

"I hope your confidence in me is not misplaced."

"*Diable*, Carton, you are being a fool! Did ever your ridiculous employer in England have cause to complain of your work?"

"No," I admitted. "Of my habits, to be sure, but not my work."

"On the contrary, I think—you made him rich! It was *you* who enabled him to win his cases, was it not? Why do you doubt your ability? *Mon Dieu*, Carton, working for a man like Aubincourt will not be like drudging for a pompous fool of a Barrister. You have the talents—let him make use of them to a good end."

I laughed suddenly. Evidently Fate, after toying with me so cruelly in my youth, was having its jest with me now by flinging me headlong into opportunity I never had sought. As I had not had the strength then to withstand Fate's blows, neither did I have it now to turn away, had I wished to, from the good fortune so fortuitously cast my way.

"Very well," said I, "I'll do it . . ."

Eléonore smiled. "Msr. d'Aubincourt," she announced, "Mr. Carton accepts your kind offer."

LA FAYETTE AND the Parisian militia arrived shortly afterward to take possession of the Bastille. To deafening cheers, a noisy, disorderly procession of carts heaped high with powder-barrels moved slowly from the square and down rue St. Antoine, towards the centre of the city. Eléonore and I joined it, after taking our leave of Aubincourt. Behind us, in the distance now as we continued down the long street, folk streamed into the Bastille still in their relentless search for arms.

The procession dispersed as boisterous groups broke away to march, shouting and singing, down side-streets and alleys. Everywhere about us the bells clanged still, rapid, monotonous, sounding the alarum, calling all within earshot to rise and defend their city. Despite this warning, the streets took on an air of celebration, as folk gleefully toasted the Nation and thrust bottles of rough red wine, tankards of beer, and flasks of *eau-de-vie* upon those who passed them, as if every one of us might have been a *Conqueror of the Bastille.*

Camille found us much later, on rue St-André-des-Arts. "They've brought powder!" he crowed. "They had twenty thousand pounds of it in the B-Bastille's store-rooms, imagine it!"

"Yes, they were taking it to the Hôtel de Ville," said I. "Did it arrive safely?"

"I suppose it did," said he, indifferent. "Have you heard of all that's happened?" Without awaiting an answer, he plunged on. "They murdered Launay—the G-Governor of the Bastille, you know. And they freed the prisoners. All seven of them."

"Only seven?" I said, thinking of the blood-curdling tales that circulated in England about French cruelty, and about the thousands of innocents who languished forgotten in French prisons.

Camille grinned. "Four forgers, one sexual pervert, and two lunatics, one of whom fancied he was Julius Cæsar and was about to be crowned Emperor of Rome. They will have to take him off to the madhouse at Charenton to-morrow and lock him up again," he added, with a burst of laughter. He clapt me on the back, kissed Eléonore's hand, and strolled away whistling into the milling crowds.

Eléonore glanced at me, the torch-light that blazed at every street-corner glittering in her eyes. "Well, Carton! Have we made a miracle or have we not!"

"The question is," I murmured, "have they begun something they cannot stop? Can anybody, even Aubincourt or La Fayette, truly command this mob?"

Eléonore impatiently waved away my objections. "Let them loose, I say! France and the Court have become as noisome as the Augean Stables— nothing less than a flood will cleanse them. Let the river overflow where it may!" She began to laugh, giddy with exhaustion. Abruptly her laughter caught in her throat and, hiding her face in her hands, she gave way beneath the burthen she had steadfastly refused to acknowledge all the day. I drew her to me and held her close whilst she wept.

At last, as her sobs quietened, I led her to her house and up the stair to her apartment. As her maid answered the door, I raised Eléonore's hand to my lips, meaning to bid her Good-night and be on my way, but she clutched at my fingers.

"Don't go," she whispered. "Stay with me . . ."

Perhaps it was the brandy and wine I had drunk that evening, from those countless bottles thrust at me along the way, which I could not have risked refusing. Or perhaps it was merely my baser nature taking hold of me, for I had not had a woman since I quitted England. Whatsoever the reason, despite my wiser instincts I followed Eléonore inside, and into her bed-chamber.

We coupled like strangers at a brothel, quick and sharp and feverish, and she sobbed as she clung to me, her splendid hair drifting over me like a silken shawl. Was she merely seeking release from the strain of that tumultuous day, I wonder, or was she imagining her dead lover in my place? I never asked her, then or since. For my own part, I remember only that I was half-drunk, and the day's events had frayed my nerves, and her body was slender, fine, and warm beneath my own.

* * *

I AWOKE IN her bed the next morning as the sunshine streamed across us. A few streets away, a lone alarum-bell clanged still. I lay silent for a moment as I recalled all that had befallen us on the day previous, then slipped from beneath the covers to retrieve my clothes. Eléonore stirred, gazing drowsily at me, and murmured "Julien . . ."

How could I respond but with silence? I glanced at her and continued to pull on my small-clothes. A moment later she flushed crimson and turned away from me, to bury her face in her pillow.

"Forgive me," said I. "I will quit you."

"You must think very little of me," she muttered, her voice muffled.

"It's I who should apologise to you. I was drunk. I presumed upon your grief, your weakness—"

"My *weakness!*" she echoed me, snapping about to glower at me. "What manner of trollop do you think me?"

"Your momentary weakness, I should have said—"

"Despite what happened yesternight, I don't invite every man who takes my fancy into my bed!" she flared. "And certainly not upon a mere fort-night's acquaintance. This will not happen again; you may be sure of that."

"Then we'll not speak of it." In my heart I felt, illogically perhaps, that by making love to Eléonore I had betrayed my chaste love for Lucie. I pulled on my boots and rose without further words.

"Those *bells!*" she exclaimed, a moment later. "I am sick to death of them!"

"I wonder if the King has learnt yet that he has lost Paris?" I murmured, glad to find myself on neutral ground. I quitted the bed-chamber and hurried into the parlour, where I threw open the shutters and stood listening at the window. Despite the single monotonous bell, the streets were quiet. Eléonore appeared shortly, clad in a becoming *peignoir.* "I hear no gun-fire," said I.

"What can have happened? Will the German regiments attack, do you think?"

The morning sunshine blazed bright in the street below us. Evidence of the three riotous days past lay all about: over-turned and broken carts; gaping holes where paving-stones had been torn up for barricades; refuse no one had collected; the ashes of bonfires; scattered, trampled hand-bills. A few shopkeepers, however, had taken down their shutters, eager to regain the losses they had suffered during the turmoil.

We both started as we heard a hurried pounding from without. A moment later Laurent burst in on us, dishevelled and covered with dust. "Léo!" he cried. "What do you think? The couriers from Versailles told us the King has ordered the troops to withdraw, and he is coming to Paris, to the Hôtel de Ville, within the week!"

"How do you know this?" demanded Eléonore. "Where have you been?"

"Manning a barrier at the edge of the city. Some others came and relieved us an hour ago—"

"Can you trust the couriers?" I asked him. He glanced at me, and from me to his sister, but abruptly shut his teeth upon the question that must have sprung to his lips.

"Well, can you?" Eléonore echoed me. "Might they not be telling us there will be no attack merely to reassure us into false security?"

He seized her hands, beaming. "Léo, the troops are breaking camp! Some of us went to the Champ de Mars to see for ourselves, and the Germans truly are quitting Paris. We'll fight no more battles—we've won!"

They embraced, laughing and sobbing all at once. I pulled on my coat and seized my opportunity to quit Eléonore ere more words passed between us. Despite my confused emotions, however, my step was light, for on that euphoric day I, even I, believed Laurent's confident words would prove true.

11

I JOURNEYED IN the public coach to Versailles a few days later to commence my work for Aubincourt. My duties did not prove onerous, for he had a clerk already. I found he preferred to use me as a discreet carrier of messages, of overtures and proposals and conciliations, and often as a sounding-board, as one with whom he could freely discuss ideas and events. I cannot say I added many brilliant insights to his perspective of the Revolution, but he claimed to find my foreigner's impressions and my knowledge of English Law useful.

"I still cannot entirely believe my eyes," he confessed to me, some few days later. "Did I not know better, I would say Maurice de Saint-Evrémonde were sitting opposite me. You're quite sure, Mr. Carton, that you are not his nephew?"

"Completely sure, Monsieur," said I, with a smile. "Charles Darnay— Charles de Saint-Evrémonde—is living happily in England as we speak."

"As far from his uncle's ghost as possible, I imagine."

"Were you acquainted with the late Marquis, Monsieur?" I enquired.

"Not well. I was a page at Court when I was a lad and saw him frequently. He must have been about thirty—and the very image of you, Carton, Heaven help you—tho' he had an evil reputation even then. Nevertheless, the old King rather liked him—I understand they often took part in each other's debauches. But then Saint-Evrémonde fell out of favour. Even the King must not have been able to stomach the rumours that found their way to Versailles. His late Majesty, lecher and whore-monger tho' he was, was never less than polite and generous to any woman he desired, be she Duchess or scrub-maid. Saint-Evrémonde, on the other hand—well!"

"Would you say," I asked him, hoping to confirm a theory I had harboured since meeting Eléonore, "that Saint-Evrémonde was capable of having his own nephew arrested in England on false evidence, in order to keep
Darnay from meddling in family scandals?"

"Entirely capable, I should say. Had Saint-Evrémonde felt that his own
interests were endangered by his nephew's interference, I don't doubt for a
moment that he would have struck back ruthlessly. I can think of no worse
representative of the Nobility of France than that man . . . altho' I've heard
it said his brother was very nearly as bad. When Saint-Evrémonde died, the
general opinion in Parisian society was that it was a wonder no one had
murdered him twenty or thirty years previous."

"Well," said I, pleased to hear my theory confirmed, "I hope you'll not
hold my face against me, Monsieur."

"No more than I would hold Darnay's blood against him, Mr. Carton.
None of us is responsible for the misdeeds of our ancestors. As they say, we
may choose our friends as we will, but we are not so fortunate as to be
offered a choice in our relatives. Now, my friend, shall we settle to business?"

AUBINCOURT SOON REQUESTED that I lodge at his house near the
Palace, for he did not wish me to spend two hours every day travelling betwixt
Paris and Versailles. After what had passed between Eléonore and me on the
night of the Fourteenth of July, I was only too glad to accede to his wishes,
for I suspected she and I both might prefer, for some little while at least, to
avoid the other's gaze. Thus I dwelt in Versailles for the remainder of the
Summer and, after a brief interlude of which I shall presently write, saw little
of Eléonore and Laurent. Camille I did encounter, for he was frequently at
Versailles. His brilliant pamphlet *Free France* appeared the day after the Bastille's
surrender (his publisher having concluded it was now safe to sell it) and was
soon disappearing faster than Msr. Momoro could print copies. Camille's
innocuous vanity swelled in equal measure with his new-found fame.

After the tumults of July, affairs in Paris and Versailles quietened. The abrupt abolition of hereditary feudal rights and privileges, the Declaration of the Rights of Man, and, more crucial still in the eyes of most folk, tidings of an excellent harvest pacified Paris further. The only visible signs of altered circumstances were the dozens of empty mansions lining the elegant streets of the *faubourg* St-Germain. Their wealthy and titled tenants had discreetly emigrated, for the Bastille's surrender had warned them that perhaps they were no longer welcome amidst a People in love with Liberty. In the provinces, however, discontent still rumbled, and I was soon to have my own vivid taste of that Summer's murderous humour.

Early in August Eléonore received word of trouble at a family estate in Normandy. The Comte de Valette, her brother Gilbert, had emigrated a week after the Bastille fell; once safe across the Rhine he proceeded to write her a series of anxious and petulant letters regarding the management of his property. Though she remarked to me that a burnt manor-house and decimated game would be naught but what her brother deserved for running away like the spineless imbecile he was, honour demanded that someone of the family attempt to regain the peasants' goodwill. Laurent had joined, and had received a lieutenant's commission in, La Fayette's new National Guard. A week's leave was out of the question during that turbulent Summer, and so the task of travelling to Caen had fallen upon Eléonore alone.

Tho' a gentlewoman travelling with two or three servants would have been quite safe on the highroads in years past, the prevailing unrest disquieted me. At last I obtained leave of Aubincourt to accompany Eléonore and Baptistine, her maid, to Normandy. He gave it me readily enough, requesting only that I should gauge the temper of the provincial towns for him and write him brief reports, for the intelligence we received from the provinces was often alarming.

We arrived in Caen on the 9th of August and drove not to the Valette estates, nor to a hostelry, but to the Abbey that sat high on a hill, overlooking the town. "I have very fond memories of the Abbaye-aux-Dames," Eléonore had explained, as we jolted past the lush green meadows and orchards lining the road that led from Lisieux to Caen. "I often visited it as a child, whensoever we were in residence at Valroche. And of course I was a pupil there."

"Were you?" As an indifferent son of the Church of England, I had but the vaguest notion of what passed within the walls of a Roman Catholic convent. "You don't mean to say you were considering taking vows?"

She laughed. "Not at all. Most convents are little more than schools for young ladies of good family; did you not know that?" I shook my head. "It's a rather frightful custom," she continued. "They shut up little girls in velvet prisons where they learn nothing important about anything, till they are scarce old enough to be wed. Then they are fetched out and thrust into a stranger's bed, and in three months the little innocents are gone from dewy-eyed chastity—genuine or feigned—to bedding other women's husbands." She laughed once again at the expression that must have risen unbidden to my visage. "O Carton," said she, "you English are so prudish. You pretend utter ignorance about subjects in which you are as well-schooled as we."

"I cannot speak for my countrymen," I said drily, "but for myself, I never claimed ignorance of Mankind's weaknesses, or condemned them. *He that is without sin among you, let him first cast a stone.* I have had above my share of frailties, as well you know."

She opened her mouth as if to retort, then closed it suddenly and hurried on. "Well . . . I don't speak of the Abbaye-aux-Dames, which has always adhered very properly to its Rule . . . but of course some convents do have appalling reputations."

She plunged into a sardonic recital of the degradation into which these houses of God had fallen. Breathless rumours flew everywhere, she claimed, of secluded monasteries whose brotherhoods were devoted to debauchery and blasphemy, to the most depraved acts with defenceless orphans of both sexes. It was common knowledge also that many convents were no better than brothels, whither girls of lofty lineage, little dowry, and no religious vocation were thrust away and forgotten by their indifferent families. "Nuns' bastards," concluded Eléonore, "are more common than pigs' bones decked out as Saints' relics—they long since gave up the thin pretence of a miraculous conception."

"And what do the more scrupulous convents teach their pupils?" I enquired.

"In truth, a lot of rubbish! I spent but two years at the Abbey. I was the eldest in my family by six years, remember, and my accomplished papa was determined I should grow up familiar with the ancient and modern authors, not to mention History, natural Philosophy, Latin, and English. Do you think I would have learnt anything of the sort, had I been educated in a place whose chief ambition is to teach silly young girls religion, manners, dancing, and *embroidery?*" Her contempt was so lofty that I could not help laughing in my turn.

AND THUS WE rolled through the great gates and into the fortress-like enclosure of the Abbaye-aux-Dames. Eléonore gave her name to a young novice and sent the girl running towards the Abbess's house. "Mdme. de Belsunce, the previous Abbess, died two years ago," she told me. "Mdme. de Pontécoulant became Abbess long after my time, but I've met her often and am very fond of her. I imagine she will offer to lodge us at the guest-house, rather than let us chance a poor reception at Valroche."

The Abbess was receiving visitors at that hour and we were promptly ushered into her study, where Mdme. de Pontécoulant and Eléonore exchanged affectionate greetings. My attention was drawn not to the austere, middle-aged Abbess but to the young woman standing behind her, eyes cast down and hands clasped demurely at her waist. She was perhaps twenty years old, tall and remarkably comely even in the plain dark schoolgirl's gown and muslin cap she wore. Sensing my gaze, she glanced at me and I caught sight of piercing blue eyes for an instant ere she hastily looked down again.

Mdme. de Pontécoulant introduced her to us as Mdlle. d'Armont, one of the Abbey pupils. Eléonore nodded. "I know the family by reputation, of course."

"You and Msr. Carton come from Paris, my dear?" enquired the Abbess. "Mdlle. d'Armont greatly desires to know what is passing in Paris and Versailles. Perhaps Msr. Carton could enlighten her." She gestured the two of us into the *salon*, where portraits of long-dead Abbesses glared down at us from the walls.

Mdlle. d'Armont gave me a brief, serene smile. "I should be very grateful for any news you can tell me, Monsieur. Every day seems to bring some startling new occurrence."

I told her all I could, particularly of those events I had myself witnessed. She listened with rapt attention, occasionally breaking with an intelligent question into my narrative, her eyes shining. When I spoke of the tremendous events that had come to pass shortly ere Eléonore and I had quitted Paris, when on the 4th of August the Nobles in the Assembly had renounced and abolished their age-old feudal privileges, her colour changed and she raised a long slim hand to her lips.

"But this is astonishing," said she. "No, it's miraculous—the beginning of a new era. This is what the Philosophers of our age dreamt of, Monsieur." Her smile faded as she sighed. "If only folk were not so blind."

"There is dissent here, then?" I prompted her, thinking to glean some tidings of the humour prevailing in Caen.

"O no, Monsieur, by far the greater part of the People is overjoyed with the Assembly, and with the news we had of the Bastille. But a few are not. Can you expect otherwise of men who will lose by our Revolution? I saw a disgraceful scene some weeks since, which revealed how easily Nobility can lose all sense of obligation and duty, and degenerate into mere arrogance."

She proceeded to tell me, icy indignation in her soft voice, of the ugly incident she had witnessed at the end of June. The day after word of the

new National Assembly had arrived in Caen, the city fathers had proclaimed a festival in one of the public squares. The officer second in command of the town garrison, however, a strutting young popinjay named
Henri de Belsunce (a cousin of the late Abbess), had no love for the
Assembly and the reforms it promised. On the festival day, Msr. de
Belsunce chose to swagger into the square at the head of a handful of blus-
tering soldiers. After insulting the citizens, the town, and the Assembly in
rapid order, he had declared the festival an illegal gathering and ordered it
dispersed.

"I was there, you see," Mdlle. d'Armont told me. "I saw the whole affair.
He is afraid, of course. And a fool as well, for he has never been popular
here in Caen, since he undertook to escort the town's grain-convoys to the
store-houses—for the poor folk think it's a conspiracy to drive up prices
and starve them—and he ought now to seek to win their favour, rather than
court their ill will. But he is not too stupid to comprehend that should the
Assembly succeed in giving us a Constitution, and should it bring some
sense and Justice into the order of things, he will lose his privileges—and
then where will he be? When careers in the army are open to talent rather
than birth, I suspect that that arrogant bully will no longer be in command
of a garrison."

She broke off as the stout door-keeper appeared once again and bowed
to the Abbess. "Madame, your nephew Msr. Le Doulcet is here to pay you
a visit."

"Dear boy," exclaimed the Abbess, as the new visitor joined us, "you have
been a little remiss in your visits, don't you think?"

"Forgive me, Aunt," said the fair-haired, uniformed young man, laughing, as he made her a smart soldier's bow. "They keep me at Versailles with
the regiment. Orders are orders."

The Abbess introduced Msr. Le Doulcet to us and he bowed cordially.
"Marie," she continued, smiling, "my nephew Gustave Le Doulcet de
Pontécoulant. Doulcet, I should like you to make the acquaintance of

Mdlle. Marie d'Armont, one of our pupils and, no doubt," she added drily, "a future Saint."

"O, Madame, I pray you," protested Mdlle. d'Armont. "She is teasing me, Monsieur."

"But already the poor folk of St. Gilles parish are calling her *the saintly lady*, and she is scarce twenty-one," Mdme. de Pontécoulant told her nephew. "What may she have become by the time she is as old as I?"

Doulcet gave the Abbess an affable grin, his brown eyes twinkling. "That's not very old, surely." He bowed to us once more. "I hope I shall have the pleasure of meeting you again ere I quit Caen. However, I must return soon to Versailles." He glanced at his watch and, thrusting it away, proffered to the Abbess the small parcel he carried. "I've no time to visit to-day, Madame, but I brought you some newspapers from Paris. I expect you and the sisters are eager to learn the latest tidings."

"Well?" said Mdme. de Pontécoulant, as the door closed behind her nephew. "What think you of Doulcet, Marie? He is not yet married. It occurred to me . . . perhaps . . ."

"O no, Madame. He would not wish a bride with no fortune." Abruptly she courtesied. "May I be excused, Madame?"

"That one," Eléonore observed, after Mdlle. d'Armont had quitted us, "will never wed."

Mdme. de Pontécoulant nodded. "I fear you are right. It's a pity, but in truth the convent is the only place for her. The family is one of the most ancient in Normandy, but they have little property and less income." She sighed and rang the bell on her desk. "Let us attend to lodging you, my dear."

ELÉONORE SET OUT for Valroche the next morning, in the company of her maid, her coachman, and a sturdy gardener from the Abbey. Having no fears for her safety, I acceded to her suggestion that I remain in Caen and observe the temper of the town. Mdme. de Pontécoulant in her turn suggested I accompany Mdlle. d'Armont, who oversaw purchases for the Abbey, in her visits to various tradesmen.

She conversed gravely of Politics and the works of the modern Philosophers as our chariot clattered down the narrow mediæval streets. Arriving at our destination, a wine-shop, she dusted off her dark blue gown and walked boldly in, oblivious to the admiring leers of half a dozen infantrymen of the Bourbon regiment who lounged about a long table.

"The Abbess keeps a respectable cellar, doesn't she?" remarked the wine-merchant, glancing over the list that Mdlle. d'Armont handed him. "And here I was thinking the holy sisters drank naught but water, as a penance. Well, I believe I'm flat out of this Tokay. —Eh, what's that, Monsieur? The reckoning?" He hurried over to his customers and as quickly returned, shaking his head. "It never does to cross a soldier, especially when he's in a quarrelsome humour. Have you heard tell what's to do at the barracks, Mademoiselle? No, of course not." He dropt a handful of small coins into the till and leant across the counter to us. "They say that young cock-a-hoop the Vicomte de Belsunce is at it again. 'Tisn't enough to swagger about the town insulting honest citizens, no indeed. No, he and the Duc de Beuvron must break up peaceful political meetings, they must, and insult our militia. I ask you, what right has he to spit on the National Guard that was approved by the King himself? Does Belsunce think he's cleverer than the King?"

"I'd not be surprised if he does," said Mdlle. d'Armont.

"To be sure, Mademoiselle. And he never was too much well-liked even by most of his own men, I hear. He'll have more trouble than he bargained for, you mark my words. Wait and see." Muttering darkly, the wine-seller trudged off to serve his other customers.

We visited a chandler, a grain-merchant, and a fishmonger without incident. Our route back to the Abbey, however, took us past the barracks. Mdlle. d'Armont signalled to the driver to pause by the parade-ground as she pointed out to me a tall, slim young officer with impeccably drest hair. "That's he. Henri de Belsunce."

Belsunce, supervising the drill, paid the onlookers no attention. Passersby who had paused to watch the manœuvres muttered angrily as he gave a soldier who had faltered in the drill a contemptuous tongue-lashing and ordered him flogged.

"Does this often happen?" I enquired, leaning out the window and catching the eye of the nearest bystander, a man clad in the uniform of Caen's *bourgeois* militia.

He nodded vigorously. "Yes indeed, too often! He punishes them for every little mistake, blunders that any other officer would let go with a reprimand. Trouble is brewing at the barracks, they say. Go into the taverns and all you will hear is soldiers cursing that strutting Jackanapes!"

Mdlle. d'Armont and I exchanged glances. "I fear this situation cannot continue," said she, her blue eyes deepening to black in the shadows within the carriage, "and I fear whatsoever happens may be ugly."

12

ELÉONORE DID NOT return to Caen that evening, though she sent word that she was safe. I ventured out alone the following afternoon to learn more of the prevailing humour. My stroll amidst the winding streets and their ancient plaster-and-beam houses led me at length to the same wine-shop, where the proprietor, recognising me, proceeded to pass on more gossip whilst filling my glass.

"Affairs are very bad, Monsieur, very bad. Msr. de Belsunce is making trouble again, the lads tell me, since this news from Versailles arrived and they're saying there will be no more privileges for the Nobility. The Artois regiment's barracks are stirred up quite appalling."

A few late-afternoon drinkers slouched about the tables in the tap-room, a handful of soldiers amongst them. I listened idly to their talk as the wine-merchant turned to other business. The words *that d__ned salaud Belsunce* caught my ear and I turned to listen, perturbed.

"You know he said he wanted to burn down the town, the high-nosed p__ck," growled one. "D'ye think he's not guessed how folk hereabout hate him?"

I quitted the counter and joined the drinkers. "What is happening?"

"Why, Monsieur, have you not heard?" said one. "There's been trouble down at the barracks."

"Some say they've called out the militia to calm matters," added another, "since the Artois regiment was ready to draw against Belsunce's men. The brave lads resolved everybody should know how he insulted Msr. Necker and the Assembly, and swore they'll take no more orders from an arrogant fool who won't admit the Assembly cut him and his fine titles down to size!"

"Aye, true enough," a soldier agreed. "Every soul in Caen has had his fill of Belsunce's strutting and his insulting the Assembly! Why, it's treasonable, it is."

"And now Belsunce is safe in his quarters," somebody grumbled, "and lets his sergeants do his dirty work."

"Yes," continued the soldier, "but there's a great noisy mob of folk surrounding the officers' quarters even as we speak. They were in a nasty humour, I can tell you, shouting threats."

"No telling what a crowd like that might do when they get their blood up, and the barracks being just timber—"

Without warning, half a dozen soldiers sprang to their feet, upsetting their benches. "Listen—do you hear it?" cried one.

"It's Belsunce's men, sure as anything!"

Two or three snatched up their hats and hastened out. The others remained a moment, locked in loud and rapid debate, then made for the door. The pot-boy dashed after them, catching the last man by his coat-tail.

"Hi, trooper! What's the rumpus about?"

"Gun-fire! Can't you hear it?"

"Gun-fire?" said I, as he disappeared down the street.

The wine-seller nodded. "Listen! That's from the barracks, to be sure. Or else from the square. That *salopard* must be behind it. Set to it, Mathieu, we're closing up." He began to hang the shutters as the boy sulkily gestured the remaining drinkers outside. I paused in the street to listen. Somewhere, not far away, the harsh spatter of musket-fire echoed.

ELÉONORE WAS RETURNED by the time I reached the Abbey. "What on Earth is happening, Carton?" she demanded upon espying me. "All is settled at Valroche. I spoke with our tenants, and they were most reasonable when they realised I was more than willing to come to terms with them—though Gilbert may not find all my arrangements to his liking! But now here in Caen—we could scarce make our way through the town. Bonfires and crowds at every corner. Is it a riot?"

I quickly told her all that I had heard whilst she had been in the country-side. "I imagine it's the fault of this man Belsunce. Folk said there was trouble at the garrison."

"I can well believe it. I remember Mdme. de Belsunce once said that her cousin was a hot-headed young fool. Bah! *I* shan't insist upon rescuing him."

"You think it may come to that?"

"I think it will come to our dear Msr. de Belsunce taking to his heels, and none too soon. Good riddance to him!"

"We would be prudent to quit Caen now, to-day, ere this riot spreads," said I.

"To-day? But it's near evening already."

"Would you not rest easier, if you were half a dozen leagues from here?"

"Carton, this ground we stand upon has always been a sanctuary. No mob would dare attack the Abbey."

"A month since, we might have said that no mob would dare attack the Bastille. Can we ever again be sure of anything?"

"I can be sure of one thing at least: that we will be safe here to-night. We may quit Normandy to-morrow, if you like. But I don't care to spend any more nights at inns than are necessary."

"I am thinking only of your welfare—" I began, but she interrupted me.

"*Mordieu,* what am I that I should need such coddling? It was you, not I, who insisted that you come upon this journey. As you can see, I have completed my errand unscathed, and without calling upon your assistance in any way. Now let me be. Let us enjoy a good dinner with Mdme. de Pontécoulant, and a good night's sleep, and set out for Paris in the morning."

I SLEPT UNEASILY that night and awoke with a start at daybreak, to the sound—the all too familiar sound—of many bells. I guessed by the

light that it was past the hour for early Mass, yet the bells of Caen's church-
es were ringing with a steady, monotonous clangour that floated to me clear
and sharp in the cool air, the echoes trembling in the Abbey guest-house's
sturdy stone walls.

I threw open the shutters, leaning outside. The Abbey's park was empty
and silent, the lawns grey with dew in the morning twilight. In the town,
though, as I strained to hear above the interminable alarum-bells, occasional gun-fire yet rent the stillness, and below it the muffled roar of many
voices.

"It seems you were right," said Eléonore, clad only in her *peignoir,* without
warning sweeping into my bed-chamber. "The town is surely in an uproar.
Tho' I say still that we could be no safer than here within the Abbey walls."

"A month ago I might have believed that," said I, pulling on my shirt,
"but no longer. I am going to alert the sisters."

"The nuns? Why?"

"Did you not tell me, during our journey, that Abbey lands, and villages
under the Abbey's jurisdiction, make up a large portion of the holdings in
this bailiwick? Times have changed—men have changed. We know how the
townspeople here regard Authority at present. If a mob gets its blood up
then they may very well intend harm towards the Abbey."

"Dear God, I'd not thought of that. Of course we must warn them. I
must dress. Hurry!"

THE DOOR-KEEPER was at her post already, for it was near Prime and
the nuns were drifting about in the cloister. "The Abbey may be in danger,
Sister," I told her. "Are the gates locked?"

She glared at me. "Of course they're locked! This is a convent, isn't it?"

Catching one of the nuns on her way to the holy Offices, I repeated my
warning. The woman nodded and hurried off to the Abbess's quarters.

Even from atop the hill, I could see little. Eléonore soon joined me, breathing hard from her climb up the slope, as several young nuns and novices converged on the path. "What . . . what . . . d——n these stays . . . what is it? Have you learnt anything?"

"There is trouble in the town, I shouldn't wonder," said one of the elder nuns. "Come, come, it's no business of ours." She herded the chattering, excited girls towards the church doors.

"I suspect Msr. de Belsunce has given more trouble," I murmured to Eléonore. "Who knows what may have happened by now?"

The nuns were just emerging from Prime when I espied the first signs of the mob approaching the Abbey. I hastened back to the gate-house, where the door-keeper sat stolidly, telling her beads. "A crowd, most likely dangerous, will be here in a moment," I told her. "Don't open the gates, whatsoever you may do."

A dozen nuns joined us, curious and flustered by the morning's unexpected uproar. Mdme. de Pontécoulant, tranquil and majestic as a Queen, glided down the hill to stand alone, facing the gates as the mob hammered at them.

"The Abbess!" somebody shouted. "We want the Abbess!"

Mdme. de Pontécoulant glanced at the door-keeper. I shook my head, divining her intent. "Don't open the gates, Madame. They may mean you harm."

"We've something for you to see, Madame l'Abbesse!" cried a woman from beyond the gates. "You and all the idle sluts here in your brothel!"

A handful began to bellow a verse of an obscene drinking-song, something having to do with a nun and a pair of monks. "Open up! Open up! Open up!" the rest chanted, above the lewd song, pounding at the gates still. Mdme. de Pontécoulant compressed her lips.

"Somebody must answer them or they may break down the gate."

"Then I shall," said I, altho' I did not like the sound of the mob. "Madame, the sisters should not be here. Take them to a safe place."

She nodded and shepherded them towards the church. Steeling myself, I fetched the door-keeper's stool and, using it as a step-ladder, climbed the wall.

"What is it you wish?" I demanded, boldly enough, tho' in truth I was trembling as if I had the ague. "What do you want of these religious?"

"We want the Abbess!" one of the mob screeched, espying me. "We want Mdme. de Belsunce!"

"Mdme. de Belsunce died two years since," I declared. "Leave the sisters in peace. They are women of God; they pray for you and they care for the poor. What do you wish of them?"

"We brought the old hag something to think about!" shouted another voice, as rough, drunken laughter echoed him. The filthy, interminable song grew louder yet. "Take a good look, Monsieur!"

"I tell you Mdme. de Belsunce has lain in her grave for two years . . ." I began, but choked on my words as I saw what was approaching me. Above the heads of the cheering mob, an object dipped and wavered for a moment as they passed it forward from hand to hand. At last they thrust it before them, white and bloody and horrible: Henri de Belsunce's head, impaled upon a pike, held triumphantly aloft scarce an arm's length from me.

"Belsunce isn't so pretty now, is he? Take a good look!"

"Jésus-Marie, what have they done?" cried the door-keeper, hurrying to my side. I snapped "Don't look!" at her in a tone that sent her running, head down. But I could not turn my own fascinated, nauseated gaze from the staring eyes, the missing ear, the slack features that bore no trace of the agony and terror Belsunce must have endured in his last moments, the thick hair that was yet grotesquely, immaculately curled and powdered.

"May God have mercy on his soul," said I, breaking the menacing silence that had fallen. "And on yours."

"We cut his b_ll_cks off!" howled a man. "Don't you want to give them to the sisters?"

"Do they get enough p__cks to satisfy them? Take his!" a woman screeched, as behind her a few began to sing their obscene verses once more. "We know what they do, rutting there behind their high walls whilst they live on the tithes and rents they screw from us!"

Some distance away a man, covered in blood to his elbows, heaved some thing else overhead, a shapeless mass dripping from the tines of a pitchfork. "We all swore the *salaud* was a gutless peacock," he roared, "but we were wrong! May be we'll stuff our sausages in them, eh? Carve up the leg they chopped off and we'll have a nice bit of meat there!"

Another woman clawed her way to the forefront of the mob. The same bloody stains streaked her hands and spattered her bodice. "He's done for and so are they! Tell them that when we catch them, we'll rip out their hearts as we did his!" She paused, dissolving into drunken laughter. "We grilled his heart at the cook-shop—it was a tasty mouthful!"

I could bear no more. I leapt down from the wall, sickened, and found myself face to face with Mdlle. d'Armont. "Why are you not in the church with the others?" I demanded. "Dear God, come away from this."

She lowered her gaze, for she had been staring at the top of the wall, had seen the mob's grisly trophy. She bore a queer stunned look in her eyes. I could guess her thoughts: all her visions of a bright future had not prepared her for the bloody thing swaying at the point of a pike.

I seized her arm to lead her to the church, but she twisted from me and fled through the garden. Thwarted, the mob turned away in search of easier prey and at length its raucous song faded.

I followed Mdlle. d'Armont, my own thoughts in turmoil. Howsoever detestably Belsunce had comported himself, surely he had not deserved so horrible a fate. He had been young, vital; and now that handsome youth was a dismembered, gutted, bleeding corpse. How, I wondered, the bile rising in my throat, how had they kept the blood—so much blood—from his powdered hair?

Abruptly I stumbled and sank trembling to my hands and knees amidst the fragrant beds of tarragon and marigold. No fashionable young Aristocrat would have his hair drest already at such an early hour of the morning; the mob, that bestial mob, had forced some unfortunate to wash and dress and powder those bloody locks after they had hacked Belsunce's head from his body.

My empty stomach heaved in a rush of horror. Crouched in the middle of the path, retching, I closed my eyes and covered my ears, shutting out the hideous world as the morning brightened about me.

ELÉONORE FOUND ME towards midday in a distant corner of the Abbey's park. Hearing her approach, I glanced up at her but could find nothing to say. She sat herself down beside me on the weathered stone bench and clasped her hands in her lap.

"I have just spent an hour with Marie d'Armont," she told me. "I know what you must have seen."

"Do you?" said I. "You cannot possibly imagine it."

"No."

"I am going home."

"Yes, my business is done here. We shall depart for Paris to-day, if you like."

I shook my head. "Not Paris. *Home.* To England. I've had my fill of France."

"Carton, you can't."

"What is to stop me?"

"Nothing but your conscience."

"My conscience!" I echoed her, with a bitter laugh. "What my conscience tells me is to quit this benighted Hell-pit of a Kingdom ere I aid in dragging it further towards Anarchy!"

"Don't be a blockhead," she snapped. "Nothing that you and decent folk like you have done was the cause of what happened here to-day. Wrongs and hatreds a thousand years old have come boiling to the surface, yes, but the Revolution will ensure that the causes of those hatreds are abolished."

"If they've not learnt yet . . . if Revolution means no more than brutality and madness and men slaughtered in the streets . . . if that is what is in store for us, I wish no part of it."

"That's where you are wrong," she interrupted me. "If decent folk don't act, who will hinder the vicious ones from making a mockery of our dreams? I am not surprised that Aubincourt chose you at such a moment, Carton . . . beneath that armour of yours, you are sharp as a needle and courageous and steadfast. Anybody who is a judge of character can tell as much. You must play your part in ensuring that the dark side of Revolution, of Mankind, doesn't destroy the dream. It's folk like you, and me, and Laurent, and Camille Desmoulins and Aubincourt and all the rest, who must ride out the storm so we can bring something better from it in the end."

"Ride out the storm," I echoed her, glancing up at her. "That is what Aubincourt said."

"You see now why you must stop on in France?"

Slowly, I nodded. "You make everything so clear for me . . . Eléonore." I touched her cheek, drawing her closer to me, our lips meeting. By tacit agreement we never had spoken of that night, the night of the Fourteenth of July. "All I ever have wished," I murmured, after a long moment, "everything, might be here in you—"

"No," said she. She pushed me away, gently. "You mustn't. Julien . . ."

"Fleutry? Fleutry's death did not prevent you from inviting more than a mere kiss from me once."

"I thought we were not to speak of that," said she, turning her gaze from me, her colour rising.

I closed my eyes and turned away. I scarce knew my own heart in such a matter. How, after pledging my love to Lucie, the only human creature I trusted with my soul's secrets, could I betray that pledge by reaching out to another? No matter that she was far from me and would never be mine— I cherished her regard and compassion for me like a priceless jewel.

"I—I do value your friendship," said I, at last.

"As I do yours," Eléonore concurred, hastily. "Let us remain as we are, Carton. Were we to be lovers, I imagine I would end by discarding you like a worn-out stocking when our ardour had cooled. Let us remain friends— something more than friends, and less than lovers."

"Forgive me," I muttered, rising. "I must think. Forgive me." I strode off down the hill, hands thrust deep in my pockets and shoulders hunched.

I WALKED AIMLESSLY through the town for an hour or two, taking a vague pleasure in the sunshine and the light cool breeze. Word of the riot must at last have penetrated to the severely respectable quarter about the Hôtel de l'Intendance, for no carriages were abroad and the elegant couples, who had promenaded so blithely beneath the over-hanging half-timbered houses but the day before, had vanished. Despite the unnatural stillness, however, no traces of violence or Revolution manifested themselves in those staid ancient streets. How far from the morning's blood and terror I seemed there, I thought, where the pale Sun shone placidly on the cobbles and somewhere above me, distinct in the silence, a harpsichord tinkled a familiar air.

> Non più andrai farfallone amoroso,
> Nott'e giorno d'intorno girando;
> Delle belle turbando il riposo,
> Narcisetto, Adoncino, d'amor!

I paused to watch a family of sparrows hunt for crumbs scarce two feet from a sleeping lion, a large tawny Tom-cat dreaming peacefully in a patch of sunshine. I envied the sparrows, I realised, imagining a life with no obligations, no troublesome choices: a carefree life, thinking ahead no further than the moment and flying with the currents of the wind.

> *Non più andrai farfallone amoroso,*
> *Nott'e giorno d'intorno girando—*

The silly pleasant tune possessed me, as such things do, and I had no choice but to whistle it softly under my breath.

> *. . . Narcisetto, Adoncino, d'amor!*

A nearby window slammed shut, waking the cat and scattering the sparrows. I continued down the street. My old life in London had, I realised, been like that of the sparrows, and it had been far from carefree. Birds led lives as uncertain as those of men; they were only denied the ability, whether gift or curse, to imagine the future.

I trudged back past the church of St. Gilles to the Abbey, in my reverie scarce nodding to the door-keeper as she opened the wicket-gate to me. I found Eléonore in the guest-house and halted in the doorway as she turned expectant eyes to mine. "Very well, then," said I, and sighed as I plunged my hands deep into the pockets of my riding-coat. "Let us depart, to-morrow morning, for Paris."

PART III

Sins of the Fathers

1789–1793

13

COULD MY OLD acquaintances have seen me that Summer of 1789, they might not have recognised me in the tidy, earnest fellow copying confidential letters in Aubincourt's study, or seated opposite him in his carriage, in charge of a despatch-case crammed with papers. Members of the Assembly soon came to know my face as I passed continually betwixt Aubincourt's house and the Salle des Menus Plaisirs (where the Assembly sat), delivering messages, taking notes, sounding opinions.

One day outside the Hall I encountered a slight, dapper, bespectacled young man who seemed to know me, and who approached me uncertainly. After an instant's confusion, I recalled Camille's never-ending gossip and recognised Robespierre, unknown and disregarded still at that early date. He greeted me warmly and remarked with a tolerant smile (and a touch of envy, I think) how well Camille had succeeded in making a vulgar spectacle of himself.

Eléonore made good her promises in late September and came calling one day with a sheaf of proofs for the first numbers of *Le Flambeau Parisien*. Tho' her grief at Fleutry's death had faded, her anger had not, for her journal was a litany of silky vituperation aimed at the selfish and stubborn Nobility of the Court.

I knew what she expected from me and I had scribbled, in idle moments, a few thoughts of my own regarding the Assembly and the Revolution. My principal impression (tho' it was not a new idea in Paris) was that the royal family, isolated as they were amidst the splendours of the Palace, could have no conception of what the ordinary Frenchman thought and dreamt, and still less of how he lived—despite the Queen's famous phantasy-village in which she had played at being a dairy-maid. Take the King from Versailles,

I suggested: Let him dwell in Paris as our English King dwelt near the People, and there he would reside amongst his subjects who loved and trusted him, rather than amidst a flock of scheming Courtiers whose first thought was ever for their own interest.

I set down my ideas in coherent form and gave Eléonore the manuscript. "Why, you write very well indeed," she told me after glancing thro' it. "You think too little of yourself, Carton. This is splendid, and fit to be printed just as it is."

"Do whatsoever you wish with it," said I. So long as nothing indicates that I am the author." I had insisted I remain anonymous, for Aubincourt's sake and my own. I cherished no desire to be alternately adulated and reviled by the other journals, both fervently liberal and ferociously royalist, that since the collapse of all Censorship had sprung up like mushrooms after a rain.

"We will simply sign it *An English Observer.* Although," added Eléonore, drily, "folk do know you to be a friend of mine. It will not require brilliancy to guess who the English Observer may be."

I shrugged. "Let them guess, so long as they have no proof."

Le Flambeau Parisien appeared in the book-stalls on the 4th of October, one day ere the market-women marched to Versailles and by main force brought the royal family back to Paris. I must not, nevertheless, imply that *Le Flambeau* was responsible for the women's march; our success owed, rather, to the manner in which we had so accurately read the pulse of the times. We had called for the King and the Assembly to be removed to Paris, and lo, the thing was done, to the joy of the Parisian multitude.

Eléonore, of course, was delighted. Overnight the print run swelled from four hundred copies to above a thousand for the second number, and two thousand for the third. Tho' Eléonore's opinions were reviled in the royalist journals (and they published some scurrilous slanders against her which she did not waste her time in refuting), the subscriptions grew steadily.

* * *

IT IS A measure of my natural perversity that, there in Paris in the midst of the Revolution, after having beheld my share of the tumults of 1789, I was more content than ever I had been since my youth. For the first two years of the Revolution were peaceful enough, tho' undoubtedly folk will forget that fact whilst they remember naught but the horrors that occur daily as I write this chronicle. The great Fête of Federation celebrated on the first anniversary of the Bastille's surrender was the most joyous Festival I ever have witnessed, though wet weather somewhat dampened high spirits.

A few days previous, the three of us—Eléonore, Laurent, and I—had joined the hordes of ebullient Parisians pouring into the Champ de Mars to assist in building the vast amphitheatre for the Fête. I shovelled muddy earth with a will beneath the hot July Sun, side by side with a cobbler, a priest, and a captain of the National Guard. Eléonore, with two or three companions (young gentlewomen of Fashion clad most unsuitably in stays, dainty muslin gowns, and beplumed silk bonnets), trundled wheelbarrows back and forth across the parade-ground and Laurent heaved stones away with a half-dozen students from the School of Medicine. As the morning wore on, at last I collapsed, exhilarated, beside my friends as we all paused in our labours. Laurent accepted a bottle that a passing carter thrust at us, shouting "Come and drink if you're thirsty! Free drink for all!"

"Is it good wine?" I enquired, as Laurent took a swallow from the bottle.

"Dreadful," said he, laughing, and passed it on to me. I tasted it, grimaced, and after taking a mouthful to relieve my parched throat, hastily handed it to Eléonore.

"Look at them," said she, her countenance glowing with more than her exertions. "What a splendid gathering! Thousands of Parisians come together to work in harmony for a common goal, to celebrate a common triumph. Could we possibly have conceived this a year since?"

"I see the next number of *Le Flambeau* taking shape before me," said I, smiling.

"And why not? All France should share in this. From Oppression and Injustice we have fashioned something so extraordinary that all Europe is gazing at us in awe. From a society bound by Inequality and Privilege we are arrived at last at the age of Reason, and of Justice."

I suffered her to chatter on, whilst I leant back against a dusty Sun-warmed boulder and gazed at her. Soon she turned to me, indignant.

"Carton, I don't believe you have heard a word I am saying."

"I was thinking," said I, "of how beautiful you are when you are speaking of that which you love best."

Flushed though she was from the noonday heat, I think perhaps she coloured. "Love best . . ." she echoed me.

"Your Crusade."

She glanced at me an instant ere nodding and murmuring: "If only Julien could have seen this day."

"He helped to bring it about."

"As did we all," she exclaimed. She sprang to her feet and flung her arms wide. "O Carton, I can't help it; I am so happy I could fly to the Moon!"

Who, present that day at the Champ de Mars, could have dreamt that the Liberty and Fraternity we celebrated would within three years dissolve away to nightmare, like a restless dream?

I CONTINUED TO work at Aubincourt's side through that palmy year 1790, at his elegant Paris town-house now that the Assembly met in the old royal Riding-School hard by the Tuileries Palace. Eléonore continued to write, to publish, and to count her profits. Laurent prospered as a lieutenant of the National Guard. Camille Desmoulins earned a considerable reputation from his own free-tongued journal, *Révolutions de France et de Brabant*, which sold well though Momoro, as publishers do, swallowed the greater part of the profits.

Camille burst into Aubincourt's house one day in December of that year, asking for me, and on espying me threw his arms about me and kissed me soundly on both cheeks, in the French manner that is so disconcerting to us English. "Her parents have consented!" he sang out, black eyes shining and his grin well-nigh splitting his face in two. "They've c-consented, and her father is g-going to give her a splendid dowry, and the b-banns have been published, and I shall wed Lucile ere the year is out!"

Lucile Duplessis was the nineteen-year-old sweetheart of whom he had told me so much, and with whom he had been hopelessly in love for some five interminable years. He embraced me once again, told me I must come to the wedding, and dashed away.

I had not yet met Lucile. I attended the ceremony, curious to see this Angel whose virtues he had constantly extolled to me, and at length I saw the bride. Dear Lord, how she reminded me of Lucie. Folk might say it was only because their names were all but the same, but they would be mistaken. She looked so like Lucie on the day I saw her first that the sight of her set my heart to pounding.

She was like Lucie, that dainty porcelain doll-child, and yet unlike. Her hair was more auburn than golden, and her eyes were grey-green, not blue; but her pretty smile and her disposition, alternately gentle and merry, were Lucie's, tho' at times she could act the capricious child. Like Lucie's, too, was her capacity for love—for I would learn all too soon that she adored her husband (more, perhaps, than Camille deserved, tho' he worshipped her in his turn) with an all-consuming devotion and passion.

I slipped off at the ceremony's end, after escorting Eléonore home, and walked aimlessly along the quay-side for a time in the wintry dusk. The sight of Lucile had set me to thinking of Lucie and all I had left behind me in London, nineteen months previous. Despite my dwelling so far from her, without her quiet words to sustain me, I had done more than survive; I had prospered. I thought of her, happy and content in the midst of her family, and realised that our ways had truly parted at last.

ONE LATE AFTERNOON in the Spring of 1791 I called on Eléonore to find that she was in the midst of one of her lively *soirées*. Baptistine welcomed me inside with a smile and Eléonore beckoned me into her crowded parlour. "I expect you know everybody?"

"Nearly so," said I, noting a few faces I did not recognise.

"O, I must introduce Talma—the actor, you know—the acclaimed leading player at the Comédie, I must add, or he will be most vexed with me—and Mdlle. Candeille, his colleague on the boards. Talma has been telling us of his plans to revive Voltaire's *Brutus* in June. You know Lucile Desmoulins, of course. And do you know Msr. Hérault de Séchelles?" she enquired, with a glance at the handsome young man seated beside her place.

"Only by reputation."

"Hérault is one of my very oldest friends. Hérault, my friend Mr. Carton."

"Camille Desmoulins sometimes speaks of you, Monsieur," said I, bowing, as Hérault rose gracefully to his feet.

"O Camille!" he exclaimed with a shrug, an ironic smile playing across his sculpted features. "I shan't ask you what he says of me, Mr. Carton, though we claim to be on friendly terms."

"Camille says what everybody says," interjected Lucile. "That you are far too handsome, rich, clever, well-connected, and Heaven-blest for your own good. Jean-Marie Hérault de Séchelles, youngest and most brilliant member of the Paris Parliament in the dark days before the Revolution; Hérault de Séchelles, cousin to the Queen's favourites and accomplished courtier, with the ear of Royalty—"

"Beware, Jean-Marie," added Eléonore, "such men as you arouse envy, and attract enemies."

"I admit Dame Fortune has smiled upon me," said Hérault, with another lazy shrug, as he bent to kiss her hand and gaze languorously at her with liquid dark eyes. "But you will hold it to my credit, won't you, dear Madame, that I chose to further the cause of the Enlightenment in our Revolution: in other words, the Crusade of Reform and Progress?"

"Dear Monsieur, I expected no less of you." She patted the brocaded sofa-cushion, inviting him to return to his seat beside her. Lucile merely giggled, evidently inured to Hérault's complacent charm. I took stock of him as I accepted a cup of Baptistine's excellent coffee. He was a few years my junior, perhaps thirty-two or thirty-three years old, exquisitely clad, and undeniably one of the comeliest men I ever had met. I must confess I took an immediate dislike to that elegant young Aristocrat-Revolutionist. Was it his urbane, polished manner, his wealth, his beauty, his d__nable self-assurance that grated upon me so? Or was it, as I refused to admit to myself, his conspicuous intimacy with Eléonore?

"Yesterday I spent a monstrous wearisome time with a pair of very dull folk," Eléonore announced abruptly, breaking into my thoughts. "Has anybody, perhaps, heard of a certain Mdme. Roland?"

"O, good heavens," exclaimed Lucile, her eyes gleaming with mischief. "Don't tell me you have encountered Madame! Is she quite frightful? Camille calls her 'a climbing little *bourgeoise* who has read some Rousseau and Plutarch and now fancies herself a Scholar.' And her dreadful old husband—twenty years her senior, they say, and as humourless as a fence-post."

"I've heard of her political *salon*," said I. "Enlightened and anti-royalist opinions only, if you please, and women are *not* invited."

"So I've been told," said Eléonore. "I imagine that Mdme. Roland is determined no other Bluestockings should draw her guests' attention from her dubious charms. *Well*, thought I, yesterday, *let us see what this baggage is made of.* I called on her and spent the dreariest possible half-hour with her. Msr. Brissot, who worships her, is forever telling me that though dear Madame is a wondrous erudite woman, she modestly refrains—unlike me, I suppose—from interposing herself into her guests' conversations."

"Perhaps that is her secret," said Lucile, giggling.

"Of course that's her secret. Encourage a lot of self-important *arrivistes,* like most of the Assembly, to think themselves men of political genius. I suspect they are too much beguiled by that gracious simper of hers to realise what a—no, I shan't say it . . . what a calculating—she-cat—the creature must be. Any woman could recognise it in an instant. What fools men are!"

"Don't underestimate her," broke in Hérault, who had languidly been listening to the conversation whilst sipping his coffee. "She provides a meeting-place for every soul in the Assembly who is no longer enamoured of La Fayette, Bailly, and the King, and their attempts to rein in the Revolution. Already she has several of those *arrivistes* under her thumb." He flicked a speck of dust from the lace at one immaculate cuff and grimaced.

"Mesdames, Monsieur, I hope you cherish no desire to keep company with that strenuously respectable Harpy?"

Eléonore dissolved into laughter. "Surely not. You are marvellously brilliant, Jean-Marie—it's no wonder you were appointed King's Advocate at eighteen."

"As brilliant as you are beautiful, Hérault," added Lucile, yawning, and put an end to the subject by demanding more coffee and cakes.

I dallied a while after the others had quitted us, to discuss the next fortnight's number of *Le Flambeau.* "And I've persuaded Camille to contribute a page or two," concluded Eléonore, "if I promise to return the favour. It should do the both of us a good turn."

"And Msr. Hérault?" I enquired. "Is he to contribute as well?"

"Heavens, no," said Eléonore, amused. "Hérault is no Journalist."

"From your conversation I surmised that Msr. Hérault, blest with such a multitude of gifts as he is, could ably turn his hand to any pursuit he chose."

"I think not. Or not, at least, by inclination. Hérault is far too fond of his own pleasures," she added, drily, "to spend any great length of time at something so dreary as labour."

"Yes," said I, "I suppose a man of his species would consider it far too fatiguing to take up a pen."

Eléonore stared at me for a moment. "Carton," she murmured, "I believe you are jealous."

"Jealous? Why ought I be jealous?"

She said nothing, merely gazed at me, unsmiling. "Regarding you?" I continued. "There is nothing between us."

"Is there not?"

"No."

"Friendship, I surely hope."

"Friendship, of course. But a reasonable man is not jealous of his friends."

"Hérault and I have been friends since childhood."

"I see . . . then he has the advantage of me there, too, in an acquaintanceship of long duration—"

"I meant only that Hérault and I are friends, as you and I are friends, and nothing more than friends." She turned away from me, folding her arms. "You *are* jealous."

I sighed. "Forgive me."

"O Carton . . ." Swiftly she rose from her desk and sat herself down beside me on the sofa. "I don't mean to tease you, or to play the coquette. Surely you know that."

"Do I?"

"Why, do you think so little of me? I have my share of faults, God knows, but I hope a want of honesty is not one of them."

I was silent a moment. "All the women I ever have dared to care for," I said at last, "have forsaken me, in their varying ways . . . whether it be coldly or kindly."

Slowly Eléonore nodded. "And thus . . . thus you have concluded that such is the nature of Woman?"

"Insofar as I will never again hazard my own heart in play in which the odds are so high against me."

"Then you are the last one who should have cause for jealousy, are you not?" She abruptly rose and returned to her desk. "Perhaps we should discuss, instead, the rising price of paper." Snatching up a pen, she bent her head over an open account-book, biting her lips as she turned from my sombre gaze.

How can we be so blind to that which is before our eyes?

14

THE ROYAL FAMILY'S bungled attempt at escape across the frontier, in June 1791, shattered any remaining hopes we might have cherished that the King and Queen would reconcile themselves with the Revolution's aims. Aubincourt and his allies at the Riding-School found themselves sadly perplexed by this turn of events. The new Constitution was ready to be voted into Law—but how, they asked, could a Constitution based on a limited Monarchy be put into practice, when the Monarch had demonstrated himself to be unwilling to submit to it?

I had no answers for Aubincourt. The English answer to the problem of a troublesome King, resorted to in the matter of Charles I, was not one which many folk welcomed. (Camille, nevertheless, mentioning the subject at one of Eléonore's *soirées*, claimed he had been a Republican all his life and would have no objection to Fat Louis losing his crown—and the head might go along with the crown, for all he cared.)

The Assembly, against Aubincourt's better judgment, resolved to press on, and disbanded to make way for its successors and the Constitution. Aubincourt, once more a private citizen, no longer needed me, tho' he kindly pretended he did, for we had come to like each other well during the two years past. I quitted his service that Autumn. Eléonore promptly insisted that I work with her, writing and editing *Le Flambeau*, which now had ten thousand subscribers or more.

I returned to the Left Bank and, for the sake of conveniency, let rooms on an upper floor of Eléonore's house. My pittance of two hundred livres per quarter that I was receiving still from my father's estate, through draughts on the Paris office of Tellson's Bank, did not buy as much as once it had, but I had saved much of Aubincourt's generous salary. Could I have

173

imagined, during my hard-living days in London, that I would one day invest my salary in the Funds, rather than fling it abroad in taverns, gaming-halls, and bawdy-houses? The very thought would have started me laughing—and the steady fellow I had become would have seemed an utter stranger.

TOWARDS EASTER OF 1792 Robespierre unexpectedly paid a call on me. Always pallid and preoccupied, he now seemed unhappy and disquieted, the lines about his mouth deep-etched. (During the six months past he had continued in Politics by taking a leading rôle in that influential society of Republicans and Idealists, the Jacobin Club.) Tho' he was but thirty-three, he looked a dozen years older. "Do ever you attend sessions of the Jacobins, or of the Legislative Assembly?" he asked me, after he had politely refused my offer of a glass of Port. "You must be aware how the debates are shaping."

I nodded. "This matter of declaring war on Austria?"

"What else would I speak of? These persons in the Assembly who follow Brissot's lead, and who frequent Mdme. Roland's *salon*—Carton, that odious woman aspires to rule all of France by seducing those conceited newcomers into her *clique*."

"Seducing?"

"Not in the manner you think—the woman is a model of starched rectitude. But many of the Deputies are devoted to her, and hang on her every word. She, and they, claim all too persuasively that warring against an ancient foe, in the name of Liberty, would reunite a France sadly in want of unity."

"It is a seductive notion," I agreed.

"But not *war*, Carton! I, tho' I am very much in the minority, most categorically oppose declaring war on the Empire. Such a reckless undertaking would create many more crises than it would solve."

"That is, unhappily, a reasonable assumption."

"Might I presume to believe that you have no more desire for war than do I?"

"Of course. France should tend to her own affairs ere embroiling herself in so costly an endeavour."

"Then you might do me—and France—a service by persuading Mdme. de Clairville not to advocate it."

Indeed, I had considered the idea of war preposterous, and had written as much in *Le Flambeau* in my character of the "English Observer". Yet Eléonore, to my astonishment, had disagreed. Though decidedly cool towards the Roland-Brissot faction, she found much to admire amongst the many members of the Assembly, fervent provincial Liberals all, who were styled sometimes *Brissotins,* sometimes *Girondins.* In the same number of our journal she had ardently upheld their proposals, though she was fair-minded enough to print my objections in their entirety.

"Ah," said I, "her opinions expressed in the latest number of *Le Flambeau,* do you mean?"

"Of course. What can have possessed her?"

"Vergniaud's acumen and charm," I suggested, recalling how many times I had encountered the affable Girondin orator at Eléonore's supper-parties. "He can be most persuasive."

"Vergniaud! He is by far the most reasonable of that lot—I had hoped he would have had more sense. But no, they must plunge, all of them, into this foolhardy endeavour, like children playing at soldiers in a barn-yard . . ." He paused, sighed, pushed his spectacles to the bridge of his nose, and continued. "Carton, since I know that you share my opinions—"

"Now wait," I interrupted him. "Why should you 'know' this?"

"All Paris knows you are *Le Flambeau*'s 'English Observer'," said he, with a weary smile. "Why deny it?"

"Nobody *knows* anything. There are many Englishmen—and Englishwomen too—in Paris."

"But you cannot deny that you are intimate with Mdme. de Clairville. I pray you, Carton, use your influence and persuade her not to advocate this misguided war."

"Influence!" said I, laughing. "I have never succeeded in winning an argument with Mdme. de Clairville about anything. Nor, I expect, has anybody else."

"Then I must make the attempt myself."

Dubious, I led him down-stairs to Eléonore's apartment. She was at home to visitors at that hour and I saw Vergniaud himself, and his pretty mistress, taking their leave of her as Robespierre and I drew near. Ringing for more coffee, Eléonore seated herself comfortably on the sofa as Robespierre remained standing, hands clasped behind his back.

"No one," he began, "can have any doubt of the influence you wield through *Le Flambeau*, Mdme. de Clairville. It is rightly one of the most influential journals in Paris."

"I have many subscribers in other cities, too," said she. "Near three hundred in Lyon alone, I believe."

Robespierre compressed his lips. Eléonore's friendship with Vergniaud and others of the Girondin Deputies, who had no great love for the powerful and often fanatical Parisian Jacobins, had more than a little to do with her coolness towards him.

"*Le Flambeau* is widely read and influences the opinions of many," said he, none too patiently. "I had hoped, Madame, that I could persuade you to cease your support for an undertaking that must ultimately be disastrous for France and the Revolution."

She turned wide, innocent eyes upon him. "What undertaking is that, Monsieur?"

"This proposal to declare war."

"O, but what could be a nobler mission than to spread the enlightened concepts of Liberty, Equality, and Fraternity to all the benighted Kingdoms of Europe?"

"Madame," I interjected, ere Robespierre could retort, "I pray you, reconsider. Imagine what would occur should France declare war on the Empire. The army is unprepared, under-supplied, and lacks leadership. Half the officers have emigrated, and we may have serious doubts about the loyalties of the other half. Can anybody say in all honesty that we are fit to wage war on a Kingdom the size of the Austrian Empire?"

Eléonore smiled, like a parent soothing a child frightened of the dark. "France is the greatest Kingdom in Europe. It has the greatest army—and if a few officers have emigrated, surely more than enough talented men remain to replace them."

"But there is no substitute for experience, Madame."

"There is always patriotism!" she returned. "Perhaps, as a foreigner, you don't truly understand how we French regard our nation, and our Revolution."

"You never before branded my English birth a liability," said I. "Is it so convenient a pretext for you now?"

"O Carton, be reasonable."

"I am being perfectly reasonable!"

"Then consider our situation. All the absolute Monarchs of Europe watch our every move and would like nothing better than to see the Revolution defeated. Thousands of *émigrés* are waiting on the banks of the Rhine, raising money, massing an army, awaiting the moment when they may thrust their way into our country and destroy all that the Revolution has begotten. The Emperor is awaiting the moment when he may best despatch his own army to crush France. Why should we suffer our enemies to prepare for war on their own terms, and await their invasion? And how can you doubt, after all you have seen, both the good and the bad, that the French soldier will dedicate himself to advancing the cause of Liberty, and defending the Revolution?"

Robespierre and I exchanged glances. She had neatly trapt him; he could not admit before an adversary that he had no faith in patriotic soldiers. "We have no guarantee that the Empire will declare war on France," he said at last, once again thrusting up his spectacles.

"And what of the *émigrés*, Msr. Robespierre? They have nothing to lose and everything to gain by overturning the Revolution."

"If the Nobles who have fled across the Rhine are as frivolous and incompetent in organising an invasion as they once were in governing France, then I believe we have little to fear. The Revolution has no greater defender than I, Madame," he added, wearily. "But suffer it first to take root in France ere attempting to thrust it upon other peoples."

"I think you lack confidence, Msr. Robespierre," said she. "You should be more optimistic about the Revolution you took part in creating."

"I did not take part in its creation only to see it thrown away in this useless enterprise!" He must have seen there was no arguing with Eléonore, or with any who endorsed the war. "Good-day, Madame; Carton. I had thought," he added, venomously, as he brushed past me, "that you might have pled our case with a trifle more vigour."

"Why disaffect Robespierre?" I demanded of Eléonore, as the door shut behind him. "I, for one, should prefer him as a friend rather than an enemy."

"Because I am right."

"You are both right. Yet is Robespierre's not the more prudent course of action?"

"Carton, it's no action at all! If Robespierre had his way, we would sit and wait for the Austrians to over-run us." She sighed and scowled at me. "Why must you be so eternally *cautious?* I would scarce think it in your nature."

"Three years ago you would have been right," I agreed. "But three years ago I had nothing to lose by being reckless, nor did the Revolution. To-day . . . I foresee a future, for myself and for France, that I can ponder with hope rather than despair. And hope is such a precious thing—none but those who have endured without it can treasure it as I do."

She gazed at me a moment. "And do you think I have nothing to lose by embracing the Girondin cause? I know full well it's a perilous wager, but truly I believe we are right. We will have war, no matter what. Better we should have it on our own terms rather than those of the Enemy."

Pausing an instant, she glared at the doorway through which Robespierre had departed. "And for the life of me I cannot persuade myself to like that man, or his opinions. He may be an old friend of yours, and of Camille's, but I find him self-righteous, humourless, and suspicious, and I'll not shy from saying so."

"Who, Robespierre?" said I, remembering the gentle, owlish boy I had known at Louis-le-Grand. "In truth he is a very perceptive and well-intentioned fellow."

"I don't like him," she repeated.

FRANCE DECLARED WAR on the Empire on the 20th of April. Robespierre would take no pleasure at being proven right within a matter of weeks, as the French armies promptly and ignominiously lost every battle they fought.

I saw him next at a dinner-party given but ten days later by Camille and Lucile Desmoulins at their comfortable apartment on rue du Théâtre-Français. Beside Robespierre, Eléonore, and me, Lucile had invited Camille's friend Danton and his wife; Hérault de Séchelles, that handsome, polished, and wealthy ex-Aristocrat; and Saint-Just, a young acquaintance of Camille's from the provinces visiting Paris for a fortnight.

Lucile captured me after dinner and gratefully (for she was five or six months gone with child) eased herself into an arm-chair. "*Mon Dieu*," she whispered, with a glance at the plump Mdme. Danton, "what a bore that woman is! Danton has brains and to spare, but he is of the species of man who likes his women domestic and stupid. I can't bear another minute of talk about wet-nurses and colic!"

"Well," said I, "I imagine you will be talking about them yourself soon enough."

"Should I do so, you have my full permission to hang me at Camille's

Lantern," she told me, giggling. Camille had been styled *the Public Prosecutor of the Lantern* since 1789, when a pamphlet of his had breezily made excuse for the mob's *penchant* for hanging victims of popular Justice from a street-lantern at the place de Grève. I saw nothing in the least comical about the appellation, but Camille found it endlessly amusing.

"No, Lucile—we shall give you the chop with this new contrivance they have built," said Hérault, overhearing us and gracefully dropping beside me onto the sofa. "Don't you know we are now a scientific and humane Nation?" This intelligence sent Lucile into gales of laughter, for the *Machine* and its tireless promoter, the humanitarian Dr. Guillotin, had been incessantly lampooned in the popular press.

O God, how careless we were as the shadow, seemingly so far away, began to reach for us. As we laughed together on that warm Spring afternoon, how could we have known that within two years, two turns of the seasons, above half our company would have been devoured by that infamous, ravenous Machine?

"It took its first bow a week ago . . . did you know?" said I. "A highwayman, I believe."

"And none too soon," added Hérault. "Did you attend, Lucile?"

"Lord, no," said Lucile, wrinkling her charming nose. "I don't wish to see any executions."

"How dull of you, *chérie*. I imagine I shall go, the next time." He fixed his liquid gaze upon her. "One should always pursue the new and fascinating . . . tempt our senses, seek out heightened perceptions, intense emotions . . ."

"I fear Camille's intense emotions are all I am able to manage," said Lucile. Hérault merely smiled lazily at her. Undoubtedly he, like many of Camille's less illustrious friends, cherished a half-concealed desire to seduce the enchanting and flighty Lucile.

I excused myself, as Hérault leant closer to her, and went to join Eléonore, but found her absorbed in a literary argument with Camille. Not wishing to disturb them, I turned away, catching young Saint-Just's eye as I did so.

"Camille tells me that you were once school-fellows," said he, with a cool smile that must have set many a provincial maiden's heart a-flutter. "I imagine you must have a few anecdotes that you could share if you wished."

"You must ask Msr. Robespierre for those, Monsieur," I told him. "I quitted Louis-le-Grand some months after Camille arrived."

"Camille and near all his friends seem to have studied at Louis-le-Grand together. It's most vexing to feel oneself ignored . . . or worse, indulged."

Having borne the burthen of Stryver's gross and smug patronage for far too long, I could sympathise with Saint-Just's bitterness. I smiled, glancing about the assembled company who were all, as they say, *coming men.*

"Never before have such opportunities been waiting to be seized by men of talent," I told him. "All you need do is prove yourself."

"I intend to. Msr. Robespierre and I have been corresponding for some time now."

"You find yourself in agreement with him?"

He straightened and his handsome visage, pale and delicate as a girl's, took on the stiffness of certitude. "Msr. Robespierre is a great man."

He ran on for a few moments more about Robespierre's devotion to the Nation, and his clear-eyed perception of how the Revolution had progressed—and how it must proceed. He added that since the King's disastrous flight, and ignominious return, folk had whispered of a Republic; he, for one, deemed it inevitable if the war turned against France. "It's misfortunate," he added, "that Mdme. de Clairville, who is an intelligent woman, should suddenly show such poor judgment in political matters when *Le Flambeau* is so widely read. Her partner in the enterprise seems possessed of clearer insight."

"I'd not know," said I, and made my excuses to him ere I inadvertently betrayed myself. He remained in his place, glancing over the company one by one, his cool grey eyes thoughtful. I guessed—correctly—that, despite Saint-Just's youth, Camille and his friends would not long be humouring him.

I slipped into a corner and observed Eléonore as she playfully argued with Danton and Hérault. The elegant Hérault, whose reputation was that of an inveterate and successful seducer, appeared determined as ever to add Eléonore (had he not already done so long ere then) to his register of conquests. Unlike Lucile, she seemed not unreceptive to his urbane advances. A flicker of jealousy stabbed me and I turned away.

"And what are you brooding about, Mr. Carton, alone there in your corner?" enquired Lucile, behind me. She slipped an arm through mine and drew me away. "Are you sulking because Mdme. de Clairville has chosen to trifle a while with the exquisite Hérault?"

"Certainly not," I lied.

"You shouldn't, you know . . . they have known each other for years, but I suspect she doesn't care a fig for him. He is far too superficial, despite his more than adequate brains—too much the careless Epicure. And Mdme. de Clairville, I think, feels far too passionately about everything to have patience with such a butterfly existence."

"I told you, Madame," said I, "it matters nothing to me. Mdme. de Clairville and I are friends, nothing more."

"You believe that, do you?" she murmured, her great eyes fixed upon me. "I have seen how you gaze at her sometimes, when you think no one observes you."

"Madame," said I, vexed, "do you take pleasure in playing the busybody?"

She smiled, unperturbed. "Do you know, Mr. Carton, were I not a married woman, I believe I might fancy you? But no matter. I speak to you because I am fond of Mdme. de Clairville, as are you."

"Well?"

"If you are her friend, you will tell her that she is wagering upon a losing horse." Perceiving my momentary puzzlement, she leant closer in to me. "The men of the Gironde. O, they have pretty dreams, and they talk well, but they are not men of action. That," she added, gesturing with a jerk of her head towards Danton's massive figure, towering above the slighter Robespierre, "—*that* is the man who will seize the reins in those great fists of his, when Brissot and the rest fumble and drop them." She pressed my hand, her little doll-like visage very earnest indeed. "You think I am merely a silly child, don't you? I may be scarce more than a child, but I listen to what the men are saying, and I am not such a nit-wit as you imagine me. Camille and I are *very* good friends of Danton's," she added. "And I advise you to be, as well." She gave me a nod and tranquilly returned to her husband's side.

"WHAT WERE YOU discussing with Lucile, and with that very attractive young man?" Eléonore asked me later, as I accompanied her home. "You seemed quite engrossed there."

"No more than you," said I, "with Hérault and Danton."

"I enjoy their company. They are both remarkable men."

"Is that all?"

"What on Earth do you mean, *is that all?*"

"Hérault enjoys the worst reputation in Paris, where women are concerned, and Danton is not far behind him."

"My own reputation is quite safe, I assure you. Danton is a brilliant man, and well-read, and possesses a certain rough charm, but I don't find hulking brutes with great pawing hands to my liking. They say the Roland woman can't abide the sight of him. I shouldn't go so far as all that, but I've no desire to share my bed with him."

"And what of Hérault?"

"What *of* Hérault?" said she, turning to look at me. "Why must you bristle whensoever I speak with him?"

"To-day you were not merely speaking with him, you were—"

"Flirting with him? Yes, I imagine I was. And why should I not? He is agreeable, intelligent, and handsome, and has lovely manners."

"And how well he knows it!"

"O, you are impossible to-day. Let us talk of something else, if we must talk."

"Forgive me, then, Madame, if I evince some concern for your reputation, and your happiness."

"*Diable!*" she exclaimed. "My private life is none of your affair, Carton, nor yours mine. Pray remember that we have agreed upon that subject more often than once."

We walked on in silence, turning the corner from the cour du Commerce onto the busy rue St-André-des-Arts. "Well, what *were* you discussing with Camille's handsome friend?" enquired Eléonore, at length.

I shrugged. "O, what else does anybody talk about, these days? Politics—the war. Saint-Just felt," I added, not without malice, "that you showed poor judgment in joining your voice with that of the Girondins, in favour of war."

"You needn't say *I told you so*, Carton. It was a risk we must needs have taken. Still I say that we might be worse off yet, had we waited for the Empire to strike the first blow."

"Worse off? How the Devil could we be worse off? Our soldiers are ill-equipt and ill-trained, and already they turn and flee when the Enemy approaches."

"The army is untried—give them a little time to find their way—"

"They will have precious little time indeed, ere the Emperor's troops trounce them. How long will you cling to this blind optimism?"

"Carton, why must you criticise all I do or say?" she demanded. "We once were friends. Are we friends still, or adversaries?"

"Of course we are friends."

"Then act the friend, not the adversary."

"Eléonore," said I, pausing, "it's the rôle of a friend to voice one's concerns. You and I have been friends these three years: long enough, I believe, to know each other's minds. And I know full well that you are a fine scholar, a most astute woman, a loyal and patriotic citizen . . . and that you are stubborn as an Irish mule."

She opened her mouth to remonstrate, but was speechless. An instant later she gave a short strained laugh and said, "Pray continue."

"I have seen how you welcome the men of the Gironde to your *soirées*, and how you offer a warmer welcome to Vergniaud and his friends than to Robespierre and Camille. You have every right to do as you please—the Girondins are vastly intelligent and well-intentioned, to be sure, and popular amongst the People as well. But can you not . . . *will* you not see that should this war go against us, the Girondins' popularity must necessarily fade? How soon will public opinion hold them in as deep contempt as it does the constitutional Monarchists? They, too, were once the People's heroes. And should the Girondins fall, they may drag you down with them. I speak merely—as your friend."

She gazed at me a moment. "I am most gratified by your concern," said she, at length. "But I must do what I feel is right. Let me alone, Carton. Let me be." Abruptly she increased her stride and in a moment was lost amidst the crowds on the street.

THE FRENCH ARMIES, pressed steadily back by the Austrian and Prussian forces, fared no better in the Summer than they had in the Spring. By August the Enemy was fifty miles from Paris.

Yet the Summer of 1792 was gay enough, despite the ever-present ill tidings from the Front, and despite the popularity of many scurrilous journals by such strident Demagogues as Hébert and Marat, who did not shrink from dubbing the King a witless pig, the Queen a foreign whore, and the Assembly a convocation of blockheads, boot-lickers, and traitors. The theatres played still to thronged houses (though plays representing the downfall of Tyrants earned the greatest applause); the Palais-Royal continued to swarm with pleasure-seekers and prostitutes; fashions continued to arrive, flourish, and disappear with their usual caprice and swiftness. Even Eléonore, who paid little attention to the vagaries of Fashion, found the most peculiar of the new crazes irresistible. One hot afternoon in late July I awaited her, as we had arranged, to discuss matters of

Business at the Corazza. She appeared at last, a quarter-hour late, cheerful and unrepentant.

"I hope you were not about to give up and desert me! Where is the waiter? I must have a glass of orange-blossom water ere I shrivel and blow away like a leaf. I didn't mean to keep you," she added, as I signalled to a server, "but I saw the most marvellous ear-rings at a jeweller's and I simply could not resist them!" She pushed aside a few dark curls so that I might have a better look at her new trinkets.

"Charming," said I, with an indifferent glance.

"Carton, you scarce looked at them. Do you not see what they are?"

I peered closer and recognised a shape I had seen often in the cheap popular prints for sale at the book-stalls. "God's death," I exclaimed. "Don't you think they are rather . . . wanting in taste?"

"O, perhaps they are a trifle *macabre*, but they are quite the rage. One sees them in all the toy-shops' windows now. The jeweller assured me upon his honour," she added merrily, "that everything will be Guillotines this Autumn." Unclasping one ear-ring, she passed it to me. "Isn't the work exquisite?"

I examined the trinket, bemused. It was, indeed, a dainty, miniature model of the humanitarian Machine that folk had jocularly christened *La Guillotine* after its earnest sponsor. A Liberty-cap sat jauntily atop it whilst, beneath it all, a *fleur-de-lys* dangled upside-down. "What's this?"

"The jeweller's political opinion, I imagine. Evidently he feels as many folk do, that the *fleur-de-lys*—in other words, the Monarchy—is about to be overturned. What do you think?"

"I think you probably paid far too much for your fashionable new *bagatelles*," I told her. Eléonore laughed and our conversation turned to the knotty question of engaging a new printer.

ALL THE WORLD knows how the Summer of 1792 came to its climax with the great Insurrection of August Tenth. Paris rose; the Tuileries fell; the King's powers were suspended; and in a heartbeat Danton, who had contrived and inspired the uprising, had become master of France.

What I doubt the Historians of the next century will record are the individual tales and tragedies of those who performed their small rôles that day on the vast stage of the Revolution. They will not relate how Camille, safe at Danton's side in the Hôtel de Ville, returned home in the middle of the night in order to reassure his near-frantic Lucile; nor how Laurent, unsure whether his duty lay in defending King or Nation, bid us a troubled Farewell as he set off to join the National Guard; nor how Eléonore paced back and forth thro' her parlour during that stifling hot day whilst we listened to the crash of cannon-fire across the Seine. The Histories will tell future generations that a thousand or more, besiegers and defenders, were killed in the battle before the Tuileries; few accounts will trouble to name the dead.

Laurent d'Ambert was amongst the thousand dead of the glorious Tenth of August, amongst the martyrs to Liberty to whom the more eloquent Deputies would make so many flowery speeches; for the National Guard, despatched to the Tuileries to protect the Monarchy, had at last turned upon their ineffectual King in contempt, and joined forces with the attackers from all the four corners of Paris. Eléonore received word of her brother's death with tight-lipped impassivity, and plunged once more into her work.

THINKING I MIGHT be of some assistance to Aubincourt in those tumultuous days of August, one day I crossed the Seine to his mansion in the Marais, only to discover his servants heaping a baggage-cart with furniture and trunks. Heavy-hearted but unsurprised, I found the Count in his study, where I had spent so many hours.

He gave me a weary smile as he recognised me, gesturing me to a chair. "I am attempting to clear away the last of my unfinished business," he told me. "So many affairs to be put in order, and so many bills I regret I must leave unpaid."

"You are emigrating?"

He shook his head as his countenance grew stern. "No. I have no wish to quit my country . . . and I rather doubt I would be welcome amongst the Royalists. We are quietly retreating to La Châtaigneraye, my estate near Montbrison. I have done all the good I can in Paris—now the Revolution belongs to the Dantons and the Marats."

"Danton . . . is not a bad fellow," I admitted. "He is a decent man. He is no fanatic, no Marat: not one to call for thirty thousand heads to fall."

"No, thank God for that." Aubincourt rose and stared out the window for a moment at the brilliant Summer sky. "You are remaining in Paris?"

"I've no reason to depart. My place, I find, is with *Le Flambeau.*"

"Tell Mdme. de Clairville to be circumspect, Carton."

I nodded. "I do, though she rarely listens. But Mdme. de Clairville has friends influential in the Assembly."

"The Assembly is a cipher now. To-day Danton is the Government. Will these friends of hers hold power still when Danton is finished with them?"

"Brissot, Pétion—" I began.

"Listen, my friend," said he, sitting once again and facing me squarely. "Do you recall how, when the Assembly first sat in Paris, the Deputies chose their seats in the Riding-School according to their sympathies, and the Constitutionalists sat together at the Left of the chamber whilst the Royalists sat at the Right?"

"Of course."

"Did ever you attend any sessions of the Legislative Assembly, after you quitted my service? Perhaps you noticed that in the Legislative, the extreme Royalists had disappeared and the constitutional Monarchists found themselves sitting on the Right, whilst that new clutch of provincial lawyers who flock around Brissot and the Roland woman seized the seats at the Left."

"Yes," said I, not liking the direction in which his words were leading us.

"They say there will be a new Government, that they will cease this nonsense of 'suspending' the King's power, and depose him for once and all in favour of a Republic. There go your constitutional Monarchists—none of *them* will be found in the National Convention. And Danton and Marat and the rest will push their way into the hall until the Brissotins are dislodged and are forced to take the empty seats at the Right. Do you follow me?"

"Too clearly. You believe that abolishing the Monarchy will solve nothing, then."

"So long as this war continues, and France continues to suffer defeat, what you have seen until now will be a puppet-show in comparison with what will follow." He sighed and pressed my hand. "Tell Mdme. de Clairville to be cautious, Carton . . . and keep watch over your shoulder."

15

ON THE EVENING of the 3rd of September, Camille wandered in upon me with a muttered word of greeting, his shoulders hunched. "Do you know what has been happening at the p-prisons?" he asked me, after staring a while into a corner.

I nodded. "I have heard rumours."

"They are k-killing the prisoners. Harmless stubborn old priests, most of them. Butchering them. They murdered three hundred or more at the C-Conciergerie to-day and piled their c-corpses like firewood in the courtyard."

The September Massacres were for the most part Marat's doing, Marat and the other madmen like him whom the Revolution's tempest had cast from the depths onto the shore. Whilst the Prussians and Austrians attacked us from without (Marat and his fellow Extremists insisted), thousands of bloodthirsty Royalists imprisoned since August Tenth would break out to betray and murder the citizens of Paris from within.

"I asked Danton why he d-did nothing to stay it," continued Camille. "He is Minister of Justice, for G-God's sake. But he said there was nothing to be d-done, that it's the People's will, that folk believe they are protecting their families from traitors, and we can but suffer the fire to burn itself out."

"Why come to me?" said I. "I have no influence."

"If Danton c-can't stay them, no one c-can. I only wished to say what was heavy on my mind. Do—do you think it's worth it? All this b-blood— for the Revolution?"

"Good God," I exclaimed, "I can't give you that answer. That is for your own conscience to decide."

"Because yesterday they b-began holding elections for the new Assembly—the National C-Convention. Everybody swears to me that if I stand for election I will be voted a D-Deputy."

"I shan't make your decisions for you, Camille. Go home and discuss the matter with your wife."

"What about you?"

"What about me?"

"You c-could stand for election yourself. Folk are mentioning your name. Did you not know? They have resolved to welcome foreigners, who have distinguished themselves in the service of Humanity or of the Revolution, to the C-Convention. Thomas Paine has been invited, and Priestley, and some others. You, with your c-contributions to *Le Flambeau*—"

"My name has never appeared in *Le Flambeau*."

"—would be elected, I am sure of it. And in any event you are half French already, and have dwelt here since 'eighty-nine."

"This is surely the maddest idea you ever have hatched, Camille."

He grinned at me, his crisis of conscience having vanished with the onset of this fascinating new fancy. "Is it so very mad? Danton speaks well of you, as does Robespierre, and folk listen to them. You enjoy a reputation as a d-dedicated and honest man, C-Carton. Why not take advantage of it?"

His impetuous suggestion was tempting. As in 1789, when Aubincourt's patronage had fallen by chance into my lap, perverse Fate was once again beckoning me onward towards a situation I would never have dreamt of pursuing. *Member of the French National Convention* . . . I repeated the words to myself, trying the taste of them—but of course the very notion was ludicrous. Still, I thought, still, I would humour Camille.

"Very well," said I. "You may put my name up if you wish, whilst you are putting forward your own. I have no doubt you will be elected, my friend, tho' I am not so sanguine about my own chances."

After he had strolled off I ventured down-stairs to Eléonore's apartment. I found her huddled on a sofa, gazing gloomily into a candle-flame.

"You've no doubt heard what they are saying about the prisons," she murmured. "Yesterday when I was coming home I heard screams from the Abbaye, but I'd no notion that the prisoners were being butchered by dozens."

I nodded. From the end of the street I heard a harsh drunken yell, the clatter of pikes, and the pounding of running feet. The footsteps ceased with a sudden cry and men's voices, raised in coarse laughter, echoed outside.

Nothing to be done, I thought, *suffer the fire to burn itself out.* I shuddered, remembering what I had seen in Caen in 1789. If I could do my small part in preventing, in future, such horrors as that, and those unfolding but a few streets from me, who was I to shrink from the opportunity?

I was about to offer Eléonore some empty words of comfort when a loud rapping at the door startled us both. A moment later Baptistine hurried into the parlour. "Madame," said she, flustered, "it's Msr. de Clairville—Monsieur your husband, Madame."

"I do occasionally remember that I have a husband, Baptistine," Eléonore drily reminded her, as she rose. A big handsome man in riding-dress strode into the room and made her a perfunctory bow.

"Madame."

"Monsieur," said Eléonore. "What brings you hither?"

"What do you think brings me hither?" demanded he. "This madness of the three weeks past. No one is safe who once had a title, save turncoats like Antonelle and Montflabert." (These were Noblemen whom Revolution-fever had seized and who had dramatically repudiated their titles and their fellow Aristocrats.) "I am quitting France, Madame," continued Clairville, "and I advise you to do the same. If you care to come with me I'll do my best to protect you."

She smiled and sat down before the coffee-tray. "What has led you to think I need protection, Monsieur? Catch your breath a moment and take coffee with us. Allow me to introduce my friend Mr. Carton."

"Carton," said he, with a glance at me as I stiffly bowed. "You are the Englishman—the one they say is my wife's latest lover."

"Folk may believe what they wish, Monsieur."

"And you may do as you like, Englishman. I don't care." Clairville seized the cup of coffee Eléonore poured for him and drank it down in a few swallows. "I didn't come hither to gossip, Madame—I must be off. Will you come with me or no?"

"You don't seem to grasp, my husband, that as the author of a journal entirely sympathetic to the Revolution, and as one who counts Messrs. Danton and Vergniaud amongst her friends, I am not only in no danger, I am amongst those who could easily denounce *you*." She shook her head at the sudden alarm in his eyes. "I merely illustrate my point. Quit France, then, and God be with you. Have you money?"

"Plenty of *assignats*,"—he spat out the name of the Revolution's detested and de-valued paper currency as if it left a foul taste in his mouth—"but little gold."

"Wait a moment." She hurried into her bed-chamber and soon returned with a velvet pouch. "Eight or ten louis, gold and silver, it's all I have. Take it." Clairville did not move. "Take it," she repeated. "*Assignats* won't bribe sentries, or buy you a meal or a horse across the frontier. Go on."

With a nod he accepted the pouch, saying "I thank you, Madame," and thrust it into his coat. Bending to her, he gave her a rough kiss on the mouth and strode to the door. "You are determined to stop on here?" he asked her once again, over his shoulder.

"I told you. *Go. Now.*"

"Then suffer me to advise you this once. I understand that ere the Insurrection began, the Assembly was about to legalise Divorce. Should such a Law pass, I suggest you avail yourself of it. Even you, no matter how secure you may think yourself, will breathe more freely when your aristocratic name is no longer tied to that of an *émigré*."

"I thank you. Adieu, then, Monsieur."

He glanced from her to me, gave us a brusque nod and Farewell, and was gone. Eléonore sighed as the door snapped shut behind him. "Well," said she, and returned to the sofa, without another word.

I KNOW NOW that on the very evening whose events I have just related, Lucie, her father, and her daughter arrived at Lorry's Paris lodgings at Tellson's. At that time I was unaware even that the old gentleman was in Paris on the Bank's business, much less that Lucie was so near. Had I but known! Had I learnt then that Darnay was in Paris, imprisoned as a returned *émigré*, I cannot help imagining that with Danton's influence I might have arranged his release, and Lucie and all her family might have been well away from Paris ere Darnay's enemies could strike. But I shall not waste words in vain speculation.

Camille was elected a Deputy to the National Convention. So was Robespierre, so was Danton, so was Marat. So were Brissot, Vergniaud, and all the eager young Republicans—eloquent orators of more vigour than wisdom—who trailed in their wake, day-dreaming of ancient Rome and the austere glories of its Republic.

So was Doulcet de Pontécoulant, the Abbess's nephew whom Eléonore and I had briefly met in Caen. So was Hérault de Séchelles, who prudently lopped the aristocratic *de* from his name, but who otherwise continued to enjoy the life of wealth and pleasure to which he had been born. So was Saint-Just, burning for a career and an Ideal. And so, to my complete stupefaction, was I.

ELÉONORE, THOUGH SHE had advocated the constitutional Monarchy, proved equally as enthusiastic towards the new Republic. She wept and cheered with the rest of us when word arrived, within hours after the Republic was proclaimed, that France had at last won a decisive victory, turning the Prussians back at the little town of Valmy. *Le Flambeau* continued to appear, tho' its tone more than ever took on a distinctly Girondin flavour.

Heeding her husband's advice, Eléonore proceeded to dissolve their marriage, a simple enough matter, for Emigration was now sufficient grounds for Divorce. Without the generous allowance the Vicomte had sent her every quarter for the ten years past, she was reduced to living on the profits from *Le Flambeau*. Few Journalists, however, even the most successful (the repellent Hébert, author of the popular gutter-rag *Père Duchêne*, was an exception), could live luxuriously on their subscriptions alone. She was obliged to sell her carriage and dismiss all her servants but the devoted Baptistine, who swore she would stay on without pay, if need be, to care for her lady.

I knew that Eléonore could no longer spare me the portion of the profits she had always pressed upon me for my work, and I wished to free her from the self-imposed obligation. I found myself, too, as the "English Observer", agreeing with Robespierre's prudent proposals far more often than with the high-flown and often impractical oratory of Brissot. At last, one evening in late November, I descended to Eléonore's apartment and reluctantly told her that I could no longer lend my pen to *Le Flambeau*.

"You intend to cease contributing?" said she, staring up at me from her dainty rosewood writing-desk as if I had gone mad all in a minute. "Carton, don't be absurd. Every day I receive letters from my subscribers telling me how they enjoy the English Observer's essays. You can't cease writing now."

"I must. Attending sessions at the Convention occupies much of my time."

"Nonsense! The Deputies have far too much time on their hands, if I hear correctly. They ought to be at the Riding-School making laws, not drinking Champagne at restaurants at the Palais-Royal. Tell me the truth."

"Well then . . . I cherish no desire to associate myself with a Girondin journal, unproven though the connexion may be."

"*Le Flambeau* is not a Girondin journal."

"Is it not? In 'eighty-nine it championed Liberty and Reform. Now it seems to champion Vergniaud and his friends. For myself, I like and admire the man, but I think he is less adept at statecraft than he believes himself to be. And the rest surely are better at turning an elegant phrase than at governing a Nation in the midst of war."

"And thus you are simply abandoning me? Carton, you and I began this together. I have always published whatsoever you have written, have I not, even when we have disagreed?"

"You have," I admitted.

"Then what have you to complain of?" She thrust a few pages into my hands, covered in her firm angular script. "Look, this is for the next number, about the question of trying the King for Treason. Write whatsoever you truly think on the subject. Write that he ought to be broken on the wheel and burnt alive for his crimes—or write that he ought to be reinstated upon his throne, with his absolute power intact—or anything betwixt the two, anything at all. And I will print it, I promise you, no matter how shocking it may be."

I clasped one of her hands in my own and kissed it. "No," I told her, gently. "I cannot, no matter how much free rein you may give me. It is still a Girondin journal, and, much as I admire their Ideals and their patriotism, I don't care to be too closely associated with them. I value Robespierre and Danton's esteem too highly."

"But not mine, evidently?" returned Eléonore, withdrawing her hand.

"You know I do, and always shall."

"Do I? We seem to be forever disputing some point of contention or other. If you value my esteem, why must you always question or belittle my opinions?"

"You do me an injustice—" I began.

"*You* do *me* an injustice! I'll not be humoured by you, as if I were some silly creature who had taken a notion in her pretty little head."

"I shouldn't think of patronising you in such a fashion, or anybody. I endured my colleagues' contempt in London—do you think I would inflict such a burthen, such a humiliation upon one whom I cherish and esteem as if she were my own sister?"

Eléonore glowered at me for a moment ere snatching away the manuscript that I held and flinging it aside. "O, very well, do whatsoever you wish! Go back to the Convention and play at being a Representative of the People. If you fear reproach so, go back and hide behind Robespierre's coat-tails—I shall do very well without you. But don't hinder me in my work."

I could say nothing without quarrelling with her further, and that I did not wish to do. Silently I quitted her.

IN A MORE settled time, I suspect Louis XVI might have been glorified as the most enlightened of French Kings. His muddled attempts to reconcile the Revolution with his Absolutist's instincts, however, had brought him naught but misfortune. Now his fate hung in the balance, to be determined by the Convention.

The Girondin faction yet wished to spare his life. The Mountain, on the other hand (so styled from its partisans' habit of taking the highest seats in the hall), demanded his head. And I? I sat with the Mountain, for there were the men I knew best: Camille, Robespierre, Saint-Just. Yet I could not bring myself to vote as I knew they would. When the time came, in the course of that fantastical night in January 1793, and in my turn I mounted the tribune and cast my vote, I said merely that as a foreigner born, I had no right to decide the fate of the former King of the French, and thus abstained altogether.

I returned wearily home late on the morning of 20th January. Eléonore must have been awaiting me in her parlour, for as my tread echoed on the stair she thrust her head out the door to the landing and beckoned me inside.

We had scarce spoken for some six or seven weeks, beyond a cool exchange of salutations at our frequent encounters on the stair-case. Now she seemed determined to behave as if our quarrel had never taken place.

"Tell me," said she. "I must know . . . for the journal, you understand."

"It is over . . . he has been condemned," I told her. "He will be executed to-morrow."

She sat heavily on a footstool. "I have been expecting this. Praying it wouldn't be so, but expecting it."

"They were determined on having his blood, and they will have it."

"They will have it," Eléonore echoed me.

"I abstained. Had I chosen to vote, had I voted for imprisonment . . ." I began, but she forestalled me.

"You would not have prevented his death. You're not to blame, God knows." She sat silent for a while, staring at the leaden sky beyond the windows. A few tears trickled down her cheeks and she angrily dashed them away. "I am not crying for *him*, you understand," she snapped. "I am perfectly indifferent to that bumbling plodder's fate. But . . . a Republic that could demand such profitless vengeance, on so harmless and well-meaning a man . . . this is not the Republic for which my brother died. This is not the Revolution we dreamt of. No one meant it to end so."

"End . . . I doubt it. I overheard Saint-Just, ere I quitted the Riding-School, remarking that at last the Revolution was truly begun."

"Every King in Europe will recognise a threat to his throne. We will be at war with the whole Continent."

I forbore from reminding her that she and the men she admired had first brought the war upon themselves, and instead mentioned the Republic's military victories. She scowled once again as a new thought struck her.

"Carton, what if England should declare war on France? What will you do?"

I, too, had considered that question, from the moment I perceived the King's death to be inevitable. "I shall stop here, as long as I am welcome," I told her. "Nothing remains for me in England."

"And should you not be welcome, should they decide every Englishman is a possible spy?"

"I imagine I would go to America."

"America!" she exclaimed. "That's so far away . . . the other side of the world." She gnawed at her nether lip for a moment. "Carton, if for whatsoever reason you resolve to go to America, take me with you . . ."

These were the last words I had expected to hear from her. I wheeled about, gazing at her in astonishment. "Take you—why? What could possibly induce you to quit France?"

"What should induce me to stay? All my family is dead, or gone. And . . . and I think I have lost my faith in the Revolution," she whispered, once again staring unseeing out the window. "This judgment—it's wrong. They are going to kill Louis in revenge for his ancestors' crimes. It's the old story: *The sins of the fathers shall be visited upon the sons.* He always meant well—but because he wore the same crown as did a handful of vicious, power-mad Tyrants during centuries past, for that they are going to make him their scapegoat!" She turned her face suddenly up to mine, with a short bitter laugh. "What then, did you think I meant for you to take me away and wed me, like a schoolgirl eloping with her music-master?"

"I scarce knew what to think," I confessed.

"I can tell full well that you will never wed anybody. You never look at women. When you look at me, it's as if you don't see me, not as a woman. Even on that occasion, that day in Caen, what you wished was a friend, not a lover."

"And the night of the Fourteenth of July?"

She gazed at me a moment, her dark eyes pensive. "That meant nothing. We might as well have been strangers, you and I—I might as well have been some Palais-Royal courtesan, for all I meant to you then. We know one another better now." She looked away, with a shrug of her shoulders. "I imagine somebody once broke your heart, or you lost a lover dear to you, and you have never recovered."

"You are most perceptive," said I. I slowly seated myself and leant forward, elbows on my knees and hands clasped. "When I was twenty years old," I began, "I fell madly, ridiculously in love with Sarah Kenyon, the daughter of our nearest neighbour . . ."

I told Eléonore the tale of my callow, shattered love-affair as we sat together in her parlour on that grey January morning—and then the tale also of my secret love for Lucie.

"I see," she murmured, when I had concluded. "A girl who betrayed you . . . and then my cousin's wife! The wife of the man who could have been your twin—that must have rankled."

"I feel no bitterness towards Darnay . . . I overcame that long since."

"But still—"

"Lucie is more to me than a woman I once loved and lost." I paused, laughing a little, despite my sombre humour, at the hackneyed phrase. "No, what am I saying . . . I never lost her, for she was never mine. But she . . . she was the one entirely good and pure thing in my life, a glimmer in the darkness, when all my existence seemed an utter wreck. I never recognised it at the time, but she gave me hope. Had she not, long ago I would have disappeared into a drunkard's grave. How can I help but find other women wanting, in comparison?"

"Like me?" enquired Eléonore.

Et semel emissum volat irrevocabile verbum—*once sent out, a word takes wing irrevocably.* I coloured, wishing I could unsay my ill-chosen words.

"I meant," I said slowly, "I meant to say, women of my own station, whom I might otherwise have loved, and wedded. Or even . . . there was once a girl, an Irish wench . . . But a—a woman of your station and breeding is as far beyond me as is the Moon."

"Has not the Revolution levelled all social ranks?" said she, raising an eyebrow. "Have a care, Carton, or they will accuse you of aristocratic tendencies and counter-revolutionary remarks."

"I pray you, don't jest about such a matter."

"About accusations of counter-revolution . . . or about your wounded heart and your chaste devotion to Charles's wife? Or *was* it chaste?"

"Of course it was. What manner of swine do you think me?"

"I never thought you less than a gentleman," she murmured, "and a fine decent man, no matter how little you may have thought of yourself."

I sighed. At last I rose and bent to kiss the top of her head. "You must know how very dear you are to me . . . Léo." I believe that that was the first occasion, in the three and a half years of our acquaintance, on which I had addressed her by that affectionate diminutive. "Truly, I could have no better friend."

She nodded. "Nor I, in you." A long while later she turned to gaze at me. "Dear Carton . . . despite all, we are still, as we ever were, more than friends . . . and less than lovers. It's a comforting arrangement, is it not?"

16

A FORTNIGHT AFTER the King's execution, as Eléonore had foreseen, France was at war with England. Whilst Mr. Paine enjoyed honorary French citizenship by virtue of his contributions to American Independence, mine was a different case: I imagine I was well-regarded still in the Convention simply because most folk had forgotten I was an Englishman. In addition, my off-hand remark to Camille (who had been boasting that his father had foreseen in him a Roman Republican by naming him Lucius Sulpicius Camillus) that my own father had named me after Algernon Sydney did nothing to blemish my reputation. That season it had become fashionable for men with dull Saints' names ostentatiously to re-christen themselves after the Republican heroes of Antiquity; thus a man who had borne the name of a martyr to the cause of English liberty since the day of his birth enjoyed a certain *cachet*.

Thus passed the Winter of 1793. In March the remote, rustic *département* of La Vendée rose in rebellion against the Government that had murdered its King and outlawed its priests. On almost the same day Danton proposed the creation of the Revolutionary Tribunal, which, by meting out swift and inflexible Justice, would prevent such horrors as the September Massacres from recurring. Who—surely not Danton!—could have envisioned that the Tribunal would become the pitiless servant of Dictatorship that it now is, as dreadful in its cold efficiency as the massacres?

The Girondins, though suspicious of the Tribunal, seized their opportunity to hail their inveterate enemy Marat before it on ill-defined charges of aspiring to Dictatorship. Callow to the end, they failed to consider that Judges, Prosecutor, and Jury were the Mountain's chosen men. Marat was triumphantly acquitted and from that moment, forging an alliance with the *enragés*, the ever more violent leaders of the city Government, he contrived to bring about the Girondins' downfall.

ELÉONORE, WHO HAD taken to attending sessions of the Convention from the spectators' gallery, regretfully recognised that the Girondins were doomed ere they themselves did. A few conciliatory paragraphs crept into an April number of *Le Flambeau*, mentioning Danton and even Robespierre in not uncomplimentary terms. Shortly afterward, Brissot paid her a visit. I know not what words passed between them, but from my rooms two floors above, I could hear their raised voices. Eléonore possessed a formidable temper (tho' I had never myself felt its full sting) and she could not have taken kindly to a tongue-lashing from that censorious prig.

Troubled, I descended to the first floor in time to see Brissot back out from Eléonore's open door, his long narrow face quivering with indignation. I heard Eléonore shout "Get out! And don't come back!" A shower of papers fluttered about him to the landing. Brissot leant forward to respond but caught a glimpse of me on the stair above him. Paling, he fled.

I approached the half-open door and pushed it wide. At the creak of its hinges, Eléonore shrieked "I said, get *out!*"

"It's only I," I reassured her. I found her on her knees in the *foyer*, sobbing in rage. "Eléonore, what on Earth has passed here?"

"That—that pompous imbecile—" She paused and clapt her hands to her head as if she could squeeze her seething thoughts once again into her skull. "He came to chastise me for betraying the sacred cause of Citizen Brissot, what do you think? Because I suggested that Danton was a man of courage and insight who had much to offer the Revolution still and his leadership should not be disregarded! But no, Brissot in all his purity must needs denounce Danton because the man is corrupt—and who, *mon Dieu*, is not? Never mind that Danton brought down the Monarchy and saved the country from invasion. And because I dared show some sense, and hoped that Republicans wouldn't split into squabbling factions, Brissot proceeded to berate me as if I were a truant schoolboy, and he some pedant with a bundle of birches!"

Unexpectedly she began to laugh and sob all at once. "It's all so very horrible and ludicrous both . . . And that d__ned manuscript—the great patriot Brissot decrees that I shall retract any thing complimentary I may have written about anybody, other than Mdme. Roland's lap-dogs, and with a sober countenance expects me to re-write his scribblings to my own style and print them!" She brushed past me and with her clenched fists pounded on the nearest wall, setting the porcelain ornaments to rattling.

"The arrogance of them both!" she continued. "How anybody can abide that woman—particularly Vergniaud, and yet he tells me he thinks it would be more in the interest of the Nation, if he is forced to a choice, to take her side rather than Danton's!" Abruptly she broke into angry tears, crumpling into the nearest chair and hiding her face in the folds of her skirt.

"The fools!" she cried, between sobs. "The d__ned short-sighted fools! How can they not see that Danton is the only one who can save them, and that they are racing headlong towards destruction? Don't they *know*, all of them, that Danton would rather cast his lot with Robespierre or the *enragés* than waste any more effort in fruitless attempts at reconciliation?"

I could say nothing to Eléonore that she did not already know, so instead drew her to her feet and enfolded her in my arms. "There, there," I murmured, rather foolishly. "Calm yourself. You are quite safe here. Calm yourself, and forget Brissot. He is scarce worth your anger." I kissed her brow, a chaste kiss that her brother might have given her, and then her cheek, tasting her tears on my lips. Suddenly, like a blow to the belly, I found I desired her as much as ever I had desired any woman. I sought her mouth and kissed her once again, a lover's kiss. A little cry, a moan or a sob, escaped her and for a moment she responded to my lips. Then, violently, she twisted from me and thrust me away.

"For God's sake let me *be*! And don't mouth inanities like a nursery-maid with a fretful child!"

I retreated to the landing and silently gathered up the dozen pages of Brissot's manuscript. When I returned Eléonore had calmed, though she was trembling still. She gazed up shamefaced at me as I approached, her dark eyes haggard in the shadows.

"Forgive me. That was ill-mannered and childish of me."

"There is little to forgive," said I. "You were amply provoked."

"O Carton, what shall I do now? *Le Flambeau* has lost its purpose."

"Well, you are not Brissot's lap-dog," I told her. "You can do whatsoever you wish."

"If I did as I wished . . . I think almost I would cease printing. I take little joy in it these days. But I have no other income, and it does pay for my wants."

I nodded. Since the declaration of hostilities betwixt England and France, my monthly pittance from Tellson's Bank had abruptly vanished. My modest Deputy's pay of eighteen livres daily, however, far eclipsed my former seventy livres per month. Had it not been for the chance that had led me to the Convention, I would have been in equally dire straits.

"Yet what can I possibly publish?" Eléonore continued. "I can no longer go on speaking for the Girondins. What an imbecile I have been, not to see through their affectations! And I will not speak for the Mountain, as much as I would hope for reconciliation with them. You may understand those men, but I do not. What other choice have I?"

"Well," said I, handing her the papers I had collected, "you might return *Le Flambeau* to what it was in 'eighty-nine, and speak for yourself."

She nodded. "Yes, there is that, isn't there?" Curling the creased sheets absently into a scroll, she stared into the flames in the hearth. "Carton, I had hoped so that we—that at least Vergniaud would see which way the wind was blowing and go to Danton. Danton is not a man to nurture a grudge against an old adversary. But Vergniaud will suffer his Ideals to overcome his common sense and lead him instead towards Brissot. It's the end of them all."

"Yes, I fear so."

"But I thank you."

"For what, pray?"

"O, for being a reasonable voice amidst this madness." She glanced down at the papers and with a grimace and a flick of her wrist flung them into the fire.

THE INTERMINABLE QUARRELS in the midst of the Convention continued another six weeks. A decisive link in the chain of the Girondins' destruction was forged when Camille published his cruelly witty, slanderous pamphlets *The History of the Girondins* and *Brissot Unmasked*.

I was reluctant witness to one of the Jacobins' earlier, cruder attempts to chip away at the Gironde's foundations. One morning in mid-May, returning from Robespierre's lodgings whither some trivial errand had taken me, I was crossing the Feuillants Terrace into the gardens of the Tuileries Palace on my way to the Convention. (It had, a few days previous, quitted its old quarters at the Riding-School for the former royal theatre in the Tuileries.) Ahead of me I espied a mob of roughly-clad women, of the sort whom the Jacobin Club pays to loiter about the doors to the Convention and insult folk, particularly Deputies, whose moderate opinions are not to their liking.

As I approached I heard shouting and coarse laughter, and above it, well-nigh drowned out in the clamour, some shrill screams. These female mobs are reputed to whip folk, usually women, who especially displease them. I had no love for the crude and violent *Montagnards* who encourage such Mænads in their excesses and thus, hoping to spare some hapless soul pain and humiliation, I waded in amongst them.

They had a struggling, screeching woman in their midst, held down in the firm grip of two brawny fishwives, her skirts flung up to her shoulders to expose her bare white buttocks. The other women, two dozen or more, belaboured her with switches broken from the nearby trees and with shoes, mud, loose stones. That she was not an Aristocrat, tho' her scarlet riding-dress was of a fashionable cut, was evident from the gutter-language pouring from her lips.

"Stop it!" I shouted, reaching for the nearest Harpy and wrenching her from her shrieking victim. "Stop it, I tell you!" At last I wrested the unhappy woman, now howling and sobbing, from their grasp. "Be off with you!" I ordered them. "I am a Representative of the People and I'll have no more of this brutality!"

They drew back a pace or two, glowering and muttering. "It's naught but what the Girondine bitch deserves," snarled one of them, "the treasonous slut!"

I ignored her and set myself to calming the wretched creature clinging to me. After a moment, for her pretty face was savagely scratched and bruised, I recognised Mdlle. Théroigne, the ex-courtesan, now Amazon who devoted her energies equally to the cause of women's rights and to the embattled Girondins. I had briefly encountered that fiery young woman at the Abbaye in '89, at the beginning of her revolutionary career, and had since seen her petitioning the Convention more often than once.

The striking visage I remembered, with its fierce lively black eyes, was swollen now and bleeding in half a dozen places. A blow had chipped one of her front teeth and cut her lip, and blood streamed from her broken nose. As she gasped and sobbed into my shoulder I tugged down her torn skirt, wiped with my handkerchief at the blood and dirt on her face, and glared at the sullen fishwives. "Be off with you," I repeated. "Get about your business."

They did not stir, though they said nothing. I turned once again to Mdlle. Théroigne. "Can you walk?" I asked her. "Come, I will escort you home and fetch you a Doctor." I led her forward, towards the ring of viragoes surrounding us. They did not budge.

"Let us pass," I said, as Mdlle. Théroigne clung to me, shuddering. "You have no right to hinder the movements of a Representative of the People."

"You may go wheresoever you like, Citizen Deputy," the biggest of the women told me, thrusting out her chin and folding well-muscled arms, "but the *salope* is ours and we're not done teaching her a lesson." The others nodded, muttering.

"D__n you," I snapped, "stand aside!"

"She's *ours*, Citizen," growled another. "We'll show her who's about to lick the dust, we or a Brissotine whore!"

I opened my mouth for a sharp retort but was forestalled by a harsh, high-pitched voice behind me, one I recognised all too well from the Convention. "Having a little trouble with the honest market-women, are you, Citizen?" it enquired. "What a pity the citizenesses of Paris don't always give their Representatives the respect they deserve."

I knew not whether to be thankful or appalled. "Marat," said I, giving him the briefest of nods. "For God's sake, call off your dogs."

"My dogs, Citizen Carton? The People are not *mine*."

Marat, tho' he was nominally one of the Mountain, claimed that he belonged to no party but that of the People—*the People* generally meaning the rabble. Irascible and insolent, he appeared to hate his own fellow Montagnard Deputies scarce less ferociously than he hated his royalist and Girondin foes.

"Then prove you are the People's Friend as you claim, Citizen," I told him, "and discover if they will take heed of you. These *honest citizenesses* of yours have brutally attacked this woman. She has suffered enough."

He sauntered through the crowd, the awe-struck market-women giving way before him. As he approached me I smelt the reek of sour sweat from the tattered and stained old dressing-gown that served him as a coat. (Camille once told me that Marat, years since, had been a perfectly respectable, conventional Physician. In 1791, however, he had contracted the hideous affliction of the skin that plagued him, and had assumed his squalid costume in keeping with the rôle he had adopted of radical Journalist and Friend of the People.)

"Who's this?" he demanded. His breath was foul and the scabs and suppurating sores that blotched his countenance were enough to turn my stomach.

"Citizeness Théroigne," said I.

"Théroigne?" he snorted. "Hah. I imagine there is no love lost between us. Still . . ." He turned to the women, planting his fists on his hips. "Enough, you old Gorgons. Let her alone."

"She's one of Brissot's mob!" a woman screeched.

"This poor used-up trollop?" said he, with a glance at the trembling creature beside me. "She's harmless, Citizenesses. Go back to your herrings ere somebody whips *your* arses."

"Long live Marat!" cried somebody. In a moment they were flocking about him, fighting to touch him, though nothing in life could have induced me to touch his filthy rags or that pustular flesh. I profited from the moment to hurry my charge away, though not ere Marat had broken away from his worshippers to glare at us.

"Citizeness, it's because you fight just as courageously for the rights of Woman as you do for those posturing fools of Brissotins that you are escaping with your life to-day. Confine your trouble-making in future to female enfranchisement, and keep out of the Convention." He darted a belligerent glance at me as he said these words, ere returning to the adoring fishwives.

I hurried Mdlle. Théroigne to her lodging on rue St-Honoré and remained with her until a Physician arrived to tend to her cuts and bruises and set her broken nose. Leaving her in capable hands, I resumed my interrupted journey to the Tuileries.

I could not forget the veiled threat Marat had cast my way, a threat surely meant for Eléonore. He, unlike many others, held no grudge towards Bluestockings merely because they were women meddling in a man's world. He hated the Girondins, nevertheless, and those Journalists who favoured them, with a virulence that boded ill should he and his rabble choose to make use of the raw power they represented. As a witness to the disorderly, intemperate scenes between Mountain and Gironde, more suitable to a nursery or a bear-pit than a Parliament, that played themselves out almost daily now in the Convention, I feared such a moment would not be long in arriving.

ON THE 2ND of June, the stalemate at last cracked. The *sans-culottes*, the working-men of the Parisian Sections, Marat leading them, formed a vast mob about the Tuileries. At its centre was a small army of National Guard with cannon, and their new commander, that sottish bully Hanriot. Pushing their way inside, a number of them bawled their demands at Hérault-Séchelles, who was President of the Convetion that day.

I exchanged glances with Eléonore, a few yards behind and above me in the spectators' gallery, which was rapidly filling with drunken, scowling *sans-culottes* and the reek of onions and cheap brandy. She had gone very pale but she made no attempt to quit the chamber. Two or three hundred armed men at least were milling amongst us, and eighty thousand, or so the newspapers claimed the next day, outside in the streets. What could we have done?

Hérault perhaps felt himself secure knowing that, despite his aristocratic birth, by his sympathies he had long proven himself an ardent Montagnard. Leading a hundred nervous Deputies outside to meet the besiegers, he calmly requested the right of way from the chamber. Hanriot and Marat demanded, in the name of the People, the expulsion of twenty-nine leading Girondins; receiving an affronted refusal (for Hérault was undeniably courageous enough to defend the Government's rights against the mob's drunken *fiat*), Hanriot ordered the cannon aimed at the doors. Within half an hour the Deputies were within the chamber once again, unable to quit the perimeter of the Palace, sweating with fear and humiliation.

Couthon, Robespierre's ally, in the strained silence suggested that since all the good People wished was the purging of villains from the heart of the Nation's Government, the Deputies ought to read the indictment against the said villains. The motion passed; I voted with the rest, for I saw no other choice.

Marat, whose day it truly was, contemptuously read out the names. Brissot, without doubt. Vergniaud, without doubt. Lanjuinais, Gorsas, Guadet. Buzot, Barbaroux, Gensonné, Viger, Salle . . . They were decreed under house-arrest, and roughly shepherded away by the triumphant *sans-culottes.*

Marat yet held the Convention in his grip. He continued to denounce the Girondins and all their partisans, particularly *those scoundrels of counter-revolutionary Journalists,* he insisted, who poisoned the minds of the honest People. At length he flung out an arm and, with a fearsome grin, pointed straight at Eléonore. "At least one of these conspirators is here amongst us!" he snarled. "A woman no less meddlesome and dangerous than Roland's wife: I refer to that bitch Ambert, sitting brazenly in the gallery!"

A chorus of hisses and cat-calls swelled as Eléonore rose. Alarmed, I promptly sprang to my feet as well. "Citizen," I snapped, "if you have any material accusations to make against Citizeness Ambert, I demand you make them here and now."

He glowered at me from the tribune, his yellow, pock-marked visage twitching grotesquely. "Is this fellow, who shares her dainty feather-bed," he demanded scornfully of the chamber, "the only defender the Brissotine bitch can rally?"

"Citizen C-Carton is an irreproachable p-patriot," cried Camille in the silence. "I ask everyone p-present if he is not one of the purest amongst us!"

I heard muttered assent. "My patriotism is not in question here," I declared. "And surely neither is that of Citizeness Ambert."

"I can speak for myself, Citizens," said Eléonore, her clear voice echoing in the high chamber. "Read all the numbers of *Le Flambeau* from the three years past, if you doubt my devotion to the Revolution."

"And the numbers of the year past that proclaim your devotion to Brissot!" returned Marat.

"Citizeness Ambert severed her ties with Brissot and his colleagues six weeks since," I interjected. I quitted my seat and descended to the floor, to confront the ranks of Deputies. "Citizens, this is an Inquisition, directed against a courageous citizeness whose fidelity to the Nation should be beyond question!"

"Six . . . weeks?" Marat echoed me, his voice dripping contempt. "Is six weeks enough, then, to wash away all traces of Girondin contamination from those delicate white Aristocrat's hands?"

An ugly murmur arose from the gallery and those *sans-culottes* crowding nearest Eléonore seemed to press in about her, though she did not flinch. "You may think what you like, Marat, but keep your opinions to yourself," I returned, my anger disguising the stabbing fear I felt for Eléonore's safety. "Have you nothing better to do in this hall than spew accusations against women?"

"I doubt the good faith of women who are the daughters of Aristocrats," jeered Marat, "and the wives and sisters of *émigrés.*"

"Citizen," snapped Eléonore, "one of my brothers may have fled France, but the other died for the Nation on the Tenth of August. And the very fact that I am here to-day, rather than with my former husband in Coblentz or wheresoever he may be, should be sufficient proof of my loyalties. It's a matter of public record that I divorced the former Vicomte de Clairville nine months ago, precisely because he had emigrated."

I heard a few shouts of "Sit down!" and "Trollop!" and "Meddlesome bitch!" from the gallery. With the image of Mdme. Roland (whose smug intolerance had assuredly contributed to the Girondins' downfall) fresh in their minds, the *sans-culottes* had no love for Bluestockings who would not keep to their place. Abruptly a desperate solution to our predicament sprang to my mind fully formed and I seized it like a shipwrecked sailor grasping at the remains of his vessel.

"Citizens!" I cried, turning about and addressing the chamber and the galleries once again. "A moment ago, Citizens, you expressed your confi-

dence in my patriotism. For my part, I cannot better express my own confidence in Citizeness Ambert's unimpeachable patriotism . . . than to tell
this Assembly that a week ago I asked her to grant me her hand in marriage,
and was accepted."

To my astonishment, the gallery erupted in wild applause. Denied his
support, Marat attempted one final thrust.

"All this talk of patriotism from a foreigner," he sneered. "Has anybody
here forgotten that Citizen Carton is no more than a mongrel Frenchman?"

"Speak for yourself, Marat," I told him, for he, half Sardinian and half
Swiss, was no Frenchman at all save by virtue of many years' residence. A
titter arose from the Deputies' seats. Flushing a savage brick-red, he
stormed down from the tribune.

"From to-day," he hissed in passing me, "you have an enemy, mongrel."

I turned away as the stink from his filthy clothes assailed me and silently returned to my seat. Around me the chamber dissolved into delirious
relief after the day's frightful tensions. My countenance carefully tranquil,
I nodded as Camille slapped me on the back, congratulating me, and wondered with an uneasy heart how I might brave Eléonore.

17

THE INTERMINABLE SESSION closed. I climbed to the gallery and placed Eléonore's arm in mine ere she could speak a word. Together, brittle smiles on our faces, we walked arm in arm out of the Palace, enduring hand-clasps and congratulations. When at last we were well away amidst the tangle of narrow streets betwixt the Tuileries and the Louvre, safe amongst the oblivious, excited passers-by, she turned upon me, her colour high and her eyes glittering in anger.

"You—you—*salopard!*"

Without further warning she drew back and, with all her might, slapped me across the face. *"Gredin! Scélérat—"*

"My God, what is the matter with you?" I gasped, seizing her wrist as she was about to slap me again. "Calm yourself, for Heaven's sake."

"You do this to me," she hissed, "and you expect me to *calm* myself?"

"What have I done? I meant only to protect you. What would you have done in my place?"

"Anything but *that!*"

"I had no choice."

"Of course you had a choice! You might have suffered me to fight my own battles!"

"You were in peril—I wished only to help you—"

"By wedding me? Did you conclude, then, that you could drag me into your bed no other way?"

"I never—" I began, astonished, but she plunged onward, deaf to my protestations.

"Don't imagine I've not seen how you've eyed me of late! You had your taste of me once—have you now, after four years, decided you wish more?

214

Or is it merely that I'm more likely to be free of disease than the whores at the Palais-Royal?"

"You insult us both by such a suggestion! How could you imagine I meant more than a marriage in name only? I had no thought whatsoever of luring you into my bed, only of your safety."

"Didn't you?"

"Of course not!"

"Did you not tell me once that every woman you cared for had, in time, spurned you? Your fiancée, and your precious Lucie, and God knows how many others? And here before you is a woman who also has refused you, upon more than one occasion: a woman who you think cannot now refuse you, for fear of her life!" She drew breath and continued ere I could stammer out some lame demurral. "Well, I'll be d__ned first! Algernon Sydney Carton, you may go post-haste to the Devil, for I'd rather be dragged before the Tribunal than meekly play your game!"

She whirled about, her light muslin skirts whipping at her ankles, and stormed away down rue St-Thomas-du-Louvre. Stunned, I stared at her retreating back and attempted to set my chaotic thoughts in order. Perhaps, I realised, her reproaches held some truth. I could not deny that I found her desirable, or that my manœuvres, extemporaneous as they had been, might have been inspired by some covert motive. Yet how could I desire Eléonore without acknowledging to myself that my passions must be more than carnal? And how could I love another without breaking faith with my love for Lucie?

"O, God's death," I whispered, and set off in pursuit of her. She snatched her arm away as I touched her wrist, and continued walking at a furious pace towards the Seine. I seized her arm again and she twisted about to glare at me.

"Let me go, d__n you, or I'll scream for the nearest constable. Don't you touch me!"

"Eléonore," I implored her, "will you not listen a moment? I am heartily sorry if I caused you grief. Truly I meant no insult to you. But do you yet realise the danger that threatened you?"

She tossed her head. "Bah—of course it was a troubling moment—"

"Troubling moment!" I snapped, my nerves wearing thin. "You might have been arrested then and there. Or, failing that, those *sans-culottes* might very well have beaten you cruelly, perhaps killed you. Do you not remember what befell Mdlle. Théroigne? I saw what they did to that poor creature ere Marat persuaded them to let her alone. But I doubt Marat would be as generous towards you."

"You cannot be serious."

"I am perfectly serious!" I clasped her hands in my own and drew her nearer me. "I feared very much for your safety, and it was the only solution I could conceive in the few moments given me. What better way for an ex-Aristocrat to prove herself a good citizen than to wed a mere *bourgeois?* And the thought of a wedding immediately touched their emotions in the gallery. One must never forget that these folk are often as heedless and sentimental as children." I gave way to a wry smile, adding: "A marriage of convenience, Eléonore, I promise you—a subterfuge only. Will it make so much difference in our manner of living, after all? You and I have spent so much time in each other's company that we may as well have dwelt in the same apartment for the two years past. And you know full well that everybody has long believed us to be lovers."

She scowled at me a long moment. At last, with a brusque nod, she looked away. "Yes—very well. What difference will it make, as you say."

"There is peace between us?"

"Yes."

"And you will wed me?"

"Yes. I haven't a choice, have I," she added.

I offered her my arm. Silently she accepted it and we proceeded sedately towards the Pont-Neuf.

"I shall have to give up my own rooms and remove into yours, for the sake of appearances," I told her.

"If we are to maintain this masquerade," said she, without looking at me, "then we ought to share our bed-chamber. For the sake of appearances. None but lords and ladies in châteaux have separate bed-chambers."

"Agreed."

"But separate beds."

"Of course."

"What a d__ned silly farce it will be!"

"My friend," said I, pausing and turning her face towards my own, "I am sorry for this, truly, but your safety meant more to me than any thing else. You know how dear you are to me. Do you think I would have placed you in such awkward circumstances on a mere whim?"

Her countenance softened by a fraction. "No . . . I ought not to be ungrateful."

"Were it not for you," I told her, "I might be copying letters in an attic for my living, not representing Paris in the National Convention. I owe you all I have achieved here, and I always strive to repay my debts. The least I can offer you is my protection, whatsoever its worth."

"Protection," she echoed me. "For years I have insisted that I needed no protection from anything. Perhaps I do. From my own self." She nodded, raising a hand to forestall me as I opened my mouth to speak. "I know what you are about to say. It would be prudent to cease publishing *Le Flambeau*. Would it not?"

"Yes," said I, regretfully. "Tho' I shall be sorry to see it disappear."

"So shall I. I never had any children," she added abruptly, a moment later. "I suppose *Le Flambeau* was the nearest thing I ever shall have to a child, that I nurtured to strength and vigour." She paused, with a burst of wry laughter. "What sentimental rubbish. Had I had children, like everybody else I would have been quite glad to pack them off to a wet-nurse, until they were sufficiently grown to be presentable. And now that *Le Flambeau* has out-lived its usefulness, and its purpose, I ought not to have any hesitation about sacrificing it as a liability. You needn't worry, Carton . . . you know that, in the end, I am relentlessly rational."

I WEDDED ELÉONORE on the 13th of June. It was a civil marriage, of course, performed by an official at the Hôtel de Ville as was now required by Law. For the sake of appearances, we invited a few friends to a simple wedding supper. Robespierre seemed stiffer and more abstracted than in previous months, yet he was frigidly polite as ever, even to Eléonore, whom he had never liked. Camille and the vivacious Lucile were as cheerful and boisterous as I expected, drinking too much Champagne and making jokes of questionable taste.

When the last guest had quitted us, Eléonore seized a three-quarters-empty Champagne-bottle from the dining-table and dropt onto the sofa. "Well!"

"Well?" said I, joining her. Her cheeks were flushed and her manner a trifle giddy; I suspected she had drunk more wine than was her custom.

"I feel no different."

"Ought you to?"

"When I wedded Clairville, I was dizzy with excitement, and terrified, all at once." She poured herself out a glass of flat Champagne and gulped it down.

"You were sixteen years old."

"Yes, I was sixteen and he twenty-seven . . . and I had the misfortune to fall in love with him. I realise now it was but a schoolgirl passion, of course—but it was my first, and I felt it so very deeply, as girls do. He was handsome and dashing, with all a gentleman's accomplishments, like a Prince in a fairy-tale. They might as easily have married me to some nasty middle-aged creature with disgusting habits and desires! And Clairville was kind enough, and never denied me anything, and came to my bed once every week as a gentleman should, but there was no love in it, none at all."

She up-ended the bottle, found it empty, and seized the nearest half-drunk wine-glass to drink down its contents ere continuing. "I was wretchedly unhappy for two years at least, until I compelled myself to admit that he had kept company with the same mistress for half a dozen years already. I ought to have no illusions, I told myself, that he was in love with me—no matter how I might delude myself into believing that every chance word, every careless gesture, every moment spent in my presence rather than in hers, meant at last he was beginning to love me and not her."

"Such wounds never quite close, do they?" I murmured.

"No, not completely."

"But you are no longer sixteen, my friend," I said drily, hoping to distract her from hurtful memories. "Why should you feel different by having wedded me? Nothing between us has changed."

She looked at me a moment, unsmiling. At last she reached out and put her hand on mine, her warm fingers curling gently into my palm. "Thank you, Carton. For being my friend."

We remained there on the sofa for a while as the shadows outside deepened into night, without speaking, together yet apart, as ever. Her hand lay lightly in mine still, her fingers scarce brushing it. Despite my reassurances to Eléonore that nothing had changed, I was conscious in myself of old emotions stirring, affections long-buried and disregarded. Could it be, I thought, that I was capable still, despite all constraints to the contrary, of loving her?

"Well," said Eléonore, at length, as I wrenched my thoughts back from their distant questing flight, "I am going to bed. Good-night, Carton."

She squeezed my hand and quitted me, calling for Baptistine. I waited a discreet quarter-hour after Baptistine reappeared once more ere joining Eléonore in the bed-chamber. She had left a candle burning for me on the table beside the camp-bed we had installed, until the fine new bed we had ordered to match her own should be ready. The heavy plum-coloured velvet curtains on her own bed were pulled shut about her, dark and silent.

22 Floréal (11 May)

TO-DAY THEY judged Mdme. Elisabeth, the late King's sister, in order to complete their royal hand of cards. None but the little Dauphin, now titled by the Royalists Louis XVII (who, I fear, will never sit upon the throne of his ancestors), and his sister Marie-Thérèse remains of that unhappy family. Even the Committee of Public Safety, nevertheless, may shy at executing a child of eight and a helpless girl of fifteen. The Revolutionary Tribunal is not so barbaric as to condemn children. But it remains to be seen if some over-zealous Jacobin will devise a plan to do away with these *inconveniences* in a manner more discreet.

ALTHOUGH MARAT, AT that terrible session of the Second of June, had told me outright that we now were enemies, I never learnt if he would make good his threats, for precisely a month after I wedded Eléonore, he was dead.

I should think all the world knows the sensational circumstances of his death. The astounding tidings sped like lightning through Paris: he had been stabbed in his bath-tub by a young woman from the provinces, from the *département* of Calvados, who some declared was a Royalist, others a fervid adherent of the fallen Girondins. I heard this intelligence with equal measures of repugnance and relief.

The next day was the Fourteenth of July, the fourth anniversary of the

Bastille's fall and the occasion of the annual Fête at the Champ de Mars. When the ceremonies had concluded and I rejoined Eléonore in the spectators' stands, I found her oddly grave and preoccupied. She remained so thro' our journey home and, once we were arrived at rue St-André-des-Arts, paced restlessly about the *salon* until I was tempted to ask her if she had murdered Marat herself.

An hour later Baptistine announced Doulcet de Pontécoulant. Though we had been on cordial enough terms, we were not well acquainted, for he had sat with the Girondins and shortly ere their fall had discreetly departed the Convention. Eléonore intercepted him ere I could make a gesture and drew him into the parlour.

"*Is* it true?" she demanded. "A woman named Charlotte Corday murdered him?"

"Quite true," said he. "I felt I should warn you both." Clad in a nondescript suit of clothes and his bright hair hanging untidily about his face, he bore a hunted, uneasy look about him. "Altho' I see you have come already to the same conclusion as I," he added.

"Yes. Are you safe, Citizen? Do you need any assistance, money?"

"No, I'm safe enough. A friend is concealing me. The greatest service you can do me, Madame, Monsieur, is to forget you ever saw me to-day." He brushed his lips across her hand and hurried out. Without a word, Eléonore darted into her study and slammed the door behind her. A few minutes later I smelt the acrid tang of smoke and, disquieted, tapped at the door. Receiving no answer, I stept inside and found her crouched on the floor, a fire-pistol beside her, feeding papers into the little brazier that warmed the chamber during the Winter months.

"What on Earth do you do there?" I asked her, mystified at her behaviour.

"I am burning letters," said she, without a glance at me.

"I see that. What's the matter? What had Doulcet to tell us?"

"What I've suspected since this morning." She dropt another letter into the flames.

I knelt beside her and seized her arm. "Whose letters are these?"

"Do you remember Mdlle. d'Armont, whom you escorted about Caen one day?"

"Yes . . . the young apprentice nun who was so enthralled by the Revolution."

"She and I have exchanged some letters in the past."

"Call me a fool, then," I admitted, "but still I don't understand."

For answer, Eléonore thrust one of the letters at me. It was dated six months previous. Aside from a line or two that betrayed the writer's horror at the King's execution, it seemed a harmless, gossipy species of letter, of the kind that women are always exchanging. "If you mean she was a Royalist—" I began.

"Look at the signature, Carton."

I looked at the bottom of the page to find a name signed in bold strokes: *Marie de Corday.* "But her name is Armont," said I.

"Her name is Marie-Anne-Charlotte de Corday d'Armont."

"God's death . . ." That afternoon at the Champ de Mars I had heard the name on everybody's lips. How obtuse could I have been, that I had not remembered even in which of the new *départements* Caen now lay? "Charlotte Corday. The woman of Calvados."

"Who yesterday stabbed Marat through the heart with a kitchen-knife. The imbecile!" Eléonore snatched the letter from my hand and thrust it into the brazier. "What good has it done?" she demanded, continuing to feed the flames. "By killing him she has probably sealed the Girondins' fate. Hébert and the *enragés* will use this crack-brained murder as proof of a great conspiracy against the Convention. Even if there is nothing to find, they will find something, or pretend to. And anybody who has ever spoken with her, or written a letter to her, will be suspect."

"God's death," I repeated. "Did you know she was in Paris?"

"No, of course not. I've had no letters from her for above two months."

Since June, thought I. Many of the expelled Girondin Deputies had fled Paris after their overthrow and had made their way to centres of dis-affection in the provinces. Undoubtedly Mdlle. d'Armont had been enflamed by the Injustice dealt them, and her unswerving Idealism had demanded an act that she had naïvely believed would save France from Dictatorship.

"And you have written to her in the past?" I persisted.

"Yes." She threw the last of the letters into the flames and I saw her hands tremble.

"Let us hope she had the sense to burn her own letters ere travelling to Paris."

"Even if she did so, they will interrogate everyone who knew her in Caen. Perhaps Mdme. de Pontécoulant—anybody. They may very well hear my name, and even yours. They will not forget that Marat named you an enemy before the Convention, either. Folk have been sent to the Tribunal with less evidence."

"But it's preposterous. I met the girl four years ago and I've not thought of her since."

"So you say, Carton, so you say. How do you prove the negative? You can only deny, and deny, and perhaps they will believe you and perhaps not."

"At least it's common knowledge that I am no Girondin."

"Thank God for that." Abruptly she hid her face in her hands. "What am I saying? They are my friends. They are men I invited to my home. What kind of times are these, when we abandon our friends out of fear, without a second thought?"

"Eléonore," said I, "you can do nothing for them . . ."

"I can assume my share of responsibility for their faults, because God knows I had a hand in encouraging them . . . and I can stand by them."

"And what good will that do them?" I demanded. "If they are doomed, they are doomed. Your noble gesture will not change that in the least; it will only destroy you with them."

"Does that matter so much?" she cried. "I have nothing any more to live for. *Le Flambeau* is gone and the Revolution I dreamt of is a travesty—is becoming a den of cannibals eager to devour each other. My brother—my family—every soul whom ever I loved is long dead, or is fighting against France. A fortnight ago I saw them taking a childhood friend to the Guillotine—he had been captured fighting in the Prussian army. You yourself—I am but a danger to you. You ought never to have wedded me."

"Do you think I would have forsaken you?"

"You should have."

"Impossible."

"Why is that? You said yourself just now that since I could do nothing for my friends, I should avoid becoming entangled in their fall. Do you not heed your own advice?"

"I could never have stood aside when you were in danger," I insisted, "because I was terrified of losing you. Don't you understand, after so long? I need you, Léo."

"Need me?" she echoed me, uncomprehending.

I seized her by the shoulders and shook her, as if by that I could convince her of my urgency and sincerity. "Good God, woman, do you not realise how much I need your strength? You have the force and ardour, the zest for living that I have always lacked. You are my strength—my strength and my inspiration. I told you once before that I owed you everything I have achieved here. That is God's truth. Without you I would be nothing." I paused, suddenly knowing that I must say the words I had thought never to say again. "Eléonore . . . I love you."

She flinched as if I had struck her. "You love my cousin Charles's wife!"

"Yes," said I, "yes, I do. Yet should that mean I cannot love you?"

"O, I see—since you will never have your perfect Lucie, you have at last chosen to settle for the poor substitute that's within your reach?" She gasped as soon as she had said these words and burst into tears. "O God, Carton, I didn't mean that. It was hateful. I didn't mean it. But I am so—so poisoned by despair and fear and misery that I feel I will infect the very air around me, like a sickness . . ." Stumbling away, she sank onto a footstool and gave way to sobs.

Eléonore was not one to easily admit her fear of anything. Absurdly helpless, I knelt beside her. "I pray you—pray understand," I stammered. "Lucie is—she has become an Ideal to me. I don't believe I could now bring myself to regard her simply as a woman, to be courted and wed and bedded, even were she not married to Darnay. It would be . . . blasphemous, almost. You, though, you are here beside me, and living and breathing, flesh and blood, and surely the most courageous and extraordinary woman in Paris." I pulled out my handkerchief and dabbed at her tear-streaked face with it, feverishly speaking still. "I know you have never loved me, Léo, not as a lover, but I beg you to understand that my love for you is—is a thing different and apart from my attachment to Lucie. I don't—would never consider you merely a surrogate for her."

"Look at the pair of us," she gasped thro' her tears. "You tell me this as if it's a confession wrung from you by torture. You and I both have been so ill-used by love that we no longer dare suffer ourselves to seize it when it comes to us. And in times like these," she added bitterly, "love seems a very trivial matter."

"Do you think so?" said I. "But what if . . . what if love is all we have left to find hope in, and to cling to?"

She said nothing for a long while as she stared into the blackened curls of ash in the brazier, tears sliding down her cheeks. At length, wordless, she blindly reached out and all at once she flung herself into my arms, clutching me with a fierce grip.

"I do love you," she sobbed. "Since the moment I told you I didn't wish us to be lovers. The instant I said it I knew I was wrong, but I was too proud. And Julien had been dead but a month—I would have betrayed his memory." She drew a deep shuddering breath. "I have been deceiving myself for years. I thought I could be content in having you nearby. I told myself I was, and I believed it for a time. And then you told me of Lucie and I knew you didn't desire me, or desired me only in your bed."

I silently held her, imagining her humiliation when she found herself with no choice but to accept another marriage with one who would not return her love. "Forgive me," I murmured.

"If you will forgive me."

I kissed her mouth, lightly and gently, and then again, more slowly, and once again, burying both my hands in her luxuriant hair, and found I was trembling. *"Tecum vivere amem,"* I murmured, *"tecum obeam libens."*

"I . . . I've forgotten much of my Latin . . ."

"With you I should love to live," said I, without completing the verse, and bent to kiss her again ere enfolding her in my embrace. She returned my kisses and began to fumble with my cravat and the buttons to my waistcoat. Rising, I pulled her to her feet and swung her into my arms. "I think," I told her, as I carried her out the door, "we may cancel our order with the upholsterer."

Eléonore suddenly smiled, blinking back the tears that yet glistened in her eyes. "Never mind," said she, with a soft laugh. "The bed's not yet paid for."

QUITE SOME TIME later, as we nestled together in Eléonore's big bed festooned with smirking gilded cherubs, I drew her hand to my lips, kissing the tips of her fine slim fingers. She sighed and huddled nearer me. "O, Carton . . . we cannot hide here from the world forever. Nothing can change the fact of Marat's murder."

"I think, truly, we are quite safe," I assured her, clasping her in my arms. "We have friends, and Danton has far too much sense to believe any foolish rumours about us. He'd not suffer us to be placed in danger."

"Danton?" said she, with a short bitter laugh. "Danton has no more power to-day than do you."

I remembered belatedly that Danton had been voted out of the Committee of Public Safety (that until then had been nick-named *the*

Danton Committee) four days previous. "He will always be the Man of August Tenth," I insisted. "He has great influence still."

"It's Robespierre who is in the ascendant, Carton—we must admit it. And I do not think he will ever forgive me for laughing at him."

I rolled to my side and kissed her once again ere replying. "I am a member of the Convention, my love, and no one would dare touch either of us."

"The Girondins—"

"I sit with the Mountain. Robespierre and Danton and I are all comrades. Why should they wish to attack us? And so long as I am safe, you are safe."

"Yes," she murmured, though she sounded unconvinced.

18

WE LIVED IN a state of what I can perhaps best describe as desperate happiness for some two months. *Forbear to ask what to-morrow's dawn may bring, Horace tells us, and count as profit every day that Fate allots you.* Beyond rue St-André-des-Arts the Revolution continued to flounder on; within the sheltering walls of our apartment we attempted to forget it.

A dreadful fascination drove me towards the place de la Révolution four days after Marat's death, to see his murderess brought to Justice. In these dismal days as I write this chronicle, we have become cruelly accustomed to the sight of three or four of Sanson's carts, or sometimes more, every day wending their dreary way towards the square and the scaffold. In July of '93, however, even a single victim—forger, deserter, luckless General, *émigré* captured fighting for the Enemy—was novelty enough still to provoke curiosity, and a fresh young girl clad in the red smock of a murderer was a sight not to be missed.

She was as serene and comely as I remembered her, though the Executioner had cut short her thick chestnut hair, baring her neck for the blade. *Poor noble Marie-Anne-Charlotte de Corday d'Armont, I thought, you will go to your death sadly deluded, believing you have destroyed the Mountain and saved the Girondins with one thrust of a kitchen-knife. And in truth you have done the opposite. I hope that when you and your doomed Idols meet once more in whatsoever world it is that lies beyond this one, they will not reproach you for their deaths.* I slowly walked the long route home, wondering if that great-hearted, misguided young woman had indeed sealed our own death-warrants.

THO' I DID not speak my doubts to Eléonore, since the Second of June I had begun to have misgivings about the road the Convention had taken. On

228

28th July, after Saint-Just's ringing denunciation of the Girondins, it decreed Outlawed those Deputies who had fled to the provinces. I voted with the Mountain, though my conscience rebelled. Outlawry is a swift and sure death-sentence, for one labouring beneath it may be executed with no other trial than a brief identification. I feared such a decree would set a terrible precedent.

When, in mid-September, the Committee of Public Safety proposed the Law of Suspects, I knew I could no longer vote blindly with the Mountain and preserve any traces of my self-respect. A law that branded Suspect all those who did not actively support the Revolution, though they might never have resisted it, seemed to me the first step towards Tyranny.

"But it's an emergency measure," protested Camille, when I voiced my doubts to him as we walked together that afternoon towards the Left Bank. "We are at war, C-Carton—we must beware of spies and c-counter-revolu-tionaries. Of c-course a law like that would never be p-passed in peace-time."

"There is no reason such a law should be passed at all," returned I. "We are no longer threatened by foreign armies. The war is once more on the Enemy's soil."

"The uprising in La Vendée—"

"Will never be more than a revolt of peasants too ignorant to realise that half the Nobles and priests who lead them are merely seeking a return to Absolutism. France does not love the rule of the Committees, I agree. But it will never return to the old *régime*, and the Vendéans will never re-take France."

"The law is necessary," said he, obstinate.

"I intend to vote against it."

He paused and stared at me as the warm breeze whipped at his lank black hair. "You c-can't . . . you are one of us. You have always voted with us."

"Have I not the right to vote my own conscience? Camille, I'll no longer peddle my honour to the highest bidder in return for my security. If I con-tinue docilely to vote as everyone else about me does, then I will be no bet-ter than the Marsh-toads, who don't dare croak for fear of their lives and who always vote with the majority." The Mountain, derisively, had long termed the silent, biddable centre of the Convention *the Marsh* or *the Plain*. "Is that what you would prefer, Camille, that I prostitute my conscience, that I go and join the toads?"

"We should stand united," he muttered.

"We *are* united. You know I will stand with you on most matters. But this law should not be passed. Why are we oppressing the People for whose benefit we proclaimed the Republic?"

"For the man who is just and firm of purpose, neither the heated passions of his fellows ordaining something dreadful," said he at last, *"nor the countenance of the threatening Tyrant before his very eyes will shake him from his stern resolve."*

"Horace," said I. "The *Odes*."

"Yes." He said nothing more and we continued silently towards the Seine.

THE CONVENTION DECREED the Law of Suspects on 17th September, as I knew it would. Eléonore, who had shared my opinion of the proposed law, nevertheless was of two minds about the vote.

"How did you vote, in the end?" she asked me when I arrived home that night.

"Against."

"And the others?"

"How do you think?"

"The law passed." She sighed and leant on the back of a chair, turning her gaze from me. "Carton . . . perhaps you ought to have voted with the rest."

"I couldn't have," I told her, slipping my arms about her waist. "Not after the Second of June, and the outlawing of the Girondins . . . I simply could not have done it again."

"I understand that. The thought of such a law terrifies me. It's as bad as *lettres de cachet*, as any abuse that ever we had in the old *régime*. But did you pause to think," she continued, "that by voting against this law, you may very well cast yourself as a Suspected person, under its terms?"

"I considered it, but I think it unlikely. Deputies are immune from arrest, and my prior record in the Convention speaks for itself. It will take more than one dissenting vote to cast any suspicion upon me."

"Deputies are *not* immune, not if the Convention passes an indictment against them."

"Léo, Léo, my love," I assured her, kissing her, "I am quite safe. You worry too much."

"No more than you have worried for me."

"O my love," I sighed. I pulled her closer, to brush my lips across her hair. *"Tecum vivere amem . . ."*

"I have remembered the rest of that verse," said she, jerking herself away to gaze up at me, her eyes grave. *"With you I should love to live, with you be ready to die.* Has it come to that, Carton? Has it?"

LATE ONE EVENING perhaps a fortnight afterward, as we sipped our coffee around the dying fire, Baptistine told us that Citizen Saint-Just himself had come to call on me.

"Saint-Just?" said I. "What can he want of me?" I had scarce spoken with him since June, when he had been elected to the Committee of Public Safety. Robespierre had been elected a month later, and the two were wellnigh inseparable.

"Ought I let him in?"

"Yes, of course." A moment later she ushered in our unexpected guest and I gestured him to a chair. "Citizen? To what do we owe this visit?"

"I have a proposal to make you, Carton," said Saint-Just, after accepting the cup Eléonore silently offered him. He sipped cautiously at it, his austere mien abruptly softening. "Real coffee . . . where do you find it these days? My servant can't get me any for love or money."

"Our domestic is a woman of great determination," said Eléonore, calmly. "But surely you didn't visit us to learn whether we were illicitly hoarding coffee."

"No." He set the cup down and fixed me with his unwavering, icy-grey gaze. "You do know, I hope, that I like you, Carton."

"I am flattered." Had I returned the compliment and told him that I liked him, I would have lied, but neither did I bear him any particular ill will.

"I do like you," he repeated, "and I respect you, as does Robespierre. You are a man of unwavering integrity, and there are few enough of us in the Convention. In fact, Robespierre has told me more often than once that, were it not for some insurmountable obstacles, he would have nominated you for one of the Committees."

I inclined my head. "I thank you, and Citizen Robespierre, for your good opinion of me."

"Unhappily, as I said, there are obstacles. You are English."

"That's no secret, Citizen."

He gave me one of his rare smiles, which for an instant illuminated his girlish features and revealed the pensive young man beneath the mask of the Zealot. "Certainly not. But I must tell you in strict confidence that the Committee will soon present a decree for the Convention to ratify, which concerns English subjects in France. All English subjects who are not residents of long standing are to be detained."

"Arrested, you mean," Eléonore interrupted him.

"Merely detained, Citizeness, not judged. We are, after all, at war with England. They will be in no danger unless they prove to be spies or criminals."

"Am I to be 'detained', then?" said I.

He raised a slim hand, shaking his head. "No, no, no, no, certainly not. You have dwelt in France for years, you are part French, and your patriotism is indisputable." He paused, took a swallow of coffee, and sighed. "But when our decree regarding British subjects is voted into Law—"

"You are very sure the Convention will approve it," remarked Eléonore. "Perhaps it will not?"

"The Convention has reposed its confidence in the Committee. It does not often refuse us its approval."

I studied his fine, arrogant countenance a moment. Forestalling Eléonore, I asked him quietly: "What have you come to tell me, Citizen?"

"Robespierre and I agree in believing that once British subjects are ordered under arrest, your position in the Convention may become precarious. Out of our regard for you, therefore, we thought it right to apprise you of the situation, and provide you the chance to resign your seat in time, should you wish to."

"Resign!" exclaimed Eléonore. "Ere you have him expelled like the Girondins?"

"Citizen Carton may have enemies in the Government, Citizeness, but Robespierre and I are not amongst them. Carton, I am here because of our esteem for you, not because of any antagonism. Believe me when I tell you it's not the Committee that's your enemy. The *enragés*, however, see an adversary in any man who does not vote faithfully with the Mountain—and they have not forgotten your quarrel with Marat. A lunatic like Hébert might even concoct some preposterous phantasy of revenge that would link your name with Charlotte Corday's, merely because you and Marat traded insults on the Second of June."

I could not forbear from glancing lightning-quick at Eléonore. She sat as if petrified, her face a pale mask that betrayed nothing. "And should I resign," I enquired, "should I return to private life and not meddle in your Politics . . ."

"Then we will use whatsoever influence we enjoy to ensure that you live undisturbed. I assure you, this is not a threat—merely a proposal for your own safety."

"A proposal that conveniently rids the Mountain of a dissenting voice," said Eléonore. "If my husband resigns from the Convention, he will no longer have a Deputy's immunity from arrest. I suppose you have considered that, too?"

"If Citizen Carton resigns, his enemies will no longer have any motive to wish him ill," came the calm reply.

I gazed at him, weighing his words. Certainly all I knew thus far of Saint-Just bespoke a steely integrity. He had undoubtedly told me the truth, whether or not he had neglected to admit the advantage to the Committee that Eléonore had so bluntly stated. "Suffer me to consider it."

"My dear Carton, you need not report to us for our approval. You may resign or not as you wish, and give any pretext you like." He drank down the last of the coffee. "I do envy you your cook, and her talents in finding supplies. It's late—I'll not disturb her. I can let myself out."

"I will let you out," said I, accompanying him, for I thought he might have some thing else to say to me alone.

He did. Gesturing me out to the landing, he shut the door behind us and stept close to me. "Carton," he said softly, his handsome countenance scarce visible in the gloom, "I didn't wish to distress your wife, but if anybody is in grave danger, it's she rather than you. Hébert will never forgive her for espousing the Girondins, or for the number of times she ridiculed him in *Le Flambeau*. He and the *enragés* at the Hôtel de Ville gain influence by the day, as well you know. Add to that all the circumstances that she cannot help: her birth, her *émigré* husband and brother, Marat's hatred of her . . . do you follow me?"

"But hers was one of the first journals to champion the Revolution in 'eighty-nine. And her younger brother died attacking the Tuileries on the Tenth of August. Surely that must count in her favour."

"Does it?" He shrugged. "These days, any black mark against one of the Suspected will be seized upon and dwelt upon until it's grown to monstrous size, whilst the other side of the balance-sheet is often ignored. It's an unpleasant truth, and one that many of us would do away with if we could, but . . . there it is."

"If I give up my seat in the Convention," said I, "they can no longer accuse my wife of exerting her corrupting influence upon a Representative of the People. What else do you suggest we do?"

"I don't know that the two of you can do anything. Quit Paris, perhaps, and bury yourselves in the country. Are your travelling papers all in order, and your identity papers, and your cards of good citizenship—yours and your wife's both?"

"Travelling papers . . . it's years since either of us has ventured farther from Paris than perhaps a Sunday holiday at Fontenay or Bourg-la-Reine— forgive me, Bourg-la-République."

"You will find it more inconvenient to travel now, I suspect, than ever it was before the Revolution. Your papers will need to be impeccable— hers in particular—should you attempt to quit the city for the provinces. If they are not, come to me: perhaps in some small way I can help you, tho' I can promise you nothing. We can bring little influence to bear over the municipality in such mundane matters, and I fear Citizeness Carton has many enemies at the Hôtel de Ville." He paused, sighed, and continued. "Your wife's presence, despite your best precautions, may prove a great danger to you. She is a mill-stone about your neck, and the greatest favour you can do yourself is to distance yourself from her. Divorce her."

"That is unthinkable," I snapped. "I could not possibly abandon her."

He sighed. "I will do for you what I can. Good-night, Carton." He turned away and hurried down the stair. Reflecting on all Saint-Just had given me to ponder, I remained there, leaning on the stair-rail, gazing into the shadows.

"WHAT SHALL YOU do?" Eléonore asked me when, at length, I returned to our bed-chamber and began to undress.

"I think I must heed his advice," I admitted.

"You may be leaving yourself open to all kinds of dangers."

"Yet Saint-Just is perfectly correct in saying that if I return to private life, no one will trouble himself about me. And if this detention of English subjects does become Law, I shall have little choice in the matter. Resign now or be expelled in a few weeks' time, undoubtedly in the midst of an ugly dispute that would call far too much attention to both me and you." I blew out the candle and slid beneath the bed-covers as Eléonore wriggled against me, laying her head on my shoulder. "I must confess it's a relief. I shall welcome not having to vote with the Mountain's whimsy, and not feeling Robespierre's eyes on the back of my head."

"But he likes you."

"Only for so long as he thinks I will follow his lead." I kissed her brow and smiled in the darkness. "O yes, my love, it will be a relief to represent the People no longer."

"What will we live on?" she murmured.

"I am well-versed still in French Law. I shall find work with some Advocate or other."

Eléonore did not answer me, though she heaved a deep sigh and nestled closer to me. Neither of us spoke, but a long time passed ere we fell asleep that night.

I DETERMINED TO concoct some plausible explanation and resign my seat in the Convention within a fortnight of Saint-Just's visit. Reluctantly, I began also to ponder how Eléonore and I might best quit Paris for the countryside without attracting undue attention upon ourselves. Circumstance, however, forestalled me.

I can scarce bear to set down what I must now write, for it is shameful to think how quick we ever are to believe the worst of folk and to play the part of the fool—and how quick we may fall from rectitude to degradation. And when one such as I has succeeded at last in struggling from the pit of Despond, it is doubly degrading to feel oneself slipping helplessly back towards its dark depths.

I thought little of it when, two days afterward, Eléonore returned to the house much later than was her custom, with no explanation. In the course of our usual conversation I asked her whither she had gone that day, but she was uncharacteristically evasive. "Walking," said she, with a shrug. "To the Palais-Royal. The Palais-Egalité, rather."

"I hope you restrained your extravagance," I told her, my smile belying my severe tone. "Soon we shan't have my Deputy's pay to live on, you know."

"I bought only half a dozen handkerchiefs. I needed handkerchiefs."

I laughed. "I think we can surely afford a few handkerchiefs."

She did not answer me. When, a few moments later, in curiosity I looked away from my desk, where I was composing my letter of resignation to the Convention, she was gone. I heard her moving about in her boudoir and returned to my writing, baffled but untroubled by her brusque manner.

The next afternoon—O God, how I loathe writing this!—I returned from the Convention during the dinner-recess to find Eléonore awaiting me in the parlour, rather than fussing affably with Baptistine betwixt the kitchen and our little dining-table as was her recent custom. She was sitting in the centre of the sofa, her hands folded in her lap and her back very straight.

"What's this?" said I, reaching for her. "Are we not dining? Has Baptistine fallen down-stairs, or drowned in the soup-kettle?"

"No," said she, without offering me her hands, "we are not dining. I do not think you will wish to dine with me in future."

"Léo, what on Earth are you saying?"

She rose to face me, pale and expressionless as a statue of a Saint on the cathedral's portal. "I am leaving you."

I stared at her. "I don't understand. What is this, a joke? Who thought it might be funny? Camille?"

"It's not a joke. I had a lover long ere I wedded you—"

"Fleutry—" I began.

"After Julien," she interrupted me. "You of all folk should know that I did not sleep alone every night since Julien's death. I was . . . a certain person's mistress once. He wishes me to come back to him."

"You—when?" I stammered. I had known nothing, seen nothing, nothing at all.

"Our *liaison* ended ere I wedded you. I never deceived you, Carton."

"Until to-day." I found I could scarce breathe.

"I don't know anything else I can do. You and I both know that I have been treading a fine line for the six months past. You will comprehend my motives for seeking protection from one who is better able to provide it than you."

I blindly felt for a chair and grasped at it, sudden nausea clawing at my belly. "Who?"

"Does it matter?"

"*Who?*"

"An influential member of the Convention."

"Hérault," said I, remembering how often during the two years past had that handsome, polished philanderer cast a lingering gaze towards Eléonore, how often he had trifled with her, touched her. Hérault, who was a friend of Danton and who now sat on the all-powerful Committee of Public Safety with Saint-Just and Robespierre. "It's Hérault, isn't it. Tell me."

"His name does not matter."

"It *is* Hérault."

She shook her head. "Carton, I am not going to tell you. I don't wish you to come battering your way into his house to challenge him, like Rodomont in the Italian comedy. Should you kill him, what would become of me? And I think I would die," she added, softly, "if he killed you."

"Do you love him?" I demanded.

"No. I did once, but no longer."

"Then *why*, in God's name?"

"I told you. I am afraid. Certainly for my liberty, perhaps for my life. Now that you will no longer be a *Conventionnel*, you will have no influence to shield me. He does."

My countenance must have betrayed my emotions, for she turned away from me. "I shall say it, if you will not. Yes . . . I am no better than a whore. And a fine man like you should not tolerate a whore for a wife. So I will spare you such humiliation by going away. Stop on here if you wish—he is quitting Paris soon to go on mission for the Convention, and he has asked me to come with him." Turning back to me, she gave me a brief, imploring glance. "I do love you still. Truly. I beg you to believe that."

Sarah Kenyon had said much the same, twenty years since. For a moment her face, her cold, porcelain beauty filled my gaze, ere melting away to the woman I had loved far more than ever, in my shallow youth, I had loved Sarah. A great surge of rage and anguish swept through me, leaving me trembling. "Is that what every woman says," I demanded, "when she peddles her honour and betrays the man who has worshipped her? Do you all tell him you love him, at the moment when you spit in his face?"

"I am sorry, Carton," said she, without looking at me. "*Mon Dieu*, you can't know how sorry I am. But I had no other choice . . ."

"*I am sorry?*" I hissed. "Can you find nothing more to say than that?" I seized her arm, my hand raised. She did not flinch but stood bleakly awaiting the blow. An instant later I released her and thrust her away from me, revolted at her and at myself both, for I had never yet, even in my basest, drunken hours, struck a woman. "Never fear," I managed to tell her, "I'll not touch you. But if you imagine I will stop here amidst your leavings, you are mistaken. Live with your whore-monger or not, as you like. I only wish never again to see any thing of yours." So saying, I stumbled past her and into our bed-chamber, where I found a valise and crammed clothing at random into it.

She did not turn as I passed through the apartment for the last time, but remained where she stood, pale, rigid, impassive. I halted for an instant, pulled off my marriage-ring, and flung it at her feet. She did not move. As if in a trance, I shut the door very quietly behind me and descended the stair.

Above me, ere I reached the door to the courtyard below, I heard hurried footsteps at the landing, and her voice.

"Carton—"

I did not respond, or even turn my head, for we had nothing further to say to one another.

"Carton, you must listen a moment. I must tell you this now, for you may never see me again. You must go to Champagne. Do you hear me?" Her voice was breathless, anxious. "Go to Champagne, and find your mother's people—begin at a village called Méry. You must, Carton. For truth's sake. Go to Méry in Champagne!"

In my consuming misery I scarce understood her words. *Go to Champagne*— what rubbish was she telling me?

My haphazard steps led me southward through the crooked little streets of the Left Bank until I found myself near the summit of the Mont Ste-Geneviève, with the dome of the Panthéon looming above me. Blindly I pressed on, over the crest of the hill to the reeking, crowded knackers' and tanners' quarter that stretches between rue Contrescarpe and the old church of St. Médard. Pedlars and butchers' boys hurried past, taking no notice of me as I slowly descended the hill by way of the slippery, ordure-slimed cobbles of rue Mouffetard.

A little way along its length I espied a sign, tacked on a door, proclaiming rooms to let. Opposite it was a wine-shop, a dark and dirty hole of a place. A devouring desire that I had not felt in some years, a desperate need to smother away the demons that writhed and shrieked in my brain, drove me towards the open door. Wretchedly, I blundered inside and slapped the counter to draw the server's attention. *"Eau-de-vie* . . . leave the bottle."

I drank half a dozen glasses of the vile brandy one after the other, numbing my senses, but I could not forget a word Eléonore had said to me. At length I gave up the attempt and stumbled across the street to the lodging-house. Ere I attained it my outraged stomach rebelled. I staggered into the nearest stinking, offal-strewn alleyway to puke up the brandy I had drunk, over and over again until I could do no more than lean trembling against the stone wall beside me and retch, as if I might vomit up the memory of her into the gutter.

PART IV

And the Truth Shall
Make You Free

1793–1794

19

I HAD MEANT, with a brief speech, to bow myself gracefully out of the Convention. Eléonore's betrayal, however, left me so disheartened that I no longer cared what my fellow Deputies might think. A few days later, when I had sobered somewhat and collected my wits sufficiently, I composed a terse letter, in which I explained that because of urgent personal matters I could no longer fulfil my duties as a Representative of the People. I sent one copy to the electors of the Section du Théâtre-Français and delivered the other myself to the Tuileries.

I encountered Saint-Just on the stair there, on his way to the Committee's meeting-chamber in the southern wing. He greeted me courteously and enquired if I had considered his advice.

"I have already taken it," said I. "I just now delivered my letter of resignation to the President."

"And your wife: she agrees with you?"

"Citizeness Ambert has anticipated the matter you were so kind to point out to me privately. She has chosen to seek the protection of an old lover who has more eminence than I."

"I see," was all he said.

I had nothing more to lose by verifying my suspicions. "Saint-Just, you would do me a very great service by giving me the address of Citizen Hérault-Séchelles."

"Hérault?" he echoed me. "Is he the man? I am scarce surprised." He leant an elbow on the massive marble baluster beside us, his visage thoughtful. "In fact I don't know where he dwells—somewhere in the *faubourg* St-Germain, I fancy. As you may imagine, we don't keep the same company. But if your intention is to confront him, I fear you have come too late.

Hérault quitted Paris for Alsace two days since, on mission for the Committee—"

"The craven . . ." I could not help muttering, betwixt clenched teeth.

Saint-Just shook his head. "I fear I must defend him in that regard. Evading you was not his purpose—or, shall we say, not his principal purpose. His mission was proposed in the Committee weeks ago. As you may recall, dozens of Deputies are quitting Paris at present to inspect the armies at our frontiers. I am leaving on mission myself within the week."

She had said her protector was quitting Paris, and she with him. I nodded. "No matter. It merely confirms my belief."

"A word of advice, Carton," he added, as I turned away. "Should you be thinking of challenging Hérault when he returns . . . he was born a Noble, remember, and given a Nobleman's education." His voice took on a disdainful edge to it, as if he, the Spartan revolutionist, held the Epicurean Aristocrat in as much contempt as the Aristocracy had once held the *bourgeoisie.* "He may be a Magistrate rather than a soldier, but I imagine he has been well-trained in the use of a sword. He could probably cut you to ribbons."

"I've no intention of challenging him," said I. "I'd not waste my time. I merely wished to stand face to face with them both, and tell him he was welcome to his second-hand goods." So saying, I quitted the Tuileries for the last time.

A DINGY ROOM in the lodging-house on rue Mouffetard became my home. So, I confess to my shame, did Le Vieux Chêne, the Sign of the Old Oak, the disreputable wine-shop across the street. Once a drunkard, always a drunkard, the Puritans say, and I imagine they are right.

I found work soon enough with an elderly Advocate in the rue du Roule. Though my dour manner and drink-reddened eyes must have given Maître Tabary cause for reflexion, I did the work he set me, for the most part concerning dull law-suits over property-boundaries, as competently and indifferently as ever I had digested Stryver's depositions. He paid me a modest wage and I was satisfied to be let alone.

The days turned shorter and colder. The Convention, in its infinite wisdom, turned its back upon the superstitious, antiquated Christian calendar and gave us a new one; from the year of our Lord 1793 we were now suddenly in Year II of the French Republic. What once had been October now was divided between Vendémiaire, the month of vintage, and Brumaire, the month of fog: then followed Frimaire, Nivôse, Pluviôse, a host of others I did not trouble to commit to memory.

I cared not by what precious nonsense the days and months might be styled, for they were all the same to me. I passed them in a numb, alcoholic haze. Though the Executioner's carts creaked past my employer's very windows on their way to the scaffold, rarely did I bestir myself to more than apathy to the grim affairs proceeding apace elsewhere in the city. The haggard Queen was brought to trial, sentenced, and executed. A fortnight later, twenty-two of the leading Girondin Deputies shared her fate.

I saw them passing, hands bound behind them and hair shorn off for the blade, on that dismal wet morning of All Hallows' Eve. The customary *toilette* of the Condemned had denied them their individuality, had reduced them to uniform stick-figures clad in torn white shirts sagging open at the throat, yet they bore themselves like victors rather than vanquished. Despite my listlessness, some bleak and bitter curiosity led me to follow the carts to the place de la Révolution and the final moment of consummation at the Guillotine.

Vergniaud, Brissot, Lasource, Lehardi, Duperret . . . I had known them all, had known them to be Republicans as sincere as Robespierre. I watched their heads fall one after the other and remembered Vergniaud's famous prophecy: *The Revolution, like Saturn, will devour all her children.* Vergniaud himself had now been devoured by that insatiate Goddess—who would be next to follow him?

So, too, silent and unlamented, died Eléonore's former husband, the ex-

Vicomte de Clairville, captured fighting in the *émigré* army against his country and despatched to Paris to be judged. So, too, died Philippe Egalité,
once First Prince of the Blood Royal and then a member of the
Convention, detested and mistrusted by Royalists and Republicans alike;
so, too, died Mdme. Roland, as composed as the ancient Roman whom she
imagined herself; so, too, died Mdme. du Barry, old Louis XV's mistress,
who rode ignobly to her death (or so the newspapers gleefully claimed)
struggling and shrieking for mercy; so, too, died Barnave, Duport, Bailly, so
many of the leaders venerated in the long-gone first days of the Revolution;
and General Biron, the ex-Duc de Lauzun, who had commanded the
Republic's armies; and Dietrich the Mayor of Strasbourg, in whose house
"La Marseillaise" had first been sung—men who, a year or two previous,
had been heroes.

And I? Soon I did not care. I had lost all interest in the fates of others,
and surely cared least of all for my own fate. A patrol might have pounded
on my door in the middle of the night, as they so often did in that season
of fear and uncertainty, and escorted me off to the Conciergerie and the
Tribunal, and I would not have uttered a word in protest. Saint-Just had evidently kept his promise to me, however, for I remained as disregarded as if
I had never existed. It was a sour irony, I reflected every evening into my
brandy, as I slouched at a solitary back table at the Old Oak, that the very
precaution that had guaranteed my safety had cost me the essence of my
life.

By chance I encountered Lucile Desmoulins one grey, wet afternoon
in late November (or Frimaire) as I trudged home from Maître Tabary's
chambers. When she spied me she thrust her market-basket into her maidservant's hands and came running to me, smiles wreathing her pretty, childish countenance.

"I've not seen you for ages!" she cried. "Camille told me you had resigned
from the Convention—is it true? But why?"

"I am more English than French—I would not long have been welcome there."

"Why, so you are," said she, with a peal of laughter. "And Eléonore—she is well?"

"I've no idea."

"I don't understand. Has she quitted Paris?"

"She is gone to Alsace, as Hérault's mistress."

She stared at me a moment, her smile fading away. "I seem to have been dreadfully tactless," she murmured. "Forgive me."

"You could not have known."

"No—I did know, though not—not the particulars. It was rumoured Hérault had secretly taken a woman to Alsace whose husband was an *émigré* Noble." She glanced away as her cheeks turned pink. "Former husband, I suppose. It must have made a terrible scandal in the Committee. Maxime—Robespierre—was fuming about it when he came to dinner some time ago. They don't much like Hérault, you see. They cannot forget he was an Aristocrat, and they don't trust him. Tho' of course I never imagined the woman in question could be . . . forgive me."

"No matter."

"You are no longer dwelling on rue St-André—pardon me, rue des Arts, then? Or I would have seen you already. Where do you live?"

"In the *faubourg* St-Jacques . . . rue Mouffetard."

"That horrid quarter, in the midst of the knackers' yards?" she exclaimed, wrinkling her nose. "How noisome and dreary it must be. Come take supper with us to-night. Camille will be delighted to see you again."

"Very well," said I, shrugging, and thinking that in exchange for Lucile and Camille's chatter I would at least eat a decent meal, a welcome change from the fare at the chophouse where I supped each evening. "Why not?"

I followed her and the maidservant to the apartment on rue du Théâtre-Français, where Camille greeted me effusively ere realising that I might have no call to feel merry. "C-Come in here," said he at length, gesturing me into his cramped, untidy study. "I should like you to read something I've done—"

"Another pamphlet?" said I, in no temper to humour him. "Whom are you slandering to-day?"

He glared at me, wounded, and abruptly dropt his gaze. "I suppose I deserved that. I know full well my *History of the Girondins* k-killed them. I wish to G-God I had never taken up a pen."

"Your remorse is not of much use to them."

"But perhaps to others, in prison for less c-cause. I am starting a new journal, C-Carton," he told me, with his old peculiar half-proud, half-sheepish grin. "I shall call it *Le Vieux Cordelier*. To remind folk what the C-Cordeliers Club once represented, and the Revolution, too."

The Cordeliers was the political Club in which Danton had first seized fame. During the turbulent year past, however, the *enragés* and rabble-rousers of Hébert's stripe had dominated it. A journal entitled *The Old Cordelier* might awaken memories that would be a slap in the face to the blood-thirsty Demagogues who now controlled it.

"It was you who first set me thinking," he added, eyeing me, as if hungering for approval. "When you refused to vote for the Law of Suspects. And then what one sees now every day. Nothing is g-glorious, merely ugly or pitiful. I see a woman often on the street, when I c-come home for dinner. She always wears grey. The shop-keepers say she g-goes by every day without fail at half past one, and returns at half past four. Sometimes her little g-girl comes with her. I spoke with her once and asked her whither she went every day—she told me her husband was imprisoned in La Force, and she waited there in the street in the chance that he might see her from an upper window. He is an *émigré* Noble, she said, but he had quitted France years before the Revolution and c-came back in 'ninety-two with no suspicion that *émigrés* were banned from returning."

I wonder if ever Lucie had any inkling that the pleasant, clumsy young man who once questioned her on a street-corner was *the Public Prosecutor of the Lantern.* Sweet Heaven above, how could I have guessed he spoke of Lucie, when I imagined her, and my adored Lucie-Anne, and Darnay, my friend of twenty years and more, tranquil and happy in England?

"The poor fellow doesn't belong in prison at all," continued Camille. "How many other folk are held on such weak g-grounds? She is a beautiful, gentle, golden-haired c-creature, very sad and lost, and of course qu-quite harmless. What has she or her husband done to deserve suspicion?" He shrugged, with a sigh. "And then Danton c-came to me and told me I had a duty to take up my pen again, in the service of patriotism."

"And what do you feel you have a duty to write about now, in your *Vieux Cordelier?*"

He raised his head and gazed at me in surprise, as if he had naturally expected me to follow his ramblings. "Clemency," he said.

CLEMENCY!

Lucie, of all the weary and anxious folk in Paris, must have dared to pray for deliverance at last when the first numbers of *Le Vieux Cordelier* appeared in the book-stalls. For the first time in well-nigh a year, a voice had dared to speak out, to declare that too much blood had been spilt for trifling causes. In his brilliant No. 3 Camille progressed to condemning the spirit itself of the times, the Terror that Robespierre had accepted as necessary for the protection of Revolution and Republic. Danton boldly proposed that the Convention should create a Committee of Clemency, which would examine the cases of prisoners held on trivial charges of Incivism. And Paris went mad with hope.

THE FUROR OVER *Le Vieux Cordelier* made no difference to me. I might have sleep-walked my way through the Winter and into that bloody Spring, indifferent and ignored, had not an errand of my employer's sent me to Tellson's Paris office, newly-housed in a splendid mansion on rue Taranne. Since the commencement of hostilities between England and France, the

Banque Tellson et Fils could have had little or no communication with the English house; its workings, nonetheless, continued as smooth as ever, mute witness to the fine impartiality of Finance.

It was 29 Frimaire—19th December; naught but four days had passed since Camille's incendiary No. 3 had appeared in the book-stalls, and already folk were paying three times the price for a second-hand copy. I plodded into the Bank, conducted my brief legal business with one of the clerks, and was about to slouch out again when, to my utter amazement, I found myself face to face with Jarvis Lorry.

He was as much astonished as I. He stared at me a moment, joy illumining his kindly features, and wrung my hand, exclaiming: "Darnay! Howsoever did you—"

"No, not Darnay," said I, more amused than vexed, shaking my head. "Tho' I've not been mistaken for him for some years now. How do you do, Mr. Lorry?"

"*Carton?*" he breathed. "Good Heavens, Sir, what has brought *you* to Paris?"

"Don't talk in English," I told him. "I imagine you have a chamber where we may speak privately?" He nodded and led the way, speechless.

"I have dwelt in Paris for the four years past," said I, after he had shut the door behind us. "Ever since I quitted Stryver's employment." Tossing my greatcoat over a chair, I seated myself opposite him.

"But Lucie said you had gone to America."

I shrugged. "I changed my mind. What brings you hither, and—dare I say it?—how have you avoided imprisonment with all the other British subjects in the city?"

"Indeed, I was arrested," he admitted, tugging at his little flaxen peruke and steepling his fingers in the manner I knew so well. "I spent the better part of a week in the Luxembourg. Happily, Manette's influence soon freed me. He enjoys a certain celebrity as a former Bastille prisoner—"

"Dr. Manette?" I enquired. "He is in Paris, too?"

Lorry heaved a profound sigh and began to fidget with his sand-shaker. "They are all in Paris, Carton: Manette, Lucie, the child, even Miss Pross. They have dwelt here above a year, since the week of the Prison-massacres."

"What on Earth . . ." I began, a shudder of both dread and joy thrilling through me at the sound of Lucie's name, but he interrupted me.

"Darnay is in prison."

"Prison!" I echoed him stupidly. "Not that old business again—" His grim, troubled aspect alerted me to the truth. "*Here?* He is in prison here, in Paris?"

"Yes. At La Force. He returned to vouch for an old servant who had been imprisoned, and was arrested himself as an *émigré.*"

"An *émigré?* Why should they concern themselves—" I stopt short as I remembered the truth.

"He is—" began Lorry.

"The Marquis de Saint-Evrémonde," said I. Suddenly I remembered, also, Camille's description of the golden-haired woman in grey. "God's death . . ."

I saw the old gentleman staring at me and gave him a wry smile. "I've not become clairvoyant, Sir," I added. "By chance I met . . . a relative of Darnay's, who told me his true name. He is well?"

"As well as can be expected, in that foul place. Manette sees him frequently—he has become Physician to several of the prisons—and obtains him as many favours as he can."

"Yet he cannot secure Darnay's release? I should think, as a victim of the Monarchy, he could demand nearly any prerogative from the Republic."

"Nearly any," agreed Lorry, "but not that. The Revolutionary Tribunal is jealous of its quarry."

I buried my face in my hands a moment. Once again ill fortune had thwarted me: for had I known, but three months previous, that Darnay was a prisoner—had I by chance encountered Lorry or the Doctor or Lucie— as a *Conventionnel* I might have been able at least to have him brought expeditiously to trial on those unsubstantial charges of emigration, and as quickly released. Or had my friends recognised my name in the roster of Deputies—but that would have been an unlikely circumstance, for what is one name amongst seven hundred and more, a not uncommon name, moreover, as likely to be a French name as English? No, had they chanced upon the name *Carton* in the daily report from the Convention in the *Moniteur* (and I had not been of that species of Deputy ever ready to thrust his name before his public with a peevish interruption or a fine speech), they would have passed over it without a second thought, for their friend Carton (as he had told them) was years gone in America.

"And the servant Darnay meant to aid?" I enquired at last.

"Was acquitted and released only a few days since, on Darnay's testimony. These Jacobins have preserved at least a semblance of Justice."

"Perhaps," I mused (for, despite all, I was not without friends), "I might yet be able to exert some small influence of my own, on Darnay's behalf . . ."

"You?"

"Fate and circumstance are queer things, Mr. Lorry. I don't suppose you ever could have imagined that twenty years ago I studied at the Collège Louis-le-Grand with a couple of boys named Robespierre and Desmoulins, and have since dined with them more often than once."

"I never was enamoured of your peculiar sense of humour, Carton," said he, after a moment. "You'd not jest, though, would you, about such a matter?"

"Certainly not."

"Then I beg you to do whatsoever you can. To see Lucie, after fifteen months of this—it's heart-breaking. She is so thin and pale . . . and they have little money, for of course they are obliged to pay for Darnay's prison-lodging. She and Miss Pross have been taking in sewing and embroidery to make ends meet. And the child creeps about their apartment like a lost little ghost. I help them in any modest way I can, of course, but I fear to wound the Doctor's pride. He promised Lucie that his influence would soon free Darnay, but thus far, to his chagrin, it has been unavailing. I often worry if this strain of mind may not bring back the *dementia* that had hold of him in the Bastille. You know of what I speak?"

"She once told me of it."

"In those eighteen years in prison, he forgot even his own name, and turned to making shoes. Lucie brought him to himself; she needed almost a year. And when he is under some strain of mind, that old cloud sometimes descends upon him once again, and he believes himself the shoemaker in the Bastille." He sighed and rubbed at his nose, blinking. "You would hardly recognise them all, Carton."

A clerk tapped on the door, interrupting him, and told him he was wanted. With a word of apology he went off with the fellow but as quickly returned. "It's the Doctor, and Lucie. I didn't know what to tell them . . ."

"Don't tell them I am here," said I, scarce knowing why, and rose to my feet. "They need not know, unless I can perhaps aid Darnay."

He nodded and went out, soon returning once again. "I fear you have appeared too late, Carton—we are come to the end of this at last. Manette has just told me that Darnay is to be transferred to the Conciergerie to-night, and summoned before the Tribunal to-morrow. I pray the Doctor's prestige will aid him."

"From all you have told me, I am confident it will." I retreated to the little ante-chamber where Lorry's clerk was copying letters into his letter-book. I would have quitted the Bank then, but realised I had forgotten my greatcoat and was perforce obliged to stop on until Lucie and her father had come and gone.

"I think," said I, re-entering the old gentleman's office, "I may be of more use even at this ultimate moment than you might expect. An old friendship with the author of *Le Vieux Cordelier* ought to stand me in some good stead." So saying, I pressed Lorry's hand and departed.

The mere sound of Lucie's voice, muffled through the heavy door, had lightened my heart and set the blood to singing in my veins. With an energy I had not felt all through the course of that dismal Autumn, I strode along rue Taranne to rue du Théâtre-Français. Camille was at home and welcomed me inside with a glass of Port.

"I have come for a favour," I told him, cutting short his cheerful prattle. "Do you remember telling me, three weeks past, of a woman whose husband was imprisoned in La Force?"

"Of c-course. I see her still, now and again."

"And do you remember Charles Darnay, who was my dearest friend at Louis-le-Grand?"

"Yes . . . the fellow you styled your looking-glass twin—how could I forget? What of him?"

"He is her husband—the *émigré* Noble of whom you spoke."

"Noble?"

"His real name is Marbois; he is the former Marquis de Saint-Evrémonde." I raised a hand to forestall his exclamations and continued. "Lucie is the daughter of Dr. Manette, the Physician who was a Bastille prisoner in the 1760s. I've no doubt Dr. Manette will secure Darnay's acquittal—the charges are very weak—but his cause couldn't be harmed by a good word from another quarter. You are the sensation of the moment, and your endorsement of Darnay's good faith would go far."

"Well . . . poor Darnay, he was an agreeable fellow . . . I could c-call at Fouquier's this evening, and request that he tread lightly with him. I doubt Fouquier would refuse me, particularly as it's plain that Darnay c-can't be much of a c-counter-revolutionary if he has wedded Manette's daughter."

"You know Fouquier-Tinville?" I enquired, pleasantly surprised to learn that I might have some indirect influence with the fearsome Public Prosecutor.

Camille grimaced. "He is my c-cousin, in some degree or another. In fact I secured him his position, although sometimes I regret recommending him—he is so very single-minded."

I laughed for the first time in months, though my laughter was bitter enough. "Then I think Darnay has nothing to fear."

AT THE PALAIS de Justice I crowded into the Salle de Liberté (an ironic name for a hall which ever more prisoners quitted only for the scaffold) with the usual throng of curious spectators. Darnay was the third of four men to be tried that day. The two who preceded him were not as fortunate as he; in short order they were found Guilty of correspondence with enemies of the Republic, and condemned to Death.

Camille must have kept his promise to me, for the Public Prosecutor, whilst brusque as ever, was not over-hostile towards Darnay. He must have considered the workaday case of an enlightened young Nobleman, who had renounced his title years before and returned to France in good faith and ignorance, to be unworthy of his fearful energy.

The counsel for the Defence pled his case very well indeed, tho' he could scarce have done otherwise with such a Witness as Dr. Manette to vouch for the Prisoner. The good Doctor cut a striking figure, his white hair and gaunt features silent testimony to all the torments he had endured in the Bastille. The crowd alternately cheered and wept, and the stolid Jurymen nodded thoughtfully.

By the moment the Doctor had concluded, I knew Darnay would be acquitted. The testimony of the second Witness, the elderly estate-steward to aid whom Darnay had returned to France, seemed trivial by comparison. I might scarce have remembered him or his apologetic statements had not his name struck a chord in me, like a song from childhood half-recalled at the edge of one's memory. Where before, I wondered, as the throng about me restlessly stirred and whispered, had I heard the name Gabelle?

The Jurymen turned to confer and within a minute the trial had concluded. The spectators cheered their approval as each man in his turn rose and said *Not Guilty*. I waited long enough only to watch Darnay step down from the Prisoners' bench and clasp first the Doctor, then Lorry, in a warm embrace.

Once again, Darnay, I reflected, *I have played my part in saving your skin*—and despite my bitter apathy, I could not help smiling for his sake, and for Lucie's. Satisfied enough with my success, I shouldered my way out through the crowd to the bustling Salle des Pas-Perdus, meaning to return straight-away to Maître Tabary's chambers. Much as I would have wished to con-gratulate Darnay on his deliverance, and—yes, confess it, Carton—to see Lucie once more, I thought it better that our paths not cross. Our ways had parted four years previous and I would gain nothing (save, perhaps, to re-kindle some old memories best forgotten) by intruding my presence amongst them once again.

I had advanced but a few steps in the vast hall, echoing with the countless footsteps of Advocates, guards, curiosity-seekers, and prisoners under escort, when somebody in the crowd seized my arm. I glanced back to find Msr. Gabelle beaming at me. "Msr. Charles—Citizen, rather," he corrected him-self hastily, "I cannot tell you how grateful I am, and how overjoyed . . ." His voice trailed off uncertainly as he had a better look at me.

"Darnay is over yonder, with Dr. Manette," said I, and stept aside, attempting to disengage myself from the little man's grasp ere Darnay or the Doctor espied me.

"*Mon Dieu!*" he exclaimed, looking from me to Darnay and back again. "But—but you could be his brother, Citizen."

"I am well aware of that. Pardon me."

"A moment—a moment." He elbowed his way into the noisy throng and in an instant returned, a handsome woman of sixty at his heels. "My wife, Citizen. My dear . . ."

She turned her gaze to me and gave a little gasp of surprise. "But— M'sieur Charles . . ." she murmured.

"Yes, yes, my dear, there he is, with the Doctor. And this—is—" He ges-tured helplessly at me. I paid him scant attention, for my own gaze was drawn to his wife, who seemed strangely familiar to me.

"You—you are a kinsman of M'sieur Charles?" she asked me. "A Saint-Evrémonde cousin?"

"No. The resemblance is mere chance, Citizeness." Though the lined countenance beneath the simple linen bonnet was kindly, I found it unsettling. Surely I knew her, and yet—and yet each of us was patently a stranger to the other. Abruptly I muttered an apology and strode away towards the Galerie Marchande, hoping to escape them, but Gabelle scrambled after me.

"I cannot believe you bear no kinship to Msr. Charles. Surely you are related in some way—"

"I doubt most emphatically that I am in any way connected to the family of an ex-Marquis," I snapped. "My father was an English tradesman and my mother a Notary's daughter from Champagne. Good-day, Citizen." Exasperated, I plunged into the crowd once more, seeking the nearest egress. The crush ahead of me pressed me back as a half-dozen guardsmen came tramping through, a solitary figure in their midst. Impatiently I glanced about me, seeking another route as the guards and their prisoner drew nearer. An instant later I stood paralysed, the breath catching in my throat and my blood turning to ice, for the prisoner was Eléonore.

20

SHE COULD NO more have avoided seeing me than I her. Her countenance, so composed an instant before, paled to a sickly white. We stared at each other for a single swift moment ere her escort cleared the way and they proceeded onward. Abruptly she tore her gaze from me and continued walking with a measured step betwixt the guards.

I had presence of mind only to intercept the last of the escort and mutter to him, "I pray you, whither are you taking this woman?"

"Preliminary interrogation," said he, not uncivilly.

"Preliminary to what?"

"Trial to-morrow before the Tribunal, of course." He shook me off and hastened after them, leaving me suddenly trembling like a tree in a gale.

Eléonore—there—awaiting trial? But she was quite safe—could not have been more so, in the company of a member of the Great Committee. Had Hérault tired of her so soon, callously abandoned her to her fate?

"Citizen," said somebody to me, tugging at my sleeve—Gabelle again— "Citizen, I beg your pardon, but I believe—"

"For God's sake let me be!" I shouted, twisting away from him and fleeing down the nearest stair-case. Somehow I found my way out to the May Courtyard and paused to catch my breath and collect my wits. I would go first to Camille, I decided, for his house was not far away. I strode off, running almost, pushing my way through the passers-by.

Lucile opened the door to me, her little son in her arms. "Camille—I pray you, is he here?" I demanded, ere she could offer me a word of welcome. "I must speak with him."

"No, he is out," she told me. "I think he is gone to the printing-shop, and thence to the Convention. What's the matter, Citizen?"

"Eléonore—she has been arrested," I stammered.

"Arrested! But she was with—she was in Alsace—"

"Nevertheless, she is a prisoner, on her way to the Tribunal—I saw her myself."

"I believe Hérault is returned to Paris," said she. "Very recently, perhaps yesterday or the day before. Could he not help you better than could Camille?"

"Had he cared to defend her, she never would have been arrested," I began savagely, but stayed myself. "No, you are right—I must find him. Do you know his address?"

She set little Horace on a chair and scribbled the address down for me on a scrap of paper. "You care for her still, don't you," she murmured, as she pressed it into my hand.

"O God," I whispered, closing my eyes. "Still . . . always . . . tho' I persuaded myself I despised her . . ."

"I will tell Camille when he returns. Perhaps he can ask another favour of Fouquier?"

I thanked her and sped away. Hérault dwelt in an elegant house on rue du Bac, west of the Luxembourg Palace. I tugged on the bell-chain with all my might and pushed my way past the disdainful manservant who answered the door. "I must speak with Citizen Hérault immediately," I said.

"Citizen Hérault is not at home to visitors," began the lackey. I turned on him and seized his waistcoat at the throat.

"I must speak with him *now*, d__n you. Take me to him."

Cowed, he led me into a dainty little cream-and-gilt *salon* where Hérault, a dressing-gown about his shoulders, was enjoying a late breakfast with a ravishing young lady *en négligée*. They turned, at my arrival, from whispering endearments over the silver chocolate-pot to stare at me in well-bred astonishment.

"Hérault," I snapped, wasting no precious moments in the niceties of social intercourse, "d__n you, how can you sit there indifferent when

Eléonore is to appear before the Tribunal to-morrow?"

"Eléonore," he echoed me, perplexed, raising his perfectly sculpted eyebrows. "Eléonore d'Ambert?"

"Who else would I mean? My God, you must save her!"

He raised a napkin to his lips and languidly wiped them ere replying. "I am sorry for you, Carton, and particularly for her, tho' I don't see what I can do to aid you. Why come to me?"

"You swine," I cried, "she went to you for protection! She sacrificed our happiness to give you what you wished, and now you repay her by casting her aside like a soiled glove?"

A frown puckering his brow, he dropt the napkin on the table and rose to his feet. "A moment, *chérie*," he murmured to his startled companion, and grasped me by the elbow, guiding me into an ante-chamber and shutting the door behind us. "Carton, I've no notion what you mean. Kindly enlighten me."

I clutched at my forehead, imagining I was going hopelessly mad. "You were Eléonore's lover. Can you deny it?"

"No," said he, shrugging. "Why should I?"

"And can you deny that she travelled to Alsace with you, as your mistress, two months since?"

He stared at me as if I had, indeed, gone mad. "That I most certainly do deny. Who told you this?"

"She told me herself," said I, a horrible misgiving clutching at my vitals. "She told me she was in danger, and that an old lover, a Conventionnel, could protect her. Moreover, he was quitting Paris and taking her with him."

He shook his head. "It wasn't I."

"Who could it have been but you?"

"God knows, Carton, but I will swear to you on all that's holy that it was not I."

"Did you not take a woman, whose husband was an *émigré*, with you to Alsace?"

"Yes," he admitted, with a nod towards the door, "my charming friend there in the breakfast-chamber. Citizen, I don't know what mis-understanding may have arisen here, but I shall be frank with you. Eléonore and I were lovers in 'ninety-two. Our *liaison* endured a few weeks only, as we soon found each other's tastes and opinions disagreeable for a connexion deeper than simple friendship. That is the truth, on my honour. I don't suppose I have been alone with her since, save for the day she came to call on me . . ." He paused, frowning. "I had almost forgotten. It meant nothing at the time. She did pay a call on me, perhaps a week ere I departed for Alsace. We did nothing more than exchange tidings—tho' I recall she seized upon my statement that I was soon quitting Paris. That is all I can tell you."

I glared at him, as if I could wrest the secret thoughts from his mind, and he gazed tranquilly back at me. I could detect no trace of deceit or guilt in his patrician countenance. "She lied to me," I whispered at last. "God only knows why."

"I don't know, Carton."

"But this changes nothing. She is a prisoner in the Conciergerie, and is to be brought to trial to-morrow."

"I'd not known. I returned but three days since."

"Surely you can do something for her," I insisted. "You are a member of the Committee. You can order the trial suspended, or have the charges against her re-examined."

He plucked absently at the rich lace at his wrist. "I don't know that I can."

"You must!"

"Carton, I don't know if any order I signed as a Committee member would be carried out, or even acknowledged. We do not see eye to eye, Robespierre and I, and the others cordially detest me. I have seen enough in two days to warn me that I may not be a member for very much longer."

"God's death, Hérault, you must at least try! You loved her once!"

Without meeting my eyes, he began to straighten the lace at his other wrist. "I regret that I . . . that I am not in a position to call attention to myself by defending a suspected citizen. To be brutally candid, Carton, I don't care to risk my own head in a probably fruitless attempt to save hers."

He might as well have kicked me in the belly. I swallowed back the nausea rising in me and drew breath, suppressing the temptation to strike him. "Robespierre," said I. "He claims to like me. Perhaps . . . no, better Saint-Just—"

"I fear Saint-Just is on mission still in Strasbourg."

"Then I must see Robespierre."

"Better you than I," he murmured, as I hastened away.

I PLEADED WITH Robespierre, knelt at his feet almost, and he would not help me.

"The Revolutionary Tribunal is beyond reproach," he told me, as he dusted powder from his waistcoat and straightened his immaculate cravat. "If your wife is innocent of the charges she will be freed, and if she is guilty, condemned. Surely, as a patriot, you would not wish to continue an alliance with a woman adjudged an enemy of the Republic."

"Eléonore is *not* an enemy of the Republic," I insisted, tho' in my heart I knew my pleas and arguments were useless with him. "She was one of the Revolution's most dedicated advocates."

"So were Brissot, Bailly, La Fayette. I'll not deny their rôles in the making of the Revolution, or your wife's either. We must judge them, however, on their subsequent actions."

"What subsequent actions? What has she done? What is she accused of?"

He adjusted his spectacles and gazed at me fretfully. "I have no idea, Carton. That is a matter for the Tribunal to decide. I had no notion, even, that she had been imprisoned. Since she discontinued publishing *Le Flambeau*, I've not considered her a threat."

"Then who has?" I demanded.

"Hébert, perhaps. Or my colleagues Billaud or Collot."

I would earn no sympathy, I knew, from those sour fanatics. I quitted Robespierre, my mind in turmoil, and walked slowly eastward along rue St-Honoré in the gathering twilight. My last hope now was Camille. Signalling a fiacre, I rode once more to rue du Théâtre-Français.

"He's not yet returned from Fouquier's offices," Lucile told me, upon seeing me. "Won't you come inside and wait for him?"

I followed her and sat drinking glass after glass of Port whilst she watched me uneasily, rocking the baby Horace in her arms. "She never went to Alsace," said I at last, knowing I must break the heavy silence or go mad. "I was deceived. Hérault denied it."

"Naturally he would. He is accustomed to jealous husbands. He has tried to seduce me any number of times."

"No . . . I believe him. It was a different woman. She lied to me. It was all a lie . . . for what?"

"If Eléonore never went to Alsace," Lucile ventured, "then how long may she have been in prison? Perhaps these two months and more, since you separated?"

"What do you mean?"

"Well . . . Eléonore is one who confronts the truth head-on, without illusions. What if she had been warned she was about to be arrested, and . . . and feared she would endanger you by her presence? It's what I would do. If I knew I were in danger, I should try to escape, of course, but I would go as far away as possible from everybody I loved, so I'd not endanger them also. But how could I do that to Camille without his learning the truth? I know he'd never quit me. I think my only choice would be to pick an artificial quarrel with him, and drive him away."

Abruptly I remembered Saint-Just's words to me on the landing, his statement of the brutal facts: *Your wife's presence may prove a great danger to you. She is a mill-stone about your neck, and the greatest favour you can do yourself is to distance yourself from her.*

"O dear God," I murmured. She had overheard him, or guessed what he was about to tell me. "What a fool I have been. Of course you are right."

Lucile glanced at me, tears suddenly shining in her wide grey-green eyes. "It's what I would have done, you see. Because I love him beyond reason, the great foolish child that he is. I would do anything to keep him safe, even hurt him terribly, were there no other way." The baby woke and began to whimper. She busied herself with calming him, without meeting my sombre gaze.

Camille trudged in soon afterward, kissed his wife, and dropt into a chair, avoiding my eyes. "Fouquier is seeing no visitors this evening," said he, "not even me. That means he is very b-busy, and probably at work on a c-case he has been instructed to win at all c-costs."

"What else can I do?" said I, forcing away the panic that threatened to engulf me. "Who else will help me? Danton?"

"He might—"

"Danton," Lucile interrupted him tartly, "will speak at length in the Convention about folk imprisoned unjustly, and Committees of Clemency, but I have never known him to bestir himself unduly for a particular prisoner. Nor does he have the authority to free anybody on his word alone. He is advocating Moderation chiefly because it will make him more popular than Robespierre."

"You think it would be fruitless, then, to see him."

"No, of course you must see him. You can't afford to neglect that chance . . . tho' I think your hope of success is not great."

"No," I murmured, and quitted them. As I pulled open the door to the passage, I perceived Lucile gazing after me, blinking away tears.

DANTON WAS NOT at home. I left an urgent message for him, without much hope, and plodded bleakly away along the darkening rue des Arts. A few minutes brought me to the corner of rue Gil-Cœur, where I stood gazing up at the windows I knew so well. As I lingered there, a smart calèche came rolling up. The porter hurried out to assist the driver in throwing open the gate and caught a glimpse of me as the calèche clattered through the *porte-cochère*.

"Why, Citizen Carton," he exclaimed. "You're returned from your journey, then?"

"Journey?" said I.

"The citizeness said you had quitted Paris on business. On mission for the Convention, she said."

"Yes," I agreed, having no desire to explain the matter. "Citizen, may I go up-stairs? Or have they sealed it?"

"Sealed, Citizen?"

"The Section Committee, or the Committee of Public Safety—"

"Lord, why should they wish to seal an empty lodging?"

"Empty?"

"Why, yes. She sold some of the furniture and packed the rest and left, she did, with her servant. Within the week after you'd gone. Surely you knew that."

"The . . . letter must have gone astray," said I. "Do you know whither she went?"

"She left no address, but Citizeness Baptistine let fly a word about the Section des Gravilliers. A street opposite the Temple, she said, and didn't she complain about the quarter not being fit for a lady like her mistress!"

The Temple district, I mused—which I never had had a reason to visit in all the years I had spent in Paris. I gave him a few sous and slunk off into the darkness, dull misery bitter as bile in my throat.

She had known me better than I knew myself. She had seen the danger to herself, accepted it, and dispassionately set about shielding me from it, even to avoiding a chance encounter between us. Clear-eyed, relentlessly logical Eléonore: she had remembered all I had told her of Sarah, remembered my ever-cool bearing towards Hérault, had known precisely how to ensure that I would quit her and never return, never learn of her peril and imperil myself by attempting to save her. She had played me as skilfully as

she might have played upon a well-tuned harpsichord, and I had responded as mechanically.

And now, knowing the truth, I was powerless to save her.

SHE DEFENDED HERSELF well. Though without illusions, she was
by no means resigned to death. Yet to what avail were her shrewdness and
her spirit in the face of a merciless Tribunal determined to condemn her?

Conspiracy with the Girondin Traitors, to subvert the Republic and
assassinate the patriot Marat; publishing writings injurious to the safety of
the Republic; aiding an *émigré* and enemy of the Republic to flee the country; this last they must have learnt, by chance, from Clairville at his own
brief trial. The charges, insidious in their distorted half-truth, fell on my
ears like a death-knell, and I was powerless.

They pronounced but two death-sentences that day, hers and that of a
shabby, surly forger of *assignats*. She did not speak or cry out as she heard
the sentence, tho' I saw her draw a long breath and let it out again. Then
the guards took charge of her, escorting her away to the spiral stair-case
that leads down to the Conciergerie, and I saw no more.

Somehow my leaden feet carried me out of the chamber and down the
Grand Stair to the cour du Mai, where the Executioner's cart stood waiting. Despite the wind and the icy mist, the courtyard slowly filled with loiterers, with the idle and the curious.

They escorted the Condemned out an hour later, shortly after the great
clock by the quay struck two. A priest accompanied them, reciting prayers
as he paced beside the sullen counterfeiter.

She seemed alien, a stranger almost, oddly youthful and intense like the
portraits of Joan of Arc, with her splendid dark hair cut close to her head.
Tho' I knew she was thirty-six, she looked no older than twenty-five. She
wore only a plain woollen gown and I saw her shiver in the chill breeze.

It was no hard task to recognise Sanson, the black-clad master
Executioner. Silent and courteous, he steadied her as she climbed into the

cart. He offered a helping hand to her companion, then a moment later turned back and stept into the cart with them, to pull off his overcoat and drape it about her. She gave him a grateful smile and a word of thanks.

I watched these preparations in a stupor, my mind scarce according what I saw. *Surely,* some part of me cried, *this is no more than a nightmare, from which I will soon awaken, and find my Léo beside me.*

It was a nightmare, indeed, tho' it was no dream.

I straightened as best I could, tho' I felt myself feeble and weary as an old man who has lived too long, as the driver clucked the horse into a walk. I could not tear my gaze from her. In a moment she espied me and her mouth quivered. She mastered herself in an instant, however, and with a brief sad smile her lips silently formed the words *I love you.*

I kissed my hand to her, not caring who might denounce me for showing sympathy to the Condemned. She smiled again, bowing her head for a moment, and turned away.

Even to the last, she was determined not to compromise me. She knew me in every other particular—did she not know that I no longer cared to live, that my life was worthless without her? At that last terrible moment, I could not forsake her. Dazed, I stumbled after the cart as it rolled through the great gates.

Never, during all my mis-spent life, had I comprehended the true nature of Hell until the endless hour that I followed Sanson's cart through Paris. Quai de l'Horloge, Pont-Neuf, rue du Roule, the excruciating interminable length of rue St-Honoré. The Palais-Egalité, once the Palais-Royal, where I first had met her; Riding-School, Jacobin Club, place des Piques. The stolid respectable house in which Robespierre dwells with his stolid respectable hosts. I flung a silent, savage curse at him, at the solemn boy who had grown into a frigid Zealot for whom Mankind was everything and men nothing.

And at last rue de la Révolution, and the Treasury to the left of us as the street opened into the square, and the Guillotine standing gaunt against an empty sky the colour of cold iron. A few dozen idlers waited hard by the rail that keeps a space clear about the scaffold. I joined them, melted into the crowd, tho' every particle of my being wished only to fly from that place.

Ancient courtesies remained unchanged; women, all during that bleak Autumn, were granted still the privilege of going first, that they might be spared the sight of blood. Sanson handed her from the cart and guided her up the steep steps to the platform, steadying her as she trod on her skirt and stumbled. His gentleness and solicitude were somehow horrifying.

I kissed my hand to her once again as she paused for an instant, glancing swiftly across the meagre crowd that had gathered to feast on Death, but I know not if she saw me. No one about me glimpsed my incautious gesture, for their eyes were fixed upon the knife. I forced myself to watch still, whilst they strapt her pale slim figure to the plank, as if my gaze might lend her strength. Then they tipped the plank forward and she disappeared beneath the blade, and I turned my head away, and that sharp metallic sigh and crash echoed in my ears, the sound of my fragile world shattering down about me, and at last I blindly shouldered my way through the men and women listlessly applauding, and fled.

21

I STUMBLED INTO the first Apothecary's shop I saw and bought a quantity of opium.

"How much do you wish, Citizen?" the proprietor asked me, when I had blurted out my demand.

"Enough to make me forget," said I. "To forget for all time."

"Have you made a habit of taking opium heretofore, Citizen?"

"Never."

He took my measure—haggard countenance and eyes blood-shot from want of sleep—nodded, and disappeared into the rear of the shop, to return with a heap of brown powder in a saucer. "So much," he told me, pushing aside a small quantity with a spatula, "taken with a little water or wine, in twenty or thirty minutes will induce sleep and lethargy. This much,"—and he augmented the quantity—"will produce deep sleep or unconsciousness for many hours, perhaps a day." He doubled it and poured the measured amount carefully into a phial. "You have here four draughts at least. I pray you, take care. Taken all at once," he added, without looking at me, as he sealed the phial, "particularly with an excess of spirituous liquor, it will kill a man. I trust you comprehend me, Citizen?"

"Perfectly," said I.

I made my way somehow back to rue Mouffetard, an hour and a half's walk or more, feeling naught but a chill howling emptiness as the early Winter dusk enveloped me. Like a sleep-walker suddenly awakening, I came to myself in the fusty room I called my home, with a bottle of *eau-de-vie* and the phial of opium waiting before me on the table. I poured out a glassful of brandy and gulped it down, welcoming its sting.

So simple it would be, to swallow that double spoonful of brown powder, to fall into a deep peaceful sleep and never awaken. In a few hours' time I could be with her again, on the far shore of the dark River; I could be far from their cursed Revolution and this world that had toyed with me so cruelly. What, God help me, had I to live for?

I could think of nothing as I sat there in my dingy room, monotonously refilling my glass, hearing the bells of St. Médard and St. Etienne-du-Mont toll the passing hours, hearing the thud of the Guillotine's blade echo again and again and once again in my ears, and yet I could not do it. Half a dozen times I reached for the phial, lifting it, staring at it, unstopping it, sniffing it delicately like a *connoisseur* with a fine wine, and half a dozen times I closed it up again undisturbed.

Well, Algernon Sydney Carton, I reflected at last, *you have ever suffered yourself to be blown hither and thither by the winds of Fate, at the mercy of Circumstance. Not once in your life have you truly chosen your own path, even to the achievement you so briefly tasted. How should such a one, who never made the effort to attain more than was within his reach, find the self-mastery to determine his own fate? Truly you are yet the man you always were; you lack the resolve even to kill yourself.*

I stopt up the phial and slipped it into an inner pocket of my greatcoat. Then all at once the horror overcame me and I hid my face in my hands, weeping, the tears running down my cheeks to drip one by one onto the table, and into the glass of brandy before me.

IT WAS A day more, a day I do not remember save as a long nightmare of cart-wheels turning relentlessly towards their goal, ere I awoke with a lacerating head-ache from my brandy-sodden Purgatory. Some blurred hours later I remembered, with a guilty pang, that Eléonore had not dwelt alone. Drinking down a half-bottle of wretched sour wine (tho' it did nothing to dull the memories or the pain), at length I staggered outside and found a fiacre that would take me to the Section des Gravilliers.

Twilight had fallen by the hour I reached the Temple and stared up at the forbidding mediæval tower where the King's orphaned children are imprisoned. Opposite the fortress's gates stretched a filthy, uninviting street, rue des Fontaines. I rang the bell at the first house on the street and began my enquiries.

I wanted little time to seek out the lodgings of Citizeness Poisson at No. 6. I climbed the rickety stair and tapped upon the door. A moment later it opened a crack and a fearful face peered out at me.

"It's I, Baptistine," I told her. "Don't be afraid."

"O, M'sieur!" she exclaimed, forgetting to call me *Citizen* in her agitation, and beckoned me inside. "O M'sieur, M'sieur, they came and took everything that was hers! What's to become of her? What's to become of us all?"

The tiny apartment was bare, with but a few shabby sticks of furniture that must have been abandoned there in the rooms when Eléonore let them. I saw nothing in the feeble candle-light that I recognised save a few of Baptistine's possessions.

"Tell me what happened after I went away," said I. I could not bring myself to tell her the truth.

"She told me you had been called away unexpected, on business for the Convention I think she said, and you could no longer afford to let Madame's apartment so we must change our lodgings. Then we came hither, to this miserable district, and a fortnight later they came pounding on the door and arrested her! And they searched thro' everything—every drawer, every box, even under the mattresses, M'sieur—and they took away all her papers. And then yesterday they came again and took away everything, and told me it was confiscated to the Republic. Everything! M'sieur, what shall I do?"

I sank onto a rickety stool and tried to collect my thoughts as a score of demons clawed at the inside of my skull. "M'sieur," Baptistine added timidly, taking a sealed letter from the depths of her sewing-basket and pressing it into my hand, "she gave this to my keeping two days ere they arrested her. She told me . . . she said, if ever I should see you, should you come hither, to give it to you."

It bore no name, no writing. I turned it over in my hands, fearful of what I might read should I open it.

"Baptistine," said I, "you have kinfolk in Sèvres, have you not? Go to them. To-morrow morning. Take all you need. You are in no danger, but you can do nothing for your mistress here. I will write to you, or your mistress will write to you, when she needs you again. Did she leave any money with you?"

"A fair bit—perhaps a hundred livres, for the housekeeping . . . she'd let the rooms for the quarter . . ."

"Take with you what remains." My grip tightened upon the folded letter in my hand. "I pray you . . . suffer me a moment alone now."

"Yes, M'sieur." She slipped into an adjoining chamber. With trembling fingers I cracked the seal and unfolded the letter. As I did so, something fell from it and dropt with a flash of gold to the floor, its faint metallic chiming very bright in the bare room. It was her marriage-ring.

My own was there, too, enfolded in the stiff paper, and a lock of her hair. I retrieved her ring from the floor and clutched it very tightly as I read the handwriting I knew so well.

The 24th October 1793

My dear friend,

If you are reading this letter, you must already have learnt the truth, from Baptistine or by some other agency. I pray you can find it in yourself to forgive my cruel deception. The truth would have been crueller yet; I thought— perhaps I was wrong?—I thought it better you should hate me and forget me than live in agony (as I would have done had our positions been reversed) knowing I was in prison, as I suspect I soon shall be, in the shadow of the Guillotine. You would have fought for me, pleaded for me, no doubt all in vain, and such persistent effort on behalf of one of the Suspected would surely have cast suspicion upon you as well. I am no sentimentalist, to see a touching glamour in our dying together like Shakespeare's star-crossed lovers. Rather, my love for you forbade me to suffer you to share with me that fate which I fear is inevitable.

My dearest, believe me once again when I say to you that I love you, above Life itself, and shall always love you, no matter what fate may part us. If it is my destiny, as I fear it may be, to die at the hands of the public Executioner, I shall go to my death consoled and strengthened by the love you and I have shared. How many folk have been so fortunate to have tasted, for even such a brief moment as we did, so profound a happiness?

Live, then, dearest love; I would not seek to have you follow me. Live and turn your talents, your integrity, your courage to a worthier purpose: that of guiding the Revolution to the dream of Hope and Promise that once we knew. The change will come, the tide must inevitably turn, tho' I fear it may turn too late for me. But this reign of the Guillotine cannot last forever. As I told you once, long since, it is your responsibility—nay, your duty—to ensure that the evil brought forth by the Revolution does not destroy the good that it has engendered. Do this for me, my love; you could build me no greater a monument.

I can think of nothing else to say. Or rather, there is everything still to say to you, and I should never cease writing, and my tears, in the end, should wash away the ink.

Adieu, my love, adieu.

I FOUND, AS I numbly folded away the letter about the pair of rings and the curl of glossy dark hair, that I had no more tears, else I should have broken down weeping at her last words to me. Enveloped in my deathly calm, I hid away the letter in my coat and bade farewell to Baptistine.

"M'sieur," said she, "I near forgot . . . but she said something else to me, ere she went off with the patrol. She told me to tell you. *Go to Champagne,* she said, *to a village called Méry, and find your mother's folk.*"

Go to Champagne? She had said the same to me, on the day we parted, and her words meant no more to me at that moment than they had three months previous.

"I don't understand. What did she mean?"

"I don't know, M'sieur. I've never heard of this Méry. But that's what she told me to tell you, and very insistent about it she was."

I could not think of her inexplicable message at that moment, or of a village in Champagne, but only of my last glimpse of her, of her pale face, her short-cropped dark hair, her neck bared for the blade.

"I will write to you," said I, touching Baptistine's shoulder, and turned and hurried away.

I would break that promise, I knew, as I trudged slowly southward along the murky rue du Temple. Better that Baptistine knew nothing of Eléonore's fate until Time might soften the blow. Had it not been for our chance encounter at the Palais de Justice, I, too, might never have known the truth, might never have found myself wandering the desolate streets of Paris, knowing I had not been able to save her.

. . . *I love you, above Life itself, and shall always love you.*

And I had not been able to save her.

I COULD NOT yet bear to return to rue Mouffetard. At length my aimless steps led me towards St. Germain-des-Prés. I remembered then that Lorry might very well have his lodgings in an upper floor of the magnificent *hôtel particulier* that housed Tellson's.

He greeted me warmly, beaming, tho' his countenance sobered when he saw me better in the firelight. "Good Heavens, Carton," he exclaimed, "what has happened to you?"

"A personal matter," said I, unwilling to speak of my grief for fear I should break down before him and sob like a child. "A death. There is nothing to be done."

"If I might lend assistance in any way . . ."

"You might be so kind," I told him, "as to give me the Manettes' address—*her* address. I should like to visit them, now. I need to recall that

Hope yet exists for some of us, and for the future, in this sorry world."

"Of course. They are dwelling on the second floor of the big stone house in the cour du Dragon, Number three, not far from here. You can't miss it."

"Darnay is well?"

"Lucie and he . . . are mad with joy."

I nodded. "I should very much like to see them."

"Go, then," said he, pressing my hand. "I have some business here that must be attended to, but I shall call there by and by."

I quitted him and stumbled the few short streets to the cour du Dragon, drawn by a desperate yearning to seek comfort in Lucie's kindness. I wished only to fall to my knees before her and weep out my grief and my shame in the safety of her arms.

The hour was late and the street deserted but for a handful of men, two in National Guard uniform. To my dull misgivings, they and I converged on the door I sought. "Stand aside, Citizen," one of the Guards told me, as he pulled the bell-chain.

"Wait, he's the man we want," said the other. "It's Darnay. I saw him at the Tribunal."

"I am not Charles Darnay," said I, mechanically. "What do you want of him?"

"No use denying it, Citizen," said the Guard, "I know you."

I felt in the breast-pocket of my greatcoat. "I assure you I am not Darnay. Here are my papers."

He took them and inspected them minutely by the light of a torch, at length handing them back to me with a grunt. "Death of the Devil! And not his twin brother, either. I never saw the like. Well then, stand aside."

"What do you want of Darnay?" I repeated, with a dreadful foreboding.

"Under arrest, by order of the Section Committee."

"Under arrest! But he was only just acquitted by the Tribunal! What has he done?"

"He has been denounced, Citizen." The porter answered the door and they pushed their way past me into the house.

I can only imagine Lucie's horror and misery upon learning she was to be separated once more from her husband. I was conscious, in myself, of simple rage, overwhelming my despair, which found its outlet not in curses or futile gestures but in a trembling energy. Slipping into the shadows, I waited until they returned from above, a quarter-hour later, with Darnay in their midst. When they had disappeared in the direction of the Luxembourg, I turned and hastened back to Tellson's.

"Darnay has been re-arrested," said I, as Lorry opened the door to me. "Ten minutes since. I saw it."

"Re-arrested!" he echoed me, astounded, and sank into a chair. "I quitted them not two hours ago—after supper—"

"Nevertheless, it is a fact." I dropt into an armchair opposite him and balanced my chin on my clenched fist. "He has been denounced, they told me. Who in Paris would care to denounce him?"

He patted uneasily at his peruke and shook his head. "I do not know."

"Contrary to what you may think, folk are not denounced and arrested merely because they are ex-Aristocrats. *Petite Noblesse* are active everywhere in the Revolution: Magistrates, Administrators, Journalists . . ." With an effort I forced away thoughts of Eléonore and continued, as if speaking would keep me from remembering. "They are in the Convention, on the Committee of Public Safety even, and two former Noblemen sit on the Jury of the Tribunal itself. The Revolution needs such men—they are the proof to the rest of Europe that the Republic is not ruled by a pack of ditch-diggers and brigands."

"Then what motive could anybody have for denouncing Darnay?"

"I've no idea—and that worries me. Darnay is the most inoffensive of men. He has seen no one, wronged no one, has been safe in prison since the day he arrived in Paris fifteen months ago, after ten years' absence. What manner of resentment—should an old resentment possibly exist—would linger for a decade? I don't understand it, Mr. Lorry."

"Nor do I."

"The good Doctor's reputation preserved Darnay once. Let us hope it will do so again. But I fear his influence may be ebbing, if he was unable to prevent this arrest."

"Then what can we do?"

"Nothing, now. I can perhaps learn who has denounced him and why, and prepare a defence against the charges; but the rest will be resolved, as it was heretofore, at the Tribunal. God will that Dr. Manette's influence stand him in as good stead as it did two days since."

Lorry turned troubled eyes to mine. Suddenly, tho' he always had been the spryest of men, he seemed old and shaken. "And should it not?" he asked me, very softly.

"Manette's name carries far more weight than does mine. But I will exert what little influence I yet possess with men capable of freeing Darnay. At present, once again we can but wait."

He nodded and reached for his coat. "I must go to Lucie. Will you not come with me?"

"No," said I, tho' in my consuming wretchedness I ached still for the sight of her, for the solace of her compassion. But what cold comfort could she offer me at such an unhappy hour? "My presence would accomplish nothing but to trouble her further."

He quitted me and I remained there, wrapt in my sombre thoughts, as the fire died to embers and ash. I felt I could see faces in the dwindling flames: Eléonore's, Darnay's, Lucie's. I had failed Eléonore—of all the souls on Earth, I could not fail Lucie as well. I gazed into the dying coals, silently repeating their names, until at last my grief and exhaustion overcame me and for a short while I slept.

* * *

I SENT A message to Camille about Darnay's re-arrest. I could think of nothing else to do until I knew why he had been imprisoned once again, and when he might be brought to trial.

Maître Tabary reprimanded me severely for my unexplained four days' absence when I shuffled into his chambers the following morning. I listened stonily to his tongue-lashing, then turned and betook myself to the chambers of one of his colleagues. In half an hour I was employed once more, not as a legal dogsbody but as a mere clerk and errand-runner. The pay was sufficient for my scanty wants and I did not care.

As I have mentioned ere now, this work took me often on errands to the Palais de Justice. I shall not write of all the pitiful sights I saw there. The Winter months claimed few illustrious victims, unlike the Autumn. Those condemned in the Winter of Year II of the Republic were the faceless, dying shabby deaths for petty, shabby crimes.

For weeks I dreamt of her, and of Lucie. I dreamt endlessly of my last glimpse of her, of her pale still face, of the axe sliding down—and sometimes her face became Lucie's, her dark hair Lucie's golden curls, hacked away for the blade's icy kiss. At such moments I awoke sweating, gasping for breath, the cloying darkness clinging to me like Paris mud. Then I would reach for the brandy-bottle that stood constantly beside my bed, and gulp down the vile stuff until my throat burnt and my senses swam and I fell into a leaden slumber.

Le Vieux Cordelier's fourth and fifth numbers appeared, despite all. Poor warm-hearted, childish, heedless Camille. For Danton, leader of the faction of Indulgence, political expediency far outshone compassion for the unjustly accused; I believe Camille, however, was sincerely troubled by events and by the three or four or a dozen Condemned who were trundled every day to the place de la Révolution. Certainly Robespierre grew more and more resentful of the dissatisfaction the journal stirred up against the Committee of Public Safety, which now, in fact if not in name, ruled France.

Camille sent me a message one day in January, inviting me to a late supper the next day and intimating that he had some information for me regarding Darnay's case. I duly called at rue du Théâtre-Français the following evening, only to learn from an apologetic Lucile that her husband had not yet returned from an evening session of the Jacobin Club.

He arrived at last, an hour late, flushed, breathless, trembling. Lucile, more sensitive to his mercurial humours than I, took his coat and poured him a glass of Claret ere quietly asking him what had happened.

"I was furious, and I m-made a d__ned fool of myself," he confessed, noisily drinking down half the glassful. "No, I m-made a fool of Robespierre before the Jacobin Club, which is far stupider." He set down the glass, his hand shaking still.

"Camille," murmured Lucile, worried, "what did you say?"

"He was g-going on about *Le Vieux Cordelier*, claiming it's irresponsible and c-counter-revolutionary—he is uneasy, you know, because half the C-Club members read it, and agree with me. He said I was a child with poor judgment and I had been led astray by bad c-companions. And he ended by suggesting they *b-burn* it, like pornography!"

"Burn it?" she echoed him, astounded. "How could he?"

"What should I have done? I c-couldn't suffer him to ride over me so, rough-shod. And I remembered words that someone had said once, ages ago, before the Revolution, and I thought it would teach him a lesson. So I said it to him: *B-Burning is not answering.*"

Lucile paled and clutched at his shoulder. "O God, you didn't!"

"He d-deserved it," muttered Camille. "But he g-gave me a look as if I had been a snake that had stung him. I apologised afterward, but he wouldn't listen to me."

"Unhappily," said I, "that clever remark of yours was made by the sainted Rousseau. Do you not know he is Robespierre's God?"

Evidently he did, for he turned a stricken face to mine, his great black eyes dark hollows in the shadows of the firelight. "O Lord, no. Rousseau . . . of all folk. I had c-completely forgotten."

"And you threw that in his face."

"O Camille . . ." whispered Lucile.

"Don't worry, love, Maxime won't order me arrested for a thoughtless remark . . ."

"Are you quite sure of that?" she asked him. She gazed down at him with a fond rueful smile ere adding that she must help Jeannette with the supper, and quitting us.

"I had some intelligence for you," said Camille, at length. "About Darnay. He is now imprisoned in the Luxembourg, and was denounced on the second of Nivôse—that's December the twenty-second—for Incivism. By three people. Two, a husband and wife, are residents of the Section de Montreuil, and the third is a resident of the Section des Qu-Quatre-Nations—that's his own Section, is it not? Probably an envious neighbour. That's all I c-could learn. I will mention the case to Fouquier if you like, tho' I don't suppose he will be so indulgent when your friend c-comes before the Tribunal for a second time. *No smoke without fire*, is what he will think."

"Nevertheless, we must do all we can. *I* must. Perhaps the greatest service you can do Darnay, and all the prisoners, is to continue with *Le Vieux Cordelier*. Perhaps a few innocent lives may be spared."

He glanced at me, his clever boyish visage haunted suddenly by doubt and remorse. "C-Carton . . . I know that *Le Vieux C-Cordelier* failed—that *I* failed to save—O God, perhaps I have saved no one with my fine writings and I am merely deceiving myself. If truth be told, most likely I have accomplished nothing, this month past, but to draw Robespierre's ire. By G-God, I am sorry . . . I did all I c-could think to do . . ."

"Do not speak of it, I pray you," said I, more roughly than I had intended, for only by thrusting away my grief and my memories could I keep myself from going altogether mad.

"I . . . I shall talk to Danton. Nobody regards me very highly in the C-Convention, you know—I am out of my depth as a statesman and the world knows it—but Danton's name c-carries some authority still. He might be able to do something, c-call in an old debt, perhaps have Darnay's *dossier* conveniently misplaced. That might be for the best. After all, they c-can't do anything worse to you once you are in prison, save to send you to—" He crimsoned and hastily looked away. "I shall do what I can."

22

I T W A S N O T long after my conversation with Camille that I espied John Barsad outside the Conciergerie.

I had, at day's end, delivered a sheaf of papers to a Prosecutor at the Palais de Justice, and was about to trudge home to my indifferent supper and my nightly bottle of bad Bordeaux wine. As I passed through the cour du Mai, I saw a man whom I thought I recognised, tho' I could not think how. Glancing about him, he sidled from the archway in the corner of the courtyard through which prisoners arrive at the Conciergerie, or quit it for the scaffold.

After fourteen years' passage, I did not, of course, remember him. I felt only that his ferret face seemed familiar, vexingly so, and thus (for what better had I to do?) I followed him as he glided from the courtyard to the street. He did not go far, only to the Left Bank and a squalid wine-shop on rue de la Huchette. I elbowed my way inside as he joined a companion at one of the tables, and sat myself at a nearby table in a beam's shadow.

His companion, too, seemed monstrous familiar to me. I listened as best I could in the blare of conversation about us and succeeded in overhearing some of their dialogue. What I heard was enough to persuade me that the two of them were engaged in the contemptible trade of prison-spy and informer, or *mouton*, as the popular *argot* has it. And in another moment, remembering a pair of Affidavit-men connected with an Old Bailey trial that I had cause not to forget, I had recognised them both.

John Barsad and Roger Cly, of all the shifty scoundrels who ever had lied themselves blue in the face for a handful of lucre. With an effort I restrained myself from a burst of sour laughter. Had they perjured and spied themselves to such odium in England, I thought, that they were obliged to ply their unlovely trade in a France whose suspicious rulers—whether Monarchist or Republican—would welcome such men with open arms? Evidently they had concealed their true nationality from their employers, for they spoke French with barbarous Créole accents redolent of New-Orléans or Martinique, which undoubtedly served to disguise a British twang.

With the suspicion that acquaintance with, and a modicum of power over, a *mouton* at the Conciergerie might one day be of use to me, I followed Barsad out of the wine-shop and across the Seine to a seedy house on rue de la Tixeranderie. I waited below until I saw his candle flickering in a fifth-storey window and decided I had, indeed, tracked him to his lair. Satisfied enough with this new discovery, I trudged home to rue Mouffetard and my night's bottle at Le Vieux Chêne.

ROBESPIERRE, THE INCORRUPTIBLE, never will interfere in the workings of what he calls Justice (save perhaps when it is in his own political interest to do so), and I knew from bitter experience that my pleas for his intercession on Darnay's behalf would go unanswered. I learnt, however, that Saint-Just was at last returned to Paris. With little to lose, I wrote to him. A fortnight later I received a terse note informing me that he regretted he was far too busy to examine individual cases. I ought, he added, to petition the Committee of General Security, which oversaw such matters, or perhaps—with acid reference to the political rival he disliked and distrusted—Danton.

Pluviôse passed uneventfully, tho' in retrospect I realise it was the unnatural stillness that precedes the earth-quake; even Camille ceased publishing *Le Vieux Cordelier* for some weeks. I plodded from rue Mouffetard to Maître Haniquet's chambers to the Law Courts to the Old Oak and back again, performing my duties and deadening my senses with the dreary regularity of an automaton. Using any means I had at my disposal, I attempted to gain word of Darnay, but learnt nothing; my hands were tied as utterly as

those of the Condemned—the half-dozen forgers, hoarders, dishonest
army-contractors, deserters, so-called *conspirators*, who every day stumbled
wretchedly from the Conciergerie into Sanson's carts.

In mid-Ventôse I chanced to be crossing the cour du Mai just as a small
four-wheeled carriage with blinds drawn rattled through the gates. Such a
vehicle usually indicated a new prisoner's arrival at the Conciergerie and,
despite my wiser inclinations, I paused to watch. To my numb despair, I
could not mistake the tall figure and the head of thick white hair as the
prisoner alighted. Approaching, I cried "Citizen Aubincourt," and reached
out past the guards who were escorting him to the door.

He heard me and turned about, warmly pressing my hand. "Carton. I
thought never to see you again. I heard—perhaps I was mistaken—that you
had been elected to the Convention?"

"I was. But I resigned my seat."

"And Citizeness Clairville—pardon me, Citizeness Ambert—I understood she ceased publishing *Le Flambeau?*"

"Eléonore is dead," I told him, very quietly. "Six weeks since."

He did not need to be told how she had died. He nodded and released
my hand as the guards, impatient, prodded him onward. "I shall soon join
her, I imagine," said he. "Adieu, Carton."

"But what ill fortune has brought you hither?" I asked him, following
them. "You retired to Montbrison—"

"Montbrison rebelled against the tyranny of the Republic, my friend,
and your charming Citizen-Representative Javogues came to quell the
rebellion in his birthplace by guillotining everyone with whom he had
quarrelled in years gone by." I remembered the rumours about Javogues
that had crept to Paris during the previous Summer, and how disgustful
Robespierre had found the Deputy's bloodthirsty licence. "He has sent me
to be judged by the Parisian tribunal, and there will be an end to it. These
citizens must not be kept waiting," he added, with a glance at his escort.
"I am glad to have seen you once more, my friend." He tipped his

hat to me as they led him down the steps and into the Conciergerie.

The Tribunal condemned him to death a fortnight later. I did not see him again. I could bear no more.

AND GERMINAL ARRIVED, and with it the promise of an early Spring in the jonquils and violets for sale at every street-corner. The *enragés*, smarting under the Committee's whip, fomented an Insurrection that died a-borning; within three days Hébert, Ronsin, Vincent, Clootz, all the leaders of the rebellious Commune and its armed forces, were in prison. On the 4th of Germinal they, too, climbed into Sanson's carts, to the onlookers' contemptuous glee. They say Hébert—who had ceaselessly jeered at the *proud and insolent* bearing of the Condemned—wept and fainted repeatedly during his own last journey through Paris to the place de la Révolution.

On the 5th, the faces in the streets seemed a trifle brighter. Perhaps my own did, too. And I am certain Lucie was gladdened by that ray of Hope, as golden and welcome as sunshine on a bleak Winter's day. How could we not imagine that the *enragés'* fall betokened the true beginning of Danton's celebrated Clemency?

Yet nothing happened to confirm our hopes, and within the week Danton, too, was in prison, and Camille with him.

In the space of a night the faction of Indulgence lay shattered. The Committees arrested Lacroix and Philippeaux as well, Deputies allied with Danton's cause, and tied his name to the tarnished one of his *confrère* Fabre d'Eglantine, that disreputable actor-playwright turned revolutionist, bond-speculator, and swindler. Hérault-Séchelles, arrested weeks before on some nebulous denunciation, was also thrown amongst them for no better reason than that of having been Danton's friend.

I hastened to the Desmoulins' house the evening following, as soon as I heard the breathless tidings repeated throughout Paris. A tearful Jeannette told me that her mistress had rushed out early that morning to fight for

Camille's freedom. As I was quitting the house Lucile returned, her doll-like features wan and haggard.

"I have called on half the Convention, and every member of the Committee of Public Safety, and even those Vampires on the Security Committee," she declared, "and not one will lift a finger for me. Robespierre would not even see me. Are there no longer any *men* in Paris?"

"Were I able to do anything," I told her, "I would help you as best I could. But I am nothing."

"Robespierre likes you . . ."

"If he would not see you, he will not see me. Camille was a far closer friend to him than ever I was."

She twisted her hands together, fingering her marriage-ring. "How could he suffer them to do it? Only a fortnight ago he called on us and seemed friendly as ever towards Camille. The Judas! And I am sure he had never wished to arrest Danton, even. It was those two—Billaud and Collot—and that cold-blooded viper Saint-Just, probably. Maxime suffered them to persuade him that Danton must be destroyed. But Camille? His oldest friend?"

It would be of no use to tell her, I knew, that Camille was far too intimately associated with Danton to escape his fall. "Danton is not conquered so easily," I told her, taking her hand in mine. "Now that they have arrested him, they must try him. The Girondins likewise erred when they sent Marat before the Tribunal. If anybody can make mince-meat of a trumped-up accusation, it will be Danton."

She nodded, a flicker of hope returning to her eyes, and squeezed my hand. "Have you an hour to spare? Wait for me a moment, I pray you." Hurrying into the house, she returned shortly with the baby Horace in her arms. "I am going to the Luxembourg gardens," said she, "in the hope that Camille can see us from a window. It would comfort me if you came with me."

I walked the few streets to the Luxembourg with her and together we made our way along the gravelled paths to the lawn at the rear of the former Palace, now property of the State and used (like the many convents, *collèges,* and ancient châteaux of Paris turned National Property) as a prison for those suspected of crimes against the Republic. As we emerged from beneath the trees I shied back and drew behind a statue.

"Go on," I told Lucile. "I will join you soon."

She cast me a curious glance but strode out to the lawn, pushing her way through the little crowd of idlers to take up a place beside the low paling that keeps one at a distance from the prison. She stood but a few paces from Lucie.

I cannot truly describe how my first glimpse of her in five years affected me. She looked tired, care-worn, a trifle older, and the grey gown she wore drew the colour from her cheeks, yet she was as steadfast and beautiful as I remembered her in happier days. If Darnay could see her from his prison window, the sight could not but have given him, as it gave me, the will to survive against all odds.

I lingered in the shadows beneath the Spring-green trees, watching them both. At last she departed and I joined Lucile.

"Can he see me, do you think?" she asked me, her eyes fixed on the windows.

"I've no idea. But if he can, seeing you and the child could only give him strength, and hope."

"I will send him a spy-glass, when I send him his clean linen to-morrow—" Abruptly she bent her head to stifle a sob. "O Lord, I've not let myself cry since they took him away. But of all my friends, only you know how I suffer . . ."

I pressed her hand and we stood a while longer, watching for we knew not what at the dark windows.

I HOVERED AS long as I dared outside the Tribunal, in the midst of an immense, pushing throng, when two days later the trial of Danton and his comrades began. What can I write of that shameful affair that has not been whispered across Paris? Danton blustered and thundered, scornfully over-turning the flimsy accusations against him. And Fouquier—no doubt instructed to obtain a death-sentence at any cost—dodged, side-stept, twisted like a snake.

Despite Danton's roars of outrage, his demand for Witnesses in his favour, his ferocious attacks upon Fouquier and his masters, by the trial's third day I suspected, with a sinking heart, that he was lost. My employ-ment and the fine weather, however, kept me from the Palais de Justice that day; instead Maître Haniquet kept me on the Right Bank to deliver half a dozen messages and parcels, the last to the Ministry of Justice on the place des Piques. Trudging back along rue St-Honoré as the shadows began to lengthen, by sheer chance I encountered none other than Robespierre and Saint-Just, walking together towards their respective lodgings not far from the square.

Very pinched and strained and paler than ever, Robespierre started as he spied me, and drew back as if I might attack him. Saint-Just, ever self-possessed, bowed and calmly bade me Good-evening.

I gazed at them a moment without responding. "Why did you not take me with them?" I demanded, scarce knowing what I said. "It would have been a blessing."

"With . . . Danton?" said Robespierre, a muscle in his cheek twitching. "Why should we?"

"Because I agreed with him. Because Eléonore d'Ambert was my wife, and because I worked with her for years on *Le Flambeau*—yes, I'll avow it now—and because my behaviour in the Convention was suspect. Because I was Danton's and Camille's friend."

"You were not arrested for the same reason that Legendre, and Thuriot, and Bourdon were not arrested," said Saint-Just. "We have no desire for needless deaths. And, quite frankly, you were not worth the trouble."

"You are too generous," I snapped, and strode on. A moment later, as I paused at a street-corner whilst several waggons passed me, I heard hurrying footsteps behind me. It was Robespierre.

"Citizen," he panted, "perhaps you could do me a very great service. We received in the Committee to-day," he continued, his voice low, "a report from the Luxembourg, which claims the prisoners are plotting to escape, and to massacre the members of the Convention."

I shrugged. "One hears such wild rumours every day."

"It also reports that Lucile Desmoulins has twice been seen in the Luxembourg gardens, in sight of the windows."

"Naturally she was there, hoping Camille could gain some solace by seeing her, and the child. I went with her once myself."

"It claims she was signalling to the prisoners."

I stared at him, a horrible suspicion taking hold of me. "That's nonsense. To what purpose?"

"To communicate aspects of the plot. This Laflotte, the informer, claims she is to distribute money about Paris to raise an army. Then General Dillon and some other prisoners will foment an uprising in the Luxembourg, break out, free Danton, and with this army destroy the republican Government."

"That is the most ludicrous concoction of rubbish that ever I have heard."

He nodded, convulsively. "So I thought, too, but Saint-Just said it would solve everything. He read the report to the Convention and—for fear of the danger, you see—they passed a decree that will permit Fouquier to have the Prisoners removed from the Court, should they cause a disturbance, and to end the trial at any time he wishes."

I stood speechless for a moment upon hearing this stunning and appalling disclosure. "How convenient for you," said I, when I had recovered my wits. "Why trouble with a trial at all, the next time?" I swerved away from him but he caught my sleeve.

"Citizen—I have thrown myself unwillingly into this battle, but it's a battle to the death. I will not—*cannot* suffer Danton to go free now. We must use this advantage."

"Well?"

"Don't you understand, Carton? We have chosen to accept the fact of a conspiracy in the Luxembourg. We shall have to arrest Lucile as a conspirator, as well."

"No," I whispered. "God's death, no!"

"She will be arrested within the next twenty-four hours, possibly to-night."

"You cold-blooded little—" I began.

"I have no more wish than do you for her blood," he interrupted me, fidgeting with his spectacles as his cheek twitched violently. "Yet what can I do? We have made our decision. Were somebody to warn her of her danger, however, perhaps conceal her, somebody quite beneath the Committees' notice . . ."

"Yes," I agreed, nodding once. "Perhaps somebody will." I turned and sped away.

It was near eight o'clock when I arrived at Camille's apartment. Jeannette admitted me and led me into the parlour, her kind, foolish countenance lined with worry. Lucile and her mother rose as I entered. I bowed perfunctorily and drew Lucile into her husband's study, where the books and papers strewn across the floor bore mute witness to the swift thorough search the arresting patrol had made thro' his effects.

"I have just spoken a moment with Robespierre," I told her. "Danton is doomed, Lucile. They cannot suffer him to be acquitted, or their own lives would not be worth a cracked sou. Now they have fabricated a story of a plot, which will end the trial and give the Tribunal the perfect opportunity to convict him." I paused. She stared straight at me, her lips a little parted. "Do you heed me?"

Her voice was scarce audible. "Yes."

"They have included your name in the plot, because they say you have been signalling to prisoners in the Luxembourg. And to be believed, they shall have to arrest you, too."

"Arrest me," she echoed me, expressionless.

"If you come with me now," I told her, "I can hide you away at my lodgings. No one will find you there—no one cares about a brandy-soaked wretch like me. Borrow one of Jeannette's dresses and give the child to your mother's care. You will be completely safe, I promise you. Robespierre sent me himself. You have my word that he wishes no harm to come to you."

"I thank you," she murmured, "for courting such danger for me."

"There is no danger—" I began.

"You ought not to have such confidence in Maximilien Robespierre's assurances."

I seized her hand. "Come, you must quit this place immediately. Change your dress and—"

"There is no hope for Camille?" said she, without meeting my gaze.

"I fear not." I reached out to smooth her hair and wipe away a tear that trembled on her eyelashes. "Danton and he are too close-linked. I am sick thinking of it . . . he is a dear friend."

"Yet Robespierre hopes to salve his conscience by suffering me to escape."

"Yes, I imagine that is how he sees it."

"He can't have that satisfaction!" she cried, whipping about and clenching her fists. "If he is to have Camille's blood, then he can have mine, too, and I hope he strangles on it!"

"Lucile," I insisted, "this is no game. To-night, in a few hours, they will arrest you . . ."

She shook her head. "No. I shan't run away."

"Lucile, it's your death if you don't!"

"And Camille's death?" she demanded. "Can Robespierre change that? Will he offer to help *him* escape?" She drew a deep breath and closed her eyes for a moment. "I don't care any more. I would far rather follow my husband."

"But your child?"

"My mother will care for him." Sighing, she clasped her hands beneath her chin, as if she were praying. "I told you that you were the only soul who could possibly know how I am suffering. Can't you understand? I am twenty-three years old—and they are going to murder my husband, the only man I ever loved, or will love. How much time have I—thirty, forty, *fifty years* without him? It would be unendurable. I love Horace because he is Camille's child—but I cannot live without Camille." She glanced up at me, abruptly calm once again. "Go on, I pray you, ere they find you here with me."

"I cannot—"

"If by some miracle Camille and Danton are saved," she told me, impatient, "then what will it matter should I go to prison for a few days? But if he dies . . . then I should like nothing better than to join him."

The pretty, giddy doll-child I had known for three years had matured over-night to this resolute stranger. I gazed at her a moment and at last, without further words, lifted her hand to my lips. She gave me a sweet, melancholy smile, a fleeting reminder of the playful Lucile I once had known, and pushed me gently towards the door. "I have made my choice, Citizen Carton. Now go, I pray you."

We returned together to the *salon*, where Lucile bade me Good-night and turned tranquilly to her mother, speaking of some trivial message from Camille's printers that had had to be answered. As I paused, turning back in the doorway, she raised a hand to me in a silent gesture of Farewell.

23

THE DAY AFTER I paid my fruitless visit to Lucile, 16th Germinal, the 5th of April, the Tribunal condemned Danton and all his companions to Death. Disheartened, unbelieving, I slunk out once again to the place de la Révolution. It was a warm, fragrant, perfect Spring day and the crowd was vast—but silent, silent as the grave, showing no triumph, not daring to show its dismay.

Sanson seemed particularly grim, as if he sensed he were about to guillotine the very essence of the Revolution. In the green park-land of the Champs-Elysées the lilacs were in bloom, their scent drifting on the soft breeze towards the scaffold.

Camille was weeping. "They are not content with my blood—they wish to murder my wife also!" he had cried at the Tribunal, upon hearing the decree read that would send him to his own death. Hérault, Aristocrat to the end, evinced nothing more than well-bred indifference and smiled as his mistress waved Farewell to him from one of the Treasury's windows. He had survived Eléonore by a mere three months.

The axe fell fifteen times that day. Hérault was the first to die, climbing the steps to the platform as if he were visiting a lady's bed-chamber. Avoiding the executioners' touch as long as he might, he shrugged away their reaching hands until they bound him to the plank, that bloody bed upon which his ultimate mistress Mdme. Guillotine would render him his last embrace.

Camille, poor brilliant, foolish Camille, followed him. I remembered the bright-eyed child I had befriended so many years since and my throat clenched in pain as I tasted a bitter tang in my mouth. At the final moment he somehow mastered his tears, despite the terrible suspicion that his Lucile would not long survive him; tho' he cried her name in anguish at the instant the blade plunged down. Had someone cruelly told him they had arrested her during the night, a few hours after I had quitted her?

Danton they kept until the end, to endure fourteen drops of the axe, fourteen cascades of blood, and he stonily watched them all. When at length his own turn came and they pushed him to the plank, he twisted about and growled his magnificent final words to Sanson:

"Show my head to the People—it's worth your trouble."

And it was done. I stood in the midst of the staring, speechless crowd, gazing at the dripping thing Sanson held at arm's length, and I knew then our last hope had perished.

I might have taken my turn upon that fatal platform any time those five months past, I brooded, yet Fate, mocking me once again, had spared me. But to what purpose? To live wretched and disregarded in a city ruled by Death, envying those I loved who had died beneath the axe?

Yet a few whom I loved remained still; tho' I feared to take myself near Lucie, feared that in some fantastic manner I might carry the taint of the Guillotine about me like a contagion. Perhaps, I realised, remembering my promise made to her so long since on a Summer's evening in London, here was the purpose for which Destiny had spared me. I made a solemn vow to all the Powers above, whilst the whispering crowd dispersed and Sanson's men sponged down the scaffold, that no matter the cost I would save Darnay, my friend, the husband Lucie loved so dearly.

To be sure, I knew not how I might fulfil my vow. With the Indulgents' fall, Clemency was scarce a remembered dream. If Darnay's chance of a second acquittal had been slender ere then, it was negligible now that the Committee of Public Safety ruled unopposed, and Robespierre spoke for it.

I wandered, dispirited, along the river-side as the blood-red Sun sank behind me: past the Tuileries gardens, fragrant with the soft scents of Spring, and the great gallery of the Louvre; past the public bath-houses and the naked, squealing children bathing in the shallows; past the laun-dresses on their flat-boats and the shouting barge-men at the water's edge; until I found myself hard by the Pont-Neuf and crossed it to the Ile de la Cité. The three dunce-cap towers of the Conciergerie loomed ahead of me. I slouched past them, turning with a dreadful irresistible impulse towards the gate to the cour du Mai, through which so many folk—so many faces I have recognised—have ridden to their deaths. As I did so I espied Barsad again, slipping with the furtive grace of a weasel through the indifferent passers-by.

He might indeed be a useful man to know, I reflected, retreating a few paces so he would not notice me. A *mouton* under threat of denunciation as an enemy spy could do me any number of services, even, were such a feat possible, to executing an escape.

I wandered on, turning, unwilling, back towards Maître Haniquet's chambers. Their faces swam before me, the memories stabbing like rapiers. Stinging tears welled from beneath my eyelids, despite my efforts to squeeze them back.

I was in no frame of mind to return to my employer's tedious business. I entered the first tavern I saw, ordered *eau-de-vie*, and slouched over it at a shadowed table in the common-room. For some reason some thing in the place—the tilt of a beam, the dingy, tarnished looking-glass on the wall, the flea-bitten tabby-cat skulking beneath a bench—reminded me of the Tudor Rose, that for five years had not seen me and I doubted would ever see me more.

By a natural association of ideas I remembered the evening following Darnay's trial at the Old Bailey, and how insufferably I had behaved. Upon how many occasions had I glared at my reflexion during those wasted years, hoping against Hope to see my looking-glass image, so similar and so different, rather than my own? I heaved myself to my feet and gazed gloomily into the glass, as if I could extract some inspiration from it. My face, pale and weary, shadows staining the hollows beneath my eyes, stared back at me. With a bitter smile I fancied that Darnay, after nineteen months' imprisonment, could look scarce better than I. At last we might be the same man, truly twins, equals, as alike (as the French say) as two drops of water.

Then I knew, if worse came to worst as I feared it would, what I must do.

9 Prairial (28 May 1794)

THAT NIGHT, RETREATING to my fusty room, I began this chronicle of my life. To-night, seven weeks later, as I glance at the heap of paper beside me, I am amazed to discover what a quantity of ink may be spent even on such a worthless life as mine. Lucie would say otherwise, that my life has possibilities to be tested still; but I think I have done all the good I ever shall do, and it was not much. And one cannot deny I failed where I needed most to prevail. Eléonore, Aubincourt, Camille, Lucile . . . their faces haunt me still, will haunt me to my last day, and no one now living—save Lucie, perhaps—will weep for me when I am gone, or even remember me.

EIGHT DAYS AFTER Danton and Camille died, Lucile followed them, with twenty-four others implicated in the dubious Luxembourg Plot. She looked radiant as a bride, clad in a fresh white gown, smiling, her cheeks aglow. Far from bewailing her own fate, she was endeavouring to console the sobbing woman beside her in Sanson's cart. I remembered her last words to me and I could not find it in me to weep for her, seeing her happiness, but I felt a terrible rage and despair that a young woman who might have had everything to live for could find her felicity only in death.

I stumbled home that evening drunken with horror. If so passionate a love could lead that charming, capricious doll-child to forsake life for her beloved's sake, then I had no doubt it could lead others to the same melancholy conclusion. A day only after Lucile went to her death, a woman cried out "Long live the King!" in the midst of the Tribunal itself, a moment after she saw her brother condemned, and was herself condemned and executed within twenty-four hours. Would Lucie do the same, to spare herself a lifetime of aching empty years, to remain at her husband's side thro' Eternity? I think she might. Should I fail to save him, I fear she would gladly seek to join him.

This time I cannot, must not fail.

11 Prairial (30 May 1794)

THIS ACCOUNT OF mine must now of necessity become wholly a journal, in which I shall recount the days as they pass until I may act at last, God willing, to save Darnay, to save Lucie, to save all those whom I love who remain to me. Meanwhile, I wait. I keep watch on Barsad, tho' I have not yet confronted him; it would not do to frighten him off ere I have occasion to make use of him. I can prowl about the Palais de Justice and gather what information I may, for they are accustomed there to the sight of me and they know I am harmless.

14 Prairial (2 June 1794)

To-day is the anniversary of the fall of the Brissotin traitors (or, more tamely, the expulsion of the Girondins from the Convention). No doubt somewhere they celebrate the great day in the usual manner with much high-flown oratory.

Folk talk of nothing but the great Festival of the Supreme Being that Robespierre has advocated, which will be celebrated on 20 Prairial, the 8th of June. From the *enragés'* Atheism the Convention has returned to conceding that there is a God, though the Christian God, with his Papist superstition and flummery, evidently will not do. I have overheard one or two impertinent young men observing that Robespierre wants to be not only King but also Pope. Meanwhile (for the renewed existence of God has not disposed the Tribunal towards an excess of mercy), Sanson's carts took thirteen men to the scaffold yesterday, and thirty-two to-day.

I have had no word yet regarding Darnay.

17 Prairial (5 June 1794), five o'clock in the morning

YESTERDAY MORNING YOUNG Chartier, one of the clerks at the Tribunal, told me that the ex-Marquis de Saint-Evrémonde is to be judged to-day, and I ought to secure myself a good place in the chamber to watch the *entertainment.* At last it is begun.

With this knowledge, yesterday I visited my Section head-quarters, where, with some patience, a few discreet livres, and my card of good Citizenship, I had my travelling papers *visé*'d for Calais. As evening fell I returned to the cour du Mai and waited for Barsad. As he hurried through the courtyard, I put myself carelessly in his path. Colliding with me, he muttered an apology and attempted to dodge away, but I had firm hold of his sleeve.

"I should like a word with you, Mr. Barsad," I murmured in his ear, in English. He gave a violent start.

"What do you want?" he demanded. "You must be mistaking me for somebody else, Citizen."

"Not at all. I have a good memory for faces, and yours, Sir, is a face not easily forgotten."

"Who are you?"

"Take a good look," said I, keeping hold of him and continuing to speak softly in English. "Think back to the trial of one Charles Darnay, a Frenchman, at the Old Bailey in 1780."

"Darnay," he muttered. "Darnay . . . Treason! The Frenchy, the one they acquitted." He twisted in my grip and for the first time had a clear look at me, his sharp ferret eyes widening in panic. "Now, now, look, Sir, that was years ago. Don't you go holding that against me. 'Twasn't a personal grudge, Sir, I was only doing a job, see?"

"O, I understand your motives pretty well, friend, but I am not Darnay."

"The lawyer?" said he, after a moment's reflexion. "The spit an' image of Darnay; it's what got him off."

"The same. I congratulate you on an excellent memory. Now, Mr. Barsad, I should like a little talk with you."

"Don't say that name!" he hissed, changing once more to French. "And don't keep on talking in English, for the love of Heaven. I am Gilles Dubœuff here."

"A good French name: for a good Frenchman and excellent patriot, of course. So dedicated to the Republic, in fact, that he takes a virtuous delight in denouncing its enemies wheresoever they may be found, even in the prisons. But then you have had extensive experience in such work, have you not, across the Channel?"

He cringed. "What do you want of me?"

"Let us find a congenial place to talk a little, and I shall tell you." I released him and he retreated a pace or two, shaking himself.

"Why should I go anywhere with you?"

"Really, Mr. *Barsad*, I can't say, if you can't."

"You've got nothing on me that I've not got on you," he declared, tho' I saw him pale. "What do *you* do in Paris? You're as English as I am."

"You think so? In fact I am for all intents a French citizen, and I have a valid card of Civism made out in my own name—which, by the way, is Carton—and signed by Robespierre himself."

He scowled at me a moment ere dropping his gaze. "Well then," he muttered, "tell me what you want."

"In good time." I had thought of leading him back to my room, but remembered that Lorry's lodgings at Tellson's were far closer. "Come take a walk with me."

LORRY EXCLAIMED AT the sight of me, for he had seen nothing of me since the night of Darnay's second arrest, five months since. "You remember this fellow, perhaps, Sir?" said I, as I ushered Barsad inside.

"I seem to have an association with the face . . ."

"I told you you have a remarkable face, Mr. Barsad," I drawled. "Witness at the Old Bailey, Mr. Lorry."

He stiffened and drew back as if before some species of vermin. I gestured Barsad to a chair and turned to the old gentleman. "Darnay is to go before the Tribunal again, to-morrow."

"I know. Manette came by, an hour since."

"What said he? What he sanguine of another success?"

"He spoke hopefully, yet he seemed troubled."

"As am I," I confessed. "The first charge against Darnay was only emigration, and he was not an *émigré* in their strict sense of the word. This time, however, he has been denounced. The charge is the usual one of Incivism and Conspiracy. Tho' it's certainly false, the Doctor cannot explain such a grave accusation away so easily."

"But what else can be done?"

"Very little. We must trust in Dr. Manette's reputation to save Darnay once again. If it is not enough, however . . . I imagine Mr. Barsad, here, can be persuaded to lend his peculiar talents, and knowledge, and privileges, to our cause."

Barsad cast me a sharp glance. "What did you have in mind, Sir? Escape? It's impossible."

"Is it?" said I. "Then how do rumours begin, Mr. Barsad?"

"There have been one or two escapes from the Conciergerie," he admitted. "But by ordinary inmates awaiting trial, not by prisoners condemned to Death. You don't know the place, Sir. None of *them* could escape in a hundred years."

"You are very certain of that?" demanded Lorry.

"I tell you, Sir, it can't be done. If your Darnay was an ordinary prisoner in the Conciergerie, and we'd had a month to plan it, then we might— *might* have managed something. But one of the Condemned? Never."

I sighed, suspecting he spoke truth. Escape had been a faint hope at best. "Very well. I can make use of you still, never fear."

He eyed me suspiciously. "How?"

"Let me first see how I can persuade you to lend us your aid," I told him, and seated myself comfortably at a table on which stood a decanter of brandy. "Mr. Lorry, you might be so kind as to fetch me a couple of glasses. Now, then, what have we here? An Englishman abroad in Paris, when all British subjects are fondly imagined to be safe behind bars. —A glass of brandy, Mr. Barsad? No? Then you'll not mind if I indulge myself, will you? —An English Affidavit-man, in fact, long in the pay of the aristocratic, despotic English Government, or indeed anybody who would grease his palm, who is now a *mouton* in the pay of the Republic, under a French name . . ."

I drank off the brandy and poured out more. "Nor is he alone in Paris, but from time to time sees an old acquaintance, another Englishman equally disguised and equally honourably employed as a prison-informer." From the corner of my eye I saw him start, tho' he hid his discomfiture well. "The inference being, undoubtedly, that the two of them are enemy spies still in the pay of the aristocratic, despotic English Government, now at war with France. Agents of a foreign plot, in fact. Robespierre has spoken of such men, and such a plot, for months."

Barsad squirmed. I smiled at him and poured myself a third glass. "I believe nothing would be easier than to denounce you to the nearest Section Committee. What do *you* think?" I drank off the glassful as he watched me narrowly, gnawing his lip.

"I hope you'd not be so rash, Sir. What would it profit you?"

"What indeed? No, you are more valuable to me alive than dead. And you can remain alive if you are disposed to grant me a small favour."

"Don't waste your time asking me to help your friend escape the Condemned cell," he insisted. "It would only put my head in the little window, too, without fail, and I'd far rather take my chances with being denounced, thank you very much."

I poured out a fourth glassful of brandy. "Did I request you to plan an escape? What I have in mind is quite insignificant: as I said, a small favour."

"What favour?"

I rose, glass in hand, and leant against the mantel-shelf, thinking how best to word my demand. He was, of course, right in telling me that too dangerous a task might send him to the Guillotine more surely than would denunciation; I could not request over-much of him. I sighed and put the glass to my lips. The brandy's acrid reek, however, abruptly set my stomach to churning. Instead I slowly poured it away in a thin golden stream upon the hearth.

"Let us speak alone." I gestured him through the first door I saw and shut it behind me. "Now then. Charles Darnay is my friend. Should it go ill with him to-morrow at the Tribunal, I've no wish to see him publicly executed. If escape is impossible, better he should die peacefully in prison than beneath the axe."

"Ah . . . you wish him to cheat Sainte Guillotine, do you?"

"Precisely."

"That's simple enough," said he, shrugging. "Give me the dose and I'll be sure to pass it on to him. A quick poison is best. What d'you have?"

"Opium."

He nodded. "Opium's good. If they misjudge the dose, at least they are dead asleep, or so far up in the clouds they never notice a thing. It's happened ere now. Let's have it."

"Not you. I. I will give it him myself, or not at all."

He gaped at me as if I had sprouted a second head. "You? But why not—you can trust me to do it, Sir."

"Trust—*you?*"

"Now, look, Mr. Carton, why complicate matters—"

"You will not change my mind. I wish a quarter-hour alone with Darnay."

"You are asking me to get you inside the Conciergerie," protested he. "It's not done. It's never done."

"Arrange it."

"Maybe . . . you are an Attorney. Maybe I could get you in to see to the prisoner's last wishes, some thing of that order. Still, I can promise you nothing."

"Find a way," said I, "or the next day I call on the Committee of General Security and tell them the shocking truth about one of their informers."

"No, Mr. Carton, Sir—I swear it! I'll do it somehow. I will get you in, the Devil knows how."

"There, that is a much better attitude, Mr. Barsad. I am confident in your ingenuity. You may use my name, should somebody enquire. They know me well at the Palais de Justice."

"It would be a deal simpler if only you'd let me give it him myself," he muttered.

"I expect I shall have a message for Darnay from his wife. Do you imagine I would care to soil it by sending it by way of your mouth?"

"Now that's unkind, Sir," said he, wounded. "We all have to live as best we can."

"So we do, Mr. Barsad, so we do. Very well. Should Darnay be condemned, you will obtain me a quarter-hour's private visit with him. If you do exactly as I say, you will have nothing to fear from me."

"And if he is acquitted?"

"God will it be so! Tho' I fear the worst. But if he is acquitted, then our bargain is void and you may go your merry way, Citizen Gilles Dubœuff. As you said, what would it profit me to denounce you?"

"I'll get you into the Conciergerie," he promised me. "Somehow."

I saw him out of the apartment and watched him scuttle down the *hôtel's* sumptuous marble stair-case. When he had disappeared, I turned to Lorry, who had come quietly up behind me.

"What have you arranged with that man?" he asked me.

"Nothing much. If Darnay is condemned I shall be able to visit him, once."

"But that will not save him?"

"I never said it would."

He bowed his head. "Poor Lucie."

"You have told her nothing still of my presence here?" said I.

"Nothing."

"Good, it's better so . . . well! The hour is late; we can do nothing more until to-morrow. Your business is done in Paris, Mr. Lorry?"

"It was done weeks since, if truth be known. I am ready to quit France. Naught but the Manettes' plight has kept me here."

"Your papers, your pass to quit the city?"

"In order. I think I might quit it at any time I wish. I am too old to be an enemy spy, God knows."

"Because if Darnay is condemned, they must quit Paris as soon as possible. She must not wait here to mourn him. She might, in her grief, be indiscreet, place herself in danger; she might be purposely indiscreet."

"Purposely?"

"Lucile Desmoulins knew she was to be arrested, and chose to follow her husband to the scaffold rather than flee."

He turned horrified eyes to mine. "I will do whatsoever is within my power."

"You are a brave soul, Sir," I told him, pressing his hand. "I am glad they may rely on you."

"And on you, Carton. I must confess I would have been at a loss, alone."

"Yes, well, perhaps. You know me, Mr. Lorry . . . you know I am not often good for much. Yet I might be able still to do her some trifling service or other. You are going to them now? She will need comforting to-night."

"I was about to go when you came."

"Then I will walk with you to her door, Sir. You will see me again to-morrow. Don't look for me at the Tribunal, but I shall be there."

"Carton, I had all but forgotten," said he, suddenly, as he pulled on his coat and straightened his peruke. "A fellow called on me, months since, asking for you. It was Darnay's old steward, Gabelle—the man he came to Paris to vouch for. The porter tells me he has returned half a dozen times since."

"Gabelle?" I echoed him, all amazement. "What could he want of me? I have scarce met the man."

"He said as much, that you had scarce met, yet he claimed he needed to speak with you. A matter of some delicacy, he said. You had left me no address wherein I might find you, so I could do nothing save tell him your name. But he seemed already to know it."

"How odd. Tho' I expect he was startled at the sight of me in December," said I, dismissing the matter. "Probably he wishes to tell me that he thinks I am Darnay's long-lost twin brother, stolen by Gypsies from my cradle."

Lorry smiled, despite his anxiety. I walked with him to Lucie's house in the cour du Dragon and lingered a while at the *porte-cochère*, thinking how every day she had quitted that door for the long walk to the Right Bank, to La Force. A wistful impulse drove me to follow her footsteps thither and stand where she had so often stood.

Gabelle . . . what faint association have I with that name?

I arrived at the Marais, at length discovering the spot where I think Lucie must have waited beneath the prison windows, at the corner of rue des Droits de l'Homme and the little passage that links it to rue Antoine, by a wood-sawyer's shed. He was sitting on the door-sill, enjoying his pipe in the warm Spring night, as I strolled by. I responded civilly as he bade me Good-evening and he grinned at me. "A popular place for looking at the prison, eh?" said he, with a glance up at the forbidding wall. "Other folk look up at the windows, too. Once a pretty citizeness used to come hither, every day, rain or shine. Her husband was locked up there, she said. Too bad!"

"A pretty citizeness?" said I, indifferent.

"Beautiful, Citizen, beautiful! No longer in her first youth, but still the sort of dainty golden-haired wench a lonely widower dreams of. Too fine for the likes of me, though. But she doesn't come any more. Her husband went to the Tribunal, is my guess. But I wouldn't know; I haven't the time to see them at the Tribunal."

"No?"

"I've work to do. It's all I can do to spare an hour to see the show at the place de la Révolution."

"You go thither every day, do you?"

"Every day, whensoever I can. It's a free show, no? Sixteen shortened to-day, and carried off very nice, without a hitch. To be sure, like that it becomes a mite dull."

"Dull?"

"They never make a fuss any more. Not like du Barry, who squalled like a roasted cat." He sighed. "But Danton was a fine sight. He had b_ll_cks, he did. Pity . . . Have you been to see it yourself? Go watch Sainte Guillotine at work when Sanson has a good batch, fifteen or twenty. It's quite a sight to see, how smooth they manage it! But they've had plenty of practice, eh?"

"Indeed they have," I said, bidding him Good-night.

I could not have slept. Instead I walked, slowly but steadily, my footsteps echoing like heart-beats in the dark streets. Rue Antoine; the place de Grève; the corner at rue de la Vannerie where Camille's notorious Lantern-bracket innocently hangs still, having out-lived its namesake; rue Honoré.

Outside the new Comédie-Française at the Palais-Egalité, amidst the cheerful throng of theatre-goers, I assisted a woman and child across the muddy street. I paused there a moment, remembering Eléonore, and the Revolution's rosy dawn. Realising then that if I walked on, I would retrace the route she had taken to the scaffold, I turned with a shudder and walked instead towards the Tuileries and the Seine. The evening session at the Convention had concluded a few minutes previous and the Deputies were strolling out to the place du Carrousel as I approached. No one recognised me, unkempt and disreputable as now I appear; the Deputies, engrossed as they were in braving the tempests of war without, and war within, and discord amongst themselves, had long since forgotten me.

My drifting path took me across the river and once again to the corner of rue Gil-Cœur and rue des Arts. The heart-ache that never had quitted me since that terrible Winter day was duller now, and I could bear to gaze up at the walls that once had sheltered us.

In my pocket I fingered the phial of opium I had carried with me always since that day, tho' I had a better purpose for it now. Remembering how intent and yet how perversely unwilling I had been to avail myself of its dubious blessing, I wondered anew if Fate—or God, if I truly believed still in a benevolent God—had preserved me for the task to which I had pledged myself.

It was well past midnight. I might have returned home then to rue Mouffetard and attempted to snatch a few hours' sleep, but I was wakeful still. Instead I glanced once more at the windows that once had been Eléonore's, breathed a tender Farewell to them, and turned westward along the quay. Half an hour's walk brought me to the bridge that ere the Republic's birth had been named after Louis XVI, which leads to the place de la Révolution.

I crossed the vast square to the foot of the scaffold. The pair of National Guards posted there to protect the Republic's property leant, snoring, against the beams supporting the platform. One man woke as I approached, tho' he said nothing, watching me with sleepy, incurious eyes as I slowly made a tour about the paling erected to keep out the crowds and sensation-seekers.

The blade and its drop-weight were missing. Undoubtedly they must take it away every night to be sharpened. In the wan moonlight, without that sombrely gleaming steel triangle the Guillotine possessed a certain grace, a spare elegance in its long, precise lines. Draped in the folds of the oiled canvas that protects it from the weather, it might have been a triumphal gateway, raised to celebrate the Revolution's glory.

I gazed at it, at the towering twelve-foot frame and the empty span at the summit where the blade ought to have been, imagining that razor-edge slashing through my flesh. They have claimed, since the Guillotine was first put to use two years since, that it gives no pain, only mercifully quick death. Yet how can anyone know with absolute assurance that this be true? Something tightened in the pit of my stomach, sending a shudder through me, as I stood studying it.

So many of those whom I had loved and cared for had preceded me thither. So many men and women I had known had looked upon their last sight at that spot, had climbed those steps, had gazed up at those twin beams just as I was doing. So many Ghosts might hover about that place, lamenting lives vainly cut short. Eléonore, my Léo whose death had left me lost and helpless as an orphan child. Lucile, Camille . . . Aubincourt . . . Danton, Hérault, Vergniaud, Brissot, Charlotte de Corday . . . so many I had known, and so many more whom I had not.

Pallida Mors æquo pulsat pede pauperum tabernas Regumque turris—Pale Death kicks her way equally into the hovels of the poor and the castles of Kings. So many, peasants and Royalty alike, have been led uncomprehending to that spot, that blood-sodden patch of ground. So many, their names and faces already half-forgotten. They have travelled that road; why do I dread so to follow them?

At last I tore myself from those dark contemplations and returned the way I had come, without looking behind me. The sentry, bored and suspicious, watched me gloomily as I passed.

24

ONLY EIGHTEEN HOURS have passed since I last added to this journal, yet it seems an age.

As the pale dawn broke over the roof-tops, I trudged home to rue Mouffetard. I slept a little, then sifted through my few belongings, thinking to pack my valise. At last I placed in it a single change of clothes and the only articles that had any meaning for me: this account of mine, and Eléonore's last letter to me.

In the morning I left the valise at Lorry's lodgings and went on to the Palais de Justice. As I edged my way into the rear of the Salle de Liberté, I glimpsed Barsad, who quickly looked away.

I endured well-nigh a dozen trials and condemnations that morning whilst I awaited Darnay's appearance. At length the Tribunal adjourned for dinner and the chamber slowly emptied. As I strolled out with the rest of the spectators, I perceived a man and woman standing together at one side of the chamber, having moved not an inch from their places. Both of them, the woman especially, seemed grimly determined to remain. At length he touched her arm, glancing towards the doors, but she shook her head *No*. I remembered that Darnay had been denounced by a husband and wife from the Section de Montreuil—part of the *faubourg* Antoine—and guessed those roughly though decently-clad *sans-culottes* were his denouncers, altho' I could not imagine their motives.

I sat an hour in an eating-house, tho' I could not touch a mouthful, and returned. As the session began, I saw Lorry enter, and I saw Lucie at the forefront of the spectators, on her father's arm. As the prisoners appeared, were judged—so deplorably quickly!—and disappeared once more into the corridors beyond the chamber, she grew ever paler until I feared she might collapse.

In all, eighteen men and three women passed before the Judges that day, the charges so monotonous and hackneyed I might have been reading the accounts of a hundred other trials. Conspiracy against the People, remarks tending towards the re-establishment of Royalty, fraudulent provisioning of the armies, conspiracy and correspondence with the enemies of the State, plots to destroy the national Representation, conspiracy to cause famine, conspiracy in a house of arrest. Twenty-one men and women were condemned to Death before my eyes to-day and I abruptly grew sick with horror that I could do nothing for them, that at best I could save one man of the hundreds, thousands who had been and might be condemned.

At last Darnay appeared, as the clocks struck four. The loving, tranquil smile Lucie turned towards him heartened me as much as it did him, though she could not have known it.

Fouquier himself, who knew full well (for it would have been there in the *dossier*) that Darnay had spent but two days at liberty in the space of twenty-one months, seemed doubtful of the accusations, but impatiently rattled out the charge: Incivism and Conspiracy to overthrow the Republic. As he called the citizens who had denounced the Prisoner, the man and woman whom I had earlier seen came forward: Citizen Ernest Defarge, wine-vendor of the Section de Montreuil, and Citizeness Thérèse Defarge, his wife. Then the third name was read—"Alexandre Manette, Physician, resident of the Section des Quatre-Nations"—and the chamber gave way to one concerted gasp and murmur of astonishment.

The Doctor rose, protested, swore it was a vicious calumny. Dumas, the presiding Judge, sharply told him Lucius Junius Brutus had sentenced to Death his own sons who had conspired to overthrow the Roman Republic, and his duty, if necessary, was to do the same. This admonition done, he called Defarge to the stand and bade him give his testimony.

I listened, a heavy certainty weighing down my heart until my whole being was leaden with despair, as Defarge recounted his discovery of the crumbling journal hidden in the Doctor's old cell in the Bastille. Listened as the journal was read, as the Doctor's own words told the fantastical and horrifying tale of his imprisonment, of the dying peasant girl and boy to whom he had been called to administer: the peasant girl who had been savagely raped and beaten, and the brother who had defended her only to be spitted like a hare by a contemptuous Aristocrat's blade.

(My memory stirred. "Ugly rumours . . ." Darnay had said to me, above twenty years since: "They say he prefers little girls, tho' he'll take any woman who strikes his fancy . . . he enjoys deflowering them, corrupting them, hurting them . . .")

Of the husband who had died of abuse so a covetous Seigneur might have his way with the young wife; of the unborn child that had died with its mother; of the father whose heart had failed him at his son-in-law's death and his daughter's defilement; of the young sister who had disappeared, been hidden away, the only survivor of that doomed and wronged family.

("A couple of prostitutes whom he had beaten nearly to death . . . he was a murderer two or three times over . . .")

Of the bestial, arrogant, and indifferent Nobleman who had raped the chaste young peasant wife, and the scarce less vicious brother who had aided him, who had connived at the abduction and who undoubtedly had taken his turn with her.

("His uncle was a consummate beast, and his father was scarce better . . .")

Of the Doctor's troubled report of the rape to the Minister of Justice, and the Nobleman's casual resolution of this inconvenience, by forever burying in prison the sole witness to the crime, as carelessly as he might flick away a fly.

("It must have been something uncommonly revolting . . .")

Of the name the dying boy had snarled with his last breath: Saint-Evrémonde.

I watched Darnay. He was deathly pale. I recalled once again how his fruitless efforts to make restitution for a dreadful iniquity, the shameful family secret, had for years taken him back and forth from England to France and set all our paths to crossing.

". . . And them and their descendants, to the last of their race, I, Alexandre Manette, unhappy Prisoner, do this last night of the year 1767, in my unbearable agony, denounce to the times when all these things shall be answered for. I denounce them to Heaven and to Earth."

In the frozen silence, the Clerk of the Court placed the manuscript's last page on the desk before him. Someone amongst the spectators screeched "Death!" and many voices took up the cry. As Dumas's bell rang futilely in the clamour, Fouquier shrugged and turned to the Jury. "Have you any doubt, Citizens," he shouted above the uproar, "that the descendant of such men, who misfortunately have escaped earthly Justice, is capable of betraying the Republic, the Nation, the People of France? What other proof need you?"

The Jury had hardly turned to confer ere their foreman rose and said "Guilty." The tumult increased. My heart lay like a stone within me; I could scarce breathe.

"The Revolutionary Tribunal finds Charles-Félicien de Marbois, former Marquis de Saint-Evrémonde, called Charles Darnay, guilty of conspiring against the liberty of the French People," Dumas bawled, "and sentences him to Death within twenty-four hours. The Tribunal is adjourned!"

As his bell rang and the crowd pushed excitedly towards the door, I caught a glimpse of the Defarges. The husband appeared stern, adamant, uncompromising; the wife, however, bore an aspect I have never before seen on any human visage, a look of savage joy and hatred and consuming hunger all commingled. This, I thought, this was more than the common resentment of the *sans-culotte* towards a man more prosperous than he. This was a ravenous private hatred, a matter of vengeance, a blood-debt. Could this woman be the missing younger sister of that peasant family, now mercilessly calling in that debt?

The crowd poured out of the chamber, babbling still. As it thinned, I elbowed my way to Barsad and nudged him towards Lucie, murmuring: "Suffer them a moment together, it will harm no one—then go and make your arrangements for me. We've not much time."

He did as I said and vanished into the prisoners' corridor, towards the stair to the Conciergerie. I waited in a shadowed corner, behind a knot of arguing enthusiasts, as Lucie and Darnay embraced.

Within five minutes Barsad returned and hurried to me. "Thank God for that bloody long journal of the Doctor's," he muttered.

"What nonsense are you saying?" I demanded. "It was Darnay's death-warrant."

"You think he'd not have been condemned without it? Open your eyes. But it's given us some time. The session lasted so long that Sanson's been and gone already with to-day's batch. They'll hold Darnay till to-morrow."

I drew a long breath. "Very well," said I. "Arrange a visit for me, then, for to-morrow morning."

I APPROACHED AND lifted Lucie in my arms, her golden hair spilling like a waterfall across my sleeve, after Darnay was led away and she collapsed at her anguished father's feet. I bore her to a fiacre waiting outside the Palais de Justice and it swiftly conveyed the four of us from that ill-omened place.

Lucie-Anne, the poor child, came racing out to the landing to meet us, caught a glimpse of me, and shouted *"Papa!"* A moment later (seeing me better in the light from the window) she stopt short, stared, and began to weep, a thin desolate sobbing that tore at my heart. "It's not papa, sweetheart, it's Mr. Carton," I told her, as I laid Lucie gently on a sofa. "Don't you remember me?"

"O, Mr. Carton!" cried she, and flung herself upon me. "I thought you had gone away forever. You went away *ages* ago, when I was little."

"You are no longer little, are you?" said I, kissing her brow. "A great girl of ten." I turned as Pross came hurrying in, to stop open-mouthed at the sight of me. "The worst has happened, Miss Pross," I told her, choosing my words carefully before the child. "She has fainted. It would be kinder not to revive her for a time." She nodded and sat beside Lucie, wiping away a tear with the corner of her apron ere taking up one of Lucie's hands in her large bony ones and stroking it.

"Mr. Carton, something dreadful has happened, I know it!" sobbed Lucie-Anne, clutching at my coat. "Why won't they tell me? And why hasn't papa come home? Mamma said they would free him to-day. Is—is that why she is so ill—because they won't let papa come home? Can't *you* go and fetch back my papa for us? Grandpapa promised me and promised me that he would fetch papa out of prison, but he doesn't. Why can't he? Papa's done nothing wrong. He couldn't. He's a good man."

"Yes, sweetheart, indeed he is," I assured her. "But his father and uncle committed some very terrible crimes, and other folk say that your papa must be punished for what they did."

"But that's not *fair!*"

"No," I murmured, "no, it's not fair."

"Can you help papa, Mr. Carton? I miss him so, and mamma does too. What's happened to make her so ill? Is she—is she going to—*die?*"

"No, my love, your mamma is not going to die. And your papa will come back to you, I promise you."

She threw her arms about me, gulping away her tears. "You promise? *Really* promise? Cross your heart?"

"I promise. Cross my heart."

She hugged me closer and I knelt to embrace her. "Do you think," I asked her, "I might kiss your mamma ere I quit her?"

She gravely nodded. I bent and kissed Lucie's lips, pausing a moment to caress her cheek with my fingertips. "You told me once that you loved me, and I pledged my life to you," I murmured, in the softest of whispers. "Remember that . . . Lucie."

The child, her blue eyes round and solemn, watched me depart. I shut the door behind me as I stept into the adjoining chamber, where Lorry and Dr. Manette awaited me. "The Doctor is no less a man of famous reputation after all this," Lorry told me, urgently, "and his name and influence might accomplish something still . . . yet the Executioner may be leading poor Darnay to the scaffold at this very moment, as we speak."

I shook my head. "We have been granted one boon at least. To-day's victims quitted the Conciergerie whilst Darnay was before the Tribunal still. We have until to-morrow afternoon. Doctor, Dumas and Fouquier are not indifferent to your reputation, I believe?"

"We have met . . . they know me."

His slow speech and dazed manner worried me. "Then let your influence at least be tried once again. Go to the Palais de Justice, go to Dumas. Go to the Committees and try to gain an audience with Lindet, or Le Bas, even Barère. Not all the Committee members are savages or Zealots—you may find a sympathetic ear amongst them."

"I will go to Robespierre himself, if I must."

"Yes, if you must, tho' I doubt you will succeed there. Nevertheless, we must grasp at every straw."

We arranged that we should meet again at Lorry's lodgings to-night. As I was about to follow the Doctor out, Lorry touched my wrist.

"I have no hope," he whispered.

"Nor have I. I have gone upon the same errand, not so long since, with perhaps as much influence in my own way as his, and failed."

"Influence?" he echoed me, a spark of hope kindling in his countenance.

"No longer. I once had a certain reputation amongst those men . . . but reputations are fragile, here in Paris. They would spare not an instant for an ex-*Dantoniste,* a drunken Englishman of dubious associations and questionable patriotism. The Doctor may yet succeed where I would undoubtedly fail, tho' I think it a remote possibility at best." I sighed, adding: "Yet Lucie must not imagine, some day, that a chance might have remained still, and was wasted." I pressed Lorry's hand and, with that ever-present numb dread clutching at my vitals, walked slowly down the stair.

ONE LAST SLENDER hope remained to me, and I was determined not to squander it. I hurried the short way across the river to the Tuileries and the Committees' meeting-chambers. There a secretary curtly informed me that Citizen Saint-Just had been absent from the deliberations to-day.

Acknowledging defeat, I trudged out of the Palace and into the twilit gardens, where I sat slouched on a marble bench amidst the fragrant rose-beds. I remained there for perhaps half an hour, as the velvet shadows deepened about me and the strolling passers-by disappeared one by one. At length the crunch of solitary footsteps near me on the gravelled walk interrupted my gloomy thoughts and I glanced up to see, to my astonishment, the very man I had sought.

"Good-evening, Carton," said he, courteous and distant as ever, and continued towards the Palace. I sprang to my feet and hurried after him.

"Saint-Just—I beg you—you must prevent a terrible injustice at the Tribunal."

"To what, and whom, are you referring?" he enquired, offering me no encouragement but pausing in his stride.

"An ex-Noble, a good man, was condemned to Death to-day because of the hatred some citizens bore his family. He has done nothing himself to incur the Republic's displeasure. I pray you, Saint-Just—I *beg* you—have the case reviewed and you will see I speak the truth."

He sighed and without looking at me flung himself on the nearest bench, elbows on his knees, his long hair hanging like a curtain to conceal his countenance. "Tell me."

I told him all I knew of Darnay, from his family's evil reputation and his efforts to escape it, to his outrageous trial at the Old Bailey, to his exemplary and hard-working career in London, to his trial and re-arrest of six months previous, to the frightful trial of to-day.

"Surely Darnay is a man whom the Republic might proudly commend as a model to other ex-Aristocrats," I concluded. "He would uphold the Republic as staunchly as you would yourself. He, of all folk, does not deserve death of it."

Saint-Just did not reply. Head bowed, he sat still as a statue for some time in the failing light. At last, rising, he spoke with no trace of emotion. "I cannot help you."

"D__n you, *no!*" I cried, hastening after him as he strode away. I seized his sleeve and swung him round. We were of a height and his grey eyes, impenetrable as ice, bored into mine. With his visage mere inches from my own, I saw how over-work and a crushing burthen of cares had left their mark: the dark crescents beneath his eyes from want of sleep, the unhealthy pallor of his skin, the fine lines that marred that stern youthful countenance. "You, of all folk, who speak incessantly of Justice!"

"It's not my place to interfere with the Revolutionary Tribunal."

"The Devil it's not—the Committee rules France!"

"We make laws, Carton. We do not rule arbitrarily."

"You think not?" said I, with a sour laugh. "The Committees may do anything they please. You have the power to free a condemned prisoner as easily as you might arrest him."

"And if I did? What, then, would that say of the Tribunal's Justice, that it's worthless, that it may be over-ruled?"

"It would say the truth—that it's no Justice at all. That your precious Tribunal is no more than a panel of bloody-handed Executioners. God's death, Saint-Just, you were once a man of integrity. How can you stand aside as the Tribunal butchers this man—as it butchers hundreds of innocents!"

"Do you think I don't know what is happening, Carton?" he snapped. "Do you think me as ignorant, or as stupid, as all that? And do you think

I never learnt of your wife's fate? Had I been in Paris, do you think I'd not
have tried to save her?"

"Then why not Darnay?" I shouted.

"Times have changed. It is gone too far to be remedied. In December—
Frimaire—a prisoner had a fair chance of acquittal still. But now? I know
full well that the Tribunal has become no more than a slaughter-house."

"Then *do* something!"

"How? What would you have me do?"

"Cease these executions of harmless, innocent folk—"

"And then? Then should we artlessly admit that a dozen—or a hundred
dozen—blameless folk have been condemned out of malice, or over-zeal,
or sheer oversight? Should we suffer citizens' minds to irrevocably associate
the Republic with Tyranny rather than with stern Justice, and thus incite
them to destroy it? This is not the way I would have established the
Republic, God knows, had I the choice. But we are still at war and our
country is still in peril. Having travelled so far along this path, we cannot
turn back and admit our errors."

He looked away and suddenly, with a swift passionate gesture, dashed his
hand across a full-blown, fading rose, sending crimson petals flying. "I fear,
as do you," he added, with a despair in his voice that I had never before
heard, "perhaps more so than do you, that these incessant judicial massacres
may very well deal the Republic a fatal blow. Yet all I know is that to confess they have gone too far, much too far, to admit our guilt—would strike
the death-blow more surely. I will not sacrifice the Republic to save your
friend, or anybody. Were it a question of my own life I would not do it. I
regret this, Carton—but you will not change my mind."

He turned on his heel and strode away. I did not delude myself into
imagining that I would profit by pursuing him.

THOUGH MY LAST faint hope had failed me, I had been granted a
few unexpected hours to perfect my plans. Thus I thought it wise to

remind the Defarges that half a dozen men resembling Darnay might walk the streets of Paris, for I had not forgotten the malignity in Mdme. Defarge's countenance.

It was a few minutes before eight o'clock when I returned to Tellson's, thinking first to take a mouthful of supper at Lorry's lodgings. As I approached the gates, however, I espied the *concierge* conversing with a little elderly man whom, after a moment's puzzlement, I recognised. What on Earth, I wondered, did this Gabelle wish from me? I toyed with the notion of confronting him but abandoned it, for I had far more pressing uses for those few precious hours. Instead I hailed a fiacre and proceeded to the *faubourg* Antoine.

I supped at a chophouse, then with little trouble found the Defarges' tavern. Wandering inside, in halting French I ordered a pint of red wine from Defarge and settled myself comfortably at a well-lit table.

The shop was empty save for the proprietors and a man and woman who leant on the counter to converse with them. After a moment Mdme. Defarge approached me and, giving me a hard stare, asked me what it was I had ordered.

I repeated my request, stumbling in my French and speaking with the strong German accent I had heard from any number of Alsatian Deputies to the Convention.

"You are foreign?" she enquired, raising an eyebrow. She must once have been quite beautiful, tho' hatred and the passage of the years had hardened her features. I could not help but notice the tiny Guillotine of pot-metal that dangled from a cord about her neck, where once a Crucifix might have hung. Her hand crept continually up to it to touch it, stroke it, as if it were a live thing.

"I am from Alsace, Citizeness," I replied, after a moment of feigned confusion, "and a good citizen of the Republic."

She nodded and turned away. Defarge served me the wine and subjected me to another keen stare. I toasted the Republic in my comic-opera accents and he returned to the counter, shaking his head, as I took up an abandoned copy of the *Gazette de Paris* and made a pretence of struggling thro' it.

They paused in their conversation, I suppose glancing at my back. Earnestly labouring through the newspaper, I paid them no heed.

"I've seen *her* many times, too," continued Mdme. Defarge, thoughtfully. "Outside La Force, every day, in all weathers. Sometimes with the child, sometimes with the old man, sometimes without. For what but to signal to the prisoners? I can swear to it—and that fool of a wood-sawyer can swear to it."

"I'll wager she was only hoping to see her husband at a window," muttered Defarge. "Did ever you see her making a sign or a signal?"

"Even if she stood still as the dead," said the second woman, "the colour of a shawl or a feather in a hat can be as much a signal as any gesture."

Mdme. Defarge nodded. "What other proof does the Section Committee need of a plot to break open the prisons? The day after to-morrow, when they are mourning his death, insulting the Republic's Justice, we'll denounce them—the pack of them."

"I still say let well enough alone," Defarge cautioned her. "To-morrow you'll have Saint-Evrémonde's blood at last. Why not stop there?"

"Because there are still Saint-Evrémondes," said she, in a soft, dangerous tone that chilled me.

"The daughter of our good Dr. Manette . . . and a child of ten."

"You," she hissed, "you would save even *him*, if you could!"

"Never! One of that cursed brood? What do you take me for? But I say stop there. How can the Tribunal condemn a little girl, ten years old? No one would stand for it. Thérèse, my Angel, tell me truly: you'd not kill a child?"

"Did the Marquis have your scruples?" demanded his wife, in a fierce whisper. "Did he shrink from killing the child in Ange's belly when he raped her—did unspeakable things to her—and beat her and left her to die? What do you know of it, husband? Not one of the Grosjean family, save for me, was left alive after that monster was done with them. My sister, my brother, my sister's husband, my sister's child, my father—those dead are *my* dead, and that blood-debt is mine!"

I had suspected as much, when I saw her at the Tribunal. My hand trembled a little as I raised my glass.

Defarge pled feebly for the sake of the Doctor, who had suffered so much, and his innocent daughter and granddaughter. His wife gave a harsh laugh. "My folk were as innocent. The Saint-Evrémondes took all my family to feed their filthy pleasures, and I'll have all of theirs in return, to the very last of them."

A few customers ambled in and I seized my opportunity to depart, after enquiring helplessly for directions to the site of the Bastille. Thrusting the stocking she was knitting into a pocket of her apron, Mdme. Defarge stood with me in the doorway and pointed out the way along rue de Charonne. I dare say had I worn a weapon about me, or had I not had a more urgent purpose, I might have rid the world of that woman then and there, if indeed one can slay Nemesis.

I strolled off comfortably enough, tho' once at the square, I hailed a fiacre and bade the driver take me with all speed back to Tellson's. The *concierge* plodded out to meet me as I alighted in the courtyard. "Are you Citizen Carton," he enquired, "the friend of Citizen Lorry the Englishman?" He thrust a soiled scrap of paper at me. "You've had folk asking for you. One of them left this note. He wouldn't leave his name."

I glanced at the paper. It bore but a few words, hastily scrawled: *Ten oClock, to-morrow, in the cour du Mai. B.* "And the other?"

"The other, he said his name was Gabelle. He hoped you might grant him an interview to-night when you returned, or to-morrow. He left his address."

Will that persistent little man never leave me in peace? Yet perhaps he may have for me some intelligence regarding Darnay, perhaps even (tho' I dare not hope it) some miraculous evidence that may save him, which I cannot afford to ignore.

I found Lorry in his lodgings. He told me he had only just quitted Lucie's side, in the hope of meeting her father. Dr. Manette, however, had neither arrived nor sent any word, and Lorry felt it his duty to return to her.

It is near midnight, or past it, as I conclude this day's account. I have waited here in Lorry's sitting-room for some two hours and have had neither word nor sign. Dare I hope this may betoken triumph on the Doctor's part, that he has succeeded in gaining a sympathetic audience amongst those scant few who could over-rule the Tribunal's sentence? I fear to hope for too much. I can but wait.

25

18 Prairial (6 June)

IT IS SIX O'CLOCK in the morning as I write these words. All the events of yesterday seem to belong to another lifetime, or another man. In how brief a moment can one's universe, one's whole existence turn a corner!

In as brief a moment, perhaps, as the world changed for us all on the Fourteenth of July?

I SLEPT A little during the hours I waited here in Lorry's rooms for the Doctor, and continued this journal. At last I heard a footstep on the stair and eagerly threw open the door.

It was Lorry. "I have heard nothing," said he, shaking his head, ere I could enquire. "And you?"

"Nothing."

He settled wearily into a chair. I returned to my seat by the cold hearth and fell into an uneasy doze. Some little time later I felt him shaking me. "I hear somebody on the landing," said he.

An instant afterward the door creaked open and the Doctor stood framed in the doorway, regarding us with a vacant stare. Lorry took an eager step forward. "Manette . . ."

"Where is my work?" he mumbled. "I can't find it, and I must finish the shoes. Where is my bench?"

Lorry and I exchanged a swift horrified glance and, as if reading each other's thoughts, in concert coaxed the old man gently to a chair.

"Do you think—" began Lorry.

"That he succeeded? I doubt it. This is his old *dementia,* is it not? You said that he has had relapses ere this?"

"Yes, when under great strain of mind."

"How long have they lasted?"

"A few hours, the space of a night . . . once for nine days." He glanced at Dr. Manette, his visage drawn. "God help us, it's as if . . . this is the same wreck of a man whom Lucie and I brought to London nineteen years since."

I slowly nodded. "Well. Our last chance is gone—it was never much. Mr. Lorry, Sir, will you now do exactly as I tell you?"

"Anything that may be of use, I will do."

"You have your travelling papers in order."

"Yes, for some time now."

"And the Doctor's, are they in order? Let us see." I felt in his coat and in his pocket-book found what I sought. "Thank God. Look here, a pass made out in his name and those of his daughter and granddaughter, all signed and stamped, quite legal. Keep it for them. And here is mine—you see, it's stamped for Calais." I pressed the papers into his hands and paced the length of the chamber, setting in order the plan I had worked out yesternight whilst wandering the silent streets. "To-morrow morning, as early as ever you can, you must hire a coach, a post-chaise, for Calais, and have it ready and waiting in the courtyard at the cour du Dragon by ten o'clock. The three of them, and you, too, must be inside it, ready to depart as soon as ever I join you. Pross and your manservant should follow in a smaller chaise; by doing so they may overtake us and order fresh horses at posting-stations along the way for us. Do you follow me?"

"Yes, indeed. But why this haste, Carton? It will be cruel enough for Lucie, to-morrow—and would they not call unwelcome attention upon themselves by fleeing?"

"They must," I told him. "They must risk it. The Defarge woman intends to denounce them all, within days. She is the last survivor of that peasant family described in the Doctor's testimony. Her revenge is not yet done with the family of Saint-Evrémonde."

"Dear God!"

"Follow my instructions, Mr. Lorry, and you shall save them. *We* shall save them. Tell Lucie, if you must, of the danger threatening them, that under no circumstances must she remain to mourn him . . . or to share his fate. Tell her that her child and her father are in as much danger as she. Tell her . . . tell her it's Darnay's wish."

"I will," said he, pressing my hand. "And you?"

"I shall see Darnay in the morning," I reminded him. "My appointment is at ten o'clock; expect me at half past ten or thereabouts. Wait for nothing but for my arrival. The moment I come, take me into the carriage and drive away."

"I wait for you under all circumstances?"

"Yes. Absolutely under all circumstances. And delay for nothing else, Mr. Lorry, *nothing*, no matter what."

"But you will be present to take charge of affairs."

"Present, yes," I said easily, "but you know my weaknesses, Sir—after taking my leave of poor Darnay, I may be in no condition to help you." I turned, as if to emphasise my admission of my frailties, and poured myself a thimbleful of brandy from the decanter that stood on the table still.

"Carton," said he, after a moment of silence, "forgive me . . . but am I right, in remembering how matters stood in the past, in London . . . am I right in supposing that your concern in this matter is more for Lucie's sake than for Darnay's?"

I could not help a rueful smile, as I faced him once more. "Darnay is my friend. But nothing much escapes you, does it, Mr. Lorry?"

"Don't mis-understand me," he continued. "I know full well you would not deliberately abandon Darnay to his fate, in order to possess Lucie. But . . . should Darnay perish, despite our best efforts—it's not inconceivable, is it, that Lucie should, in the end, turn to her most faithful friend for consolation."

I gazed at him, and said nothing.

"I ask only," he hastily added, "because I love Lucie like a daughter. I ask you to—to be worthy of her."

His words abruptly set me to pondering matters I had thrust from my thoughts long ere I had made my vow on the 16th of Germinal. Lucie could be mine, I knew, should I wish it. And I knew now, for Eléonore and her unwavering assurance in me had proved it so, that I could indeed be worthy of her.

I might still, I thought, give up my last mad, perilous hope of saving Darnay and turn instead to comforting Lucie in her grief. I might turn my back on Death still, turn my back on that fate that lay heavy in my belly like a sickness, and once again welcome Life instead. So simple and so easily attained that path would be, so bright with promise after my long dark night.

But I had made a vow to myself and to Lucie, and—despite my many other faults and errors—I do not break my word. With an effort I tore my thoughts from that beckoning path, though my whole body trembled a moment at the alternative, and shook my head; for all at once I knew it was only Life and not Love that beckoned me.

Lucie, dearest Lucie, it was you, so long ago, who gave me that faint spark of Hope that encouraged me to flounder on, when I might more easily have followed the shorter route to the end of my miseries and died a drunkard's unlamented death. Had you not offered me your friendship and your extraordinary faith in my long-debased and prostituted gifts, I should never have survived to go to France, to discover unlooked-for opportunity in a career, and happiness in Eléonore. You and your kindness made my brief felicity possible, and for that I am indebted to you.

I love you, Lucie, as another man may love God, or his guardian Angel. But even at this very moment when you are within my reach still, indeed offered me for the taking like a jewel on a satin cushion, I may truthfully say that I choose instead, without an instant's indecision, to renounce the prize that I dreamt for years of attaining.

All these considerations coursed through my thoughts in far less time than it requires to set them down. Again I slowly shook my head. "No . . . too much has come between us for that."

Lorry gazed intently at me a moment, a little frown puckering his brow, ere slowly nodding. "I see."

"Well," said I, drinking down the last swallow of the brandy. "All's done, I think. You promise me, Mr. Lorry, that you will do exactly—*exactly*—as I have told you?"

"I swear it."

We shook hands. As I stept away, he pressed my hand a moment longer, his old eyes sad and bright. "For her?" he murmured.

Our hands clasped still, I looked at him a moment. "You would not try to stop me, would you?"

"How could I? But no. I have not the right. Whatsoever you may do, you do of your own free will. For her sake?"

I nodded, turning from his gaze. "For her . . . for Darnay. Because— because I found that I was, indeed, capable of doing some good in this world, yet it all came to nothing in the end. Because all I have ever dared to love, save for them, has turned before my eyes into dust and ashes." I drew a deep breath and blinked away unbidden tears. "Ask me no more, Sir."

Betwixt us we led Dr. Manette, whimpering for his work-bench still, back to the cour du Dragon. When Lorry had gone above with him, I lingered alone in the darkness of the courtyard for a few moments. At last, murmuring a blessing towards Lucie's window, I resolutely turned my head away and trudged out to the street. I was restless and wakeful, as taut as a soldier on the eve of battle.

I might now respond to Msr. Gabelle's entreaties, I suddenly thought. It was past one o'clock and I felt that rousing him from his bed at such an hour would repay him for his vexatious persistence.

The *concierge* had given me an address on rue de la Pologne, a dilapidated alleyway at the furthest reaches of the *faubourg* Honoré, towards Mont-Martre (now styled, God help us, *Mont-Marat*). I hailed another late-going fiacre and set out past the boulevards.

A frowzy, sleepy wench of sixteen at length answered the door in response to my determined knocking. "They're long abed," she objected, when I told her I wished a moment with Citizen Gabelle, but plodded away with her candle and in a few moments Gabelle himself appeared, grey hair rumpled beneath his night-cap. Rubbing the sleep from his eyes, he hastily greeted me and invited me to sit down.

"I am here, as you wished," said I. "What do you want of me?"

"I wished—well, in truth it's a delicate business, Citizen," he admitted.

"Has this anything to do with Charles Darnay—Charles de Saint-Evrémonde?"

"No . . . and yes, in a fashion."

"Will it save him from the Guillotine?"

"The Guillotine?" he echoed me, startled.

"He was re-arrested, and yesterday sentenced to Death."

"Dear Lord," he murmured, crossing himself. "M'sieur Charles, of all folk . . ."

"If you can tell me nothing that will save him," I interrupted him, "then our interview is at an end." I bowed curtly to him, bidding him Good-night.

"Wait, I pray you!" he implored me, seizing my sleeve, and turned to the servant-girl. "Agnès, run and wake your mistress, quick now! Stay a moment, Citizen, and hear us out. For my wife's sake."

"What have you to tell me?" said I, wearily.

"I believe we are related."

I stared at him. "Related by marriage, I should say," he added. "You told me you were the son of an English father and a French mother, a

Notary's daughter. Was your mother's name Marie-Virginie Leblanc?"

"Yes," I stammered. "Yes, it was."

"Then my wife . . . is your aunt, you see. Your mother's sister. Elisabeth Leblanc."

"I knew I had recognised her," I whispered. "My mother's countenance . . . and the name Gabelle. I knew I had a connexion with the name." She must have spoken of her sister in my hearing when I was a child, I thought, tho' I had never known anything of her family.

I heard a footfall behind me and turned to meet Mdme. Gabelle's gaze. My heart trembling within me, I now saw my mother's features reflected faintly in hers. She raised her candle to have a better look at me and once again drew a quick breath.

"My dear," said Gabelle, "you remember Citizen Carton, who you said must be your sister's son . . ."

"Carton," she murmured. "That was his name, the Englishman she wedded. Joseph Carton. When I saw you that day, I could only think—but then you told me you were no kin of the Saint-Evrémondes, that your English father had wedded a Notary's daughter, and I began to wonder . . ." She paused, changing colour.

"That was my father's name," I agreed, as she clasped my hand betwixt her own.

"My sister—is she well?"

"My mother died thirty years ago, when I was a boy."

"Ah—poor Virginie. Poor, poor Virginie. I never had a word from her, you see, not since I saw her last, at my wedding forty years ago and more." She exchanged glances with her husband, who shrugged. "Citizen— nephew—may I ask you one thing: when were you born?"

"When was I *born?*" I echoed her, nonplussed by the unexpected question.

"I pray you, Citizen."

"The thirteenth of February, 1752."

She let out a long sigh. "Then—I was right. And you were right," she added, turning to Gabelle, the hands that clutched my own suddenly trembling. "O, *mon Dieu*, my poor Virginie . . ."

"Right?" said I, looking from one to the other. "About what? Something having to do with my mother?"

"Pray let us all sit down," said Gabelle, guiding us to chairs. "Citizen," he began, "we have dwelt here in Paris for six months only, since the Tribunal freed me, for our house was burnt to the ground during an uprising in 'ninety-two. You know, perhaps, that I was once steward of the Saint-Evrémonde estate at Méry in Champagne—"

"*Méry?*"

"Why, yes," said he, staring at me. "It's a village, in Champagne—"

"I know," said I, feeling an icy hand clutching at my heart. *Go to Champagne,* she had said: *begin at a village called Méry, and find your mother's people.* "Go on."

"I am not a native of the province. But my wife's family had dwelt there for generations, as notaries, customs-officials, the like. I came to Méry as the post-master, was offered employment by Saint-Evrémonde, and settled there. I wedded Citizeness Gabelle soon afterward." He glanced at his wife.

"My sister Virginie had wedded the Englishman already," said Mdme. Gabelle. "Four years previous, I think it was. It was very sudden. He came to Méry on a business matter—something to do with glazes and porcelain—and six weeks later Virginie wedded him and he took her away to England. We loved each other dearly and I wrote to her often, till I told her I, too, was about to wed. I begged and pleaded with her to come to my wedding and at last she agreed."

I frowned, vexed in my bewilderment and impatience. "What is it that you must tell me about my mother? And what has any of it to do with me?"

Mdme. Gabelle bent her head, gazing at the hands folded in her lap. "I had my suspicions, you see, when she married so suddenly. Virginie was— God help her—she was very beautiful. I saw he had his eye on her, at Mass, in the village, whensoever they chanced to meet. I think she wedded the Englishman in order to escape him." A tear trickled down her cheek, though she seemed oblivious to it.

"Escape whom?"

"The Marquis, Citizen. He who was M'sieur Charles's uncle. He was very handsome, you see, with a fine way of talking and lovely manners, but he was bad all through. The dirty things they whispered about him . . . and he wished—he wished to bed her. He wished her for his mistress. But she was the Notary's daughter—of respectable family and reputation, not some peasant wench he could carry off and tumble at his pleasure. So he hounded her, pursued her, gave her no peace till she went away to England."

"Well?" said I, more bewildered than ever, but at the same time shackled by a horrid anticipation.

"Then she came back. She'd been wed four years, and had a child—"

"My brother—"

"Yes, he was a darling mite—she brought the child with her. And he knew she had come to visit us, of course, for he came to the wedding. Such an honour for us, everybody said, when the Seigneur attended," she added bitterly. "And then Virginie quitted us suddenly for England and I never saw her again, or had a letter, or any word from her." She paused a moment, gazing still into her lap. "I suspected, but never knew until this hour . . . I think he—the Marquis—I think at last he seduced her then, or worse. He might have—he might have raped her—"

"*Raped* her?"

"—and she carried that foul secret with her to the grave, it seems. Poor Virginie! I can't blame her for never again wishing to see Méry, or any thing that might remind her of that horror."

"*Raped* her?" I echoed her again. "How dare you suggest—" Yet all I had learnt, from Darnay and Eléonore both, about the late Marquis de Saint-Evrémonde suggested Mdme. Gabelle's abhorrent notion might indeed be the truth.

"Now finally I've set my mind at peace about it, thank God. It was *he* . . . that brute, that monster. I had wondered so often, you see, if it were because of some fault of mine that she never wrote a word more to me."

"But still," I protested, loath to accept such a stain on my mother's memory, "*mon Dieu*—still—how can you—what proof of this can you possibly have?"

Twisting her hands together, at last she glanced up at me. "You yourself are the proof. Don't you see?"

I perceived then what she must mean, and sat stunned, unable to say a word.

"You were born nine months after my wedding, after your mother's visit. And you might be twin-brother to M'sieur Charles, or to the Marquis himself when he was young. You are the image of every Saint-Evrémonde whose portrait hung in the picture-gallery at the Château."

Dear Lord, what a blind fool I have been all my life.

My pulse roared in my ears in the icy silence. "Are you saying," I stammered, "that—that the Marquis de Saint-Evrémonde was my *father?*"

"Yes, Citizen," she whispered.

I lurched to my feet. Turning my back to Mdme. Gabelle, I reached for the nearest wall to steady myself, and clutched at the door-post. Scarce aware of what I did, abruptly I struck at it with my clenched fist, hammering blindly at it until I came to myself and found I was sobbing.

Eléonore—O yes, Eléonore had known, had guessed the truth in almost the first hour I knew her; she had guessed it the moment I had revealed, so carelessly, that my mother had come from Champagne, home of the family of Saint-Evrémonde. She had perceived the ugly truth that must have been in plain sight for all those who cared to piece it together. All those like my father—or rather the man I always had called father—

He, too, had guessed the truth, guessed it long ago, or a portion of it. He had seen his son, the son born nine months after his wife's journey to France, grow into a boy who resembled him not at all, neither in his person nor his character: a lad of quick wit, handsome countenance, and a tendency towards indolence and debauchery . . . Perhaps even he had once met the Marquis, when he first met my mother, and in time recognised the resemblance I bore him. But undoubtedly he had perceived the truth. That coldness towards me, that coldness I never could fathom, had surely begun on the day he had concluded I was no son of his.

Hence the indifference, the fault-finding, the quarrels; hence the rancour he must have fostered towards this interloper, this proof of his cuckoldry, another man's bastard. Hence his resolution to bequeath the fortune for which he had worked so long to my cousin, to a man who was, if not a son, at least his blood-kin. Hence my vanished inheritance—no, never mine at all—my wasted years in London, my aimless path in life that at length had led me by chance back to Darnay and closed the circle once more.

And the man who had sired me, whose blood courses through my veins, whose tainted name is my true birthright—

I thought for an instant that I might vomit as I stood there. I clapt a hand to my mouth and in a moment the nausea passed, leaving me trembling. "*Why* did you tell me this?" I gasped, without looking at the Gabelles. "Why bring this foulness to light?"

Mdme. Gabelle touched my shoulder. "Forgive me. But . . . it is the truth."

"The *truth*—what can this truth bring me beside sheer horror?" I twisted about to face her. "Adieu, Citizeness. You will not see me again." So saying, I threw open the door and fled, leaving them silent behind me.

I stumbled down the alleyway, her words echoing relentlessly in my ears: *You are the image of every Saint-Evrémonde. The image of every Saint-Evrémonde. You— you—you—*

Saint-Evrémonde, I thought, with a shudder. *My father?* Saint-Evrémonde, the handsome, polished, vicious Aristocrat who had defiled countless peasant girls and children too much terrified of him to resist him; who had tortured women in the course of his depraved pleasures; who had coolly destroyed at least one innocent family in order to possess the woman he desired, only to fling her aside when he had done with her, like a child with a broken doll. The man who, in ridding himself of an inconvenience, had thought nothing of condemning a blameless man to a life-long Hell in prison, or of betraying his own blood-kin to the likelihood of a shameful and horrid death. The man who had raped my mother. My *father.*

Increasing my pace, I sped on as if I could flee the truth. At last I paused to heave a painful breath as I drew near the cemetery of La Madeleine, where King Louis and his unhappy Queen lie, in ironic company with the Girondins, and Hébert, and Charlotte de Corday, and the two or three hundred faceless victims who died at the place de la Révolution during the Autumn and Winter past—and with Eléonore. Above me rose the great gates, locked forever against intruders who might seek relics, for the cemetery is choked now with the dead; these days the executed are buried elsewhere, at Les Errancis to the North, where Danton, Camille, Lucile, and their friends lie. A neat, austere placard hung from the gates, its lettering just visible in the grey light of the Moon. *Death is an eternal Sleep.*

Then again (I mused, pondering the words before me), what, truly, did Mdme. Gabelle's revelation matter? I had resolved long since to save Darnay by any means within my power, even to the sacrifice of my own life. The question of my paternity, this odious truth, would mean nothing in another day's time, when Mdme. Defarge's blood-debt was paid.

Paid in truer coin than she could know, I realised. And as I stared unseeing through the cemetery gates, all at once I felt an immense burthen lifted from me, as if all my life I had struggled thro' a murky wood to emerge now at last onto a bright beckoning shore. I laughed aloud for sheer relief, standing there stock-still in the middle of the empty, dirty street, for in surrendering to the tyranny of Fate I had found instead that I was free.

I turned away, laughing softly still, and upon some extravagant impulse spun about and flung my arms wide, as if I might welcome all the stars in the heavens into my embrace. And tranquil at last, I walked easily, steadily

onward then, beneath the old monks' bridge that gives rue de l'Arcade its
name; past the Benedictine monastery, its inhabitants driven out and scattered; past the foundations of the old, long-demolished church to St. Mary
Magdalene; past the Treasury into the place de la Révolution. As I did so,
a long-forgotten memory flickered to life, a memory of my father—the
man I had called father—reading his Bible.

If ye abide in my Word, then are ye truly my Disciples, he had read. *And ye shall
know the Truth, and the Truth shall make you free.*

The same sleepy guard eyed me as I approached the scaffold and gazed
up at the framework looming black in the moonlight.

"Well, Sainte Guillotine," I murmured, "it seems you and I have a tryst
to keep . . ."

LITTLE MORE REMAINS to be told. I wandered to the river-bank
and, all at once monstrous weary, like a traveller at the close of a hard journey, slept a few hours on a rough plank bench. The first grey light of dawn
roused me and I made my way through the waking streets to rue Taranne.
Lorry, true to his word, had gone out already to procure a post-chaise. I
changed my clothes, ate a few mouthfuls of bread, and turned my hand to
this journal, to these last few lines I shall write. When I am done I shall
place these pages in my valise with the rest, and with those few sad relics
that remain to me of Eléonore, and leave a note to Lorry asking him to
carry them safe back to England.

I trust him to do as he thinks best. Perhaps he may find Kitty, my daughter, if she is to be found, and deliver this journal to her as the sole legacy—
this, and the truth—that I can bequeath her.

The morning is passing. Lucie, Charles, if you should read this, you now
know all, even to that which I did not know myself but the space of a day
ago. What else remains to be said? I will add no more than to ask that you
hold me in your hearts now and then and think kindly on my memory.
Should God grant you more children, you could do me no greater honour

than to give a son of yours my name, for I know your child will bring it more lustre than ever I did.

Non omnis moriar . . . I shall not altogether die; what's best of me shall escape the tomb.

My dearest friends, when first I debated choosing this path, I imagined that, tho' all I ever had loved was gone from me, I might yet earn a lasting place in the heart of another human creature, and earn what I most desired, the right to be wept for. I find I was wrong. Remember me, I pray you, yet do not weep for me: for should one be pitied who goes so willing to his necessary destiny? Think, rather, that I seek a far better rest than ever I have known.

I have said enough, and it is near time for me to keep my appointment with Barsad.

26

I THOUGHT I had done this morning with my chronicle, but Circumstance has offered me one ultimate opportunity to set pen to paper. Perhaps these last pages will find Lucie; if not, at worst they will provide me a means of passing the slow hours.

HALF AN HOUR ere I was to meet Barsad in the cour du Mai, I bought a bottle of good Claret at a neighbouring shop. Remembering the instructions the Apothecary had given me months before, I shook a portion of the opium I carried into the bottle and corked it once again. I carried it to the Conciergerie's gate and passed it to a gaoler with instructions to deliver it to Darnay, saying only that it was a last gift from a friend; for the opium, I remembered, would need some little time to produce its effect.

I met Barsad a quarter-hour later and together we hurried down the steps into the Conciergerie. According to my instructions, he sent one of the turnkeys to fetch us another bottle and a pair of wine-glasses. The wine arriving and duly paid for, he led me to a forbidding iron-bound door and beckoned to the gaoler to lend him his ring of keys. "The Condemned wait here till Sanson comes for them," he muttered to me, unlocking the door. "He's been there alone since yesterday—I made sure of that. Be quick, now. There's no telling when they'll send to-day's first down from the Tribunal."

"Wait for my call," I told him, and stept inside the cell.

Darnay was lying on a bench, an arm flung across his eyes against the bright solitary sunbeam that shone from a barred window high up in the wall. He was coatless and had laid aside his cravat, awaiting the fatal hour.

He stirred and sat up, his visage betraying his astonishment as he recognised me in the shadows. "Carton!" he exclaimed. "Of all men on Earth—"

"You least expected to see me?" said I. To my relief, as I set down on a battered table the bottle and glasses I carried, I perceived he had drunk much of the wine I had sent in to him. "Rest assured," I added, as dismay flickered in his countenance, "I am not a prisoner. I have the grudging acquaintance of one of the *moutons* here, and I came to offer you a means of escape, should you choose to take it."

He shook his head, with a regretful smile. "I fear you are come for no purpose. Escape is impossible from this place. One quits this room only for the scaffold."

"I said nothing of escaping the Conciergerie. Yet you may escape the scaffold still, my friend, should you wish to."

In a moment he comprehended my meaning. "I see," he murmured. "What do you offer me, then?"

"Poison—a quick poison."

"Quicker than the Guillotine?" he enquired, with a wry twitch of his lips.

"More merciful, surely, than the stares and jeers of the crowd. More merciful," I added, "to your wife."

"Lucie," he whispered, and closed his eyes for an instant. "Give it me, then. Thank you."

I reached for the bottle, pushing aside the papers and ink-stand lying beside it. "What's this, letters?"

"For Lucie, and Mr. Lorry, and the Doctor. Would you deliver them for me?"

"If you wish." As he turned away, by a stroke of good fortune I succeeded in pouring out the drugged bottle rather than the one I had brought in with me. For appearance's sake, I took the phial of opium from my pocket, poured a pinch more into his glass, and let it sink to the bottom. "A toast, then," said I, offering him the glass.

He stared at the wine a moment ere replying, as if, thanks to the opium he had taken already, he was slow to comprehend my words. "A toast?"

"Don't be obtuse, Darnay," I told him, remembering another occasion long past on which we had drunk a toast together. "To the name on the tip of your tongue."

"To Lucie, then. To my dear wife." Abruptly he seized the glass and drained it in a few rapid swallows. With a long sigh, he very carefully set it back on the table. "How soon?"

"Soon," said I, fervently hoping that the opium would complete its work in short order.

"Carton," he began, speaking in a rush, as if he feared he might not be granted the time to say all he wished to say to me. "I would be a very dull fellow indeed, had I not seen the depth of your regard for Lucie. Perhaps you have changed towards her across the years . . . but if not, I ask you—I ask you only that you make her as happy as she deserves."

"You are mistaken, my friend," I told him. "She was never for me."

He stared at me, baffled. "But you—" Abruptly he pressed one hand to his forehead and with the other reached for the table to steady himself. "I feel . . . light-headed . . ."

"Sit, then." I pushed the chair towards him, easing him into it as his legs gave way. "You'll feel no pain."

"Carton—tell her I love her . . ."

"Tell her yourself . . . cousin."

I know not if he could have heard me. He collapsed onto the table, head on his arms, his breathing slow and heavy.

Chance had smiled upon me. We both were wearing the English riding-boots so favoured by the French, and our breeches were of a similar enough colour and cloth to make no difference. I needed but to exchange waistcoats with him, carelessly knot my cravat about his throat, and gather back my untidy hair with the ribbon that had tied his, whilst shaking his own hair negligently about his face. A moment more sufficed to dress him in my coat.

Barsad came in like a shot in answer to my call. He darted a glance at me as I stood leaning, in my shirt-sleeves, against the table; then at the man clad in my coat who lay unmoving beside me; then at me once more. "What the Devil?" he began, aghast. "You bloody fool, you oughtn't have let him take it till we were well away. You'll be for it, and me too, helping a prisoner escape the Razor."

"He is not dead, Barsad," said I. "Nor, I devoutly hope, will he be."

"What the—what have you *done?*"

"Nothing that need worry you," I told him. "You escorted in a visitor. You will simply escort him out again—tho' in a worse state of health than when he arrived."

"*Him?*"

"Him."

"You said—you tricked me, d__n you!"

"And would you have agreed to our arrangement, had you known my true design?" I shrugged. "The thing is done, Mr. Barsad. I suggest you make the best of it and do your utmost to avoid detection. What here should arouse suspicion? You escorted in a visitor; the visitor, overcome by emotion, has fainted; you will carry him out again, with a suitable profanity or two for your added trouble. I foresee no danger, if you are prudent."

"You're stark mad," he muttered. "Why not throw yourself off a bridge, then, if you wish to make an end to yourself, and keep me out of it?"

"No, I'm not mad. Merely fulfilling a promise . . . and a duty. Take him out."

With a brusque nod he strode to the doorway. "Once and for all, you realise what you're doing?" said he, turning back to me. "You're a dead man the moment he passes through that door."

"Stop wasting time. Take him to the carriage waiting in the courtyard of Number three, cour du Dragon—you know the cour du Dragon, near St. Germain-des-Prés?"

"Yes, yes. Number three."

"Mr. Lorry will be awaiting you, and Darnay's wife. Tell them to leave him sleeping, that he will wake by to-morrow; remind Mr. Lorry of his promise, and tell him to be off, with no protestations or regrets. Go."

"You'll not betray me?" whispered Barsad, glancing back at me once again.

"At such a late hour as this?" said I. "You need have no fear of me, Mr. Barsad. Tho' I suspect Sainte Guillotine will embrace the like of you soon enough, without my help."

He paled and hurried out, returning in a moment with a pair of turnkeys. I retreated into the shadows as they heaved Darnay onto a plank and lugged him off, punctuating their work with not a few rough jokes and curses. Barsad glanced back once at me as they vanished through the door, and was gone.

I am alone; an hour or more has passed since they quitted me. I have heard no alarums, no uproar, nothing to indicate that Barsad did not safely remove his charge from the prison. Finding the paper, pen, and ink Darnay left behind him, I have occupied myself with this last fleeting chronicle. Lucie, you and yours have, I think, by this time passed the Barrier unscathed and are on your way to the sea-coast. I no longer fear for your safety, and my hand is steady.

THE EXECUTIONER HAS come and gone, to return inevitably in a few hours' time. He entered without warning, a short while since: a tall, not unhandsome, sombre man. I recognised him and bade him Good-day.

"Citizen," said he, with a brief nod. "Pardon me . . . I must cut your hair."

"You do me too much honour, Citizen Sanson," said I. "Is this not a task for your subordinates?"

"It falls to me at times," he told me, and loosed my hair from its ribbon to clip it short. When he had done, he cut away my shirt-collar and stept away. "Thank you."

"I trust you will not yet tie my hands?"

"No, not until all is ready."

"Until another two or three hours have passed, you mean, when the Tribunal has sent you another dozen clients?"

"Regrettably, yes, Citizen."

"Sanson," said I, "I have heard what they say of you, that you are a better man, and a kinder one, than your masters. I understand the last letters of the Condemned are not delivered, but despatched to the Tribunal's records."

"Since you know it, there is no purpose in my denying it."

"You might do me a very great service by taking charge of these pages yourself, when the time comes for us to depart, and sending them to their destination."

"And that is . . ."

"In care of the Banque Tellson et Fils, on rue Taranne. They will keep them safe, I think, until they may be sent on to England."

He nodded. "If you wish."

"I thank you. It's kind of you to trouble yourself so."

"Kind?" he echoed me, as he reached for the door. "You call *me* kind, Citizen?" He shook his head, sorrowfully, and quitted me.

THEY HAVE BROUGHT the first of my fellows in. He is middle-aged and black-clad, a priest I think. He silently scrutinised me for a moment ere retreating to a corner to mutter prayers over his rosary. I shall not disturb him in his devotions.

OTHERS HAVE JOINED us. A pair of rough-looking men in tattered army uniforms, deserters evidently, converse sullenly together in English rendered all but incomprehensible by a thick Irish brogue. Occasionally their voices rise in a barrack-room oath and I overhear a few words of their dialogue. They wonder, over and over again, if they would have done better to stop and starve in Ireland than to have gone to seek their fortunes in France.

Another pair are, I think, man and wife. They sit side by side on a bench, clasping each other's hands, saying nothing. Half a dozen, four men and two women, are manifestly Aristocrats; the men lean against the cold stone wall, arms folded, grim and aloof, whilst the women pray quietly together.

As invariably upon espying me these folk shy away from me, perceiving in my cropped hair and torn shirt the fatal foreshadow of what is soon to come, I make no effort to speak with them. It is perhaps better that I do not, so I will not betray myself. Thus I did not expect to hear a voice behind me murmur "Citizen Saint-Evrémonde."

I turned, startled, to discover a slight, pallid, hollow-eyed young woman gazing at me, twisting her hands in her apron. "Citizen?" she repeated. "I was with you at La Force. Toinette, the sempstress. Perhaps you remember?"

"I—I forget what you were accused of," said I, rising.

"Plotting," said she, with a sad little shrug. "They said I made counter-revolutionary remarks. It may be I did say something, but I don't remember. And who would plot with *me?*"

I clasped her cold hands in my own. "I am sorry, Citizeness," I murmured, "so very sorry . . ."

"I am not afraid," she told me, a touch of defiance creeping into her soft voice. "You're a gentleman. You don't know how hard life is for the like of me. I think it will be easier to die, than to work and work and work always, and wear out my eyes over a needle for a few sous like the other women, and never have enough to eat. There's no work to be had these days in the *modistes'* shops. I've had to work the streets since Madame shut up the dress-shop and emigrated, but I don't earn very much because I've never been pretty. And when you're plain, and poor, and past twenty, you might as well be dead. Only the poorest and the barge-men will have you. And then one of the dirty beasts gave me the pox, and now I'm good for nothing." Her mouth trembled a little and in the light from the solitary window I saw the faint sores about her eyes and lips that betrayed lurking

Syphilis. "The Guillotine will be easier," she added, "and quicker."

I think she is very probably right; the moment of her death may be the most merciful instant in an unforgiving life that has brought her naught but poverty and ill-use.

"Come sit by me," said I, guiding her to my chair, and drawing across a stool for myself.

"I—I say I'm not afraid, and it's true." She hastily crossed herself and clasped her hands once again, white-knuckled, over her belly. "In my mind it's true. But—but I think our poor bodies wish to *live*, no matter how hard and cruel it is—and I feel sick, right here . . ."

I pulled out my handkerchief and leant towards her to wipe away the tears that threatened to spill down her cheeks. As I did so her eyes widened and she gasped. "You—you're *not*—are you?"

"Hush," I whispered, raising a finger to my lips. "Never you mind who I am."

"But—what's become of Citizen Saint-Evrémonde?"

"He is safe, I hope, and soon to be far from here."

"And you . . . have taken his place?"

I nodded. She stared at me a moment, then seized my hand in both her own and kissed it. "I ought not to be afraid at all, then," she murmured, "if you go to it willingly." Unexpectedly she showed me a timid smile. "Would you let me stay beside you, so I'll be brave when the time comes?"

"With all my heart."

I made her take a few swallows of the glass of drugged wine I had poured out for myself but had left untouched. After a while she fell asleep, leaning against my shoulder.

WE NUMBER TWENTY-SEVEN in this room. It is a strange-assorted gathering of beings, from the grim and imperturbable Nobleman who holds himself like an officer accustomed to command, to the four or five men who are as surely simple day-labourers or domestics, like my poor companion caught heedlessly in this vast web of suspicion and betrayal that the Revolution has become. How many of them, of these men who may have fought and bled on the Fourteenth of July or the Tenth of August, deserve so ill of their Revolution? For it was, once, *their* Revolution, though most now have forgotten that.

This cannot continue very much longer; suspicion and fear will do their work and the strangle-hold the Committees have upon the Government and the Tribunal will be broken. I see no other course. They have a matter of months, or perhaps weeks, ere their inevitable ruin. I think Saint-Just and Robespierre and their comrades will travel the same route as I shall travel to-day, and as Danton and Camille, and Brissot, Bailly, Vergniaud travelled before them. It is a pity. At another time, such extraordinary men as Saint-Just and Danton might have done much good for the Nation, rather than suffer it to sink into this cess-pit of blood.

I CANNOT HELP but dwell, in the brief time remaining to me, upon the truth I learnt last night. I am heir by right of blood to that accursed and doomed family of Saint-Evrémonde as surely as is Charles Darnay, my friend, my kinsman, my looking-glass image. And from my initial revulsion I have travelled so far as to embrace this bitter truth, in perceiving how it must fall into its place in the great Plan, perhaps fore-ordained from the moment the Marquis's libertine gaze first fell upon Ange Grosjean, or upon my mother.

The blood spilt by the Marquis and all his forebears can be washed away only with blood. The living and the dead to whom it is owed shall, indeed, receive their libation of Saint-Evrémonde blood. *Delicta maiorum immeritus lues,* the poet tells us: *Undeservedly you shall atone for the sins of your fathers.* Mdme. Defarge would have Darnay's innocent blood in return for that of her family; how much the more fitting that she should have mine.

These thoughts occupy me without cease, yet, far from troubling me, they calm me. I think I shall meet Death with composure, eagerness even,

when at length we quit these shadows of the prison-wall to pass once more
for a brief while into the daylight. It grieves me a little that I shall not forever rest in the same ground as Eléonore; yet those who have preceded me
to Les Errancis are not unworthy companions. If another, kindlier world
exists beyond this one, she and I shall find each other there, I think, and be
content.

Toinette is asleep at my shoulder still, her hand on mine. I pray I may be
granted the capacity to sustain her courage when she awakens. The time
cannot be long now.

SANSON HAS JUST returned, his men behind him, with their scissors
and ropes. It is time to lay down my pen. Adieu.

> *A.S.C.*
> *At the Conciergerie*
> *18 Prairial, Year II of the Republic*
> *Three o'clock.*

HISTORICAL NOTE

THE TERROR ENDED on July 27th, 1794, six weeks after the close of this novel, when Robespierre was at last shouted down in the Convention by his opposition and captured and guillotined the following day. Saint-Just and eighty-one others of his most ardent partisans followed him to the scaffold. Fouquier-Tinville (the Public Prosecutor) and a dozen judges and jurors from the Revolutionary Tribunal were guillotined the following May, while the power of the Committee of Public Safety was greatly reduced.

With the deaths of Robespierre and Saint-Just, the Terror that they had created had devoured the last revolutionary leaders of significant political ability and vision. A coalition of opportunists and second-rate talents who had survived the purges of their various parties inherited the Revolution after the crumbling of the Committee; the social reforms that Robespierre had championed were ignored in the wave of reaction following the end of the Terror. The National Convention limped along for another year until superseded first by the Directory and after that by the Consulate, which was soon to be dominated and then made irrelevant by its most famous representative, the victorious general Napoleon Bonaparte.

Anne Théroigne became increasingly unstable and was committed to an insane asylum late in 1794; she died in 1817 without regaining her sanity. Madame de Pontécoulant survived the Revolution unmolested but never again mentioned Charlotte de Corday's name. Doulcet de Pontécoulant became a peer under Napoleon, witness to two more revolutions in 1830 and 1848, and one of the last surviving Conventionnels, dying in 1853 at the age of eighty-nine.

DICKENS'S VIVID, THRILLING, but often distorted portrayal of the French Revolution in *A Tale of Two Cities* has become the unshakeable cliché-myth of that period. The image that most people call to mind when thinking of the Revolution—an indiscriminate slaughter of aristocrats, conducted by leering *sans-culottes* and bloodthirsty old women knitting at the guillotine—is at bottom Dickens's creation. For Dickens, the French Revolution is the Terror and only the Terror, a fallacy enthusiastically compounded and embellished by Hollywood and a dozen Scarlet Pimpernel novels.

One can scarcely blame Dickens for this; the sheer gripping theatricality of the Terror ensures that the more hopeful, less eventful years of the Revolution are often ignored by authors in search of drama. But the five years between the fall of the Bastille and the fall of Robespierre were by no means all riot and mayhem and heads tumbling into the basket. It was not until 1792–93, when the war with Austria and Prussia (which Dickens never mentions) threatened the nation, and Louis XVI's execution irreparably divided it, that France was thrown into true turmoil. The Terror (rechristened "the Reign of Terror" by conservative nineteenth-century historians of lurid imagination) was not anarchy but rather its opposite: a series of rigorous emergency laws passed to preserve the Republic in the midst of this turmoil, by combating the crises of foreign war, civil war, a tottering economy, and pervasive discontent.

Most modern readers leave *A Tale of Two Cities* under the impression that the Parisian Terror was the eighteenth-century version of the Holocaust, responsible for the deaths of thousands upon thousands of helpless innocents. In fact about twelve hundred people perished in the September Massacres and about twenty-six hundred (including many petty criminals guilty of prosaic, non-political crimes) were condemned to death by the Revolutionary Tribunal. The guillotine itself was not used until three years after the Bastille's fall, while the Terror, by the most extravagant estimates, lasted no longer than the fourteen months between 2 June 1793 (the fall of the Girondins) and 28 July 1794 (the death of Robespierre). And although Dickens seems to imply that the Parisian "Great Terror," with its forty or fifty executions daily, was the standard for a year or more, in reality it lasted only for about eight weeks in June and July 1794. Dickens specifies that the final chapters of *A Tale of Two Cities* take place in December 1793; according to the Revolutionary Tribunal's records, however, a total of sixty-nine prisoners were executed that month, an average of two or three per day—somewhat fewer than the famous fifty-two of the novel.

The scale of bloodshed during the Revolution may be quickly put in its proper perspective if one reflects that at least twice as many French citizens died for Napoleon's glory in the twenty-four-hour Battle of Austerlitz than were guillotined in Paris during all the fourteen months of the Terror. It was not in the number of the dead, but in the wasted potential of those many extraordinary individuals whom the Terror devoured, that the true tragedy of the Revolution lay.

SELECT BIBLIOGRAPHY

Bernier, Olivier. *Pleasure and Privilege: Life in France, Naples, and America, 1770-90.* Garden City, NY: Doubleday & Company, Inc., 1981.

Christophe, Robert. *Danton: A Biography.* Garden City, NY: Doubleday & Company, 1967.

Curtis, E. N. *Saint-Just, Colleague of Robespierre.* Morningside Heights, NY: Columbia University Press, 1935.

George, M. Dorothy. *London Life in the Eighteenth Century.* London: Kegan Paul, Trench, Trubner & Co. Ltd., 1930.

Grose, Captain Francis; Eric Partridge, editor. *A Classical Dictionary of the Vulgar Tongue,* 3rd edition (1976). New York: Dorset Press, 1992.

Hampson, Norman. *The Life and Opinions of Maximilien Robespierre.* London: Gerald Duckworth & Co. Ltd, 1974.

Hibbert, Christopher. *The Days of the French Revolution.* New York: William Morrow and Company, Inc., 1980.

Hillairet, Jacques. *Connaissance de Vieux Paris.* Paris: Editions Payot & Rivages, 1993.

Lenotre, G. (Théodore Gosselin); Frederic Lees, translator. *The Tribunal of the Terror.* Philadelphia: J. B. Lippincott Company, 1909.

Manceron, Claude. *Blood of the Bastille.* New York: Simon & Schuster, 1989.

Methley, Violet. *Camille Desmoulins.* New York: E. P. Dutton and Company, 1915.

Morris, Gouverneur; Beatrix Cary Davenport, editor. *A Diary of the French Revolution.* Boston: Houghton Mifflin Company, 1939.

Palmer, R. R. *Twelve Who Ruled: The Year of the Terror in the French Revolution.* Princeton, N.J.: Princeton University Press, 1941.

Restif de la Bretonne, Nicolas-Edmé; Linda Asher and Ellen Fertig, trans-
lators. *Les Nuits de Paris or The Nocturnal Spectator.* New York: Random
House, 1964.

Robiquet, Jean; James Kirkup, translator. *Daily Life in the French Revolution.*
New York: Macmillan, 1964.

Sanson, Charles-Henri; Monique Lebailly, editor. *La Révolution Française Vue
par Son Bourreau Charles-Henri Sanson.* Paris: Editions de l'Instant, 1989.

Schama, Simon. *Citizens: A Chronicle of the French Revolution.* New York: Alfred
A. Knopf, 1989.

Shearing, Joseph (Gabrielle M. V. Long). *The Angel of the Assassination. Marie-
Charlotte de Corday d'Armont, Jean-Paul Marat, Jean-Adam Lux: A Study of Three
Disciples of Jean-Jacques Rousseau.* London: William Heinemann Ltd., 1935.